What They Want

A Novel

Omar Tyree

Simon & Schuster Paperbacks

New York London Toronto Sydney

SIMON & SCHUSTER PAPERBACKS
Rockefeller Center
1230 Avenue of the Americas
New York, NY 10020

Copyright © 2006 by Omar Tyree

First Simon & Schuster trade paperback edition June 2007

SIMON & SCHUSTER PAPERBACKS and colophon are
registered trademarks of Simon & Schuster, Inc.

For information about special discounts for bulk purchases,
please contact Simon & Schuster Special Sales at
1-800-456-6798 or business@simonandschuster.com.

Book design by Ellen R. Sasahara

Manufactured in the United States of America

1   3   5   7   9   10   8   6   4   2

The Library of Congress has cataloged the hardcover edition as follows:
Tyree, Omar.
What they want : a novel / Omar Tyree.
p. cm.
1. Male models—United States—Fiction.   2. Man-woman relationships—
Fiction.   3. African Americans—Fiction.   I. Title.

PS3570.Y59W47 2006
813'.54—dc22
2006045020

ISBN-13: 978-0-7432-2869-5
ISBN-10:   0-7432-2869-3
ISBN-13: 978-0-7432-2873-2 (Pbk)
ISBN-10:   0-7432-2873-1 (Pbk)

For those of us
who think we know what we're doing
and for those
who understand that we don't.

Hey man, just shop until you drop
don't stop
and don't let your bubble get popped
love to rock
then roll
and make sure you be extra bold with it
whip it
crash it
wreck it
get naked
whatever's clever, brother.
You know what I'm talkin' 'bout?
Fuck it!
It ain't nothin' but pussy.

—*The Player's Ball,*
OMAR TYREE

Contents

What They Want

Under Pressure

I DON'T KNOW WHAT TO DO."
   That's what she told me. This was several years ago in the prime of my modeling career. I was twenty-seven years old and on a break at a photo shoot in Cancun, Mexico. We were relaxing at the beach on a beautiful late afternoon right before the sun had gone down over the Gulf of Mexico. The sky was light blue mixed with fluffy gray clouds and a fading orange sunlight. The sand was warm, and the slight breeze was just enough to get your attention but not enough to cause a chill. The entire scene was as beautiful as a naked girl in a perfect picture. And I was loving every minute of it.

"Did you hear me?"

Of course I heard her. But at the moment, I was busy framing the sandy brown skin of the local Mexican mommies against that beautiful backdrop. They continued to walk by and sneak peeks at me under our oversized umbrella. They were more interested in me than the white boy models. Ten of us were there for a summer swimsuit issue of *Fabulous* magazine, and I was the only black man. I guess you could call me the token sex god.

"Terrance, I'm talking to you."

No, it was more like she was bothering me, and I didn't feel like dealing with her conversation. I was taking a much-needed break from my hustle, and I planned on enjoying it. Talking about the future of a tug-of-war relationship was work. Now why would any guy want to work in such beautiful surroundings unless he absolutely had to?

"This is what I'm talking about. You never acknowledge me when I'm trying to talk to you. You're so fucking rude. You know that?"

She was being rude to me. I had been working my tail off down there in the baking heat of Mexico. But did she care? Evidently not. She only wanted to address her issues. I was rarely the type to argue, but that never stopped her from trying to provoke me.

"Hello? Is anyone home? Earth to Terrance."

I finally looked into her Gucci sunshades, under her straw sombrero, and asked her, "Andrea, what do you want me to say? I'm not gonna tell you what to do. I thought you told me you were a grown woman. Well, you make your own decisions then."

As much as I was paying attention to the local girls, who were shaking their tail feathers with purpose and flirting all around us, Andrea's beauty was stunning. There's nothing like a fine black woman with a history of strong mixed genes. Everything about her look was perfect; five-nine, one twenty-five, flat stomach, strong thighs, pretty feet, luscious lips, long, thick hair, flawless skin, photogenic like a baby, and curved like sculpture. But none of that mattered to me. I wasn't going to allow her looks and insatiable attitude to hold my emotions hostage.

"I'm not asking you to tell me what to do. I know I make my own decisions. I just want to discuss things with you."

She paused to see if I would respond to her, but I wasn't up to it. Discussing things with women took a lot out of a guy, especially when those things involved relationships. It wasn't the kind of shoot-from-the-hip discussions I would have with guys about our feelings for a woman. You said what you felt and moved on. But discussing relationships with a woman held infinite consequences. Every single word you used was a trap. So I learned to use my words sparingly with most women.

"Do you want me in your life or not?" Andrea asked me. "Just let me know something."

I turned away from her. I liked the girl, I really did. But I didn't want to be bonded to her. We were doing just fine with our loose arrangement. I go on a job, take her with me, love her down, and keep it simple. Then another guy came along and started putting pressures on her, which she in turn passed on to me. Only I wasn't up for playing that game. I refused to compete with another guy over a woman. There were too many women out there for that. So I pleaded the Fifth Amendment and remained silent. I knew that anything I said to her could be held against me.

"Well?"

Instead of answering her question, I thought about the other guy she had started dating on the side. I hated jealous guys. If the girl wasn't into you, then let her be. It's that simple. But this guy Jayson Walker, one of those briefcase carrying number crunchers, had made it his personal mission to try and take her from me. There were plenty of other fine women out there to choose from, but he just had to chase after her.

Guys who live and die for the dollar swear that everything, including every woman, has a price tag. So I blamed Andrea for even getting involved with the guy. Then again, a girl had to eat, and I was not offering her free access to my bank account, like he was. But even with all his money, I held the keys to her heart. That only made him chase her harder, and I wanted no part of that game.

Andrea finally lost her patience with me. She stood up to leave and I didn't plan on stopping her.

"You know what? I don't even know why I'm trying so hard with you."

Once she climbed to her feet, she looked down and noticed my lack of urgency. "So, you're not even gonna try and stop me. Like, you don't even care."

Actually, I did care. I just wasn't willing to allow my feelings for her to get in the way of what I wanted for myself. I loved my freedom, and I wasn't willing to sacrifice it to make permanent room for her.

Despite Andrea's beauty, the girl was struggling to launch her modeling career next to mine, and she hadn't been successful at it yet. What can I say? Modeling was a tough business, not everyone could create a solid living from it. I was one of the fortunate few who could. Nevertheless, I couldn't stand the pressure that she was putting on me because of Jayson Walker and his income. But how could I tell a woman that I didn't want to afford her? I mean, I could. With my five-figure-a-day rate for modeling jobs, I definitely had enough in the bank to carry her for a while. I just didn't want to.

Why should it be necessary for a guy to economically provide for a woman? She needed to find a regular job to hold her over until she could catch her break. She had plenty of time on her hands. She was only twenty.

In my grand scheme of things, since I knew she liked me so much, I figured I would allow Mr. Walker to continue to provide for her while she snuck off for rendezvous around the world with me. Crazy, ain't it? But that's what I was thinking at the time. I was young and very cocky.

I was so cocky that I didn't believe she had the courage to leave me. She had tried to leave me several times in the past year, but she always came crawling back. I guess she was hooked on my stroke and my character.

Yeah, she wasn't going anywhere. She was only bluffing.

Before she strutted away from me, she said, "You know, he asked me to marry him. He even bought me a ring."

That got my attention. I looked up into her sunshades. "He did what?"

I didn't believe her.

Instead of her trying to convince me, she dug inside her beach bag and pulled out a black ring case to hand over to me.

You believe that shit? She must have had it all planned out to surprise my ass with. I was afraid to even touch the thing. But I was curious.

I opened the case and found a nice-size diamond engagement ring.

It was all round and raised like a dome. It looked expensive as hell, too. That changed everything for me. The shit was serious!

I looked up and asked her, "So what did you say to him?"

She continued to stare at me through her sunshades.

"What do you want me to say?"

It was another trap.

I said, "He didn't ask *me* to marry him. What are you talking about?"

She wasn't going to get me that easily.

She said, "Well, you know I don't want to do that, but . . ."

She was still undecided.

I said, "But what?"

She shrugged her shoulders and looked away.

She looked back at me and said, "I've just been thinking about this modeling and stuff lately and . . . these racist people just won't let me in. I mean, they know I have the look. It's like they only let two or three black girls in at a time. And while Naomi and Tyra's still around . . ."

I had been around plenty of black women who called themselves models, but I couldn't really say that many of them made a solid living from it. Modeling was still an aspiration for most of them, and a part-time high. Then again . . .

"And please don't start talking to me about that music video shit and all of these freaky men's magazines, because I'm not interested."

They say beggars can't be choosers, but Andrea was one choosy broad.

I chuckled and said, "Look, we both know that you can work if you really wanted to. What's wrong with showing a little bit of your ass? It's a nice ass, and if they're willing to pay you to show it . . ."

"Whatever," she said and cut me off. "You want everybody seeing what you get?"

I shrugged. "Everybody sees what *you* get."

I was practically naked in some of those swimsuit shots. But I didn't mind it. It was my body to show off, and if they wanted me naked, then so be it, as long as it was a straight magazine. I didn't go the other way. That was about my only limit. I didn't need any extra bullshit coming my way on account of a few thousand dollars. I made enough money not to have to bend.

"Anyway, so what do you want me to say to him?"

We were back at square one, talking about her ring and marriage proposal from another man.

"Look, if you don't like this guy like that, then tell him no. You're not ready to get married. You got a whole life in front of you. You're not even legal to drink yet," I told her.

I was only telling her the truth.

She said, "I know."

"There's no more to talk about then."

The shit was obvious to me. This numbers cruncher was crazy. He was really getting under my skin. I swear, he was doing it all for spite, just to get to me. I even asked her about it.

"Does he still talk about me all the time?"

She smiled. "Of course he does. He said your pretty ass needs to get a real job. He said you probably can't keep a real job because you're too much of a faggot for real work."

Shit like that made me want to kick Jayson Walker's ass. I knew he couldn't beat me. That skinny motherfucker looked like the type who would pay someone else to fight for him. But allowing that asshole to talk about me like that made me pissed off at her as well.

"And what do you say when he talks about me like that?" I asked her.

She still thought it all was a joke and had a locked smile on her face.

"He knows you're not gay. He's just jealous of you."

"But how do you just let him talk about me like that?"

She shook her head. "It means nothing to me. I know when a man is jealous of another man."

I said, "Yeah, but it means something to me. You let this guy continue to disrespect me like that, and you think it's all a game. Looks to me like you still got a lot of growing up to do," I told her.

"*You* still got a lot of growing up to do," she snapped at me. "I mean, here I am all the way the fuck out in Mexico, trying to get you to see that I still love you, and all you can think about is these beach bitches walking around, and how you don't want him to have me, but then you won't lock me down."

Then she snatched the ring case away from me.

I asked her, "Why should I lock you down? If you say you love me, then you lock yourself down."

"That's what I'm here trying to do."

"Well then, do it!"

People were starting to stare at us. I wasn't the type to argue with a woman. I usually stated my position and moved on. But when a woman gets to you . . . That's when I realized how dangerous Andrea was. I couldn't have her even if I wanted to. She could mess up my whole career worrying about her. I had a carefree lifestyle with no dependents. Even my family knew to leave me alone. I was out there on my own island.

She glared at me and said, "You are such a coward. If you want a woman, then get a woman. At least he's real about it."

"Real about what?" I snapped at her. I don't even know why I asked her that. I didn't care anything about that guy. She had me reacting impulsively instead of thinking things through.

"He shows that he's serious about me. You're just out here fuckin' around with me. This ring is real. So don't talk about somebody needing to *grow up!*"

She got me to thinking. J. Walker had two kids with two different women, and he *still* didn't have his act together. He was already paying a truckload of child support, and both of these other women were in their early twenties, like Andrea. What made it worse was that she *knew* about them. She told me everything.

This numbers cruncher had screwed up a couple of young

women's lives, and he was ready to screw up hers right along with them. But *I* was the bad guy. *I* was the one who wasn't doing the right thing. At least I knew I wasn't ready to be serious.

That girl was out of her mind to deal with this guy. He must have been a part of her game plan to get me to do what she wanted. But I wasn't going for it. So I gathered my emotions back into my bottle, and I told her to kiss off.

I said, "You know what? I don't think it would be a bad idea for you to settle down. I mean, you're definitely gorgeous, but like you said, this modeling game is a hard one. So if you think this guy is gonna give you a better life and a chance to breathe while you try to establish your career, then go for it."

That was some cold shit for me to say to a young woman who was extending herself to me like she was. Andrea was the type of girl who would put everything on the line, and she had been doing that with me and her modeling aspirations, it just hadn't paid off for her yet, the steady modeling jobs *or* me.

I was doing her the same way the industry was doing her. Wait, wait, wait, and I may have something for you next season. *Possibly.*

After my line of truth mixed with bullshit, instead of going through another round of arguing, Andrea said "Fuck you" and got to stepping. I guess she finally said to hell with it then.

Her exit was so abrupt that it didn't register with me right away. I was still waiting for her to hang around and argue her point until the sun went down, but she didn't. At first, I felt this big relief in her absence. Then, all of a sudden, I became paranoid.

What if she actually marries this asshole? What would I do then? I asked myself. *Nah, she wouldn't do that. She'll come to her senses. Marrying that guy would be crazy.* And I went back to enjoying my perfect view of the ocean. It may have been a boring life to some, but I liked keeping things simple. Peace, quiet, and independence was what I liked . . . I just didn't know what I had just lost.

Still Strokin'

I DIDN'T EXPECT ANDREA to fly back to the States just like that. I figured we would at least have another night or two in Mexico to mull things over. But she surprised me and broke camp immediately. What could I do at that point? I wasn't gonna call her back and beg her to stay. That was probably what she wanted me to do. Me calling her back would have been her dream story. I just wasn't her dream maker.

So I went on my merry way with my modeling career and didn't hear a peep from the girl for a couple of weeks. I even called to check up on her a few times with no response. I didn't sweat it though. She was known to disappear on me for weeks at a time before she would resurface with an abundance of energy. I had gotten used to that, and it served me well. I liked having my little space, too. But once the weeks turned into months, and the months turned into a half a year without me seeing or hearing from her, I began to lose hope of her ever returning.

After more than a year with no word from her, I finally wiped my hands with the girl. I told myself, *Well, I guess she went ahead and married the guy.*

I figured he had told her never to contact me or talk to me again as a part of his deal with her. The devil usually negotiated for your soul, and more than just your mind and body. I assumed he wanted her

9

total loyalty, nothing less. I didn't even hear about her in my modeling circles anymore.

I admit, I had little spells of thinking about the girl that got to me.
But when I realized that it was over, it didn't bother me as much as I
thought it might have. I always had women around me anyway. I was
still in the prime of my career, so I was pretty busy with new jobs to
keep my mind moving forward, never backward.

SEVERAL YEARS LATER, I was still happily single and living real
swell with a penthouse in the heart of Atlanta's Peachtree Street. I had
three national ad campaigns: Johnson's International Furs, Class-A
Jewelry, and M. O. Clothing. Things were smelling real good all over
me. I even went out and bought one of those Mercedes CL coupes; a
silver one, with the AMG horsepower package. I had no reason to
complain in life.

I got a call one afternoon from an old friend who was in town. He
wanted to do drinks and grab a bite at the Cheesecake Factory. He
was a guy I had met years ago in Chicago. He heard I had settled
down in the Atlanta area, so he called around and got my number
through mutual contacts. Since I was not exclusive to one modeling
agency, I kept my line of communication open to as many friends and
associates as possible. You never know when a contact may bring in a
new job.

Anyway, this guy, Corey Sanders, had been a football player, a
model, an aspiring actor, and finally a security agent for celebrities. I
had first met him during his transition from football to modeling. He
had the passion for the job, but he was maybe too much on the bulky
side and not attractive enough for most clothing lines. So instead of
doing big man's clothes, athletic wear, fitness ads, and calendars,
Corey tried being an action hero/stuntman in films before settling
down in security. Whatever works for you, I guess.

Once I arrived at the Cheesecake Factory and joined him at his
booth, I extended my hand to greet the giant of a man. Corey had to

be at least six-foot-five, two hundred forty-five pounds. That was several inches taller and thirty pounds heavier than I was.

He said, "Hey, Terrance. How are things going for you? I guess real well, because I keep seeing photos of your work everywhere."

I smiled. "Yeah, things have been good for me."

It was a Thursday night. I had to fly to Miami the next morning, but the night was still young. My bags were already packed and I didn't need a lot of sleep. So I ordered a drink, sat back, and relaxed.

Corey was wearing a dark sports jacket with a bright white tee underneath, just like I was.

I grinned. "I see you're still following the latest fashion trends," I said to him.

He grinned back at me from across the table. He held a glass of dark wine in his huge right hand.

"Denzel makes it work, so why can't we?"

I nodded. "If you wanna be the best, you gotta copy the best."

"Dig it."

Our male waiter stepped up to the table to see if we were ready to order our food. I had barely looked at the menu.

"Give me another minute or two," I told him.

"Yeah, give us a few minutes," Corey repeated.

Our waiter nodded, wearing a wavy ponytail, white button-up shirt, bright orange tie, and a black apron. He stared at me and grinned.

"Excuse me for staring, but aren't you Terrance Mitchell, the model?"

I nodded. "Yeah."

"Well, I love your work. You don't mind if I get an autograph before you leave, do you?"

"I have to sign my check, don't I? Unless I pay for this in cash," I joked to him.

He chuckled with an abundance of tickle in his bones.

"Oh, I mean, like, on a different piece of paper. I wanna tape it up on my wall."

I looked at Corey, who was already shaking his low-cut head. I had gotten a haircut that day myself.

"Yeah, I can do that. Get it before we leave," I told our starstruck waiter.

"Oh, thank you very much. Thank you."

As soon as he left us, Corey smiled and said, "You get that a lot down here, don't you? It's a gay man's heaven in Atlanta."

I said, "You know you're still on top of your game when the lollipop patrol likes you. 'Cause they don't lie to you. If you're not lookin' good, they gon' let you know in a heartbeat."

Corey laughed and said, "The lollipop patrol. I've never heard that one."

"Yeah, you don't have to worry about me though," I told him. "I mean, I'm flattered by it, because it's the nature of the business, but God knows I love me some pussy."

Corey continued to laugh, but I was just being frank.

On cue, my cell phone went off. I was expecting the phone call. I flipped it open and looked down at the number. Then I smiled back at Corey.

"See what I mean? Here comes pussy right now. Hello," I answered.

"Where are you?"

It was Danyel Addison, a young model in her early twenties. Her agency tagged her "Danni," and she was definitely on her way up the ladder. She was sexy, slim, and yellow, with light brown curly hair, and gray eyes. And she was already spoiled like a budding super-model.

"I'm over at the Cheesecake Factory," I told her.

She got excited. "Oh, I'm close by. Are you with a guy or a girl?"

I wondered for a second how she would have responded had I said a girl. Instead of thinking of a cat fight fueled by jealousy, I automatically thought of a night with two women. Danni was experimental that way. That's why I liked her. But instead of cooking up my fantasy, I mumbled the truth.

"I'm with an old buddy of mine from Chicago."

"You mind if I crash the party?"

I smiled and thought about Corey. I didn't mind showing Danni off to him. I was sure that he would like her. The girl had an infectious hold on men of all creed, class, and color. But the thing I liked about her most was that very few men could fuck her. I was one of the few who could.

I told her, "Come on through. My boy would love to meet you."

"Okay, I'll be there. And I'll let you see my new ride."

Danni liked to show off. She had me wondering what kind of new car she had bought.

As soon as I ended the call, Corey smiled at me and shook his head again.

Out of the blue, he hit me with a sledgehammer.

"Whatever happened between you and Andrea, man? I saw her recently in the Big Windy with some of the biggest assholes in Chicago. Seems like she took a few steps backwards. I got a chance to talk to her for a minute, but she seemed out of it. It was like she was embarrassed to see me."

I had gotten over Andrea, or so I had told myself. But Corey bringing her up like that had taken me aback. I wondered what she was up to myself.

Our waiter arrived with my drink just in time to wet my whistle. I waited for him to clear the area before I spoke. I had forgotten that Corey was around me when I first met Andrea. She was from Champaign, Illinois, about an hour out from "Chi-town." I was from the same Midwest area, out of Gary, Indiana.

I chose my words carefully.

"She, ah, decided to deal with someone else."

I took a swig of my drink.

Corey nodded and said, "J. Walker, the stockbroker, who thinks he's in the movie *Wall Street*."

It was all humorous to him, but I would rather not hear about either one of them.

"Hey, man, I don't wanna go there right now. I haven't been around her in years."

"Well, don't sweat that. She don't look like she used to, man."

Why did I care? Like I said, I didn't want to hear about her. But Corey had me curious.

"What do you mean by that?"

"You know he stopped her from modeling."

I had figured that much on my own.

"Yeah, I know. It was getting old fast anyway."

"And I heard she had a miscarriage with his child," he told me.

It was another bomb dropped on my head. Why the hell was Corey bending my ear with that shit? Had someone sent him to do it? What the hell was the deal?

"Why is this important to me, man?"

I was expressing my frustration with the whole history of it. But how was Corey to know what I felt? I didn't know how deeply Andrea and Jayson Walker had cut me. I had simply moved on from it. Or so I thought.

Our waiter swung past the table again.

"Are you two ready to order?"

I still hadn't looked at the menu.

"Hey, man, just give me whatever today's special is," I told him.

I wanted to go back to relaxing. I had enough on my mind already.

"Well, we have two specials this evening. We have a chicken dish . . ."

What the fuck? I didn't want to hear any of that shit. *Just bring me out a hot fucking plate of food,* I felt like telling him.

Danni arrived just in time to preserve my cool.

She slithered up beside me in our booth, wearing a sky blue silk dress with a funky pair of tall white leather boots.

"That chicken sounds good," she told our waiter. "I'll have one of those."

He looked at her with disdain before he eyed me for my response.

"Is she with you?"

Danni beat me to the punch.

"Who else do you think I'm with? I'm sitting next to him, ain't I?"

She must have just gotten a big new contract. Good modeling jobs made a lot of us act foolish, and downright ugly.

He said, "Whatever," but still wanted to confirm things with me. "So have you made up your mind on your order?"

I could see that I was about to have a long night.

"I'll take whatever you bring me, man."

It was the safest thing for me to say.

"Okay, I'll have them hook you up."

When he left the table, Danni looked at me and joked, "Looks like I busted somebody's groove up in here tonight."

She looked over at Corey and asked him, "Did you see how he looked at me when I sat down? Oh, boyfriend did not want me here. Okay?"

Corey could care less what she was talking about. Danni had brought an entire aroma to our table. It was a scent I had never smelled before, and it had crept up on us from the moment she sat down. I was sure that my friend could smell it.

I asked her, "What is that you're wearing?"

Corey laughed on cue. "That's what I wanna know."

Danni smiled wide and whispered to us both, "It's, like, some new shit. They just gave it to us today. Don't it smell good?"

It smelled to me like she wasn't going to make it back home to her luxury apartment in Buckhead that night. I could use the release, that was for sure. Corey's mention of Andrea had done a job on me.

He leaned back in his seat and asked hypothetically, "Why do we always tend to whisper whenever we talk about good deals with white folks?"

Danni looked at him and frowned. It was the wrong line of conversation to use with her. She was hardly the pro-black, sister girl. Danyel Addison had been trying to move on up as far as she could in life, and race meant nothing to her.

She said, "Here we go with that black man shit. Don't even get me started on that."

Then she reached over and grabbed my drink. That was why a lot of men couldn't have their way with Danni. They tended to put their foot in their mouth, as if she brought out the worst in them. I guess a lot of guys got too anxious around her and ended up trying too hard.

"You want me to order you a drink?" I asked her calmly.

"Please."

I watched her kill the rest of mine without a word about it. From that moment on, I realized that Danni had no intention of staying there long. Her goal was to make an entrance, make a scene, and then steal me away for the night to fuck my brains out. And who was I to deny her?

"Terry, watch my purse while I run to the restroom."

I hated when she called me that "Terry" shit. It sounded less masculine to me, so I informed everyone to stick to my full name. Danni knew that already. So I figured she wanted me to be rough with her that night. It was like a cat-and-mouse game that we played. I knew her every move, and she knew just what to say and do to push the right buttons on me.

In Danni's absence, Corey smiled and said, "She reminds me of Andrea a little. Doesn't she? Or do all models act like that?"

Why? Why did he keep bringing the girl up, just when Danni had calmed me back down?

I said, "Hey, man . . ." and I just decided to let it roll. But one thing was for sure, Corey wouldn't get another drink with me. He was fucking up my mood. Andrea was in the past. I didn't want to hear shit else about her.

Danni arrived back at the table. At the same time, our waiter presented me with a notebook pad of yellow paper to scribble my John Hancock on.

"I'll be right back with your food," he told me. It was like I was the only one at the table.

As soon as he left, Danni turned to me and said, "You're not really hungry, are you?"

It was her cue for us to leave, like in right now!

I shook my head and told her, "Not really. I can get it to go." It was rude to Corey, but like I said, he had ruined his welcome.

He grinned and took it in stride.

"Well, I guess I'll see you around then, Terrance."

"Yeah, you got my numbers." That was all I had left to say to him.

When our waiter returned with the hot food, Danni wasted no time in telling him our change of plans.

"You know, we're all gonna have our food to go now." Then she looked over at Corey. "Oh, but you probably want to stay, right?"

Sounded like she was putting his thoughts in his head.

Corey continued to grin. "Yeah, I'll stay. I like it in here."

"Okay, well, nice meeting you." Danni didn't mean that shit. It was all a part of being cordial. She told me, "I'ma get my car while you get the food. I parked with the valet."

What else was there for me to say? She had already made her moves.

I nodded and said, "Okay."

When she walked out, Corey told me, "Man, you got your hands full with that one."

"Mmm, hmm," our disgruntled waiter mumbled.

"Yeah," I mumbled back to them. They just didn't understand the girl. Danni was easy. She wanted to make her own moves and feel in control of her destiny. She only wanted a man to counterpunch with tact and precision. And I was just the right man for the job.

WHEN I ARRIVED outside the Cheesecake Factory with a bag of hot entrées in hand, Danni blew the horn of a midnight blue BMW sports car and got my attention. It was shining like it had been freshly waxed. Either that or she had just driven it off the dealer's lot.

"You like it?" she asked me, cheesing.

"I like you more," I told her.

She said, "Of course you do. So where's your car?"

"It's parked in the back."

"I'll wait next to the curb for you."

Of course she would, in the middle of Peachtree Street, where everyone could see her and know that she was living the high life. However, if Danni were to stop working tomorrow, she wouldn't have fifty cents to make a phone call. She spent every dime she made so she could at least *look* like she was living how she wanted to live.

I led her back to my place, where she commented on my car's horsepower. We were walking to the elevators from the parking garage.

"What kind of horsepower does it have when it's an AMG model?"

I smiled and said, "It's off the charts."

"I have two hundred and ninety."

"I have about two hundred more than that," I told her.

She shook her head. "Guys and their egos."

"You're the one who brought it up. I wasn't thinking about it."

She grinned as we reached the elevators. As soon as we climbed on board, Danni moved close enough to nibble on my right ear. "Why can't most guys be like you?" she asked me.

"Why would I want them to be? Then they could all take you home. I kind of like being that guy," I answered.

She laughed and bit into my ear.

I moved my head away from her. "Hey, watch those teeth. I have a shoot in Miami tomorrow."

"How much is it paying?" she asked me.

"Enough to live on."

"For life?"

I stood up straight and stared at her. She knew better than that. She used the moment of silence to kiss me.

"Wouldn't you love to fuck me on the elevator?" We had to transfer at the lobby level.

"Yeah, but what do I do with the food?" I teased her.

I was cool and calm about it. Nothing surprised me. You only live once, so dream on and do it.

She took the bag of food out of my hand and set it on the elevator floor.

I said, "I think it's safer if we did that on the other elevators. The garage elevator is only three floors."

"Who said I wanted to be safe?" she asked me.

All I could do was smile at that. She was ready for whatever.

"You know I don't usually wear panties unless the shoots requires it, or I'm on my cycle. And neither one of those are the case tonight . . . Terry."

There wasn't much left for me to say. My dick was throbbing and ready to push its way into her wet pussy. Danni loved getting wet. The girl was a fucking river when she was horny.

So I went ahead and poked two of my fingers into her cream to make sure she was ripe. She bit her bottom lip and hissed at me. I gripped her by her hips and heaved her into the air to place her pelvis against mine. She hustled to undo my pants zipper. I pulled the red STOP knob on the elevator to stop us between floors. We had nearly made it to the top level.

I asked her, "What did I tell you about calling me that Terry shit? Didn't I tell you not to call me that?"

She pulled my dick through my pants zipper and tugged it in place under her dress.

"What are you gonna do about it?"

I gripped her by the back of her neck like a caveman. Her wild, curly hair fell into my face from her position above me.

I pushed into her from below, and pulled her down from above.

"I, told, you, 'bout, that, shit, *didn't I?*" I pumped into her locking body. She wrapped her long legs around my lower back like a yoga master.

"Yeah," she whimpered as I thrust into her.

I loved how I slipped into Danni's presto pussy. Her shit felt as slippery as the silk of her dress, and since she stayed on birth control, I never worried about condoms. She liked it raw anyway. The girl was wild and reckless when she fucked. And I was wild and reckless right with her.

"Why, you, so, fuckin', *hardheaded*?" I asked as I banged her into the elevator wall.

"I, don't, know," she humped into my ear. She rode my upward thrusts and held on tight.

"Yes, you do. You know why. You, want, this, shit, like, this. *Don't you?*"

"Yeeahhh," she moaned, and sucked into my eardrum.

"I know, I know, I know," I pumped into her wriggling torso. I was nailing her wild head of curls into the wall and everything.

"I didn't mean it," she whined and squirmed. She snaked her hot, wet body in mini circles on my dick. Then she bit my fucking ear, and I tore a fire to her crazy ass.

"What, the, fuck, are, you *doing*? Didn't, I, tell, you, not, to *do that*? Didn't I, didn't I, *didn't I*? I gotta *shoot* tomorrow!"

My dick felt like it was pushing up into her stomach. Danni lost control of her body as shit started popping and cracking and twisting in her bones. She didn't have that much meat on her body to protect her from my constricting grip and violent pumps to begin with. And when I came, the cum shot out of me so strong that I didn't care if she died from a seizure.

Danni tilted her head to the roof of the elevator and howled like a werewolf.

"UUUUUUUU!"

She wanted it fucking rough. Then she started panting like she was insane.

"Uhh, uhh, uhh, *uhhnn*."

Sweat was dripping out of her hair and into my face. And she was changing colors. I guess she came as strong as I did. She dripped all over the front of my pants and made a mess, that's for sure.

After all of that, she gripped my wet head inside of her arms and started crying.

"You gon' make me miss you, Terrance. You gon' make me miss you."

All I could think about was my right ear at that point. The shit felt like I had been stung by a wasp.

I pulled her down off of me. "Look, we gotta get up to my freezer and get me some damn ice for my ear."

She laughed and leaned into me, extra weak from fucking. Her legs were not stable yet. She had a case of rubber thighs. She was leaning up against me to stop herself from falling over. She didn't even care about her dress being cum-stained.

I zipped my shit back inside my pants and I planned to hide us behind the bag of food. I pushed the STOP knob back in on the elevator and it began to move.

"Oh, shit. You're gonna have to carry me to your place," Danni joked. I couldn't even lean down to pick the food up with her full weight against me. I was worn out, too. I had just pumped over a hundred pounds at least fifty times into the air.

"Come on now, stop it," I told her.

"I'm serious. I can't stand up," she whined.

As soon as she said that, I could hear people talking above us as the elevator reached the lobby floor. I quickly grabbed the bag of food from the floor and held it in front of us.

The doors opened up, and at least three of the building's staff were standing there to greet us.

"Ah, sir, was the elevator stuck?" the white security guard asked us.

Danni started laughing. Only the white security guard even bothered to ask. The two black guys walked away from us in embarrassment. We looked and smelled like sex.

I said, "Yeah, we'll be all right. You don't have to file no complaint or nothing. We're fine. We're just a little exhausted from the gym."

I didn't know what the hell I was saying. We weren't even dressed for the gym.

The security guard nodded and said, "Okay," and walked off.

When we climbed into the second elevator to my floor, Danni leaned up against me and mocked him.

"Ah, excuse me, sir, was the elevator stuck?"

She started laughing again. Then she looked me in the eyes with more seduction in mind.

"You wanna get this elevator stuck, too?"

I was still rubbing my right ear to take the sting away.

I said, "I think you had enough elevator for one night."

Fortunately she agreed with me. "Yeah, you're right. I probably need vanilla ice cream over the kitchen counter now. Do you have any of that, or do we need to order?"

I shook my head. That damn girl was wild. That's probably why I liked her. I could fuck her any way I wanted.

Nightmares

DANNI TORE ME UP for two more howls at the moon that night before I fell asleep and into a deep coma. She could have bitten my ear off completely, à la Mike Tyson, and I still wouldn't have gotten up. That's just how out of it I was. I was deep into what scientists call REM sleep, the dream level.

And that's what I did. I dreamed about a ménage à trois. Or I guess that's what happened. I didn't actually have sex in the dream, I just assumed that I had. All I remember is leaving one girl in the bedroom, while the other girl took a shower in the bathroom.

I climbed up out of bed to go join the second girl in the bathroom. The door was cracked open, so I took the liberty of stepping inside and right onto a cold, wet floor.

"Shit!" I reacted to the cold floor in my bare feet. I looked down at the water and found that fresh blood was dripping into it. I followed the dripping blood to the feet and bloody legs of the second woman, who was standing in the middle of the bathroom. Blood was trickling down between her legs in front of me. But I still hadn't looked into her face.

She said, "You see what you made me do? Do you see?"

I finally looked into the woman's face and it was Andrea. She held her bloody palms out toward me. She wore a bloodied, long white

T-shirt, with no underwear. Her loose brown hair was wet and cling-
ing to her head like in some kind of horror movie.

I said, "I didn't do that to you. I didn't."

I sounded like a punk. But you can't control what you say and do in
your dreams. It was like I was watching myself in a movie.

She screamed, "Yes, you did! You made me go to him! This is all
your fault. And look what he did to me."

It was all crazy.

I shook my head in denial. "I didn't make you go to him."

"You told me to. You said it would be better for me."

I was confused. Did I say that to her? I had said something of that
nature but I couldn't remember.

"Well, I didn't mean it," I responded in the dream.

Aw, man, I was so weak. Dreams are pitiful like that. You have no
control over how they play out in your conscience.

She said, "You did mean it. Now look at me. *Look at me!*"

Andrea continued to scream at me, while drenched in blood.

MAN, I woke the hell up in the middle of the night and was stunned.

"Fuck!" I cursed. I was nervous and shaking as chills overtook my
body.

I looked over at Danni, who was still sound asleep. Then I looked
over at the clock on my nightstand. It read 4:24 in green neon. I had to
get up and get ready for my flight to Miami by seven. The flight was
scheduled for 9:45 AM. I wasn't extra tired or anything. I usually only
got four to six hours of sleep anyway. But my mind was definitely tripping on me that morning.

"Shit," I cursed again. I thought about Corey. Had someone sent
him to put that crazy seed in my head about Andrea? Why was he so
interested in meeting up with me again anyway? I had to wonder. I
even felt like calling the guy and waking his ass up. But that would
have been extreme. How would he have taken that? He would have
thought I was a lunatic. If his actual intent was to get me to feel guilty

about my aborted relationship with Andrea, then my phone call in the middle of the night would have been a confirmation.

So there I was, stuck in the middle of the night, wondering about my old fling for no good damn reason. I didn't want her back, but if she wanted me, all she had to do was call. I still had all the same numbers.

"What's wrong?" Danni asked me out of the blue.

When she touched me lightly on the back, I jerked away from her as if she was a cold-fingered ghost.

"Shit." I wasn't expecting her to be up.

She looked at me and was confused. She asked me again, "What's wrong with you? Do I repel you or something? You never acted like that before."

She looked offended.

I shook my head and said, "Nah, nah, it doesn't have anything to do with you. I just . . . I just had a bad dream, that's all."

I only told her that because I didn't want her to feel offended. I didn't mean to pull away from her like that. She had simply caught me off-guard.

"A bad dream about what?"

That was a question I didn't want to answer. Danni even sat up in bed next to me to hear my response. But I wasn't planning on giving her one.

"I don't feel like talking about it. It wasn't pleasant, that's all."

"Was I in it?"

I didn't expect her to ask me that, but I guess it would have been a normal question after she had just gone to bed with me.

"No, you weren't in it." Then I thought I may have answered her too fast and too coldly. What would she ask me next? I could feel it coming.

"Was it about another woman?"

I had to stop her questions, so I did what every man has learned to do with women. I lied.

"I dreamt that I had gotten into a motorcycle accident and had ruined my whole face and body to the point where I couldn't model anymore. I mean, I was messed up real good and in the hospital. The doctors had bandaged up my entire head. I had hair missing and everything. It was just crazy."

To my surprise, Danni began to laugh at me. I didn't consider the story funny myself, whether I was lying to her or not. What if I was telling the truth? Is that how she would have responded to me? Or did she know that I was only bullshitting her.

I said, "That shit ain't funny, man." What was her angle?

She said, "I thought only us girls thought about stuff like that."

"I didn't think about it, I dreamt it," I told her.

"Same difference. If you're dreaming about it, that means you're trying to suppress it."

"Okay. So what? So you're saying that an athlete wouldn't think about getting injuries where he couldn't play his sport anymore? That's just not a girl thing. Everybody has those fears."

It sounded like I was fighting for my manhood. I had been doing that for years as a model, and I was still doing it on occasions like this one. Everybody had bad dreams every once in a while, didn't they?

Danni continued to smile and leaned back in bed.

"What time do you have to be at the airport again?" she asked me.

"Eight-thirty at the latest," I told her.

An hour before departure was always enough time for me because I rarely traveled heavy. But every now and then I'd be given a stack of complimentary clothes that I would have to fly back with.

Danni said, "I'm still gonna miss you," and reached out to touch my back a second time.

That girl wasn't going to miss me. Who was she kidding? She was around plenty of other guys who would treat her better than what I would. Her drinks should have worn off, so I figured she could tell the truth that morning.

"Why would you miss me?" I asked her. "Was the dick that good?"

It just slipped out of my mouth. What the hell, it was nearly five o'clock in the morning. If you can't be frank with a woman at five o'clock in the morning in your own bed, then when could you ever speak your mind to a woman?

Danni chuckled. She said, "The dick is definitely good, but I like the personality, too."

I turned and faced her. Damn, she was gorgeous . . . in the face. But her body couldn't match Andrea's. Danni was rail thin whereas Andrea had some bona fide curves.

I asked her, "Am I the last guy you've been with for a while?"

Danni stared at me for a minute before she answered.

"Do you want it to be like that? I mean, I can do that. All it is is a word."

There I was again, in a very similar situation. I didn't want Danni getting any more serious than sex. I had put my foot in my mouth by asking her about other guys. But it would be a hell of a lot safer if she was only dealing with me with no condoms.

"How many people are you seeing?" she asked me.

It was the wrong conversation for both of us.

"Honestly, I don't even want to go there. And you don't want me to."

"Yes, I do," she responded defiantly. "Are they all models?"

I paused for minute. Then I let her have it.

"Of course they are. That's all I'm ever around."

"That's not true. I know plenty of women who are attracted to you who are not models. I don't even hang out with other models, and my friends talk about you all the time," she told me.

She was telling me more information than I wanted to hear.

"What do you mean 'your friends talk about me all the time'? You tell them about us?"

It was obvious if they were talking about me.

She said, "That's one of the things that I like so much about you. I mean, you have no idea how popular you are. You just take the pictures and leave. It doesn't go to your head."

"So you tell them about us?" I repeated.

"No, I don't. I mean, they know that I know you, but that's about it."

That was bullshit and Danni was a terrible liar. She was one of those girls who couldn't look you in the face when she lied. Most of the time she didn't have to. Guys could barely get close to her. So I continued to stare at her until she began to crack a smile.

"I mean, I may have told them that I've slept with you once or twice, but not much more than that. They just keep bringing you up on their own when they see you in ads and things."

It was no big deal to me. I smiled with her.

She said, "Now tell me, how many women do you have relations with?"

I shook my head again. "We're not going there."

I laid back to get more rest before it was time to go. Danni leaned over and looked into my face, determined to get her answers.

"Is it that hard to answer me? It's not going to change how I feel about you if that's what you're thinking."

"Why even ask me then?"

"I'm just curious."

"Don't be. Because it will definitely kill you."

"Has it been that many? And you don't use condoms with any of them?"

She looked alarmed. I had to answer that.

"Oh, no, I wear condoms. But how many do *you* have with no condoms?"

We both needed to answer those questions.

She answered, "Only you with no condoms. I do have two other guys that I see, but it's not that much, you know. We're all busy doing what we do. I mean, I barely see them."

"You barely see me either," I told her. "And how would these other two guys feel if you just up and dropped them?"

"It's no big deal to them. Trust me."

"So, it's not much of a sacrifice for you then," I told her.

"Sure it is. Every girl likes to be pampered," she stated with a smile.

It sounded like a similar conversation indeed. Danni wanted me to choose her over everyone and pamper her like a legitimate girlfriend.

But at least she didn't have a guy's diamond ring to pressure me with. Not yet, at least.

"Would you cut your other women loose for me?" she asked me.

Before I answered I thought about Andrea and my bad dream that night. Would it be so bad to give Danni the illusion that I would work things out with her? Not saying that I had to, but would it really be that bad of an idea to cut off several women for the commitment of one? I was really thinking the idea over.

"Let me think about it over this trip," I told her.

She nodded. "That's fair enough. I mean, it's not like I'm asking you to give blood or anything."

I looked into her eyes to catch her smiling. If she only knew how crazy my dream was that night, she wouldn't have joked about blood like that. But I hadn't told her my real dream, and I never would.

I said, "We'll see when I get back," and I planned to leave it at that.

Celibacy

I ARRIVED IN MIAMI that Friday slightly before noon, and was surprised by my girl Judi Wells, who was waiting for me at the airport. I had told her weeks before that I had a shoot in her area, but I didn't expect to see her waiting for me in the terminal as soon as I hopped off the plane. Judi had been living in Miami, a hot spot for international models, for the past three years.

She was wearing a lime green dress, gold heels, accessories, and a golden brown straw hat, and all eyes were on her. I liked to call Judi "Essence." She had that chocolate brown, sophisticated, sister-girl look that *Essence* magazine liked to feature. She had been in several of their fashion spreads over the past five years. We had been friends and occasional lovers for six.

"Hey, I wasn't planning on seeing you here," I told her. I barely had time to free my mind from Danni and Andrea that morning.

Judi smiled with her perfect pearly whites. "I figured I'd surprise you."

She surprised me all right. I gave her a strong hug and stepped away. She smelled better than she needed to, making me think with the wrong head before I could even get out of the airport terminal with her.

"Ahhh . . . what kind of perfume is that?"

She grinned, knowing good and well what I was thinking.

"It's Jean Paul Gaultier."

I said, "It's soft and sweet, but not too much."

"Just enough is all I need," she commented.

I smiled. "Yeah, tell me about it." I was thinking with the wrong head again.

She said, "I will. Later."

I looked forward to it. But then I started thinking about Danni. How quickly I had forgotten. Maybe I had too many women to seriously try and commit myself to only one. Danni had two other guys to choose from anyway. She would be all right.

Judi looked toward the baggage claim. "How many bags do we need to collect?" she asked me.

"None. I only brought my carry-on."

She looked and nodded. Then she began to walk toward the terminal exits and parking area. I followed her out with my carry-on bag in one hand and a copy of *Smooth* magazine in the other.

Judi glanced at my magazine while she led me through the exit door. On the cover jacket was a half black, half Native American girl. They called her Thunder Horse. She had beautiful bronzed skin, long legs, and all the right curves in her purple, orange, and white swimsuit to earn her name.

"I see you kept yourself awake on the plane," Judi hinted to me.

I chuckled. "Yeah, just keeping tabs on your competition."

"She's not my competition. I don't go there."

I gave her a quick nod and decided to leave it alone. There were all different kinds of models, and whatever paid your bills was cool with me.

Judi asked me, "So what hotel do they have you staying in?"

"The Hilton."

She nodded as we headed through the parking garage in search of her car. She wasn't too talkative that day, that's for sure. Judi usually had a lot to say. She was heavy into philosophy.

I got curious and asked her, "What's on your mind this morning? You seem to be in deep thought over something."

She took a breath and said, "I've been doing a lot of meditating about my life lately, Terrance. I mean, there's just so many things that we all could be doing for the betterment of ourselves and for others, you know?"

That was another reason why I liked to call her Essence. Judi was the one woman who could bring you back down to earth with her talk about one's responsibilities to the common man. She just would not allow herself to enjoy her blessings without feeling guilty about those who were less privileged.

I asked her, "What do you want to do, a nature walk for charity?" I was trying to lighten her mood. Frankly, I wasn't in the right frame of mind for hearing any let's-go-save-the-world speeches. I was in Miami, and outside of my photo shoot, the only thing I was thinking about was hanging out at the hot clubs that lined South Beach.

My quip at least got a smile out of her.

She said, "You just keep it light, don't you?"

"Heavy only holds you down," I told her. "That's why I like traveling light and living light."

She grinned and nodded.

When we reached her car, a yellow Volkswagen Bug, I started grinning. She used to drive a black Corvette.

"I see you're downsizing with cheerful colors," I commented.

She faced me and smiled, while opening the rounded trunk to toss my bag in.

"I wanted to surprise you. I traded in the Corvette over a month ago."

"I see. And are you satisfied with the trade?"

"I'm very satisfied." She sounded very confident in her answer, too. I guess she had had to tell a lot of people that.

I climbed in on the passenger's side and found it a lot more spacious than I imagined. In fact, the yellow bug had more room than her Corvette had.

Judi climbed behind the wheel on the driver's side and said, "I find it very liberating. I have similar start speed, plus I can get in and out of spots with ease."

"You have similar start speed?" I questioned. I could believe the in and out of small spots part, but there was no way a Volkswagen Bug had similar start speed to a Corvette.

Judi smiled at me. She pulled the gear into reverse and backed out of her parking spot. Then she righted the wheel and gassed around the corners toward the parking lot exit.

I asked her, "Are you trying to prove something to me?"

She smiled and shook her head. "You always seem to bring the badness out of me."

"Aww, don't blame that on me. You're the one who started talking about start speeds. That means you had already experimented with it. And I didn't buy you that Corvette either."

I had her cheesing like normal again.

"So, you don't start shooting until tomorrow morning?"

"Yeah, we have wardrobe tonight, and then we shoot all day with a crowd in the background tomorrow."

She nodded. "What time is wardrobe?"

"Three to seven."

We hit the road and headed for my suite at the Hilton. It wasn't far from the airport.

"You wanna order room service for lunch at your hotel? I really need to talk to you about some of the changes I've made in my life."

I didn't see anything wrong with that, but her tone was ominous.

"Okay."

WE ARRIVED at the Hilton, where I checked into my suite on the seventh floor. Lucky me.

Judi walked in, kicked off her shoes, plopped her hat down on the chair, and sat in the middle of my king-size bed, good and comfortable.

"Can you pass me the menu?"

I was still standing, close to the office desk near the window. I grabbed the menu off the desk and tossed it onto the bed.

"Thank you."

Judi went ahead and ordered a grilled chicken salad, ginger ale, and vanilla ice cream for both of us. Then she patted the bed for me to join her.

That was the kind of woman she was, very self-assured and fluid with her moves. Judi wielded power without much effort. It was just in her to be that way. She was older than most of the other girls I dealt with.

Once I walked over and sat on the bed beside her, she cupped my head in her hands and stared into my eyes. She had me right up close to her. She said, "You know what I decided to do?"

She waited until I asked her, "What?"

"I decided to go celibate."

I nodded to her. "Congratulations." I didn't know what else to say. She made it seem as if celibacy was a major achievement, so I decided to treat it that way.

"How long has it been?" I asked her. I hadn't touched Judi in that way in over a year. But when you're a legitimate model like she was, the opportunities to indulge were endless.

She answered, "Six weeks."

I don't know if it was just me, but a month and a half would have sounded a lot more solid than six weeks. Six weeks sounded as if she was counting the days, the hours, and the minutes. Compared to six months, or six years, six weeks sounded breakable. But a month and a half, which is essentially the same thing as six weeks, sounded as if you were actually building something.

"Have you ever thought about it?" she asked me.

"Thought about what?"

I knew she wasn't asking me what I *thought* she was asking me.

"You know, abstaining from sex."

I said, "For what? Why would a healthy, sexually active guy want to abstain all of a sudden?"

"To stop from cheating yourself," she answered. "I mean, do you realize that sex is here to enjoy your mate unconditionally. That's why it feels how it feels and we do what we do when it's good. And can you imagine how much stronger it would be if we actually stored it up for the right person, at the right time, for the right reasons. I mean . . . You know what I mean?"

She was really trying to get me to understand her point. Her passion was written all over her gleeful face, as if abstinence and celibacy were the greatest discoveries on earth.

"But what if, after all of that, you end up with a person who just doesn't know what they're doing?" I joked. "Then what? I mean, you just wasted all that time."

"No you didn't. You didn't waste anything. You only waste it when you do it for no reason with people you don't care about."

I said, "So, you didn't care about me?"

It was a good question.

She answered, "Of course I did. And I still do. That's why I'm here with you now, telling you this. You have the potential to make a change."

"But a change for who, and for what? Why are you trying to change me? I mean, I'm happy with how I live."

"Are you really?"

She sounded disappointed in me. I guess she figured I should have been reaching for more.

She said, "Do you realize how much you could change in this world if you actually used your voice? The pictures only tell half of the stories."

I said, "What does that have to do with celibacy and abstinence? And why do you feel that people would even listen to me? We're models. We're not politicians."

"We don't have to be politicians to say something, Terrance."

"Well, anybody can say something, but to get the people to actually listen to you is something else."

I felt like she was barking up the wrong damn tree. The argument was pointless to me. There were a lot of ways a person could be helpful to the community that had nothing to do with your personal life, or your personal statements. You could start a foundation without ever having to change who you are and what you do. Celebrities did it all the time.

Judi said, "The power that you take over your personal appetites is the same power that you'll need to be true to what you're doing in the public arena."

"Well, who said I wanted to be involved in the public arena like that? That's not my world."

Judi looked at me and recoiled. "That's not your world? What are you talking about? You are in the public arena. That's why these companies pay to use your imagery, Terrance. Whether you realize it or not, you have followers. You have people who will buy certain items because you promote them. So why can't you promote a particular lifestyle to them while you're at it?"

I told her, "Look, people want to live how they want to live, Judi. They don't care about us being celibate. That's not important to them. But sex . . . that's important. And they want that. They don't want to be thinking about some perfect man or some perfect situation. That's not the desired reality."

Judi was steadily shaking her head. She said, "You're wrong, Terrance. You're wrong. We all want more control over ourselves. We just don't know how to do it."

I smiled. I said, "Well, shoving beautiful models in their face every day won't make it any easier for them."

Judi looked down into the bedsheets. She said, "That's my biggest dilemma. So I've been thinking about giving up modeling. It's hypocrisy."

I said, "Let me get this straight. You say that we have a certain credibility as models, since we're in the public eye with what we do. And we are therefore able to make an example of change through our own lifestyle changes. But then you're thinking about quitting what gives you that power in the first place, so you won't look like a hypocrite while pushing items that may not be all that good for them?"

I said, "Well, how about only modeling for products that are community-based and community positive then?"

The irony was that those items typically viewed as "good for them" were generally harder to promote because they were supported less and made less money. But the things that people seemed to like and support—sex, cigarettes, alcohol, drugs, violent films, addictive music—were in constant need of regulations and restrictions because they were craved so strongly. However, the library was free. They only charged you to bring their books back so more people could share them.

Judi said, "I've already begun to do that. I'm modeling for causes now."

"Well, that's all you need to do then. You don't need to quit. You're still beautiful," I told her.

She chuckled. "Thank you. But what about you? Are you willing to make a change?"

She was dead serious, too.

I said, "Are you asking everybody to do this? Why do you want me to make a change?"

She joked and said, "Because you're in room seven-twelve. You're the lucky one."

"The lucky numbers are seven-eleven," I told her.

"Whatever."

By then our food had arrived. I signed the bill and gave our Latino server a tip.

"*Gracias,*" he told me.

I nodded to him.

When he left the room, I joked and said, "How about giving up our food and abstaining from eating to support those who don't have food."

Judi gave me the evil eye as she uncovered her grilled chicken.

"Don't play with me. I already starve myself. That's another thing I don't like about modeling."

"Oh, so starving is not good with food, but it is good with sex?" I continued.

Judi shook her head at me as she began to stuff her face.

"You are impossible," she mumbled through her first bite of food.

"And you are trying to make the impossible happen," I told her. Then we went ahead and stuffed our mouths.

Cock Blocking

JUDI AND I DROVE OVER to a place called The Outfitters Warehouse for my wardrobe selections. I had to shoot at several Miami Beach locations for Class-A Jewelry, wearing complimentary outfits. Class-A wanted outfits that would pop. So I tried on a lot of bright colors: oranges, limes, rich golds, turquoise blues.

Judi had nothing on her schedule, so she decided to spend the entire day with me.

"I really like the orange on you. It's pretty blinding," she commented. I was trying on an orange button-up short-sleeve with a wide collar. I didn't check for the designer. I tried not to. I was into style, and the designers who created what I liked reaped the rewards of their mention in the back credits.

"Yeah, as long as it doesn't overpower the jewelry," I responded.

Henry Shoals, the stylist, and Mark Simion, the photographer, were both there.

"The white gold would work well with that orange," Judi suggested.

Henry nodded. "Hmm, she has a point. That orange shirt would overpower the yellow gold, but it would definitely bring life to the white."

Henry was a short, gray-haired white man in his early fifties who still had a young man's energy and zest for life. Mark was much younger, in his late twenties. He was just happy to be there on assignment. He had a loose, hippie style of dress and dark curls. His camera hung around his neck.

"That works for me," he told us.

Judi said, "The lime green sets off the yellow gold. But you could probably get away with an olive as well. A darker green would allow the yellow gold to stand out a little more."

Mark checked out her theory from behind the lens of his camera. I wore a yellow gold watch and link chain.

"She's good," he said with a nod.

"What about the platinum jewelry?" Henry asked her.

Judi told him, "The turquoise blue. Platinum is more of a metallic tone than gold. Blue is a metallic color, and the turquoise blue adds a little extra flavor to it."

She spoke with the same raw confidence with which she always carried herself.

I joked and said, "Are you guys planning on paying her for this?" She was doing their job better than they were.

"Yeah, I may have to hire her to help me," Henry quipped.

I said, "She lives right here in Miami."

"I sure do," Judi told him.

He said, "We'll definitely exchange numbers."

IT WAS WELL after seven when we finished with the wardrobe, and Judi and I were both hungry again. We stopped at a place called the Golden Dish, a Thai restaurant in the middle of downtown Miami.

While we waited for our food, I stared at the intricate paint job and artwork that covered the walls.

"We need to do more of this kind of thing with soul-food restaurants," I said to Judi.

"What kind of theme would you have?" she asked me. She took a sip of the herbal tea she had ordered for both of us.

I shrugged my shoulders. I hadn't thought about any particular theme, I just felt we needed something extra in soul-food spots to represent the culture.

"Maybe we should have African sculpture and artifacts on the walls."

"But would that be from soul-food culture or more Afrocentric history?" Judi questioned.

"What difference does it make? It's all the same culture. Why separate the American from the African? I mean, that's who we are, right? African Americans. So why not represent that?"

Judi nodded to me. "Good point." Then she smiled. "So why are we in a Thai restaurant? You think *they* would stop to eat in a soul-food spot?"

I thought about it and smiled back at her.

"Probably not."

"So what makes us so prone to follow other people's culture? I don't think anyone eats as much Chinese food as black people do."

I asked her, "You think someone else eats more soul food than us?"

We were playing a game of wits. Like I said, Judi was my *Essence* magazine girl, always thoughtful. She said, "I see your point."

"And what about pizza?" I asked her. "Is that still Italian food, or is it all-American food now?"

Judi laughed. She said, "You never cease to amaze me."

I didn't know how to take that.

"You mean with my intellect?" I asked her to make sure. Some folks had this idea that models were not supposed to think, as if we didn't experience the world just because we made our livings taking pictures. Judi, of all people, should have known better than that.

She said, "Sometimes you try to act aloof on purpose to stop yourself from taking your life up to that other level. But you don't have to be afraid of going there."

I said, "I'm not afraid of anything. Why can't I just be satisfied with where I am? I have a pretty good life in front of me. I have my health. I have my sanity. I have a bit of a nest egg. What else could I ask for?"

Our waitress made her way back to our table before Judi could respond. We gave our orders then resumed our conversation.

"You could have a real purpose for what you're doing, Terrance. Have you ever thought about that?"

Of course I had. "I do have a purpose," I told her.

"Which is?"

"To keep working and keep living."

"That's not a purpose. That's a function of life."

"Not for a lot of people. A lot of people don't have a function. A lot of people don't function period."

Judi was quickly tiring of my small talk. She let out a sigh and appeared ready to drop the discussion. And she was right. I didn't like battling wits for too long. For what? I figured I had nothing to prove to anyone. I knew I had intelligence; I would determine my own life values and not have someone else impose theirs on me.

Judi didn't need to convince me, anyway. She had plenty of guys who would bend over backward for her. So I moved on without thinking anymore about it.

BY THE TIME we finished our meal, it was close to ten o'clock. I had a one-track mind at that point: hit South Beach and check out the action at the nightclubs. A few of the promoters and radio guys I knew from Miami had already put my name on several of the guest lists for that night. But what about Judi?

She was pretty silent as she drove me across the bridge to the beach area. Maybe she was tired. She didn't have to hang out every minute with me. I knew how to get around by myself, and I told her so.

"Look, ah, if you're tired, just drop me off and I'll get a taxi back to the Hilton. I mean, I don't want to inconvenience you."

She didn't respond immediately. I guess she was thinking it over. To tell you the truth, I would rather go solo. With Judi's celibacy issues, I figured that going to a nightclub with me was the wrong atmosphere for her to be in. I was definitely not celibate, and I still knew how to score.

She finally said, "I don't mind."

"Are you sure?"

"Yeah, it'll be fun to hang out with you."

I didn't feel the same way. I didn't want to be rude and tell her that I'd rather see her in the morning, where she could accompany me to the photo shoot if she wanted, but that was damn sure what I was thinking.

I said, "Now, you do know there's gonna be plenty of women here who are not abstaining from anything, right?"

Judi looked into my eyes and frowned.

"I've been in these clubs, and I'm a grown woman, Terrance. I know what goes on there."

I heard her words loud and clear. All I could do was acknowledge them.

"Okay." Then I wondered how she'd react when I told her I was on the guest list of a place called Beds, where you actually partied and drank on oversized beds.

We arrived at the heart of South Beach, Miami, at 6th and Washington streets, and ran right into heavy traffic.

"Looks like they're starting early tonight," I commented.

"Lucky you," Judi responded with a forced grin.

I could tell it was forced because it didn't last long.

"Okay, where to?" she asked me.

I didn't want to start off at Beds. I figured I would shake Judi sooner or later, and then go to Beds on my own.

"Let's go to Opium," I told her. That was a safer bet.

We found a parking spot next to a meter, and walked a good two blocks back to the club. Opium was the kind of club where a lot of national celebrities hung out. The staff and bouncers at the front door were not too receptive to local nobodies. Fortunately, I was neither.

So we walked right up front and past the line of onlookers so I could give them my name.

"Terrance Mitchell."

They looked on the guest list and found me.

"Hey, you're the model guy, right?" one of the bouncers asked me. He was a beefcake white guy with close to a bald head, wearing all black.

I nodded to him as we headed toward the entrance doors.

"Yeah."

He looked like an aspiring model himself, for sportswear, body-building, vitamins, and workout spas.

As soon as Judi and I walked in, the eyes all swung in our direction. Everyone wanted to see which celebrities would walk in next. I wasn't tripping on that. I was no celebrity. I was just a good-looking guy, paid well to model, who knew the right people. Nevertheless, I looked good enough with Judi on my arm to keep the crowd's attention for a minute.

"These people need to get a life," she commented, louder than a whisper. Some of the folks who were near us overheard her. But her bold tongue only made them more curious. Celebrities were prone to dissing locals. And whenever I frequented celebrity-attended events, the locals would eat up their every word, move, or spite, in L.A. and Miami in particular. Snobbish attitudes didn't fly so well in New York, D.C., and Chicago. But Miami and L.A. pampered the stars.

I looked around and surveyed the ratio of nationality in the place. Latinos and whites ruled the numbers. Even my DJ and promoter friends were Latin.

"Hey, Mr. T. How you like it? You lovin' it, or what?"

Mario Rome faced me with two Latin mommies under his arms—one dark-haired, one light-haired, both gorgeous.

"And the night has just begun," I told him with a smile and a nod.

"You're the model, right?" his light-haired girlfriend asked me. "You think I got what it takes?"

She was right on my case. But she was a little too short and round for fashion modeling. She was more in line for hip-hop videos and swimsuit posters. But she was perfect as a significant other. She was what normal guys would go crazy for, including me.

I said, "I wouldn't worry about modeling if I were you. Instead, I would fly straight out to Hollywood and do some acting. The moving cameras would love you."

She stared at me for a second as if she were in a trance. I was used to that. The gene gods had blessed me.

Judi spoke up and said, "You're gonna need more height and less curves for real modeling jobs, Maria. That's just how it goes."

No one responded to Judi's comments.

I asked her, "What if her name's not Maria?" I was just trying to lighten things back up. Judi was taking it too seriously.

"It's not," the light-haired Latina told us. "It's Candace."

"Let me go tell Vinny Blues to give you a shout out," Mario Rome told me. I guess he wanted to get out of Dodge.

I was ready to tell him not to bother. I didn't need all that extra attention, but he was already gone, leaving his two girlfriends with us.

The dark-haired girl reached out her hand to mine.

"I'm Alex."

"Terrance."

Alex was actually slimmer than Candace and taller. She was closer to what the runway would want to see. Candace was just more outspoken.

Alex then moved on to Judi.

Judi took her hand and gave her name.

"I guess you already know my name," Candace spoke up again.

I smiled, right before Vinny Blues called my name over the microphone.

"We got my man Terrance Mitchell in the house for the ladies who love a *GQ* man. You don't see a whole lot of *GQ* men walking around, so make sure y'all give him love out there tonight. Mr. T," he called out from behind his DJ booth.

That really got the eyes of the club crowd swinging in my direction. I had always managed to get my share of attention in a crowd, based on my appearance alone, but the timely shout out made me an instant babe magnet.

"I guess I better get out of your way before they trample me," Judi commented. I couldn't call it a joke, because she didn't appear to be joking. However, Candace and Alex laughed at it.

I was trapped in my emotions for a minute, but then I reverted to what I had been trained to do; I chilled. I was used to camera lights, crowds, and women hollering and hooting, so the Miami party crowd was nothing new to me. You just had to wait until they all got it out of their systems. Then you approached who you wanted to approach.

"So, are you used to that yet?" Alex asked me.

I grinned knowingly. "Yeah, I'm used to it. Are you?"

Judi looked away from us and seemed bored with it all. I was counting the minutes until she would decide to leave.

I had become a natural with women. I can't say I always had them, I just can't remember anymore when I didn't.

Judi looked at me and frowned. She knew I was ready to turn it on. I was in that environment. What did she expect me to do?

Alex said, "I don't get it all like that. Now Candace, she's the one who gets all the attention."

Candace started laughing, but I didn't believe all of what Alex was saying. She was gaming me. I was sure she got her share of attention, she was just quieter, which probably meant she was more crafty. In her sly way, she was basically telling me to choose her instead of her extroverted friend.

"So the guys don't often look at you, huh?" I teased her to test my theory.

Candace protested her friend's game.

"Aww, man, that's bullshit. She gets 'em. She gets the good ones."

Now that I could believe. Men of higher caliber generally liked women who carried themselves with a little more tact. We prefer women who open up in private, and usually only for us. It was an exclusivity and ego thing.

"Well, I'm off to the restroom," Judi told me. I don't know if she was upset or not, but she had no reason to be. We were friends who were only part-time lovers, and she had announced an end to part-time loving. I had pretty much warned her that I was out there on the Miami nightclub scene to be me, and that included showcasing my skills with the ladies.

While Alex and Candace chatted me up for themselves, I scanned the crowd for other women who were game for my attention that night. I figured I would have some salsa in my love life. The Latinas were feeling me in there. There were a few white girls looking, but the catch of Miami were Cuban, Dominican, and Puerto Rican girls. I had done my research, but I decided to ask to make sure.

"So what are you both Cuban?" I asked Alex and Candace.

"She's all Cuban, but I'm Cuban and Dominican," Candace answered.

"Oh, a double dip, huh?"

"Whatever that means."

Mario Rome rejoined us.

"Hey man, this is a good night. Look at all the lovely ladies in here. Usually we have to hold the guys outside for a while. Looks like we can let 'em in early tonight."

That was another perk of the more exclusive nightclubs. They tended to be more populated by women, making the pickings of established men much easier.

"Hey, let's hit the VIP room," Mario told me.

I still wanted to chill with Alex myself. We both looked at each other and knew.

"I'll be here," she told me, grinning. She knew I wanted her. She touched my hand again and had me sold. But there were never any guarantees. The night was still too young.

I told Mario, "We have to wait for Judi. She just ran off to the bathroom."

I figured I could slide Alex my number just in case I didn't get a chance to make it back to her that night. In my fast-moving profession, with flighty models and their entourages, I learned to get it while it's hot, or lose it to the next man.

Mario looked at me and frowned. He said, "Candace can bring her back. She knows everybody here."

Then it dawned on me that Mario may have had his own ties to the lovely Latinas. Latinos were sometimes clingy that way. Nevertheless, he did walk them over to me. But was the introduction for his benefit or mine? They didn't act attached to anyone. Then again, if Candace would walk Judi back over to us in the VIP section, Alex would most likely accompany them. So I would find a way to slide her my number later.

"Okay," I obliged Mario with a nod. I gave Alex one more look before I moved on behind him.

"So, what's the story with those two?" I asked my friend as soon as we walked away.

Mario turned and grinned at me. "I knew I would get you open with them."

"So it was planned?"

"Not really. They're what I call sexy cohosts. I'm just trying them out."

"So a guy's not supposed to fall for them, or he is?"

Mario started laughing at me.

"They do what they're supposed to do, man. They make you feel like you can."

I shut my mouth for a minute. I knew a tease from a score. Candace was a tease, but Alex was a score. She had already stepped out of her boundaries with me. I could tell. Her telling me she would be around was my clue to let her do the work on her own. Or maybe not. Maybe she was better at her game of flirting than I thought she was.

The VIP section had more men than the regular areas. I recognized several professional athletes immediately—basketball, football, and boxing guys. Then you had your hip-hop guys and actors. Imagine that; a club full of Latin and white women with high-priced brothers all over the VIP. That was the new pecking order of America for you, and I was welcomed right into it.

"Hey, that's Terrance Mitchell, the model dude. What's happening, man?"

I nodded, shook hands, bought drinks, and mingled with them, but I won't tell no names. It's an exclusive membership thing, and a number of those guys were married.

"You probably don't even have to try to get women, do you?" one of the ballers asked me. I guess he recognized that I was more handsome than they were.

"I figured I would ask you the same thing," I told him. Athletes didn't have to worry as much about their looks. That seemed to be much stronger than game to me. Then again, a lot of women only wanted their money.

He smiled and held his drink up high in his right hand.

"It's a good life."

Despite the love they were all showing me, I didn't feel as comfortable in the VIP section as I did in the regular areas. The VIP seemed too obvious. Every woman there was looking to score with one of the ballers or rappers, or gaining points for themselves just for being inside the room. It reminded me of an old-country gentlemen's whorehouse. If you were inside the room, then you were important enough to pick a whore. Only I didn't like to think of women in that way. I still wanted there to be some mystery involved. There was no mystery in that room. The most important ballers could basically pick who they wanted, and the rest would scramble for the loose bones. It was like a documentary on mating, straight from Animal Planet.

Before I knew it, Judi, Candace, and Alex were up in the room. I knew that the VIP was not where Judi wanted to be in her present state of mind. But I was curious to see how Candace and Alex would act in the room.

As expected, Candace jumped into flirtation mode with anyone who got her attention. After talking to Mario about her, I understood

that it was all an act. I was still skeptical of Alex, though. She continued to be coy with the attentions she received.

"I can tell I don't want to hang around this place for too long," Judi
commented.

Tell me something I didn't know.

I said, "I don't like being up in here either."

Alex gave me another look right after one of the ballers was unsuc-
cessful at caressing her hand.

Judi saw it, too. "Looks like somebody likes you," she commented.

I didn't want to speak on that. How much of good friends were we?
I had never gone after another woman in Judi's presence before. But
since she was no longer on the market for my affections, maybe she
would understand. I still had those needs.

"Would you mind?" I mumbled to her. The best way to find out is
to ask, right?

Judi turned and looked in my eyes. That alone gave me my answer.

"Well, as a friend, I expected to be able to hang out with you and
enjoy your company."

"You are enjoying my company."

She paused and looked away for a minute. Then she said, "Would
you even ask me that if you thought we would have sex tonight?"

It was a good question. Judi was on to something. Her celibacy issue
had given me an excuse to be disrespectful of our relationship. I had a
lot of strange relationships with women. We were friends and lovers
who played a careful dance while in the presence of other people.

"I see your point. You are right about that," I told her.

"You think that's fair of you?" she asked me.

We were in a much deeper conversation than everyone else in that
room, and I could see Alex watching from the corner of my eye as
Judi continued to face me. Alex was really into me, and that was only
making my situation worse.

I said, "Well, when you're honest you bring out . . . more honesty."

Judi said, "So, you want some pussy that bad tonight? You mean to
tell me you can't go one night without it?"

That was out of character for the Judi I knew. It made me feel that she had already gotten a lot of flack over her decision. I could just imagine. It also made me wonder what guy had pissed her off to the point of cutting off her well.

I kept my cool and answered, "Yeah, Judi. I'm a grown-ass man."

"A grown-ass dog is more like it," she scoffed at me.

I didn't take it personally. I could tell when a woman was hurt. I felt like hugging her. But not in front of Alex. That only made me feel more guilty. I wanted what I wanted regardless of my friendship or Judi's feelings. I halfway expected her to make a scene. It was a fifty-fifty chance.

Judi said, "Well, I'ma help you control yourself tonight."

I thought about it and smiled. She was being a little bit of an ass-hole.

"Hey, Judi, what's going on?" a VIP baller asked her. He had just walked into the room.

I recognized him and was shocked. Since he didn't bother to speak to me, I immediately assumed that they had a connection. Was he the one who had turned Judi sour to sex? Again, I won't name any names, but this guy was a real popular football player.

Judi blew his ass off like a scorned woman.

"I'll talk to you in a minute."

He looked at me and nodded. "Hey."

At least he acknowledged me. I guess he had no choice. I didn't want to speak back to him though. It seemed insignificant, so I just returned his nod as he walked away.

When I met eyes with Judi, she already knew what I was thinking.

"Now how would you feel if I went off with him tonight?" she asked me.

It was a thought. Judi gets the football player, and I get Alex.

"Don't even answer that," she told me. I guess she could read my mind.

I cracked a smile. I couldn't help it.

She said, "I don't believe you." I felt like an overgrown kid being scolded by his mother. I knew I was wrong, but I couldn't stop my thoughts.

Judi said, "Well, it's not gonna happen; not tonight."

"What?" I asked her. Was she talking about her and the football player, or me and Alex?

"We came here together, and we're gonna leave together," she cleared up for me. That answered both of my questions.

Before I could stop myself, I was already shaking my head in defiance.

"Look, Judi, I understand your situation, I really do. But I'm just not . . ."

I shook my head again, contemplating the whole celibacy issue. Had it been any woman I knew outside of Judi, I wouldn't have believed her. But Judi was the kind of woman who meant what she said, every time.

"We need to get away from here," she told me. The next thing I knew, she was pulling me by the hand.

"What are you doing?" I asked her.

She said, "I'm serious about this, Terrance. Get a grip on yourself."

I watched Alex turn away, and that did it. Judi had killed the mood. Alex could now determine that it was a bad situation to get involved in. That pissed me off. Judi and I didn't have a situation.

I waited until Judi got me outside of the club to let her know how I felt. I wasn't into making scenes. I planned on being stern and discrete in private. So I led her away from the club and in between the parked cars that lined the side streets.

I faced Judi there and let her have it. "Look, had I known you would have had this much of a problem with me having . . ."

All of a sudden, I stopped and stared forward with my mouth still open. Judi looked to see who or what I was staring at.

It was Andrea, wearing an all-white two-piece with a gold belt and gold shoes. Or was it? I continued to stare to make sure. She was with a girlfriend who wore a similar white outfit, not the exact same one, but close enough. She didn't look bad from the short distance. I figured she would look busted from what Corey had told me. But she was still shapely and lively.

In a flash, I had a rush of emotions come over me. I didn't know if I wanted to run up to her and speak, or just stare her down to see if she would speak to me first. Then she turned to face me and our eyes locked in on one another. My heart skipped a beat in shock, and I anticipated anything, only to relax again and take a deep breath.

That's not Andrea, I told myself. The woman only looked like her from the side of her head. So we both looked away as two strangers and went on about our night.

"Who is that?" Judi asked me. She had never met Andrea or heard me mention her name, but we had talked about her once or twice in casual conversations. In friendship, I had asked Judi's objective opinions on a few of the other women I had dealt with over the years.

Once I determined that the woman in the distance was not who I thought she was, I looked into Judi's eyes and saw that she was hurt. She turned and walked away from me.

"You can get yourself a cab home now. And go on back in there and get your girl. Or whoever the hell you want to be with tonight."

She didn't really mean that. I felt her pain. I looked like a real asshole that night, so I followed her to make amends.

"Go on, Terrance, do what you gotta do," she told me.

I didn't say a word, I just continued to follow her. I figured that one night without sex wouldn't kill me.

"So you still want to talk about this?" I asked her.

She obviously had some issues to handle.

"What difference does it make? You don't respect what I'm doing."

"I do," I told her. "I just don't see how I'm included in that. I didn't ask to become celibate. It's not fair of you to force this situation on me. I didn't sign up for that."

She stopped and faced me again. We were out in the middle of the street.

"Your attention never swayed from me like that before I told you."

"Yeah, but that's before you told me. That's like telling a guy you have a heart condition. If he cares about you, he's gonna take it easy on you."

"Oh, so you think you're taking it easy on me by letting me know that I don't exist anymore? Is that your idea of sympathy, to outright ignore me?"

She had a point of course. I had officially moved on from Judi, right there in her face, just because she had told me there would be no more opportunities for physical contact.

She said, "Now what if I went ahead and decided to give you some anyway? Would that make everything all good for you again?"

I said, "But then you would be forsaking your very serious decision."

She stared and said, "Don't patronize me, Terrance."

"I'm not."

"Yes, you are."

Sex Crazy

JUDI DROVE ME BACK to the Hilton, where she decided to stay with me for the rest of the night. Now I had slept with women without digging into them before, plenty of times. I just didn't feel like doing it that night. I know I told myself I could do it, sleep without fucking, but for whatever reason, I was extra horny that night. I wanted Judi so bad that it was killing me. Was it because she had suddenly become off-limits? Or was I as much of a dog as she had accused me of being?

So I sat up in the dark, on the left side of the king-size bed, stiff as an unripe banana, and not knowing what to do with myself. I couldn't even leave the television on. It would have only been a distraction. I wanted to think hard about what was going on with me. How badly did I need to have sex?

I looked over at Judi who was sound asleep in one of my T-shirts, wearing shiny pink panties and no bra. Damn she looked tasty. But I had to control myself. So I left Judi alone and stared up at the ceiling. That's when memories of Andrea popped into my head. I had a normal sex life when I was with her. She was my steady woman, so I had no anxieties about anything. But it seemed that once she was no longer in my life, I was ready to fuck anyone and everyone. I hadn't thought about it in detail, but my sex life was a lot more erratic after

Andrea. Was that what the single life was all about, fucking without purpose? Maybe Judi was right.

I sighed and remained horny. *Fuck it, Andrea's no longer in my life, and I like to fuck,* I admitted. So I stopped trying to control myself, and I reached out with my right hand and rubbed it across the small hill of Judi's ass. I had no idea how she would react to it. I guess I was going to find out.

At first she didn't respond to it. So I backed my hand over her ass again.

When Judi failed to respond to my second round of ass rubbing, I got excited. Maybe she would change her mind and act like a normal woman again. So I leaned over and positioned my brown banana against her hip. I was so hard that it probably felt like a stick-up weapon against her smooth skin. I rubbed it around in circles on her hip, ready to burglarize her ass.

All of a sudden, she spoke up through the dark. "Terrance? What are you doing?"

I was stuck. Did I need to tell her the truth, or did I need to bullshit? "Ah . . . I don't know," I told her. That was a lie. I knew exactly what I was doing. I was hoping that a hard dick up against her soft skin, in the middle of the night, would remind her of her past freakiness and revert her back to the old days. But Judi turned over to face me instead.

She said, "I knew this would happen."

I tried not to say it, but my stiff Johnson made me do it anyway. "Well, why you stay with me then?"

"Because we're friends."

That was the wrong answer for me. I said, "You know what? That's bullshit. You could have driven me back to my hotel and left. You didn't have to stay the night. You're trying to test me on purpose. And for what? That's not friendship. That's evil."

Judi sat up in bed and said, "I don't believe you. So we can't be friends without fucking?"

I said, "Nah, we can be friends. But not like this. You're sittin' up in here with silky, pink panties on."

"Does that bother you?"

"Of course it bothers me. I want them off. Right now."

She started to smile, but I was serious. I wanted to stick her with my magic stick.

"Terrance, I already explained my situation to you. I'm just not into casual sex anymore. Now you said you were okay with that, but if you're not, then I need to put on my things and drive on back home. . . . And it would be unforgivable if you made me drive home at this time of night," she added for good measure.

It was after three o'clock in the morning. But Judi was a big girl. She could handle late night. She had driven home from plenty of late parties before, later than three, so I was tempted to call her bluff. But I didn't.

"Go on back to sleep then," I told her. I said it, but I didn't mean it. I wanted her to stay up and change her mind. I still wanted her to give me a little something, or at least a blow job.

"Are you sure?" she asked me.

Yeah, I was sure all right. I was sure that I was lying to her.

I said, "Unless you wanna stay up and wrestle with me."

Judi shook her head. "Guys," she mumbled.

What did she mean by that?

"So now I'm just another guy. I'm not your friend anymore?" I asked her.

"Terrance, what do you think? Are you acting like a friend?"

"All I know is that I used to be a friend who was sometimes sexual," I told her.

"Well, just look at it this way. At least I'm not giving it to any other guys. So you're not losing out on anything."

"And how long is this supposed to last? I mean, you're gonna do this the rest of your life?" It was a valid question.

She said, "Of course not. I still want to have children. I still want to get married. I still wanna do a lot of things. I just need to cleanse my mind, body, and spirit for a minute. That's all."

I couldn't really argue with that. Her game sounded solid. I nodded my approval.

"Okay, well, like I said, go on back to sleep then."

Judi gave me another stare and returned my nod.

She took a deep breath and said "Okay" before she lay back down. I took a minute before I laid down myself. But I still couldn't sleep. I forced my eyes shut to convince myself to rest, and to sleep it off.

Thirty minutes later, I was still awake while Judi was snoring.

"Shit," I mumbled to myself through the dark.

I climbed out of the bed to use the bathroom and got to thinking about taking a walk around the hotel. It was four o'clock in the morning. After handling my business in the bathroom, I decided that I would take that walk. So I tossed on the complimentary white bathrobe from the room, with white slippers to match, and I snuck out with my key, headed for the lobby.

"Crazy," I mumbled to myself as I rode the elevator down.

My photo shoot at Miami Beach was in less than five hours, and there I was, walking around in a bathrobe at my hotel in the middle of the night, without getting a wink of sleep.

As soon as I reached the lobby and walked off the elevator, there was a lone black woman waiting to go up. She nearly walked into me trying to get on.

"Hey, are you sleepwalking?" I joked to her. At four o'clock in the morning, I was liable to say anything. I was also happy to see someone else still up.

She mumbled, "I wish," and walked onto the elevator.

I turned to face her. She was wearing night clothes, a long, pink nightgown. Pink was making a comeback for women; pink, orange, and bright green.

On instincts, I grabbed the elevator door and asked her, "You wanna talk about it?"

I could tell she had something to get off her mind. So did I. I needed to talk to someone about my unfounded sexual urges. Strangers were good for odd angles. I found that a lot of your friends thought the same way you did, or completely opposite. There was a whole lot more going on than simple black or white when it came to views on sex. Or at least I thought so.

Who knows what this woman wanted to talk about. I was guessing men. Women always wanted to talk about men; men, bills, and career aspirations. The order would change depending on what they already had going for themselves.

She looked at me and paused for a minute. She wanted to talk, sure she did. But it was awkward for a stranger to ask her to do so in the middle of the night at the elevators.

Finally she said, "Talk where?"

Good question. She didn't know me to invite me anywhere, or for me to invite her.

I said, "Right down here inside the restaurant. There's nobody there now. And it's nice and quiet in there."

She wasn't bad-looking either. A little plump compared to what I was used to, but she was cute in the face with reddish brown skin and jet black hair.

She stepped back off the elevator without speaking and headed toward the the restaurant area with me.

I reached out my hand to her and said, "My name is Terrance."

She looked at me and smiled. "You model?"

I was surprised by it. "Yeah, you've seen some of my work?"

I was always flattered by the folks who noticed me. I pretty much did the work and kept it moving. Not to say I didn't know what I was doing as a model, I just didn't sweat it too hard. I liked the perks that modeling afforded me though.

She said, "I thought you looked familiar. I think I saw you in *Complex* before. My boyfriend reads that a lot."

I nodded. "Yeah, I've been in *Complex* a few times. It's one of the few places where a brother can get a decent fashion spread. But I sure wish *Code* was still around. Most of the new men's mags are about

nothing but cars, ass, and tits. Excuse my candor," I told her. Hypo-
critically, I was up late thinking about ass myself.

"Oh, don't worry about that, I've heard much worse than that," the
woman told me. She said, "And my name is Rachel."

"Well, I'm pleased to meet you, Rachel."

We walked over to the hotel restaurant and sat in a comfortable
booth, facing each other.

"So, what's on your mind at four o'clock in the morning that keeps
you up late in your nightclothes?" I asked her.

She said, "I was gonna ask you the same thing."

"So we're both crazy then," I stated with a chuckle. I tried to keep
it real but light at the same time.

Rachel didn't take offense to it. She said, "Life is crazy, and we're
just trapped in it."

"So where is your boyfriend, back out on the town or up in the
room?"

I didn't really want to be caught with her while a jealous boyfriend
was running around. So I planned to keep things harmless.

She said, "His ass is back home in Cleveland. He was supposed to
meet me down here and he didn't come. I knew I should have come
down here with my girlfriends."

I said, "So you don't live together or anything?" Rachel looked at
least thirty. Shacking up had become the norm for most couples.
Seems like most people who still lived alone were single, including
me. I had offers to shack up, and came extremely close a few times,
but I didn't take the plunge.

Rachel said, "We tried that but it didn't work out. He liked to run
the damn streets too much, and had me up worrying about him all
night."

I said, "But when he's not expected to come home every night,
you're not as concerned about it and your mind is more at ease."

"Exactly."

I knew the deal like the back of my hand. It was one of the main
things I knew about myself. If I wanted to hang, then I was going to

hang, and no woman waiting up for me was going to stop me. So it was no sense in me putting any woman through that torture.

"Does he really want to be in a committed relationship?" I asked Rachel. Some guys like to bullshit a woman just to stay close to the pussy.

She answered, "He says he does, but I don't believe him anymore. I mean, how can I? He hasn't acted like it."

I couldn't beat the guy down. Some guys couldn't afford to be honest and still get what they wanted from a woman. Each man had to do what he had to do to survive.

I asked her, "So you're down here by yourself?" It sounded like an incriminating question. She didn't have to answer it if she didn't want to.

She smiled and nodded to me. "Mmm hmm."

I smiled back. "I mean, that doesn't mean anything. I just wanted to get the facts straight."

"Who are you here with?" she asked me back.

"A celibate friend."

I found the idea of celibacy interesting to talk about, at least from someone else's perspective, because I definitely was not going there.

Rachel frowned and said, "Celibate? Why?"

"Some people just need to cleanse themselves from the whole process of lust for a while, that's all."

Rachel nodded. "I agree." Then she looked at me. "So are you celibate, too?"

I began to laugh at the question. "Not at all," I answered.

"You couldn't do it, huh?"

"That's why I'm down here now, trying to walk and talk off the energy."

"You think it'll work?"

"That's what I'm going to have to find out," I told her.

"Do you masturbate?" she asked me.

That was quite a frank question. "Well, I try not to. I try as best I can to save my juice for the real thing, you know."

She said, "But sometimes you gotta take care of what you have to take care of. And in this world, masturbating is a lot safer than anything else."

She had a point. I said, "But nothing beats the real thing."

She laughed. "Don't I know it. That's why I'm up now my damnself. I'm in a terrible heat. I had to pray on it. I don't even know if this is natural."

I asked her, "Has it happened before?" I already knew the answer to that. Of course it had happened before. Women had needs just as much as men. They just had to be more tactful about it. A ho is a ho in everybody's book.

She said, "I can't lie."

"So what do we do? We both go to the room and masturbate?"

"Whose room?" she asked me. She had this mischievous look in her eyes.

"I meant that in general," I told her.

She paused and shrugged her shoulders. "I don't know." Then she added, "You're a little slimmer than what I'm used to."

She was beginning to broadcast her thoughts to me.

I said, "I look good though, from my head to my feet."

I figured I would play things her way, but only as a counterpuncher, responding to her lead.

"I bet you do if you're modeling. But you're just a little too pretty for me," she told me.

She was doing it again. Her curiosity was getting the best of her, and she was teasing the hell out of me with it. But I maintained my flirtatious reserve.

"Like they say, you never know until you try it once," I hinted.

We were both crazy strangers, not to mention horny.

"Once, huh?" she repeated.

"Or twice, or three times; whatever," I told her. I was going to leave it all up to her.

"You mean in one night or . . . ongoing?"

She was asking me if it would be a one-night freakfest or an actual relationship.

I dodged her question and said, "Well, you know, I do travel a lot."

"That's not what I asked you. Don't be afraid to answer. You don't even know me. We're just talking about it, right? So let's talk about it," she told me.

She was pulling my card with authority. So what else could I do but step my game up a notch.

"You would want to keep seeing a man who's not your type?" I asked her. I used her words against her like women would do to guys.

"If I decided to do something then obviously I've made an exception."

I do believe I had underestimated this woman. She had me clearly on my heels.

"Well, you haven't decided on anything like that. We're just talking," I said. Or were we? We were more like feeling each other out, and both of us were very cautious not to commit any fatal moves.

Rachel started to laugh. She shook her head and said, "The games guys play."

I took a breath and was slightly offended by her assumptions. You had to play a game to stay on the court. That was what women couldn't understand. I didn't want to join the crowd in the stands and become a spectator, while holding hands with a wife and kids. I wanted to continue being a player. And the only way you stayed a player is by showing the most effective and elusive moves while on the court.

Hell, I didn't even want a girlfriend watching me. All I wanted was a rotating line of cheerleaders who were ready and willing to screw me after the game. You can call it selfish if you want, but that was my life. So what was I to tell Rachel? Could she handle that?

"Are you a big girl?" I asked her.

She smirked. "You can see that."

"You know what I mean," I told her.

"I do. And I am a damn big girl."

So let's cut the bullshit then, I told myself. *What do you want to do?*
"So..."

I stopped right there. I wasn't willing to put my cards on the table with this broad. She wasn't my type either, and I didn't want to commit to desperation. Not saying that Rachel was all that bad-looking, because she wasn't. She was definitely cute. I just didn't want to end up having her chasing me.

"What do you want from me?" she finally asked me. "If you want something, then say it. I would."

Damn she was digging into my ass. What did I really want from her? An ego boost? But I wasn't willing to outright bang her, unless she made it terribly easy for me. If I had to do any real work to get it, then I wasn't up for it.

It's funny what complications can do to a guy. All of a sudden, my alert penis fell limp. The party was over. I didn't want anything from this girl. I didn't even want to talk to her anymore. I just wanted to crawl up in my bed and go to sleep.

"Mmm hmm," she grumbled. I had failed to answer her. She said, "You know what I want?"

I just looked at her. I had an idea of what she was about to tell me.

She said, "I want a motherfucker who can say what's on his damn mind. If you don't feel like coming, then say you don't feel like coming. If you got yourself some new got' damn whore, then say you got some new whore. And if you want some new fuckin' pussy, then say you want some new fuckin' pussy."

She looked me dead in my eyes when she spit out her last sentence. But I kept my cool.

I said, "But that's not really saying what you want. That's just saying what you want a guy to do. So what do you really want?"

I was knocking the ball back in her court.

She said, "I want a man who's gon' handle his business."

I continued to stare at her. She still wasn't getting it.

"That's still not saying what you want. That's what you want a guy to do."

"Well look, what you want me to say?" she snapped at me. "You didn't answer the damn question at all."

She had another point. I had to chuckle at it.

"I don't think the shit is funny," she told me. "There's too many damn cowards out here if you ask me."

In a blink, my mind flashed back to that day in Cancún, Mexico, when I let the closest woman who ever got to me slip away. Andrea had called me a coward, too.

"So how bold should a man be?" I asked Rachel, while thinking about my past again. A man could be as bold as he wants to be, but if he's not in line with what a woman wants, it won't make a bit of difference. I was bold in saying that I didn't want to be tied down. And where did that get me? It got me out of a fine woman.

"I mean, you don't have to be nasty about it, but at least give a woman a chance to make up her mind based on the truth. That's all I'm saying," Rachel answered.

Our talk had gotten a lot deeper than I expected.

I said, "That's the man's dilemma. He knows that if he tells the truth, and that truth is not what the woman wants to hear, then he could be out of a woman."

I was speaking from experience. If I had bullshitted Andrea and told her to give me some more time, or that I had to think it over, or anything that gave her false hope, I could have held on to her. But how long would the bullshit last? Until she won, or I lost. That was exactly what had happened. I had stopped lying to her, and I lost her. Had I hung in there and fallen for her, I could have been in the stands with the kids and popcorn, and hating it.

Nevertheless, there I was in Miami at four in the morning, single, free, still on the hunt, and hating it. In fact, you only love the single life when you win. How childish is that?

Rachel was still looking into my face.

She said, "It looks like I done opened up a can of something. What's wrong, you don't want to talk about it anymore?"

She was smiling in her victory. I guess she could see that she had whipped me. I had surely underestimated her. So I went ahead and changed the subject.

"So you have nothing to get up for tomorrow?"

"Nope. I can stay in bed all day long if I want. But I'm not."

"Well, I have an early day tomorrow at a photo shoot on the beach."

"You better get yourself some rest then."

After she cut me off, it was pretty much a done deal that no magic would happen between us. At least not on that night.

She stood up and said, "So I'll see you around. How long are you here for?"

I only had another day, but one extra day was enough.

"I'm out of here tomorrow," I told her.

"Well, maybe we can go out or something when you're finished with your photo shoot."

I wasn't really up for going out. That seemed like too much work again. And I still had Judi to deal with.

I said, "I can't make any promises on that. But I'll call your room and let you know."

"You don't even know my room number," she commented.

I figured she would give it to me though. "Okay, what is it?" I was still seated at the booth while Rachel stood over me, ready to make her exit for bed.

"I'll tell you what, why don't I give you my cell phone number and let you call me that way."

"Okay, let's do it that way then," I agreed.

I took the number but that didn't mean I would call her. It only meant that I acknowledged her desire to go out with me.

Before she walked away, I grinned and asked her, "So does this mean that you're making an exception for me?"

She grinned back. "We'll have to wait and see."

Anything Can Happen

I GOT BACK TO MY ROOM and was surprised to see Judi still sound asleep in bed. I wondered if she had felt my absence at all. That disturbed me. How could she not miss me at all? So I climbed back into the king-size bed with a ruffle of the sheets to make sure she knew I was there. Judi readjusted her head on the pillows and remained at rest. But when the sun came up in the morning, and it was time for me to rise and shine for work, she awoke and asked me, "Where did you go last night?"

I smiled. She still cared about me.

"I just had to take a walk."

She nodded. "Okay." And that was it.

I TOOK CARE of my modeling business at Miami Beach, hung out for another sexless night on the town with Judi, and arrived back in Atlanta the next afternoon. I never did hook back up with Rachel. I saw no point in it. I had to admit that Judi was right, senseless sex meant nothing.

There were countless times where I chose to relax without sex while dating Andrea. But I rarely gave that option to new women. Either we were fucking or there was no sense in me even knowing them. And there were plenty of women I would meet on a whim while traveling. But that didn't mean I had to stay in touch with them all. And I didn't.

That was my life: meet them, treat them, and leave them.

Once I arrived back home in Atlanta, I dialed up my phone message service and found that I had seventeen messages. Three of them were from my mother. She was complaining about not being able to catch me on my cell phone. That's because I had to turn it off a lot. The last thing in the world a model needs is a hot line while trying to take hundreds of pictures. It screws up everyone's concentration. So when we hit the shoot, the cell phones are off or on mute. And after a while, you get used to not answering them at all.

I couldn't relax for two minutes at my place before the phone rang again. I read the caller ID, and it was my mother calling for a fourth time.

I answered the phone and asked her, "So what's the urgency, Mother?"

I loved being playful with my mother. She had such a great sense of humor. She had spoiled me something terrible, too. I had her partially to blame for my free-flowing attitude with everything. My mother had even been the one to push me into modeling. And of course, no woman was good enough for her only boy. However, she did like Andrea. I always wondered how much that had to do in the symmetry of their names. My mother's name was Adrienne.

She said, "If I died yesterday, you would never know it, would you? Have you ever stopped to think about that?"

"No. Because if you ever did die on me, I'm quite sure I would get a phone call from heaven. Either that, or you would haunt me like a ghost."

"That's not funny, boy. Have you talked to your sister lately?"

I strolled out into my living room and sat in my brown leather La-Z-Boy chair to relax.

"No. What's going on with her?" I asked.

I didn't talk to my family a whole lot. I liked the peace of mind that space and time afforded me away from my kinfolk and old friends. I mean, I loved them all, but I didn't see why I couldn't love them from a distance. Of course, I was forced to talk to my mother the most. She had made absolutely sure of that.

"Well, I need you to talk to Nita and explain to her that a guy does not want to be held hostage by a baby. And I know that firsthand because your father damn sure didn't—with either one of you or with any of his others. You would have thought he would have stopped and learned his lesson after a while."

My mother never pulled any punches when it came to my father. He was a true rolling stone with zero marriages and six kids from four women. My mother was my father's second baby's momma with two kids. I had an older half sister from his first baby's mama, two younger half sisters from his third, and a lone half brother from my father's fourth. Talk about a crazy family. That's why I loved my space and peace of mind.

I asked my mother, "What do you want me to say to her? Juanita knows how men think by now. She's had plenty of opportunities to do the right thing and to choose the right guys, but she chooses not to. Does she want to hear that from me? No. End of conversation."

"But you're her big brother."

"And I hold absolutely no weight with her. She's a grown woman like I'm a grown man."

I didn't talk about it with my mother, but I had been guilty of sleeping with at least three of my sister's high school and college girl-friends. Juanita had some good-looking friends, and they were very much into the big brother adulation thing. Should I have taken advantage of that? Probably not. But what was done was done. I couldn't put the serpent back in my pants after I had done it. And boy did I do it. I had a couple of Juanita's friends fighting over me. Mom just ignored it all. Kids will be kids.

"Well, she's just getting herself involved in the same old . . ."

My mother trailed off with her comment. I understood her though. How many life lessons were we all ignoring from those who came before us? So my sister went ahead and got involved with a professional basketball player from the Indiana Pacers, got pregnant by him, cussed out, ignored for several months, and she still wanted to have this guy's unwanted baby. And what could I do about it? I told her to have an abortion. It looked like another lifelong disaster to me. Juanita was convinced that the guy's attitude would change. Fat chance. But she wouldn't listen to me.

I said, "Mom, I understand your concerns, but this isn't your issue anymore. Juanita's making her own decisions for her own life. She's approaching thirty now."

"I don't care how old she is. You think she's not gonna ask me to babysit?"

I started smiling. My mother had a point. My wayward sister was about to make her life more complicated as well.

"Better you than me," I joked.

"Well, how come you don't have any children, Terrance?" she asked me. "You're past thirty now."

I had explained it all to my mother before, but it didn't hurt to remind her. Restating my policy was good as a reminder to myself.

"Because I make sure to choose women who are as free as I am, and who *like* their freedom. So they're all using contraceptives, birth control, and any other method short of signing a legal contract not to get pregnant. Not to mention *me* protecting myself from them.

"I'm not trying to be a rolling stone," I explained to my mother. "I like being an unattached wheel. So when I roll, I roll smoothly."

"What about that Andrea girl? Did she agree to this policy?"

I knew that was coming. Andrea was the one who had gotten the closest to everything dear to me. She had even gotten around my family members.

I said, "Well, that's why we're not together anymore. She was ready to be serious and I wasn't."

"Mmm," my mother grunted. "Well, at least you're not out here screwing up somebody's life like so many of these other guys are."

Screwing up somebody's life. I had said that myself about some guys, including Jayson Walker, who had snatched Andrea away. But I had to rethink that issue for a minute. Could a man actually screw up a woman's life without her participation in it? No; no more than a man could change a woman's life for the better without her giving him an opportunity to. Truth was, a lot of women had themselves to blame. They chose who they chose for whatever reason, and then they were forced to deal with the consequences.

I said, "Well, I hate to cut this conversation short, but I have a lot of other phone calls to return, Mom. And I already know that calling Juanita will be nothing more than in vain."

"Well, you call her anyway. Do it for me," my mother demanded. "You never know when one last phone call may do the trick."

I shook my head against the phone. *Do it for my mother.* She always got me to do something for her. Nevertheless, she had my loyalty. She was the one woman in my life who could always have her way with me—to a certain degree. So I agreed to it.

"Okay, Mom. I'll call her just for you. But please don't expect any miracles."

"I sure will," she joked back to me. "I've already been praying for it. You're my only hope now."

Absolutely ridiculous, I told myself. Was my mother serious or what?

One of my other phone calls was from a Chicago-based modeling agency. I had another job opportunity. Life was indeed good. That was the good news. I went back and forth on whether I should call the agency back before I talked to my sister. Finally, I decided to do the bad news first. I figured Juanita was not going to change her mind about her pregnancy, and after I would fail again to convince her, I would call Chicago for the good news and move on.

I dialed my sister's cell phone number from my same position in the La-Z-Boy chair. She lived in Indianapolis now, just a few hours from Gary.

"Hello," she answered.

"You know who it is," I told her.

"Mmm hmm," she acknowledged me.

I asked her, "So, what's the final verdict?" We both knew what I was referring to. The pregnancy seemed to be all that Juanita and I talked about for the past month. She was still early, in the first trimester.

"Did Mom tell you to call me?"

There was no sense in me lying about it.

"It's not fair to her no matter how you slice the cake," I answered.

"Well, who says I'm going to ask her for help?"

I shook my head against the phone again. "Juanita, come on now. You know good and well you can't raise a child on your own. And you're gonna have all of us feeling guilty by association."

"None of you have to be involved in it," she responded. "I mean, you're not perfect either, Terrance. Mom always thinks you can do no wrong just because you make a good living."

My sister sounded defensive and childish if you asked me, and she was turning twenty-nine soon. How in the hell did she get involved with a young basketball player in the first place? I could see if she was still in her early twenties, but not late. Juanita had a grown woman's curves and age, I just wasn't sure how grown her mind was anymore. So I decided to try some reverse psychology on her.

I said, "Juanita, can we be honest with each other for a minute?"

"Oh, I'm always honest."

"Okay, good. Now, in your honesty, would you call me a selfish man?"

"Definitely. We already know that. You are one of the most selfish guys I've ever been around in my life, Terrance. And that's the truth."

"Now, would you have a baby with a guy like me?"

Juanita stopped in her tracks.

"Okay, now I see where you're trying to go with this. But he is nothing like you."

"Are you sure?"

"Yes I'm sure."

"Has he ever met your mother? Because I try not to meet any parents. I don't even want that much attachment."

"Because you're an asshole."

"Okay, but this isn't about me. What about this guy? Would he be willing to admit to his stance? He probably already has."

"No, he has a bunch of friends who like to influence him. You don't even have friends."

"Look, I'm not trying to make this an argument. I don't like arguing."

"Yeah, and you only called because Mom told you to. How selfish is that?"

She was getting slightly off track.

I said, "The point is, unless you're going to be inside of a normal family setting, you're gonna create an unnecessary strain on yourself and on the rest of us."

"Well, we didn't come from any normal family setting. So what are you talking about?"

"Does that mean that we have to stay outside of the norm?" I asked her.

She said, "Well, in case you haven't noticed, single black women raising children *is* the norm now. He was raised by a single mother, too."

What in the world had happened to Juanita's mind? I couldn't understand her logic. And she was a college graduate. I was ready to stop the phone conversation altogether. What the hell was the use? She was locked in her own world.

She added, "You could have had a single mother situation, too."

I didn't plan to respond to that. For what? She had her life and views, and I had mine. That's exactly why I kept my distance from other people's chaos.

But Juanita was on a roll.

She said, "That girl Andrea was ready to have your baby, but she knew that your ass would have acted a fool, so she decided not to."

I stopped cold, but I figured my sister was pulling my leg to get a rise out of me. She had to be. At least I hoped she was.

I blew it off. "Yeah, whatever. That's impossible. I was always protected with her."

"Are you sure?"

I wasn't, but I wasn't going to let Juanita know that.

"Yeah, I'm sure."

"Well, that's not . . ."

She left me hanging.

I said, "That's not what? She would have told me about something like that. And why would she tell you?"

"I was just in the right place at the right time. Sometimes people need to just get the load off, and it doesn't matter who they do it with."

"Yeah, whatever." I didn't believe her. She was saying that just to spite me.

"Are we still being honest here, big brother? Because I'm not making this up. And you can think what you wanna think, but I know what I know."

I said, "Well, why are you telling me something like that now?"

"Because you think you can do whatever you want. But real life is not like that."

Juanita was extremely poised with her information. So I started to believe it. I even had to stand up from my La-Z-Boy chair and feel my legs for a minute. My heart started racing and everything.

"And you're telling me that you didn't try to stop her."

Not that I would have wanted a baby, but since Juanita was so adamant about having her own child, it didn't make sense that she wouldn't have fought for a child of mine that would have been her niece or nephew.

"She had already had the abortion by the time she bumped into me. We were both waiting for our separate planes at the Chicago airport."

I calmed down a minute and tried to regain my composure. "Well, she could have been lying to you. You don't know if she was telling the truth. Did she tell you not to say anything to me about it?"

"Of course she told me not to say anything."

"So why are you telling me now?" I asked.

"So you'll know that this can happen to anybody, including you. So stop judging me; you and Mom."

She still could have been making the whole thing up. I just didn't know what to think anymore. But I knew I was sorry about making that phone call to her. Then I wondered if our mother knew anything about Andrea.

"Did you tell Mom about this?" I asked my sister.

"No, I did not. Mom would have immediately told you and called that girl back up and everything. It would have been a big mess. And like I said, she had already had the abortion, so all of that energy would have been expended for nothing."

She was probably right about that. But it all left me speechless.

Juanita repeated, "So, like I said, this situation can happen to anybody, including you. And if the girl asks me why I finally decided to tell you, I'll tell her the same thing, somebody had to prove to my big brother that his ass is not invincible, and he doesn't know what he's talking about."

Damn!

CAN YOU BELIEVE THAT? I hung up the phone with my sister and was stunned. Things began to add up so quickly in my mind that I could feel a headache coming on. Andrea's miscarriage, was that my baby? Was the dream in the bathroom about losing my baby? Did Corey know about that? And why was I thinking about it as "my baby" if it never happened and I didn't want it to happen? What was my mind telling me? Was I feeling subconsciously guilty about it? Would I have allowed it to happen had Andrea told me? What was on my mind?

I just stood there in the middle of my living room with the phone in my hand.

"Shit!" I cursed myself. "I don't need this shit right now."

Things were going just great in my life. The sane thing to do would be to ignore it. Like my sister said, if Andrea had already gone through with an abortion, then what was the use in sweating it? The insane conclusion was to start a witch hunt until I tracked down the witch. And guess what conclusion I came to?

I called my sister back while searching my cluttered desk of business cards and phone books for Corey Sanders's number. He had been the first one to bring Andrea back up and plant her unsettling seed in my mind. But first I wanted to see if my sister still had any contacts for her.

"Yeah," Juanita answered.

"Do you have Andrea's number?" I asked her.

"Leave it alone, Terrance. It's already over and done with," my sister warned me. "And I wouldn't give it to you if I had it."

I was ready to argue with her, but what was the point in that?

"Okay," I told her. I hung up and moved on.

I located Corey Sanders's number and called him up. It took a few rings before he answered. I was ready to leave a message for him to call me back.

"Yeah, is this Terrance?"

"You got caller ID?" I asked him.

"Of course I do. That's the way of the world now. So what can I do for you today, Terrance? You headin' this way anytime soon?"

He was referring to Chicago.

I said, "As a matter of fact, I am. I just got the call today. I think they need me in Chicago by next weekend."

I hadn't gotten a chance to call and confirm any dates yet, but Corey didn't know that.

"Oh, well, look me up when you get to town. I know where all the new hot spots are."

"Do you know where Andrea is?" I figured I'd go straight to the business at hand.

"Why?"

"I wanna talk to her. You brought her back up to me," I reminded him.

"Yeah, but I don't have any contact for her. I wish I did."

"Well, what about the guy she married? You know how to reach him, right?"

Corey went silent for a spell. "Now, you don't want to go through him, do you?"

"I'm just trying to track the girl down."

"Track her down for what?"

Sounded to me like Corey knew more than he was willing to tell. It almost sounded like he was trying to protect her.

I asked him, "How well do you even know Andrea?"

"I don't know her that well. I just know that she was fine, and that she was caught up between two men."

"How do you know that?"

"That's what happened, ain't it? I know both sides of the story. I saw when you were with her, and I saw when he was with her."

"Well, how did he treat her? Are they still married?"

I wanted to see how much Corey would reveal.

"He paid more attention to her than you did, but he was extra possessive, too. I think she liked being with you more. And I haven't heard about any divorce, but I know they're at least separated.

"I haven't seen her around on the town with him lately, ever since the miscarriage," he added.

I said, "So how the hell do you know all these things?"

"Hey man, I do security work for the stars. I know things."

"So what were you, just infatuated with the girl?" I asked him. It sure seemed that way. I still needed to understand his angle.

He said, "I guess so."

"And you don't have any contacts for her?" If he was that connected he could do a background check, a credit check, or something to find her for me. My guess was that he didn't want to.

"Like I said before, I wish I did," he told me. "She hasn't been around anywhere lately. But hey, man, I can show you some other spots where we can hook up with some girls. That's not a problem."

I could see that I wouldn't get anything concrete from Corey. He could probably talk all night about his infatuation with Andrea and hooking up with fine women, but I didn't really care about that. So if I was going to find out what the hell was going on with her, it looked like I would have to do it on my own once I got to Chicago.

I hung up the phone with Corey and called the Chicago modeling agency to get more information about the upcoming shoot.

"Hey, Terrance, thanks for getting back to me so soon. Now this shoot, like I said in my message, is for an ad for lung cancer awareness.

Since you have such a great healthy body, representing the African-American male, we figured it would be a perfect match to get you involved."

I had known Kim O'Bannon for years, but she had only gotten involved in the modeling agency game over the last eight. It was really taking off for her, too. Kim just knew how to pitch. She made the deals happen.

"So when is the shoot?" I asked her.

"In two weeks."

Perfect, I told myself. I wanted to have enough time to develop some strong leads, and track Andrea down before I even got off the plane in Chicago. The pieces were falling right where I needed them to.

As soon as I hung up the phone with Kim, Judi called me from Miami.

"Hey, Tee. I just wanted to thank you for what you did. I really enjoyed myself with you the last couple of days. I mean, we had some confusion about everything at first, but then you mellowed out and accepted things. And I really appreciate that."

"Okay. It's all good," I told her.

It was no big deal to me. I wasn't even thinking about it anymore.

Judi went on. "You have no idea how peaceful it feels to be with an attractive man on your own terms, you know."

"On your own terms? What do you mean by that?" I asked her.

"I mean, without all the added pressure of expectations."

Here we go. I guess she was already trying to place me among the many dickless men in the world who women felt unthreatened by.

To tell the truth, I didn't even feel like having that conversation with Judi. I had my mind locked on other things.

I said, "Okay. Thanks. I'm glad you feel that way."

I was ready to move on to the next phone call. I had at least five other calls to return.

Judi detected the blandness in my tone.

"That doesn't sound sincere to me."

"It doesn't sound sincere? How do you want me to say it?"

"Say it like you mean it."

What if I don't mean it? I asked myself. Judi was ready to bark up the wrong tree.

"You're not mad at me, are you?"

"Why would I be mad at you? I'm not mad," I told her. "But I do have some other phone calls to make."

"Are you sure?"

"What, that I have other phone calls to make? Yeah, I'm sure."

"I'm not talking about that. I'm talking about you being mad at me for not sleeping with you."

I said, "Now how are you gonna go from how happy and proud you are that we were able to sleep together for two nights without doing anything, and then turn around and start feeling guilty because the celibacy thing didn't rub me too well. I mean, that situation is your life, not mine. So I don't have that much to say about it."

"But you respect my decision to do it, right?"

"I had no other choice. I wasn't gonna rape you."

"Rape me? So you wanted sex that bad?"

"Evidently not if I stopped trying so easily."

"Mmm," she grunted. "I can't believe you even said that."

"All men think about taking it on occasion. Trust me."

"All men?" she repeated for clarity.

"All men who have a sex drive and like women."

"That's a terrible thing to say, Terrance."

"Yeah, well, have you ever honestly thought about going out with a guy just because he has money?"

"Now you know you can't ask me that. I've been a national runway model. We're surrounded by men with money."

I told her, "The point is not whether you would do it or not, but that you've thought about it. That's all I'm saying. We all think about it."

Judi listened to me as I continued.

I said, "Men think about sex as urgently as women think about security. And that's a fact."

"So holding out sex on a man is the biggest crime in the world then, huh?" she teased me. I could hear the chuckles in her voice.

I said, "You already know that. That's why they call it the power of the capital P. Women already know how to get to a man. That's been going on since the beginning of time."

I said, "But I really do need to go."

"Where are you off to next?" she asked me.

"Chicago."

"Oh, I haven't been there in awhile now, ever since I decided to take my hiatus from modeling."

"Okay, well, that's where I'm off to next."

I was eager to hang up the phone. I wasn't in the mood for small talk.

Judi said, "Have fun, but not too much fun."

"All right, so I'll call you when I get back," I told her.

I was trying to end the phone call on a good note. But when I was just about to hang up with her, she asked me, "Why can't you call me while you're out there. You think you'll be too busy?"

It was a loaded question. Of course, I would be busy, but "too busy" meant that I wouldn't make time to talk to her, as if she were not on my priority list.

I said, "Judi, let me ask you a question. When I was on my photo shoot and hanging out with you in Miami, did you see me making a lot of calls on my cell phone?"

"So you're going to be preoccupied with someone else?" she asked me. That was what she wanted to ask me all along.

I said, "Why does that make a difference to you? It's not going to stop you from being celibate."

"Oh, so you are mad at me."

"No, I'm not. But I do plan to continue on with my life."

"I didn't tell you not to."

We sounded like high school kids arguing in a circle.

I finally asked Judi, "Hey, girl, what's the *real* meaning of all of this?"

Our argument seemed pointless. We weren't dating or anything. We were just friends. Or were we?

"Oh, so now I'm a girl," she responded.

"It's just a figure of speech."

"A figure of speech that I don't particularly care for."

I didn't particularly care for this conversation. I had been ready to hang up with her five minutes ago, and long before I had gotten myself into trouble with her.

I said, "Look, can we finish this conversation at another time?"

We were both wearing out our welcomes.

Judi responded, "Go on and do what you have to do then. Nobody's stopping you."

"I think you *are* stopping me."

How many times did I have to tell her that I was ready to go?

I was pacing my apartment floor growing more irritated by the minute. What exactly did Judi want or expect from me? I wasn't going celibate. It was a waste of time to even engage me in a conversation about that.

Finally, she said, "Okay. Call me whenever."

"That's a deal." I hung up the phone and paused for a minute to get my bearings. "Women," I told myself. "They're confused as ever."

By that time I forgot who else I was supposed to call.

While I still held the phone in my hand, it began to ring and startled me. I was willing to bet that it was Judi calling back for more, but I would have lost my money. I looked down and read the number on the caller ID, and it was Kim O'Bannon calling back from Chicago. She probably had more details on the photo shoot. I wouldn't have answered it if it was Judi again.

"Yup, it's me," I answered.

"Oh," Kim responded. She seemed startled by my snappy answer.

She said, "If you don't mind, Terrance, I'd like to have a moment to talk to you about something else while you're out here in Chicago."

After just hanging up the phone with Judi on some possessive-woman shit, I don't think I was in the right frame of mind for any more mystery. It didn't sound like Kim was talking business anymore. She usually talked business right out in the open.

I said, "You can't give me a bit of a lead-in?"

I didn't want any more surprises. I'd had enough of that over the past few days.

She said, "I'll tell you."

That wasn't exactly answering my question.

"When?" I asked her.

That wasn't even my style. I was usually easygoing and very trusting with Kim, but my inner alarm was going off. I had to investigate.

She said, "I'll call you back on your cell phone later on with it. I should have just . . . Well, never mind."

She was making me nervous with all of that. I could tell she didn't want to talk about it while still at the office. Then I started thinking about Andrea again. Kim and Andrea knew each other. I almost forgot about that. Andrea actually knew a lot of my old friends. I could ask Kim how to get back in touch with my old flame.

I said, "You don't have any bad news to tell me about Andrea, do you? I dun' heard plenty of that over the last couple of days. Seems like everybody got a story to tell."

I was putting it all out on the table.

Kim said, "Andrea? No. I haven't spoken to her in years. She didn't really talk to me like that. Seems like she was jealous about everything we were doing for you. I've seen her around though."

I forgot about the jealous thing. I guess it wasn't a lot that I remembered correctly.

Anyway, I said, "So what is it?" I was trying to make my asking sound bland.

Kim answered as cool as designer sunshades. "We'll talk."

Seems like the more I pushed for inside information, the more insecure I sounded. So I backed off.

"Okay, well, I'll talk to you later then. But ah, you don't know how to get in touch with Andrea either?"

I figured I had to at least ask.

"Terrance, I don't really know or talk to her like that. I only knew her through you."

It was a fair assessment, and I needed to move on from it.

"Okay, my bad. I'll just talk to you later on then."

I hung up the phone with Kim and felt a little more at ease with myself. The world wasn't out to get me after all, so there was no need in me getting involved in a witch hunt. Andrea had her own life to live now, and I wasn't a part of it. Her life was so private I couldn't even find her.

I SAT BACK DOWN in my La-Z-Boy chair and relaxed again. Before I realized it, I had fallen asleep for a few hours. I surely needed a good rest after Miami. The cell phone rang against my hip and woke me back up after seven o'clock that evening.

I looked down at the cell phone and didn't recognize the number. It was a 443 area code.

"Baltimore," I mumbled. "Who do I know in Baltimore?"

The number didn't click right away, but I did know people from B-more. How else would I know the area code? So I took a chance on answering.

"Hello."

"Hey, Terrance, it's Nicole. Remember me? From D.C.?"

"D.C.? Why do you have a Baltimore area code then?"

"Oh, I'm originally from Baltimore, but we met each other in D.C."

I began to smile. "Yeah, I remember you." I did. I remembered that she sucked a mean sausage; sucked it until it was well done and ready to pop. And boy did it pop.

"Well, guess where I am right now?" she asked me.

"In Atlanta."

"Oh, you got it on the first guess. You get extra points for that."

"Extra points toward what? I get to pick a big prize or something? How many do I have to have?"

I was already flirting with her. I was thinking about getting my sausage popped again.

She laughed and said, "They're just extra points." She was obviously teasing me.

"Well, I don't want them if they don't mean anything. You give them to the next guy."

Beautiful women loved rejection. I had gotten used to playing the game the right way with them.

She said, "Now what if I went ahead and did that?"

"Well, I'm sure he would deserve it," I told her. "And as long as *you're* satisfied, that's all that really matters. So make sure you get what *you* want."

She laughed again. "Okay, I'ma try that."

"So where are you staying down here?" I asked her. I didn't want to bring every girl back to my turf.

She hesitated. "I'm embarrassed to say. It's not like the places *you* stay at, being a big-time model and all."

"I've stayed at hotels and motels before. It's no big deal. Just make sure you bring your own sheets and towels and an air conditioner that actually works," I joked.

She laughed hard at that. "It's not that bad. I have stayed at places like that, though. And you're right, you barely wanna sleep or wash up in there."

I said, "So what's your plans? I'm not embarrassed by your room. You work with what you work with."

"But my girlfriend is staying here with me."

I hesitated after that. Where did I want to go with that information? I immediately became curious.

"You guys ah . . ."

I couldn't even finish my sentence before the girl started laughing.

"Guys. It's not even like that. We're just down here in Atlanta having a good time. So what's up? You wanna meet us downtown at the Hard Rock Cafe?"

"The Hard Rock Cafe? That's not exactly my favorite place to hang out," I told her.

"Yeah, but it's a big meeting place. And I didn't say we had to stay there. We can go wherever you wanna take us."

I noticed she kept using the word *we*. Was it a family affair? And how come the plans were all of a sudden being mapped out around me?

"How long are we all planning on hanging out? And who all are *we*, anyway?" I asked her.

I wasn't really up for a group date. I loved solo parties.

"I mean, we can step off whenever you want to. It's just me and my girl and a guy that she knows. But if you don't feel comfortable . . ."

"I don't," I told her. There was no sense in prolonging the issue. Once you get to a certain age in the dating game, you already know what you can stand. I would have been counting down to the minute I made my exit.

She said, "Well . . . you just wanna pick me up then?"

She was game, but that still didn't settle where we would go.

"How hungry are you?" I asked her.

"Very."

"For seafood, Chinese food, soul food, or what?"

"All of it," she answered with another laugh.

"Okay. We meet at the Hard Rock Cafe; I'll call you once I'm in the area."

"In what, like, thirty minutes or so?"

"Precisely," I told her. All I needed to do was change clothes and toss on some cologne, a lightweight scent. I didn't want to come off too strong, but I did want to smell good.

I hung up the phone and was already excited. I could take her just about anywhere for dinner, but where would we go afterward for dessert? I was all about the dessert.

Once I changed my phones started going crazy with calls again.

I read the phone numbers from the IDs, and none of them were business-related. My mom called me back, and Danni called. Danni I wouldn't call back until much later, but I could fill in my mother on information regarding my sister before I went out.

I called my mother and said, "Juanita's going to go through with the pregnancy, Mom, and there's nothing I could say to stop her."

"Absolutely nothing?" my mother asked me.

"That's the deal," I told her. "So you're just gonna have to hold her to her word. If she thinks she can raise this child by herself, then let her try. And she is a grown woman, Mom. So let's treat her like one."

"Mmm, mmm, mmmph," my mother grunted. "She's gonna put me in an early grave."

"Did you tell her that?"

"Not exactly, but I did tell her I'm too old to be helping to raise any new babies."

Did that include babies from either one of us? I was curious.

"What if I had one?" I was going back to what Juanita had told me about Andrea carrying my seed.

My mother said, "That's different. It's always different on the mother's side. But on the father's side, his mother is not as involved with the child, if at all."

She had a point. I repeated, "Okay, well, that's the deal. Juanita's not having an abortion."

I was ready to end the conversation and hit the town with Nicole from Baltimore.

"So, where are you on your way to tonight?" my mother asked me.

"Out," I answered, and that was all I planned to say. I had talked to my mother enough for one day. I was only calling her back to fill her in with the verdict on my sister.

My mother said, "Well, you be careful out there. Some of these women can be devious."

"I know. That's why I got my guard up at all times."

My mother paused. I wondered what was on her mind. She was still a woman herself.

"Okay," she finally answered. "I'll talk to you tomorrow."

She made it sound as if it was a foregone conclusion. But I wasn't going to argue about it. If she called and I answered the phone, then I'd talk to her.

I left my apartment dressed in beige Dockers slacks, soft brown leather shoes, a lime green T-shirt, and a lightweight Bill Blass sports jacket, wearing Escape cologne by Calvin Klein. I didn't know how Nicole was going to be dressed that night, but I remember her being pretty stylish. I figured I needed to at least match her, but I didn't want to go overboard with it.

I caught the elevator down to the garage to my car, and my cell phone went off again. I looked down and read the number. It was Danni calling again.

I didn't want to answer her calls yet, but then I got to thinking about whether I might bump into her while out on the town with Nicole. Generally, I didn't care that much about being caught with other women. I was a single man in a business dominated by gorgeous females. I had easily claimed it was business talk in the past. Whether the women believed me or not was up to them. Of course, Andrea never believed me.

Anyway, I started having recollections of Danni saying that she would miss me right before I flew to Miami. Could she have meant it? It seemed like she did. That gave me more reason not to want to call her back. I might have gotten on the phone with her and couldn't get off. So I ignored her call again.

I found my car, hopped in, and drove toward downtown Atlanta. When I arrived outside of the Hard Rock Cafe before nine, I found Nicole standing with her girlfriend and a guy near the curb.

I rolled down the passenger-side window. Nicole noticed me behind the wheel and screamed through the open window. "I just wanted them to meet you."

I nodded my head to her friends. "All right, how y'all doin'?" I didn't want to be rude to them. It wasn't their fault I didn't do the team date thing.

Nicole stated all of our names in an introduction, but I was only paying attention to when she would climb into the car. I was ready to get the hell out of there as quickly as possible. Danni was familiar with my car.

Why am I even worried about her? I asked myself. But I was worried.

Nicole finally climbed in and got comfortable. She was wearing Apple Bottom blue jeans with a netted, light brown blouse with gold-sequined heels and a matching purse. Her hair had been cut short with a slight highlight of violet. She was looking stylish and cute again.

I joked, "What are you trying to do, outdress me?"

She chuckled. "That's any day of the week."

"Confident, are we?"

"You have to be. You're not?"

Before I could answer her, she commented, "Nice car."

I still hadn't made up my mind where to take her. I did know that I wanted to get her away from the city.

"Have you ever eaten at Pappadeaux's?" I asked her. Pappadeaux's seafood restaurant was on the far east side of Atlanta, near Decatur.

"Papa who?"

I smiled. She hadn't eaten there before. I don't recall seeing a Pappadeaux's up north anywhere.

"That's where we're going then," I told her.

"Do they have good food, because I'm starving. The worst thing in the world is to be hungry with nasty food."

"No, the worst thing in the world would be a hungry person with no food."

"Well, you know what I mean."

It appealed to me that I really didn't know Nicole that well. I was just trying to make up for what I missed out on in Miami.

I slipped on the radio and Usher's "Yeah" song came rushing out of the speakers.

Nicole immediately started shaking her head in disgust. "Don't you ever get tired of hearing that song? If it's not them, Lil John and The

Eastside Boys, or Ciara, then Ludacris, the Ying Yang Twins, Trillville and Lil Scrappy."

Sounded like she named them all.

"They're all local stars in their hometown radio market. That's how it should be. Didn't they play Sisqo up in Baltimore when he was hot?"

"Yeah, and you see what happened to him, don't you?" Poor Sisqo was never able to live that "Thong Song" down.

I said, "Well, that won't happen to Usher. He has the right crossover audience and a solid album. That 'Yeah' song isn't the only one they're playing."

"I didn't say I didn't like Usher," she explained. "Don't get me wrong. I'm just saying that that particular song has been worn into the hole."

I couldn't argue with that. I said, " 'Burn' is getting pretty good airplay now as well."

WE HAD A GREAT DINNER and conversation at Pappadeaux's restaurant, and when it was time to pack up and leave, I still didn't know where to take Nicole.

"So, where do we go from here?" she asked me.

We were still seated, and my pants immediately began to rise under the table. I had been teased for a couple of nights in a row with no sex. So I was ripe. I had learned a while ago in the dating game that if a girl shot hard at you, then you needed to shoot hard right back.

I chuckled with wicked thoughts in mind. I said, "You know that guys have fantasies just like women do, don't you?"

She smiled at me. "And what kind of fantasy are you having?"

I waited a minute for a dramatic answer. "Car sex."

"Car sex?" she repeated. "You never did that before?" She was frowning at me. I guess she was a car sex pro. Or at least she had enough experience with it to wonder why I hadn't. I had in high school, but not the kind of car sex that I was thinking about.

"I mean, behind the wheel sex," I explained further.

Nicole was right with me. She grinned and said, "You mean to get blown while you drive?"

She made it sound nonchalant. It was nothing to her.

I asked her, "You've done that before?"

She looked at me with a pause. "Now, do you really want me to tell you something like that?"

She was right. I would rather find that out for myself. So I shook my head and spoke no more about it.

I paid for our meal, and walked Nicole to the car while holding her hand. Small gestures created an illusion of closeness. All the while, all I could think about was getting blown while driving.

We climbed into the car, and Nicole could not stop herself from grinning. She had something real temptatious on her mind.

"What's so funny?" I asked her.

She shook it off and didn't answer.

I got to driving on the expressway with no real destination. That's when she undid her seat belt and told me to move my car seat back.

I didn't ask her any more questions, I just did what she told me to do.

She started massaging my crotch with her left hand to make sure I was all there. And I was. Then she unzipped my pants, and searched for my brown monster.

"Looks like somebody's already excited," she commented with a laugh.

She pulled me free from my pants and started to thumb me around the tip.

Shit! Just keep your eye on the road, I told myself.

Nicole leaned over to taste my erection. I kept my cool, driving about fifty miles an hour on Interstate 20 while she worked me.

"This is where you have an advantage with short hair. I don't have to keep pulling my hair out of my face," she said and laughed again.

I couldn't even respond to her. I had some serious concentration to do to keep myself from swerving into other cars.

"Let me know if this is too much for you."

"Naw, I'm all right," I told her. I wanted her to do less talking and more sucking. But after a while, when it started to feel too intense, I didn't think it was safe anymore to keep it going while we were out on the road.

"Hey, hey, ah, let, let, let me pull over," I stumbled to tell her.

"On the highway?"

"Naw, into a parking lot or something."

I was already moving into the far right exit lane.

She said, "Oh. Because a cop might have pulled up behind us or something if we stopped right in the middle of the highway. That would have been embarrassing."

I could barely pay attention to her. I just wanted to drive into a parking lot as quickly as possible so she could finish the job without me crashing into something and killing the both of us.

I got off the expressway and pulled into the parking lot of a small shopping center. It was close to eleven o'clock at night by then, so nobody was there.

Nicole looked around and asked, "What if someone sees us parked over here?"

I turned off the ignition and the car lights. "Just keep your head down and they won't even think about us."

She looked at me and smirked. "That's another fantasy of yours, huh, getting sucked off while cars drive by?"

"There's nobody driving by in here. They're all out on the road."

"But what if a cop drives up to investigate?"

"Investigate what?" She was talking too much. I was ready to grab her head back down. I said, "Not if you're done already. But the longer you wait . . ."

She caught my drift. "I should shut the hell up and finish giving you this blow job, huh?"

I started smiling but didn't comment.

"You see how you are?" Then she went back to work on me with no more distractions. She sucked and sucked and sucked until I was ready to boil over.

"Oh, shit, you got me!" I yelled.

I panicked, thinking that she would pull away and have me spraying all over my car. So I grabbed the back of her head to make sure she got it all.

"Mmmmph," she grumbled. She didn't fight me though. So it was all good.

When she finally came up for air, she asked me, "Why you do that?"

I thought the truth may have been too tacky to bare. I didn't want to spray my leather car seats up with cum. But hell, a girl could choke and die down there if the nut was strong enough. So I was basically willing to kill a girl over my car.

I said, "I'm sorry. I guess I just . . . I just couldn't control myself."

She wiped the edges of her mouth with her hands, and took out a napkin from her purse to finish the job. Then she pulled out a pack of Wrigley's spearmint gum.

"You want a stick?"

I took one. "Thanks."

We just sat there for a minute. I needed to recuperate anyway. I couldn't just drive off. My nerves were still tingling. That Nicole knew what the hell she was doing.

She looked at me and said, "So, where are we going now?"

I still had a dilemma. I didn't want to take her back to my place, and she had already stated that she didn't like her hotel. All that was left was getting a new room at a better hotel, or going out to the clubs all night until it didn't make a difference. But I didn't feel like partying just to kill time. And I was sure Nicole wanted to get her thing off. She was waiting for me to take her somewhere where we could finish getting freaky.

Right in the middle of my perplexed thoughts, my cell phone went off. I had it on vibrate, but since there was nothing going on in the dead silence of the car, Nicole was still able to hear it buzzing against my hip.

"Your phone," she told me.

I ignored it.

"You're not gonna see who it is? It may be your woman."

I smiled it off. "And if it is, then what am I gonna tell her, that I'm not coming home tonight?"

Nicole had given me a way out, and I was surely thinking about taking it.

At first she grinned at my slyness. Then she asked me, "So you live with someone?"

If I told her the truth, then she would want to come over to my place to prove it, which I did not want. But if I lied to her to save myself the hassle of an invitation, she might have flipped out at me for taking advantage of her ignorance. But she knew I wasn't married, so how bad could she take it?

I asked her, "How much will that answer change the plans of our night?"

"Well, if you have a woman at home, then it explains why you had me suck your dick in your car instead of at your house."

She was already taking it to the extreme. I hadn't planned on that.

"You're already assuming things," I told her.

"Well, answer the question then."

It's funny how sour women can get when reality crashes down on their dreams. Nicole loved to laugh a lot, but she wasn't laughing now.

She gave me no choice in the matter. I had to stand my ground or go through the same backlash I went through with Rachel at the Hilton Hotel in Miami. So I got bold and said, "I have a woman in nearly every state. I'm single, and loving it. And I don't share space with too many people."

"How many people do you share space with? Do you have a home in every state, too?"

She was making it a lot harder than I thought it would be to clear the air.

"No. I don't have it like *that*, but I'm comfortable."

"And you're telling me that you have a woman in Wyoming and New Mexico?"

I grinned. I don't know if she was joking or what, but I joked back with her anyway.

"Those two are about the only states where I'm still looking."

"What about Oregon, Idaho, and Rhode Island?"

She was really getting into this. I said, "What are we having, geography class or something?"

"You're the one who brought it up."

"Well, it was only a figure of speech to emphasize that I'm a free and roaming man."

Nicole looked ahead and nodded. She mumbled "Okay" and munched on her chewing gum.

I didn't know how to feel after that. Did I take her back to her hotel room and drop her off or what? I still didn't feel like going club hopping.

She said, "So, I guess we can't go back to your place. I mean, I don't want to get you in trouble with your Atlanta woman. But who do you have up in D.C. and Baltimore?"

She looked me straight in my eyes. I had a few prospects in D.C., but Nicole was it in Baltimore. I mean, I knew women from B-more, but not like that.

I said, "You're my Baltimore girl" with authority.

"You didn't meet me in Baltimore," she reminded me.

What difference does it make? I asked myself.

"But you are from Baltimore," I told her.

She said, "I live in D.C. now, I just keep my Baltimore number for family and friends."

I nodded. She was taking things way out there, and I mean, literally. The whole idea had sparked her interest.

She said, "So you got somebody in D.C. already?"

Did she want the position? What was her angle? I was a little cautious with that. Women were crafty that way. One minute you think they're agreeing with your game plan, and the next minute they're calling you an asshole. I had no idea where Nicole and I were going.

I asked her, "Now what if I said I was bullshitting about everything? What would you say to me then?"

She stared into my face trying to figure me out.

"Why would you bullshit me like that?"

"I mean, you started it, talking about my cell phone," I told her.

"Because you didn't want to answer it. Not only that, but you didn't even want to look at it. I mean, what does that mean?"

She had a point, of course. I said, "Because it's rude to answer the phone while I'm out with you."

That lie didn't even sound good to me.

Nicole huffed and said, "Now that's some bullshit right there. Because if a guy wants to answer his phone, he's gonna answer his damn phone. Just like I would answer mine, or at least look to see who was calling me."

"Well, that's you," I told her.

She said, "You know what, are you taking me to your house or what? Because if you're not, and you really do have all these bitches running around and whatnot, then just drop me off downtown somewhere like a whore. 'Cause that's how I'm feeling right now. Gon' have me suck your dick in the car, talking about some fuckin' fantasy."

She said, "You really got me with that dumb shit. But I gotta give it to you though, 'cause I didn't even see that shit coming. Mother-fucker!"

That's exactly what I was talking about. Women were viperous. She was doing exactly what I was afraid of. But fuck it. If she wanted to act like that, then the sooner I got rid of her the better.

I said, "If you feel that way, then I'll drop you back off at the Hard Rock Cafe downtown."

"Well, how the fuck am I supposed to feel? You tell me!"

I had already restarted my engine. She was going somewhere, but it wasn't going to be with me.

"I mean, you acted like you did it before," I mumbled under my breath. And she heard me.

"I acted like I did it before? Motherfucker, did I say that?"

She started reaching for her purse. I had no idea if she had a gun or a blade in there or what.

I pulled over to stop before we even reached the street. "What are you doing?" I freed my hands from the wheel, ready to grab whatever it was that she was about to pull out from her purse.

"I'm making a damn phone call," she told me. "What do you think I'm doing?"

When she pulled the harmless cell phone out of her bag, I felt ridiculous.

"Scared motherfucker," she taunted me. "You need to be scared."

I couldn't believe it. The same spirited and playful girl I had talked to just a few hours ago had swung full circle into an erratic and dangerous mind.

She got on the phone and said, "Pam, I can't wait to talk to you."

Then she listened. "I'll tell you, but right now I'm still with the motherfucker. So I gotta wait for him to drop me off."

I didn't see why. She was as blatant as you could get while sitting right there in front of me. I guess I had burned that bridge. I was just rushing to get the ashes out of my car at that point.

"Yeah, he's dropping me back off at Hard Rock Cafe," she was telling her friend.

I started thinking that maybe I should drop her off around the corner from the cafe to save myself from any more drama. Who knows what her girlfriend would do. So I was speeding and thinking a mile a minute of how to alleviate more problems.

"Hope your ass get a ticket, too," she huffed.

She was itching for me to drop her ass off in the middle of the highway! It was a good thing I didn't invite her to my house if that was her attitude. It would have all come out sooner or later.

So I drove her back to the downtown Atlanta area, and I stopped the car a few blocks away from the Hard Rock Cafe.

She looked at me and asked, "What are you doing?"

"The Hard Rock Cafe is right around the corner."

At first she stared at me. Then she raised her finger to my face.

"Look, you take me back where you picked me up from!"

She was really going overboard. How much abuse did she expect a guy to take? It wasn't as if I had forced her to suck me off, at least not in the beginning.

I looked away from her and decided to try an extreme approach. I didn't even bother to face her. That's how serious I was to keep my sanity in the midst of an insane situation.

I said, "I'm not gonna ask you twice. Now, I think it's best for both of us if you were to walk back to the cafe yourself."

She studied my stern face, and gave us both a gift. She climbed out of my car without another word, and slammed my Mercedes door shut. I was quite hot about it, but as long as she didn't break the door, I was happy that it was over.

As soon as the girl began to walk up the street toward her destination, I made a swift U-turn and headed the other way. Then I called Danni back on my cell phone. I had to call and tell her something. She had paged me fives times with no response.

"Oh, you finally decided to call back," she answered. I could hear loud music in the background.

"Where are you, at a party?" I asked her. I needed to sound perfectly normal.

"I got tired of waiting, so I took myself out to have a good time."

"Where?" I repeated. I planned to pick her up if I had to, and turn my cell phone off. After the incident with Nicole, I needed some comforting for the night. Who said a man can't use a hug?

She said, "I'm at Visions on Peachtree."

That was all I needed to hear.

"I know where it is. I'm on my way to come get you," I told her.

She stumbled and said, "Ah . . . okay."

I didn't need to hear anything else. She had called me five times that night. No one else mattered to her.

A Lot to Think About

I ARRIVED OUTSIDE of Atlanta's popular Visions nightclub and watched the line move from inside my car. I definitely didn't want to pay to go inside just to tell Danni to leave with me. That Visions place could get greedy on you and charge forty dollars a head, depending on what hip-hop star had shown up to party that night. I wasn't even into the hip-hop crowd like that. And if you weren't one of them, they made you feel like a dissed groupie, male or female, which led to a clan of drug-selling egoists, who would spend hundreds of dollars a night to be a part of the in-crowd and VIP section, with video chicks and bottles of every expensive wine on the drink list. It was a big waste of money and effort if you asked me, but that was how those folks made themselves feel important.

I called Danni on my cell phone to let her know that I was outside, and that I was not coming in.

"Come on, just for a minute," she begged me.

"Look," I said, "I'm not waiting in that line to pay forty dollars after standing around like some sucker."

I had done it in my youth, like every other American guy, but I wasn't that young anymore. I didn't have the temperament for it as an older man.

Danni said, "Come on now, Terry, you know me better than that. I know the owner. I'll come right out there and get you with no money and no waiting in line. Terrance," she corrected herself in her tipsy swagger. I could hear it in her voice. It didn't take much to get her tipsy.

I said, "I'm really not in the mood for the club tonight, sweetheart. I just wanted to be with you."

"Awww, ain't that sweet. Now you wanna be with me after ignoring my phone calls all damn night. I know you saw my calls on your cell phone. So which one were you with tonight?"

Damn! When women were good they were good. She had my selfish, no good ass. That's why I was calling her in the first place, I had been busted. Had Nicole not smacked me in the face with the reality of my ways, I would have ignored Danni for the rest of the night.

I said, "Okay, I understand if you want to do you for the night, since I didn't call you back in time. But if you feel like you still want my company later on, you know where to find me."

I didn't want to go too soft, but not too hard either. Ultimately, Danni still had to want me.

I waited for her response, only to hear ruckus over the phone.

"Look, don't be grabbing on me like that, you don't know me," I heard her tell someone. "Yeah, whatever. I'll get his ass thrown out of here. He just don't know. Anyway . . .

"So, you're not coming in here to see me?" she asked me over the phone again.

"Danni, Visions is not my kind of place, unless I'm forced to be there on business, and this is definitely not business," I told her. "I would only be coming in there to see you. And I would much rather see you on more personal grounds."

"So, you don't want to be seen with me out in public now. Oh, don't even play that. Do you know how many guys in here want me. Yeah, give me another drink," she told the bartender in my ear.

She was reading things the wrong way and giving me no other choice than to walk up in there and try to play Superman.

I tried one last time to have things my way instead.

"Let's make this easy for both of us. You walk out, I meet you out-side, I walk you to your car, and I'm yours. Okay? I'm yours."

I didn't hear anything but background music and chatter from the club. I guess Danni was thinking about it in silence. That was a good thing.

"You mean that?" she asked me. She sounded serious, too, and vul-nerable.

Did I mean it? For the moment, I did. "Yeah, I mean it."

"Don't be playing around with me, Terrance. Okay? If you mean that, then mean it for real."

Sounded like she was taking it more seriously than I thought. That scared me. But I would rather have that conversation face-to-face with her.

"Meet me outside, I'm parking right now." I was willing to park ille-gally to get her the hell out of there.

Danni finally said, "Okay. I'm coming out."

As soon as we hung up the phone, my heart started racing. What had I just done? And how seriously was she taking it?

It was too late for second thoughts. I parked the car outside of the parking lot and immediately drew attention.

"You can't park there."

"I'm not staying," I told one of the parking lot workers. "I'm just getting my girl and I'm gone." I was already walking across the street to meet up with Danni.

As I made it to the front of the line with folks all positioning them-selves to get in, Danni walked out looking like a super runway model. She wore tall cowboy boots, designer blue jeans, a Louis Vuitton pocketbook, a white Von Dutch tank top, gold jewelry, and curly light-brown hair with sunshades in it. She was still tipsy, and strutting like she was on an actual stage.

By the time she made it through the crowds and held out her hand to mine, all eyes were on her, and then on us as a couple. Danni was obviously putting on a show.

"Here I am, baby. All for you."

I smiled at her and pulled her into a hug. She was making me feel proud to be the one.

She said, "You know you're making me leave my girlfriend. And with my car at that."

That spoke volumes. Danni had just gotten her new car. However, I don't think she would have been driving home that night anyway.

I said, "I'm sure your girl will take good care of it. You did give her the keys, right?"

I was already guiding her across the street to my car, and the crowd was still looking. It all made me feel like a big man on campus.

Danni was all smiles, smelling good and looking good.

"So where are we going?" she asked me.

"I want to order you dinner in bed," I told her.

What the hell, I was feeling extravagant.

She stopped me at the car and said, "I'm not dreaming, am I?"

"Why would you think that?"

"Because you . . . you . . ." She couldn't even get her words out. I guess she was trying to say that I was being uncharacteristically considerate. I usually played the I'm-too-busy-for-you-but-in-the-meantime-let's-get-naked role. Now I had all the time in the world for her. I guess the change was drastic.

Danni shook her head and strutted to the passenger side of my car.

"Okay," she told me. "Let's go."

I had planned to walk her over to the door, but she beat me to it.

I clicked the doors open with my remote, and the parking guy caught my eye before I climbed in. He nodded his head in approval with an oversized grin.

He said, "I would have parked anywhere for her, too."

I laughed. "You have a good night," I told him.

I climbed into the Mercedes and looked into Danni's curious face as I slid behind the wheel.

"Terrance, can I ask you a question?"

I paused and studied her. She was really listening for my sincerity.

"Yeah."

"Where have you been all my life?"

I just started to chuckle. Doing a woman right for a change was a good feeling.

"Yeah. Good question," I told her, and I drove off.

I GOT DANNI BACK to my place and ran warm water in my Jacuzzi. I figured we'd take a relaxing bath together, dress comfortably in my complementary robes, and have a twilight dinner from All Occasions Catering, who had a late-night taxi service for those who could afford it. These guys did all their business through credit card, with tips and driver fees all paid in advance. They would deliver full-course meals to your home, apartment, or condo up until two o'clock in the morning. Who else would do that outside of pizza and Buffalo wing joints? I thought it was a grand idea, and they had much of the wealthy, romantic crowd of Atlanta on lockdown.

Danni was floating around on air as I showed her the late-night menu of steak, seafood, veal, barbecue, sushi, et cetera.

She looked at me with the menu in hand and said, "It's good having inside connections, isn't it?"

I couldn't lie; modeling was a high-end trade when you got in good. And just like with any other profession, top-of-the-scale salaries brought all kinds of insider perks.

I said, "Yeah, but I still have to pay for the dinner."

Danni smirked. "You can't have everything for free. What else would we have left to live for?"

I nodded. "You got a point."

"Well, since I haven't really eaten all day, how about a nice juicy steak, medium rare," she told me, "with the loaded baked potato, and fresh vegetables."

"Your wish is my command. And I'll just have the warm bread pudding and a ginger ale."

She looked at me and asked, "All you're having is dessert and a soda. Why?"

"I'm just trying to cater to you. I don't need a lot to eat right now. But you've been drinking, so you could use a little something."

"Yeah, but I don't want to eat all that if you're not."

I looked over her slim, trim body and said, "Trust me, you got plenty of room for it."

She ignored me. She said, "It also slows you down. What if I need all my energy for the rest of the night?" she hinted.

I actually wasn't looking for sex anymore, just interesting company. Maybe Judi was right, sex wasn't always a good thing.

I said, "We don't have to exhaust ourselves tonight. Let's just chill and enjoy our good fortunes." My little outing with Nicole was all I could stand for one night.

Danni stared at me again. She said, "What has gotten into you tonight? Whatever it is, you need to take a daily dose of that."

"Naw, I doubt if you want that. A woman likes a sour edge on a man every now and then. It keeps you guys honest."

Danni started laughing. She knew it was true. She allowed me to order her steak dinner before we got undressed and slipped into the Jacuzzi together. It was a crafty way of me getting clean again for whatever. Nevertheless, I was no longer feeling sexual that night.

As soon as we got comfortable inside the warm bubbles and scented water of the Jacuzzi, Danni looked across the tub and asked me, "So, did you mean it?"

I had to stop and reflect before I answered. She was talking about me dedicating my loyalty to her at the club. I must admit, it was a spontaneous comment of desperation. But I was no longer desperate in the Jacuzzi. I had to reevaluate what I meant by it.

I asked Danni, "Okay, what would you have me do if you had your way with me?"

She studied the stillness of my eyes before she responded. "Like I said, I would be interested in seeing if you could have just one woman. And of course, that one woman would be me."

"So, what would I do while I'm out on the road?" I had always been able to hook up with new women when I traveled.

Danni splashed water in my face. "For God's sake, Terrance, I get guys who want to go to bed with me all the time, cameramen included, but I don't."

Here we go with that again, I thought to myself. Unless you were a whore, a good-looking woman was expected to turn down twenty guys a day. That was natural for a woman. But for me to turn down twenty women a day . . .

I could hear Judi's voice in my head again, pushing the need for abstinence. But the sex practices of men versus women were miles apart.

"So, I guess we would have a lot of catching up to do with you out of town, and then me out of town, and then both of us out of town, huh?" I commented.

It was the same predicament I had with many of the models I dated. Maybe I needed to stop dating models altogether and focus on stable career women who would be at home when I got back. But would that be fair for them? I got to travel to a lot of great places. Maybe if I could use my woman as a travel manager/agent or something . . . I don't know.

"Terrance?" Danni called me from across the tub again. "What are you thinking about? Is that a good thing?"

Was it a good thing? I wasn't so sure yet. However, heavy thinking wasn't what a lot of women wanted a guy to do. They wanted you to act, and act on what they wanted. That's why they were always interrupting a man's thoughts.

"I'm just thinking about everything, that's all," I told her.

She could already see that, but what did it matter to her? She only wanted the answers.

AFTER WE HAD DRIED OFF, dressed in my comfortable robes, unpacked our late-night meals, and settled into my bed with the plates of food, Danni was no longer hungry.

I told her, "I'll just save it all in a container then. It'll still be good tomorrow."

She handed me the plate and said, "Okay. At least I know it won't go to waste. There are plenty of people starving out there."

I took her untouched plate of food without another word and went to put it away inside the plastic containers. I planned to eat it for lunch, dinner, or even for breakfast that morning.

When I returned to the bedroom, Danni was all smiles. It was close to two in the morning by then.

She asked me, "You're not tired, are you?"

I could see what she had in mind; more hot sex on a platter.

"Yeah, I am a little tired," I told her.

But Danni didn't care. As soon as I neared the bed, she reached out and felt for my dick through my bathrobe.

"What are you doing?" I asked her.

"What does it look like I'm doing? Don't act dumb on me now. You said at the club that you would be mine."

"I did, didn't I," I reminded myself.

"Yes, you did. And I immediately asked you how serious you were when you said it. You've forgotten already?"

I hadn't forgotten, I just hoped that she would be enjoying herself too much to remember.

"I said it," I mumbled. I guess it was time to show and prove. Ironically, since I was not the aggressor, I didn't feel the same sexual energy I normally felt. But I did respond to Danni's gentle massaging of my jewels.

She pulled my robe back and bared my naked treasure. But I stopped her short of kissing it. I had enough of that from Nicole already.

Danni looked up at me in confusion. "You don't want me to?" she asked me. "We could sixty-nine if you're really mine," she added with a grin.

It became obvious that I would be forced to perform for her without the right motivation. Then I was concerned about how *well* I would perform.

"What if I let you ride him?" I suggested to her.

"Come on and get in bed with me then."

I don't know what it was about a woman being on top, but I rarely remained excited that way.

I climbed into bed, and Danni leaned over me and kissed my lips. She liked to be fingered a lot, so I slid my right hand in between her legs and softly fiddled her clit. She jerked her head and shoulders forward like a chicken as soon as I poked my finger in.

"You like that, don't you?" I asked her.

She could barely talk while I continued to work my fingertips around her clitoris. To anchor herself, she reached down and grabbed two fistfuls of my bedsheets, overwhelmed with pleasure. She closed her eyes and arched her head, neck, and back toward the ceiling.

Not a word was spoken between us, as I continued to stroke Danni with just my index finger, slightly inside, while working her spot just right. It amazed me how wet and horny she was getting from just one finger. That wasn't much work for me at all.

I leaned up toward her and kissed her light brown nipple, poking out from the fluffy white bathrobe she still wore. I kissed the other nipple, and slightly squeezed and sucked each one from left to right.

Danni wrapped her arms around my head and pulled me in closer, enjoying it all. She kissed the top of my head and allowed her curly hair to fall into my face as she held me close.

We were so soft, so subtle, so pleasing with the lights still on. There was nothing to hide between us.

Danni pulled my head back just enough to look into my face.

She asked me, "Why are you doing this to me?"

What kind of a question was that?

I answered, "This is what you want, right?" and poked my finger in deeper.

"Oh," Danni moaned and jerked forward with it. "Yeah, but . . . you gon' make me want it all the time now," she told me.

I said, "Just enjoy it now," and stroked her with my finger again. I got so hard that I was pushing up between her thighs like a weight lifter. I was certain she could feel it, but since it was all about her, I allowed her to deal with it as she saw fit. But I did hope that she would decide to put it in soon. A dick that hard was painful after awhile.

"You wanna put it in?" I finally asked her.

Danni began to work herself into a frenzy from just my finger.

"Not yet," she told me in nearly a whisper. "Not yet."

She became so wet between her legs that my full right hand was soaked. So I went ahead and slid more than one finger inside her.

"OOOHH!" she reacted to it. She grabbed my head into her breast and worked herself wild until she humped like crazy and came all over my fingers. It was a mess that I really didn't get a chance to enjoy. I figured it was all over and that she would fall limp and relax for a spell. But Danni surprised my ass by slipping me right up inside of her in the middle of all that wetness. She pushed me back down on the bed and started to work me like she was riding the horse of her life. As wet as she was, the fast-paced, slipping and sliding felt great.

"Oh, shit!" I moaned back to her. She was working it; up, down, left, right, backward, forward. I couldn't believe how much energy she still had. Then again, Danni was always pumped with energy. I wondered how much my slow, selfless foreplay had added to her excitement.

"What about you?" she asked me through her romping.

"Huh?" I muttered. I didn't want to do any unnecessary talking. I was doing just fine in my silent bliss, while she rode me like a rodeo pro.

She said, "Is this how you like it?" and balanced her hands against my rippled stomach. A great sculptured body came in handy that way.

I stuttered and said, "Just, just, just keep going."

"But I wanna know if you like it," she continued to ask me.

I don't know if she had a lack of confidence or if she was simply fucking with my head, because it was obvious that she was working the living hell out of me. How many bold-faced clues did she need?

I squealed "YEEAAAH!" like a puppet with his strings being pulled.

"Am I on the spot!" she panted. "Am I on it?"

I began to think about the tenants who lived directly below me as the bed began to bounce from Danni's hyperactive thrusting. She had a case of human hydraulics going on.

All of a sudden, she began to cramp up in perfect time with me. It felt like a rocket was getting ready to launch out of me. So I grabbed both of her slim hips and braced myself for the takeoff.

"UUEW! UUEW! UUUUEEWWW!" she squealed as she twisted the last few pumps out of herself.

That was all I needed to blast off to Jupiter.

"AAAHHHH!"

I tightened my hold on Danni's hips and wondered how much she could take before I broke her in two. That's just how intense the nut was. But the girl held her own. She could take it.

When I relaxed my fingers on her hips, with everything I had squeezed out of me, Danni fell down against my chest and kissed me there. "Hmmph," she grunted. "Now I know why I was so pressed for you to come back home from Miami."

I listened to her and smiled. I just didn't like that "come back home" part. It sounded too much like we were living together. Hell, it sort of sounded like we were married with a family. Did I want any part of that? I don't believe I did. So what the hell was I doing getting that close to a woman?

"Here you go with your deep thoughts again," she assumed of my silence. And she was right. I was basically a solitary man. After spending days at a time in front of a camera for a living, how could I not think a lot? I assumed that she thought a lot about things as well.

"I'm all right," I told her.

"Are you sure?"

She began to play with the new hairs on my chest. I didn't have a lot of them. I usually shaved them off. But that didn't stop them from growing.

"Ah," I snapped. Danni had pulled one of my damn chest hairs. "What are you doing?"

"Keeping you awake."

"I am awake."

"Are you sure?"

I was beginning to see a pattern with Danni that concerned me. How close did I really want to get to this girl? She was pretty much forecasting that life with her could very well be painful.

I said, "What if I pulled one of your damn hairs?"

She grinned against my chest. I could feel the muscles in her face rising up.

"Go ahead."

Problem was, Danni didn't have any hairs on her chest. She barely had hair anywhere. She was a slick, smooth-skinned woman from head to toe. So I went ahead and tugged on a hair from her head.

"*Ow!*" she yelped. "I didn't pull a hair from your head. Why did you do that?"

"You actually expect for me to try and find a hair on your chest?" I asked her.

She chuckled, knowing full well she didn't have any chest hairs.

"You could probably find one somewhere," she told me.

"Yeah, right."

Say What?

O VERALL, hanging out with Danni for a week wasn't all that bad. We both had new shooting dates coming up, and she never crowded me during much of my day. Turned out we both liked having our space. As for Judi and the whole idea of celibacy, I definitely didn't get a chance to practice much of that while Danni was around. I brought the subject up over lunch in Atlanta's midtown area, and Danni looked at me as if I had lost my mind. Celibacy was out of the question for her, too.

"Well, I can see if you have AIDS or a disease or something." Then she looked at me skeptically across the table. "You don't have a disease, do you?"

"No," I told her. "I just know someone who's pushing the celibacy idea pretty strongly."

"Well, maybe they have a disease."

That was it. It was a done deal for her. Danni went right back to eating her food and sipping her drink.

I didn't think that deeply about Judi having a disease. I looked at her celibacy issue more as a decision of proactive choice, not reactive guilt. Then again, it did seem that she was responding to something.

I figured I would casually bring it up once Judi and I had another chance to talk. I didn't want to call her up to instigate it just off of

111

what Danni was saying. I figured a natural conversation with Judi would happen in time.

In the meantime, I was getting set for my lung cancer awareness shoot in Chicago. We would all be wearing basic white T-shirts, tank tops, and sports jackets to show purity and innocence. I had stopped my witch hunt for Andrea. What was the point in it? However, the day before my flight to Chicago, Corey called me.

"Hey, Terrance, are you still coming into town this week?"

"Yeah. I fly in tomorrow."

I wasn't going to ask him anything about Andrea. But he decided to fill me in with the latest reports on her on his own.

"You wouldn't believe what I found out about your old girl this week, man. I mean, I can't say that it's official yet, but this is what I'm hearing."

I was ready to cut him off and tell him that I didn't want to know about her anymore. But before I could make up my mind to speak out, he said, "I hear she's into girlfriends now."

That was it for me. I said, "Look, man, I've been thinking about this thing, and I came to the conclusion that I really don't want to know about her anymore. It's all water under the bridge now."

"Are you sure, man, because I got a number for her now and everything. I mean, it's a friend of a friend, but I figured you'd be able to track her down with it if you really wanted to."

A friend of a friend? I thought to myself. This guy was hilarious. I didn't know how seriously I could take him anymore.

"Nah, man, I'm sure. I just gotta keep that girl out my mind. It's the only way to keep my sanity about it," I told him.

"What, she's been fucking up your mind lately?"

Sounded like I had given him too much information. He didn't know all the things that had gone on between Andrea and me. Or did he?

"Yeah, I'm just gonna leave it alone, man," I answered. "That's all I have left to say about it."

"Okay. So we'll just hang out when you get to town then? I'm not too busy this week."

I started to think about who he was busy with in celebrity security.

"Who do you, uh, have contracts with right now?"

"Mainly athletes," he told me. "We have plenty of them in Chicago. From the Bears, the Cubs, the Bulls, the White Sox, you name it."

"So does Atlanta," I told him.

"That's why I'm trying to get into that Atlanta market."

I really didn't feel like shooting the breeze too long with Corey, so I moved on.

"Yeah, so I'll probably call you up once I get into town if I'm not too busy, man."

"What time does your plane arrive? Maybe I can pick you up at the airport if you want?"

I didn't want to make any solid promises to him. I had to back away from that. "They already have a limo set up for me. I need to check my flight schedule anyway. And I have a few other calls to make, man, so I'll call you when I get a chance."

"All right, you do that. And I look forward to seeing you again, man."

"All right, good."

I hung up the cell and took a breath. I didn't really want to be around that guy anymore, so I planned to keep myself busy enough in Chicago not to have time to call him. Nevertheless, the guy had gotten to me again.

I hear she's into girlfriends now were his exact words. I wondered whether it was valid information. But if I was no longer involved with Andrea, then what the hell difference did it make? She could do what she wanted to do and like who she wanted to like.

I shook my head and mumbled, "I don't have nothing to do with that, so just leave it alone."

I did remember conversations with Andrea where she discussed her understandings with certain girlfriends concerning sex, life, and feminine feelings. But that was normal for any woman with girlfriends. That didn't mean they were sucking on each other. So I tried to block those thoughts out of my mind and move on.

KIM O'BANNON called me later on that night to tell me that she may ride with the limo driver to pick me up from Chicago's O'Hare Airport when I arrived in the early afternoon. From the airport, they would take me to check into the Swissôtel on Michigan Avenue. They had made reservations for me to stay there over three nights. The first day in town was for basic introductions. The second day was the photo shoot. And on the third day there was a lung cancer awareness banquet.

Kim was all giddy over the phone. "I'm really looking forward to seeing you again, Terrance. Out of all the models we've dealt with over the past few years, you have definitely been the most consistent."

"Thank you," I told her.

"Oh, you're welcome. You wouldn't believe what we've had to go through with some of these models, especially when they feel they've gotten close to you."

She said, "You know we've never been a cut-and-dry agency. We care about the models we represent. But some of these models have taken advantage of that relationship. They overextend themselves in their personal lives, and then start asking us for advances on work to come and all kinds of stuff. And you know we're not an exclusive firm, but they start offering exclusivity and everything, just to try and figure out how they can get the most out of us."

I didn't see that as a bad deal, actually. Exclusive firms had the option to pay advances based on how much work they figured a model would get in a year or over the life of an extended contract. That was normal policy. Of course, advances were usually only guaranteed to heavily booked models from topflight agencies, and those agencies rarely went out of their way for models of color.

"Anyway, I don't want to boggle you down with my struggles," Kim told me. "It's all good with you."

She was right. I was in a good place in my career. I didn't need advances or exclusivity. I had so many good connections to people in the industry that I didn't even need a manager. Managers and agents could get in the way sometimes. Then again, depending on the immaturity or eccentricities of each individual model, managers and agents actually helped to maintain more and better business.

I said, "Yeah, I'm looking forward to being back out in Chicago."

Three nights in Chi-Town, I told myself. I didn't want to harp on it, but I couldn't stop myself from wondering if I would bump into Andrea while I was there. I wondered if she even kept up with my career. It's not likely that she had stopped reading magazines—that would have been extreme. Andrea loved everything about magazines, even the printed smell, especially when they included perfume and cologne samples.

Kim brought me back to our phone conversation. "And I'll talk to you about that other thing when you arrive, too."

I hadn't gotten a chance to talk to her again in detail since I first called her.

"Oh, yeah, we'll talk about it," I told her. I wasn't concerned anymore. Whatever it was, I figured I would handle it with Kim face-to-face once I arrived in Chicago.

When I hung up the phone with her, I took a breather. I had worked out pretty good that day to get my body up to par for plenty of photos in white tees. Wearing white may be clean and pure, but it showed everything.

After my short rest, I started picking out my clothes for the trip, which I hadn't bothered to do yet. But as soon as I did I got another phone call. I needed at least two good, meet-and-greet outfits, and something more upscale for the banquet. I read the caller ID on my phone and saw that it was Judi.

"Hello," I answered.

"So, you're just about ready for your trip to Chicago tomorrow?" she asked me.

I chuckled with ties and dress shirts in hand, making final packing decisions inside my walk-in closet. "What do you have, ESP?"

"No, I just know that you're going back out of town tomorrow."

I had told Judi all about it, especially since the campaign was to support efforts, research, and awareness on lung cancer.

I asked, "You have a shoot this week as well, right, out in L.A.?"

"Yeah, and I hate L.A.," she told me. Of course she would say that. Los Angeles pushed all the things she was now against. But at the end of the day, she still had to pay the bills.

I told her, "L.A. and Miami have a lot of things in common if you asked me. They're both warm-all-year climates, they both like to flaunt their wealth, and they both cater to celebrities."

"Yeah, I don't know how long I want to stay in Miami either."

I hated to admit it to her, but Judi didn't seem too satisfied with her life. Maybe Danni was right, something was going on with her that was causing her to lash out at everything that seemed normal.

"Let me ask you something, Judi, because I'm getting really curious about this."

"Sure, go ahead."

"Ah . . . what is it exactly that would make you happy? I mean, because I listen to you, and you make sense and everything, but at the end of the day, what the hell is the point? It just seems like you have all complaints and no joy."

I said, "We all live to want things, to want to do things, to want to show off a little bit. That's what creates the challenge of life. So if you take all of that away . . ."

"I'm not telling you to take everything away. I'm just saying you need to have more of a purpose with it."

"Well, what's the purpose in a rich guy having a two-hundred-thousand-dollar Ferrari, Judi? To show off his wealth, right? You think he doesn't know that? You think he doesn't know that other people can't afford a Yugo? I mean, I just don't get it. People do what they do because they're alive and they want to."

I had Judi silent for a minute. That's when I wondered about her physical and sexual health. Was she suffering from a disease? How did diseased people react mentally and socially? Was she showing signs of it through her depressing theories about life? How exactly would I even start that conversation with her?

Finally, she said, "You're not getting me, Terrance. You're totally not getting me."

"Well, that's obvious. And I'm starting to think something's wrong with you."

I had picked several shirts and ties and spread them out across the bed. I was going with yellows, browns, beiges, and hints of black. Cancer was a sentimental issue that was serious business, so I tried to stay close to earth tones with black as a solid foundation color.

Judi said, "Wait a minute. You're starting to think that something's wrong with me? What do you mean by that?"

I had to readjust the phone to my opposite ear, while I continued to pack my things.

"Yeah, I'm beginning to wonder if you're all right. Is everything healthy? Have you been to the doctors lately? The clinic? You tell me."

"I don't believe you," she responded. "You're sitting there accusing me of being imbalanced in some way, just because I'm questioning the crazy things that so-called normal people do in America. And now I'm the one who has a problem?"

There was no sense in me backing down at that point.

I said, "Yeah, normal people have sex and drama in their life. That's always been normal. And you use to like sex."

"So, I'm being abnormal by not wanting that shit in my life? Is that what you're telling me?"

I said, "You know it already. You know you're confused. You're still trying to figure out the answers."

"Okay, yeah, let me get off this phone before we end up no longer being friends," she told me.

"You're gonna cut me off for telling you the truth?"

"You think you're telling me the truth? No, you're telling me an *opinion*. Because there is nothing wrong with me."

I had no more to say about it. Judi seemed to be getting more defensive by the minute, and I still was not convinced that she even knew what she was feeling herself. Was her ego that blind that she refused to admit her ailments? Women could be three times as stubborn as guys when it came to their feelings. A guy can admit when he's wrong, he just wants to do the shit anyway. But women, they wouldn't even admit that they were wrong. I guess they were spoiled into thinking they were right all the time. I don't know.

"Well?" she asked me.

I was confused. "Well, what?"

"Are you gonna apologize for that?"

"Apologize for what?" I asked her. Can you believe that? She was asking me to apologize, as if I had no right to express anything that was in opposition to what she thought.

"Judi, you're being ridiculous. Why do I have to apologize? Even if it is an opinion, I wasn't saying it to hurt you. I was just expressing my thoughts like you express your thoughts."

"Okay, well, I'll talk to you once you feel you owe me an apology then. Because it sounded to me like you were accusing me of having a disease or being crazy. I got your 'have you been to the clinic' shit! So what exactly are you trying to say, that I stopped having sex because somebody gave me something?"

I had went ahead and put my foot in my mouth, and Judi was making me choke on it. So what could I say to that, that Danni made me do it? I would sound like an asshole. I already looked like one. Different women had different ways of living their lives. But I already knew that.

"Well, what do you have to say for yourself?" Judi pressed me. "Are you gonna try and tell me now that that's not what you meant?"

She wasn't planning to let me off the hook easy. I had rather she hung up on me than force me to answer her. I didn't have anything left to say. I had stopped packing my clothes and everything.

She said, "It sounded to me like you were talking to some of your *friends* and they told you some garbage like that. And gon' try to make *me* sound crazy. So yeah, you owe me an apology," she repeated. "Or you still don't think so?"

She had me. Shit! I figured it was best to get it over with.

"All right, I apologize for that," I told her.

"And do you actually believe it?" she asked me.

"Believe what?"

"That a woman has to catch some foul disease before she stops having sex? Either that or she's a lesbian, right? She doesn't like men anymore. I mean, you guys are just . . . I don't believe you."

"Actually, a woman said that to me," I told her.

"Yeah, a *young* woman," she assumed. "But she'll learn. You give her five more years. Probably less than that."

She was right again. Danni was nearly ten years younger than Judi.

I said, "Okay, you've made your point." I was ready to move on. There was no sense in beating a dead horse. But Judi kept going with it.

"So you're fucking this girl?"

Her language caught me off guard. Not that I had never heard her swear before, but under the circumstances, I figured she would want to use a bit more tact.

I said, "That's not important. I was wrong and I apologize."

"But why did you even bring it up to this girl? I mean, that's *my* business."

"It was just the subject that I brought up. It wasn't like I was talking about any specific person. But look, let me finish doing what I need to do to get ready for my plane in the morning. You were right, and I was wrong. Okay?"

I wanted to cut that whole conversation short. We were headed nowhere positive. Fortunately, Judi let me off the hook.

"Okay. I'll talk to you later."

"Thank you," I told her.

"Don't mention it," she said, and hung up.

She had made her point. Obviously, I didn't know what the hell I was talking about, and listening to one woman over another would only get me into more trouble. So I shook it off and went back to packing my clothes.

I WAS WAITING at the airport in Atlanta that next morning to fly to Chicago when I received another phone call on my cell. It was a 614 area code. I believe that was Ohio somewhere. I thought about it and remembered Rachel, the woman I had met in Miami.

Did I want to answer her call? No. She was only a Miami Jones, a craving that lasted less than an hour. After the Nicole fiasco, I needed to chill a minute from hooking up with pop-up women anyway.

While I sat and waited for my plane with a copy of *Ebony* magazine in my lap, I noticed an attractive, dark-haired white woman who continued to take peeks at me. As a model, you get used to people staring at you, but since she was sitting directly across from me, it became something to think about.

Did she recognize me from one of the many magazines where I had been a feature, or was she simply into good-looking black men?

When it was time to board our plane, she finally got close enough to comment.

"I know I've seen you in a magazine somewhere, I just don't know which one," she told me with a smile. Then she flipped her long, dark hair out of her face. She looked ethnic and had model looks herself, with strong features and twinkling dark eyes.

"How many different magazines do you read?" I asked her.

I was ready to help her pinpoint where she may have seen me.

"Oh, I read so many of them."

I looked down at her empty hands. "And you don't have one now?"

She pointed to her floral carry-on bag. "I have four. I just wasn't able to concentrate."

She was admitting that I had distracted her to the point of putting her magazines away so she could continue to stare at me.

I was flattered by it, but I only nodded to her. "Okay." Then I gave her a compliment. "You look like you could be featured in a few magazines yourself."

She smiled and said, "Yeah, but they told me I was too short. Two more inches and I could have been the next Kate Moss."

"Or Eva Pigford," I told her. "They're about the same height."

"Yeah, but I'm only five-five."

She looked much taller with heels on, but so did every woman.

"So, you gave up?" I asked her. We were ready to move toward the gate with our tickets. Only I was flying first class, and she was flying coach.

"I mean, what else can I do?" she asked me.

I immediately thought about her modeling for *Playboy*, but I wasn't going to say that. I think it was just the man in me, and the practical joker. But I didn't know this woman to make jokes like that.

"Well, how old are you?" I asked her.

"Twenty-four."

"Finished with college?"

"Yup."

"Ready for the world?"

She smiled and chuckled. "As ready as I can be."

This white girl was cool, with an easygoing personality. But you never really know with those folks. Sometimes they talk to you just to prove they're not prejudiced. So I took her to the test.

"Well, if I come across any leads for a great-looking brunette, how will I be able to let you know?"

She looked up into my eyes and said, "You can call me. I'll write my number down."

She took out a business card and wrote her cell phone number on the back of it. Then she extended her hand for a shake when she gave it to me.

"Victoria Mason," she stated.

"Terrance Matthews."

She nodded, still grinning. "So, what's going on in Chicago?"

"Business," I said, and kept it at that. I wanted to see how interested she was.

"A model shoot?"

"Yeah."

By that time they were calling coach class to the plane. I had already missed the call for first class, but I could board when I wanted to. My seat wasn't going anywhere.

She said, "I still think about modeling, but you know, maybe I'll get into acting or something."

"If you do that, you'll shoot right past me. That's where the big cheese is," I told her.

"Yeah, and a much longer line to get in, too."

"You've tried out for a few things already?"

"What haven't I tried out for is more like it."

I flipped over her card to see that she worked for a Chicago marketing firm.

"So your boss pretty much puts up with it, huh?"

"Oh, they love me there. I charm all the big clients. So they were all telling me I should go for more, you know, try to get it while the getting's good."

"While you're still young and spunky, right?"

"Yeah, you know."

We finally handed in our tickets at the gate and moved down the bridge toward the waiting plane.

"Well, please, Terrance, let me know if you have any leads for a hot brunette. You have my numbers. Okay? And if you like, I can send you pictures through e-mail, too."

I said, "Okay," and we went our separate ways once we reached the plane.

I tried not to, but I thought about that white girl for a good minute. Business was business and white folks had it down to a science. I had

been around white models, male and female, who would do everything in their power to move up. Black models, on the other hand,
rarely bothered to take it to that extreme. Either you had it or you
didn't. So we tended to float more between dedication and indiffer-
ence. Those who did take modeling to the extreme were looked at as
crazy . . . unless you made it.

I got off the plane and didn't look back. I didn't want the white girl
thinking I was sweating her. I did want to get one last look at her,
though, just to make sure she looked as good as I thought she did. I
had been around enough women of all races to know when they
looked good, and this girl had the look.

Anyway, I had baggage to claim and a limo to catch. Since the plane
ended up being delayed, we were already thirty minutes late when we
landed in Chicago. So I got on my cell phone and called Kim.

"Hey, we're just getting in here," I told her as soon as she answered
her cell phone.

"I already know it. I'm down here waiting for you at the baggage
claim."

"Okay, good deal."

When I arrived at baggage claim, Kim stood out in the middle of
the floor, looking great. She wore a purple business suit with a black
blouse, French collar, and black heels that matched her black leather
purse.

I joked and said, "I thought the banquet was Saturday. Do I need to
be dressed now, too?"

I wasn't exactly slumming in my tall boots, blue jeans, and blue Air
Jordan tee, but that surely wouldn't get me into anyone's banquet like
Kim's purple suit would.

She said, "I just woke up feeling good this morning. Is that a
crime?"

"Certainly not," I told her.

Kim stood around five-five herself, and one hundred sixty pounds.
She would have been what they called a short, plus-size model.

"So how many bags do you have?" she asked me. "You probably

just have your suit bag and your carry-on with your underclothes, accessories, and shoes in it, right?" She already knew.

I chuckled and said, "You pulled my card on that."

She nodded and told me, "You're an old pro, Terrance."

I had been modeling for fourteen years, straight out of my sophomore year of college.

Out of the blue, Victoria Mason approached me.

"Hey, I hate to bother you again, but is it possible for me to get in touch with you? I mean, I know you have to be quite busy with your traveling and everything, but maybe I could, you know, leave you a message or drop you an email or something from time to time."

Since it was all about business, I figured I would introduce her to Kim, who dealt with models.

"Hey, Kim, this is, ah, Victoria Mason. She wanted to get into the modeling business but they told her she was too short."

Kim immediately pulled out her card.

"You give us a call, and we'll see what we can do about that."

Victoria took the card and looked startled by it.

"Oh, okay. So you work with Terrance?"

"Yes, we do, and he's one of our very best."

Victoria looked at me and smiled. "I bet he is."

"Nah, I'm just one of the guys," I commented. "Hey, here comes the luggage."

We all turned to walk toward the baggage belts.

"So how long are you in town for?" Victoria asked me.

I didn't know what I was feeling from her. One part of me said she was desperately trying to take care of her business, while the other part told me she was inquiring about my personal life. But she was definitely a heartthrob. I looked into her face again and confirmed it.

"I'm only here till Sunday," I told her. "Then I'm back to Atlanta."

"Are you from Atlanta? I was only visiting there for a marketing conference," she responded.

I said, "I live there now, but I'm originally from Gary."

"Gary, Indiana? Oh, so you're originally from this area."

I nodded. "Yeah."

"I'm originally from South Jersey," she told me. "My family moved to Chicago right before my senior year of high school. I hated it. But now it's kind of grown on me."

She just continued to talk to me. But why? Was I showing her any interest?

I located my bags and pointed them out to Kim. She was closer than I was.

"I got it," she told me.

I faced Victoria and told her I would give her a call. I didn't know if I meant it yet.

She said, "You make sure you do that. All right?"

That didn't sound like business. That sounded like an East Coast pickup.

I said, "All right," and caught up to follow Kim to the limo that was waiting for us outside.

As soon as Kim and I walked out of the airport exit, she smiled and said, "That white girl was all over you. Who is she?"

"I just sort of met her on the plane," I told her.

"Who started the conversation?"

"She did. She noticed me from the magazines and kept staring at me."

Kim mumbled, "Mmm hmm, them white girls don't play. They see what they want and they go right after it."

"But she was going after business."

"Business with a black man, yeah."

I smiled and chuckled at it. "I couldn't read the girl until the end. She just sounded real eager to find a way into the modeling and entertainment business."

"Or, she could find a man to date who's already in it," Kim stated.

We reached the limo and the driver popped open the trunk to put my luggage in. He was an older black man with a short, graying afro.

"How are you doing?" he greeted me.

"I'm good. How are you?"

"Hanging in there."

"Well, don't let it kill you," I told him. "In fact, let me get the luggage."

He smiled and insisted that he stack the luggage inside the trunk for me.

"Now don't take my job away from me, young fella. I've been doing this here for thirty-two years," he told me. "I remember when it wasn't too many black folks riding in limos. It was hard for me to even get to drive one."

Kim said, "We came a long way, ain't we?" and climbed inside.

"You can say that again," our driver responded.

I climbed in after her, and the driver shut the door behind us.

Kim was looking mighty peaceful in the back of the limo. She looked like she had some good thoughts on her mind.

I asked her, "So you've been feeling pretty good lately, huh?"

I could see it in her. She had a twinkle in her eyes and everything.

"I've been feeling pretty good, yeah."

I grinned. "It ain't a new guy in your life, is it?"

I had never gotten into Kim's personal life. She was one to keep business and pleasure separate. I had never even seen her with a guy. But I know she had to have one. She talked about the "hotties" too much not to. That's what she called us all. Kim knew the breakdown on many types of men, too. She studied us.

All she did was grin at my question. I didn't expect her to answer it anyway. So I moved on.

"Yeah, so what's this thing you want to talk to me about?" I asked her.

She said, "Actually, I've been thinking about children lately."

I wasn't expecting that. I had a blank stare.

"Okay," I told her. "Are you thinking about adopting or something?"

She frowned at the idea. "Ah, I thought about that, but I'd rather have that . . . that connection, you know."

In a flash, she had me thinking about Andrea and having my own children again. I guess Kim could think about having children like any other woman.

I said, "Is that what you wanted to talk to me about?"

Kim shook her head and started to chuckle. "You are so perfect."

I was then confused. "Perfect for what?"

She said, "Terrance, these days, more and more professional women are starting to think about sperm donors and artificial insemination."

She was right in my face with that. I thought those kinds of conversations only went down inside private hospital offices or clinics.

I looked into her eyes and said, "You're really serious about this, aren't you?" I began to speak in a hushed tone. I even looked forward toward our driver, but it was one of those long, stretch limos, so he was nowhere near our conversation. But still . . .

Kim nodded and said, "Yeah, I've given it a lot of thought."

I had never known her to be a practical joker. "And . . ."

I knew what I wanted to ask, I just didn't know how to ask it.

She grinned and said, "Usually, a woman would ask for an unknown donor who may have certain characteristics. But I don't trust that too well. I'd rather know what I'm dealing with, you know."

I was totally silent. I just *knew* she wasn't talking about *me* having children with her. That was totally off the radar. But what else was I supposed to think? I couldn't even nod my head to acknowledge her. I was in suspended animation, like I was watching someone else's movie. I was waiting for the next scene to happen. Kim had turned the limo ride into a sit-on-the-edge-of-your-seat-with-your-heart-racing thriller, with your eyes wide open, your mouth dry, and the hairs raising off the back of your neck.

She said, "I know I'm just putting this on you out of the blue, but I have a very short list of the kind of guys I would prefer, and it's best for me to ask you straight up to see how you would respond to it first."

So far, I had no response at all.

Kim said, "And knowing that you would keep doing your own thing is a plus, because I wouldn't want a whole bunch of complications with it, just like you wouldn't."

I sat there and said nothing at all. Then I started shaking my head and grinning like a madman. Was someone playing a sick joke on me? I felt like a man in ancient Greece with Zeus and the other gods toying with my emotions. What the hell was going on?

"So . . . what do you think?" Kim finally asked me. She said, "I know, it's crazy ain't it?"

That was obvious. She began to grin along with me. I was glad she was taking it lightly. I just didn't know how to break the bad news to her. There was no way in hell I would have been down for something like that. So I decided to break her armor down piece by piece.

"Okay, so what happens when the kid asks who his father is?"

Kim shook her head. "I won't even go there. And why do you assume it would be a *he*?"

"It's just a figure of speech," I told her.

"Well, I'll tell my child the situation, and explain that the father's identity is confidential."

"And what if this child looks just like me?" I didn't want to talk about it out in the open, but Kim obviously felt comfortable with it.

She smiled and said, "So if I decided to use you, I wouldn't be able to work with you anymore."

It sounded ridiculous. She had to be joking.

"And you think people wouldn't be able to connect the dots?" I asked her.

"I don't think anyone would care. I'm not a public figure. Why would they be investigating my life?"

She had a point, but it was still a crazy idea.

I said, "Now, how do you think I'm supposed to feel about all of this? I would know that it's my child."

"Yeah, but you don't want children, so it wouldn't matter."

"It would matter. That would be like me being a deadbeat dad. I couldn't tell myself that it's not my child. What if the child got sick or in trouble? Am I not supposed to care about that?"

What the hell was she talking about? This was the same Kim O'Bannon who made all the sense in the world before, but now she was bouncing off the walls in insanity. She may as well have been wearing a straitjacket.

She said, "So, you do have attachments?"

"Attachments? What do you mean?"

"I mean, you have the capability to actually become attached to something."

I felt a little offended by that. I mean, I may be selfish, but I wasn't *that* selfish. No way in the world.

I said, "Shit, I'm human. Of course I would have an attachment to that."

"Well, some men don't," she told me.

"Yeah, because they get twisted into the shit, and a lot of them are not ready for it, and then you actually have to start paying money for the rest of your life. So they get pissed off at the whole thing, and unfortunately take a lot of it out on the kid. But it's not the kid's fault."

I totally felt my fellow man's point of view. I figured Kim should have known that already. She knew me better than to think I would go along with donating sperm to create another fatherless child. What in the world was she thinking?

She nodded her head to herself. "Okay, so now I know how you feel. And honesty is the best policy. That's why I decided to just spring it on you in person, rather than try and coach you through it, because that would have been unfair."

I thought about that for a minute. We were stuck in Chicago traffic, heading south on Interstate 90, so we were going nowhere fast. I had all the time in the world to think.

Kim had considered my right to refusal, and in her fairness, she had lost an easy argument to me. I had to comment on that. There was a lot to be said and understood between men and women, who, in rela-

tionships, bring children and all types of unsettled issues to bare over
and over again through their cowardice. All of a sudden, my selfishness didn't seem that bad. At least a woman knew exactly where she
stood with me.

Kim sat there as quietly as I did. She was probably thinking that she
should have never brought the idea up to me. And maybe she
shouldn't have, but it was too late; she already had.

I took a breath and said, "I thank you for being that fair." I even held
her hand inside the limo. "And I'm flattered that you asked me,
but . . ."

I said, "I wish we all could be that fair to each other. But we're not.
Each and every day is filled with people trying to be as nice as they can
be just to get the other person to do what they want. Now how selfish
is that?"

Kim nodded to me and spoke on it. "That's what I thought about
with you. I know where you stand. So I knew you would say what you
had to say, and give me the most realistic view on what I'm trying to
do."

I said, "But Kim, do you understand how selfish that is to the child?
What child wants to come into the world and never know its father?"

She said, "Well, at least they are born. I mean, Tupac Shakur was
constantly bad-mouthing his father and his mother, but look what he
was able to do with his life? He's the most idolized man that these hip-
hop culture kids have."

"Yeah, and he died in a bunch of craziness, just like thousands of
other fatherless kids," I argued. "I mean, you can't sit here and look at
the exceptions as the rule. In fact, he wasn't even an exception. Tupac
Shakur had the craziest public life of any man you could imagine."

"But the understanding of his pain lives on," Kim commented. She
was as cool and calm as ever.

She said, "No matter what we decide to do, Terrance—and I'm not
in any position to force you into anything—but you have to understand that, like it or not, there has always been and will always be kids
who are born into this world without a father. All you have to do is

think about all the men who die in these crazy wars, and the kids and families they leave behind. And it's always going to be that way."

"Yeah, but I'm not in anyone's war, and I chose not to be, just like I choose not to be a father." That's all I had left to say about it. Tupac didn't want to be a father either. And he's not.

After that, Kim tried to change the subject and lighten the mood, but my sour state of mind was already set. She had disturbed me, and I no longer felt comfortable around her. So I couldn't wait to get to my hotel room and away from her. That was the privilege I would always have in being a single, fatherless, and unattached man. If I wanted to get away, I didn't owe an explanation to anyone.

Hypocrisy

K IM HAD REALLY caught me off-guard and had destroyed my mood. I didn't even feel like going to the meet and greet that night. In fact, ever since Corey had brought up my past relationship with Andrea in his visit to Atlanta, the past three weeks of my life had been crazy. So I was sitting up in my room, watching the HBO network on cable, ready to ignore my telephones for the rest of the evening. I figured I would tell everyone that I had gotten sick with a sudden flu bug, and that I had taken a truckload of medicine to sleep it off, just in time for the photo shoot.

"We didn't have a father either," I grumbled to myself. I was still thinking about my own connection to family. I figured my mother had a lot to do with making sure no man could stand her enough to stick around and help raise us. I only dealt with my mother because I was used to her. It seemed that my little sister had become just as obnoxious with her first fatherless child on the way.

Do this, do that, do this, do that—that was the problem with women, they all wanted something extra. Come to think about it, so did a lot of men.

"Buddhism," I thought out loud, "the religion of not wanting. That's what we all need to study."

Then again, how could you stop yourself from wanting things? I started thinking about Judi and her abstinence again. I still didn't know if I could ever do it. America was a twenty-four/seven seduction vehicle.

My cell phone went off, and I had no plans of answering it, but I did peek to see who was calling. I looked at the screen and read Rachel's 614 area code again.

"What the hell does this girl want?" I asked myself. I had only met her once, and for a mere thirty minutes at that. She wasn't even my type. Why did I even call her with my number?

I felt like calling her back and letting her know that I had no plans for her. Honesty was the best policy, right? But I seriously saw no use in that. Just continue to ignore the girl. And I did.

They had an original HBO movie on cable, with a white girl who reminded me of Victoria Mason, only Victoria looked twice as good. I became disturbed by that. Of all things to think about, I was up in my hotel room pondering a twenty-four-year-old white girl. I even thought about calling her.

"Now wouldn't that be a bitch?" I asked myself. Of all people to call and talk to, I thought about a young, careerist white girl.

I shook my head and tried to talk myself out of it, but I was curious. I hadn't dealt with white women much, even when I had opportunities to. They were around me. Fine white women. Topflight models. But I always had a black woman around to help me avoid the temptation. Even with salt and pepper girlfriends, I would naturally gravitate toward the pepper. But not that night.

It was a toss-up between calling Rachel or Victoria, and it wasn't even a competition. I was thinking Victoria all the way. Then I came up with a better idea, a more sane perspective.

I decided to call Danyel instead. Wasn't that what a dedicated man would do? You were supposed to do that. You do it when you're first courting a woman. You call her day and night from anywhere in the country. But who was I kidding? I hadn't courted a girl like that since my college years at Purdue. And I only stayed there for a year and a half. Once I joined the modeling world, the phone calls to my college sweetheart slowly evaporated.

I called Danni up and got her answering service. I left her a message to call me back, and wondered how long it would take her. It was nearing seven o'clock in Chicago, which meant eight in Atlanta. Danni had plenty of time to call me back before the night was over, but I felt anxious. I started wondering where she was.

"Shit! I don't want to feel like that," I mumbled. I liked feeling unattached, it kept your mind at ease.

My un-attachment was what Kim had correctly assessed about my character. But so what? I was still a free man, and I liked it that way. And if I wanted to call a white girl and shoot the breeze about life and relationships, then it was my prerogative to do so.

I took out the card Victoria had given me at the airport and flipped it over to her 773 cell phone number on the back. Before I actually dialed her numbers, I thought about Judi again.

To sex or not to sex, that was the question. But I was only calling the girl, and I was certain she would want to talk more about modeling and her career in the public eye than any personal conversation I wanted to have. So I went ahead and called her.

"Hello," she answered on the second ring.

I hesitated before I opened up with, "Surprise, surprise. This is, ah, Terrance Mitchell, from the airport."

She responded with, "Hey you, hold on one minute, okay. Let me clear my other line."

She did it all in rapid fire, just like a businesswoman would. It was nothing personal.

Immediately, I told myself that the call was a mistake, and that I would keep things short.

What the hell am I doing? I questioned. I continued to jump from one adventure to the next.

Victoria returned to the line with all of her enthusiastic energy.

"So, what's going on, Terrance? Will they have you all up under the camera tonight? Are you wearing sunshades right now?"

"Sunshades? Nah, I don't wear those much. I like looking people in the eyes."

"Oh, well, that's good. I'm an eye-contact person myself. You make a stronger connection that way."

"I agree," I told her.

"So, do you travel out of the country a lot, too?"

"Yeah, when the job calls for it, you're there."

"What are some of the places you've been to so far?"

It was a different kind of energy. I felt like she was verbally pushing me up against the wall. We were playing a championship tennis match. I had no chance to rest.

"Ah, London, Amsterdam, Paris, Italy, of course, Mexico, the Caribbean Islands . . ."

"Wow," she interjected. "That's the part I *really* admire. I mean, I wanna travel so badly. So at my job, like, any out-of-town functions that come up, I'm there. But I don't get a chance to fly out of the country. I mean, I've been to Canada once, and to Puerto Rico, but, you know, like, *Amsterdam.* That's great!"

"Yeah, it's an interesting place," I told her.

"I bet it is."

I said, "But I'm not too busy tonight. They wanted to do a meet and greet out and around town, but I just wanna relax a minute."

"Yeah, I can just imagine. You can't run on a full tank all the time. You have to settle down and refuel."

I asked her, "But what about you? What's your thing to do?" I didn't want the entire conversation to be about me.

"Oh, me, I just go. Whatever it is, I just go do it. You tell me to be there, and if I wanna go, then I'm there. And everyone knows that about me."

I was stuck for a minute. The girl seemed as if she was game, but I had to make sure I wasn't hearing things the wrong way.

"So you would just jump up and travel, just like that?" I asked her.

"Yeah, just like that."

"But what about your job?"

"I told you, they let me do it. I mean, it's not like I travel for weeks at a time or anything, but two, three days, yeah. And I come back and get right back to work. I even give them ideas over the phone when I'm gone half the time."

I kept my investigation going.

"Well, what does your guy have to say about all of this?"

"My *guy*, you mean like a boyfriend or something?"

She waited for me to answer. That meant she didn't have one. That also meant she had a story to tell about it. Women weren't that much different. If she had a boyfriend, she would have just come out with it.

I said, "Yeah, what does he think?"

"Nope, wrong girl," she told me. "I decided not to have one of those for a while, after my sophomore year at Illinois. That was the last time I had one. And everything was, 'Where ya' goin' now, and how long are you gonna be there, and who you goin' with, and I don't know about this, and I don't know about that.' In the meantime, I'm like, 'Wait a minute, this is my career, and my life, and my time, and my place to, you know, get out there and do things.' And all he wanted to do was hang out at the frat houses, drinking, and watching football and goofing off. And I can't do what I want to do because you want me here doing *this*?"

"So that was it for me," she explained. "And it's like, I have girl-friends who are always, 'Well, I know this guy who would be just perfect for you, and I met this other guy,' and I'm like, 'Come on, there're always gonna be guys around.' Guys approach me all the time, and everywhere, so I'm not impressed with any of that. I mean, I'm twenty-four years old; it's not like I'm forty. So I just wanna go out and be me for right now."

I said, "So, the last time you've been in the sack was in your sophomore year of college?"

"Ahh, well, I . . ."

I knew I would catch her off-guard with that one. We started laughing together, which was a good thing. But she was still fumbling with an answer.

"Well, you know, you don't really . . . I mean."

I let her off the hook and said, "You don't talk about it."

"Yeah, you don't." She said, "But I can tell you this, it hasn't been that many, because I don't really, you know, like a lot of people like that."

I asked, "Are we getting too personal here?" I just wanted to back up a minute.

She said, "Why, you're not gonna tell me about *your* escapades? You already got it out of me."

She was right. She was dealing with a pro who had slipped sex in on the conversation. I even think she was embarrassed by it, which was another good thing. Embarrassing a woman always brought her down to earth.

I said, "You're very attractive. A guy could definitely get distracted by you."

"Umm, thank you, but does that mean you're going to ignore my question?"

I chuckled and told her, "I make a living by taking pictures in front of a camera. Some of the pictures are sexy, some of them are not. But with most of them, women get a chance to stare at me. And if a woman is constantly staring at a guy . . ."

I left it open for her to fill in the blanks, and that got her laughing again. I made her feel guilty on purpose. We both realized that she was staring me down at the airport, so the ice was already broken.

"But you've probably never been with a black man before," I instigated.

Victoria paused and was tickled by it. She laughed and said, "You're not getting me to go there again."

I could feel her smiling through the phone. She was just melting away.

She said, "But . . . what if I have?"

I was waiting for that. She was making it too easy for me.

I said, "Then he was a very lucky man."

She paused and laughed some more.

"Okay, next subject," she told me. I had damaged her armor enough.

"Yeah, so what were we talking about again? Travel?"

"Yeah, travel, that's it. You were telling me about all the wonderful places you've been to."

"And you were telling me how you could just grab your bags and tag along with me, because you just go for it."

I had her where she couldn't stop laughing.

"Ahh, did I say that?"

"I think you did. Do I need to rewind my tape recorder?"

"Yeah, I think you do, because I didn't say—"

"You didn't say, 'If you tell me to be there, and I wanna go, then I'm there'?"

Those were her exact words, or close enough to it. I knew what she meant by it, but I was only teasing.

"Yeah, but I didn't mean like, *you* you, I just meant like . . . you know."

"You meant *you* as a whole, like in anyone," I explained it for her.

"Yeah, but not, like, *anyone*. I wouldn't go with just *anyone*, but . . ."

I had her falling all over herself, and I doubt that she was that way with most guys. I seriously doubted it. I could feel the pressure she could put on a guy when I had first met her. I was just being a great phone conversationalist.

I said, "I understand. You were just explaining your philosophy of life."

"Yeah, and I wouldn't want you to think that I was just trying to . . ."

"Come on to me," I filled in for her. But once I said it, it made it a reality. She did like me. That much was obvious.

She said, "I'm not like that."

"But you are attracted to me," I commented.

I was killing the girl. She had no idea who she was up against.

She paused again to make sure she could gather her correct words.

"Well, I have to see," she told me.

That was fair enough. It was a start, and I had successfully moved her away from a strictly business conversation. But that didn't mean I wouldn't introduce her to a few people.

In fact, I told her, "Look, we have a lung cancer banquet I can invite you and a friend to where you can show off a bit, and I'll see if I can introduce you to a few people who may want to work with you."

I didn't want to make the conversation all personal either. She was still career-minded, so I needed to respect that.

"You would do that?" she asked me.

My cell phone buzzed from the other line before I could answer her. It was Danni calling me back.

I told Victoria, "Consider it done. You got the look. We just have to work on that height of yours. So all you have to do is show up like you're serious."

I wasn't planning on using the extra tickets they had given me to the banquet anyway. I wasn't inviting Corey to the event, and I hadn't called up any of my other folks in Chicago. I was pretty much laying low. I thought about Andrea showing up, which was still a possibility. But I couldn't let thoughts about her derail my day. I had to fill my plate with other items to do. So I forced myself to move on, don't look back, and don't even think about her.

Victoria cheered up a great deal after the banquet invitation.

She said, "Oh, I'll be the hottest of the hot. And I bet that I'll make you real proud of me. You watch."

I laughed. "I hope you will. But let me take this call, and I'll call you back later on to give you all the information."

"Okay. And Terrance?"

She waited for me to respond again.

I smiled and said, "Yeah."

"Thank you."

Sincerity was her way of locking her teeth into a guy. But she would only use it with someone she felt could really help her. I guess I was in that position.

I hung up with Victoria and caught Danni on the last ring.

"Hello."

"Oh, I was just about to hang up," she told me.

"With no messages?"

"For what? You don't respond to those things. I leave you a message and you don't call back for five hours."

"But I *do* call back."

"Yeah, whatever. So are you being good out there in Chicago?" she asked me.

"Are you being good in Atlanta?"

"I'm always on my best behavior. And most of these guys hate me for it. But I do it anyway, all for you. But will you do the same for me? Drum roll, please."

I laughed. She was being lighthearted about it, but she was also getting her point across.

I told her, "You're in good shape. I'm just handling my business out here. In fact, I didn't even feel like going out to the meet and greet tonight. So I'm just sitting up in the hotel room watching HBO."

"Yeah, with a little chick about to bring you room service and spend the night for breakfast in bed."

She had quite an imagination.

I said, "Is that what happens when you're on the road?" Danni was due to fly out to Detroit for an automobile campaign the next day.

"I could if I wanted it to; every night of the week," she answered.

"But then you would be a professional garden tool," I told her.

"Whatever. I would have me a good time though."

"Is that what you call it?"

"Is that what it is?"

Danni was trying to walk me right into something. This wasn't a young white girl anymore. Danni was a seasoned mixed chick, who had been spoiled for her entire life.

I grinned. "It's only a good time when you really do care about the person. Everything else is just practice."

She started laughing and said, "You are so full of shit. So I need to go out here and do me some more practicing then."

"You don't need practice."

"Didn't you just say that's what it is?"

"For the people who need it, yeah."

"So you don't need it anymore?"

She was still trying to stump me.

I asked her, "Do you think I need practice, Danyel?"

She hesitated before she laughed again. "I think you've had enough practice."

When she finished her sentence, my cell phone buzzed a second time. I looked down at the screen and read Corey's number, but I wasn't going to answer that. I had already made up my mind. I wasn't hanging out with him.

I went back to my call with Danni and teased her. "Do you really think you can hold me down?"

She said, "I know I can. Matter of fact, do you need me to fly out there right now? I can be there by midnight. You could leave a key for me at the front desk. And I could fly to Detroit in the morning."

I hadn't even thought of that. Detroit was an hour flight from Chicago. Then again, did I want Danni being that close to my business? I mean, I enjoyed her, I really did. But . . .

"Un huh, I'm fucking up your game, right?" she assumed. "You don't wanna bring no other bitch to the beach."

I had done it before with Andrea, and with a few other women. So that was no big deal to me. I just needed more time to myself to figure out where I wanted to be. Ironically, being with a new woman was almost like being by yourself, because there were no realistic ties that could be assumed on a simple date or a one-night stand. However, Danni and I had moved past the simple date and the one-night stand. I had to figure out for myself what the next step was going to be before she succeeded in pushing that next step on me.

She said, "I'm not even packed yet for that kind of shit, so pull your drawers out your ass and chill. I won't blow your groove tonight. Go ahead and have your fun. I mean, practice."

I said, "Look, Danni, I'm not having any of that tonight. Now I will have room service, because I'm hungry, but after that, I'm gonna order a movie on TV and go to bed. You got that?"

I was coming down on her kind of hard, but that's just how it came out. She took it all in stride though.

She said, "Okay, if you say so. I guess I have to take your word on it."

"So you still don't believe me?"

"Yeah, I believe you. I'm just . . . Look, just have a good night. I didn't even mean to get into it like that. I was only playing when I started with you."

She still sounded insecure to me, but that wasn't my problem.

I said, "Danni, you're in good hands. Now how did the rest of your day go?" We really needed to change the subject. Danni realized that herself.

"Thank you for asking," she told me. "But it's been a pretty good day. I mean, it's always hectic the day before you go out of town because you're thinking about packing and getting to the airport and everything. But once you get to the airport, you're at peace with knowing that you're going to another place, you got a check on the way, and your life is still moving forward, you know. I mean, traveling is always a good feeling for me."

I smiled. I felt the same way. Travel represented forward movement.

I said, "Yeah, I know exactly what you mean."

AFTER SPEAKING TO DANNI, I felt slimy when I called Victoria back to give her the details on the banquet. I really did. But I would have been a coward not to call her after offering her the opportunity to attend. So to make peace with myself, I had to consider Victoria as strictly a business associate. Even with that, I felt a nerve of betrayal stirring inside me. There had been plenty of qualified black women I had not bothered to introduce to anyone. But there I was, ready to give this undersized white girl, whom I had just met, a red carpet affair in Chicago.

There Is Always Another One

A S PLANNED, I ignored all of my phone calls, ordered room service with ice cream for dessert, and watched a movie on cable before I fell asleep like an overgrown baby. The rest was well appreciated.

In the morning, I awoke bright and early and checked all of my phone messages, the most important of which was from Kim:

"You know, now I kind of feel like I should never have brought up my ideas about a child to you. I didn't really know how you would react to it. I just had to try it and see. But you don't have to act as if you can't talk to me anymore. We've known each other too long for that, Terrance. I mean, come on."

She was right, of course. I didn't plan to ignore her for too long, I just needed to clear my head a minute. A lot of recent events seemed to be swirling out of control on me.

"All right, I'll call her back and square everything away," I told myself.

I got up, took a shower, and by the time I had a little bit of breakfast in me, the limo driver had arrived to take me to the photo shoot at the Museum of Chicago. The shoot was set to start at 10:30 in the morning. We all had to arrive for makeup and wardrobe by 9:30.

I grabbed my things and made sure to call Kim back before I left the room.

"Are you waiting for me inside the limo again?" I asked her light-heartedly. I was calling her on her cell phone.

"Not today, honey, I'm back at the office," she told me. "But you're a big boy, you can handle it by yourself. And I'll see you guys later on tonight."

I smiled. At least she wasn't taking things personal.

I said, "About yesterday . . ."

She cut me off with her response. "Don't even worry about it. I understand."

Do you? I asked myself. I still felt guilty about turning her down, but I wasn't going to be a part of a science baby.

"I'll see you later on tonight then," I told her.

"Yeah, we'll talk tonight."

I ARRIVED AT the Museum of Chicago, a tall stone building that reminded me of ancient Rome and the many other aging buildings of art and culture. It had the high ceilings, archways, and intricate stone designs that were rarely done anymore. Modern architecture liked to deal more with shapes, colors, and different materials. But the old-school stone look was always classic to me. I'd take an old stone place over a colorful modern place any day of the week. So I walked around and felt good in there.

"Terrance Mitchell," a woman's voice greeted me. I turned and faced Paula Robinson, a makeup artist I hadn't been around in years. She had her hand extended toward me, wearing the color of the day, basic white. She looked damned good, too, with a wife-beater tank top popping out against her flawless brown skin.

I smiled and took her hand.

"What has it been, eight years since I seen you last?" I asked her.

"Yeah, at the old BET studios in D.C. I did your makeup for the Tavis Smiley show."

I looked at her again, and was amazed. Paula had to be at least fifty, but she looked thirty-five, if not younger. She had toned up her muscles with a flat belly and everything.

I said, "Are you sure you're only doing makeup? Did they bring you in here to take some healthy, cancer-free shots, too?"

She laughed and smacked my arm. "I see you still got that sharp tongue of yours. But yeah, they are gonna let me do a few shots."

"So who have you been working with lately? You still independent?" I asked her. I knew she had stopped working for BET, but that was the last time I heard from her.

"Yeah, I'm still independent, but I've mainly been working with my niece. We're getting ready to bust her out of the ranks. She's really gonna be something."

She said that with real gusto, but I had heard it all before. You can't imagine how many family members had high hopes for some cutey in the family that they felt should be taking pictures for a living. Seeing it is believing it, so I just nodded to her.

"Okay, that's good. So are you ready to start making me up?"

Her makeup chair, equipment, and mirrors were already set up to our right. Paula had a complete traveling stand that was gorgeous, with lighting and everything. She was a top-notch professional, and I was proud of her.

"Nice setup you have," I told her with a grin.

"Oh, you know I have to do my thing out here. You can't be independent and not look like you know what you're doing. Imagery is half the battle."

Before I got a chance to comment, a tall, elegant, brown-skinned girl walked up and stood beside us. She wore the same white tank top and white pants as Paula, and suddenly Paula looked her age. This girl was young and fine, the kind of girl who makes an older man wish he were twenty-four again.

Paula looked at her and said, "Oh, TaShay, this is Terrance Mitchell—the model I was telling you about."

I was immediately impressed. She had the runway height, proportions, bone structure, white teeth, slick hair, perfect brown skin, nose, lips, eyes . . .

"You were telling her about what?" I asked. I had to say something just to stop from staring at the girl. She had the kind of aura that sucked you in.

"I was telling her how long some models can maintain a career in the business when they keep themselves up and stay busy. And you've been one of the most consistent black male models in the game," Paula answered.

"She said you were around before Tyson Beckford," Paula's young niece revealed to me.

"Yeah, but just a little bit earlier. You're making me feel old," I told her. I didn't want her thinking I was older than I was. I was still very much in the game, and not a statue.

The girl smelled good, too. I asked her, "You just put something on inside the bathroom?"

She grabbed her beautiful neck with both hands. "Why, is it too strong?"

I smiled. "Nah, it's not too strong. It just has that newness to it, that's all."

"Oh, okay. Because I was ready to say . . ."

Paula said, "All right, well, let's get started making you up, Terrance."

I took my seat in her makeup chair.

"Well, nice meeting you," her niece told me with her hand extended.

I took it in mine and said, "I'm not going anywhere. You're gonna be around me for at least a couple of hours."

She laughed and said, "I guess so, right?"

When I let her hand go to get my makeup on, she slowly walked away to take in the museum for herself. And as she walked, she showed me some curves.

Paula smiled in my face and asked me, "So, what do you think about her?"

I nodded. "Yeah, you got something on your hands there. How old is she?"

"Nineteen."

"Turning twenty?"

"No, she just turned nineteen."

I nodded my head again. "Damn."

Paula started laughing.

I said, "Well, she's not . . ." I had to get my words correct to explain it right. "Well, she is exotic, but she still looks approachable. She has that in-between look. Some exotic women are just to look it. You don't really want to talk to them. It ruins the illusion. But with . . . What's her name again?" I stopped and asked.

Paula chuckled and answered, "TaShay."

"Yeah, TaShay," I repeated. "She makes you want to talk to her."

"I taught her that," Paula informed me. "I taught her that I don't want her to be unapproachable. Being unapproachable doesn't mean anything when you can't get any jobs. So I taught her how to invade a person's space just enough to where you force them to acknowledge you. Then you make your statement and move on. You don't want to be a nag, but you do want them to remember you."

I sat there and was stunned. The girl had just practiced what her aunt had preached. And it worked on me.

While Paula began to wipe off my face with a moist cleansing pad, I asked her, "Does she have a boyfriend? And I'm not asking for me, I'm just seeing how you're planning to deal with the other guys," I explained with a laugh.

Paula answered, "I already told her, 'Your boyfriend is your face, your health, your mind, and your body, so make sure you learn to love you before you love anyone else.' "

She had the right approach. I laughed and said, "Yeah, because if she's gonna invade people's space like that, they're gonna want to invade her space right back."

"Don't I know it. So I told her that she has to be extremely head-strong about what she's doing and why she's there."

Sounded like a plan to me. And before I knew it, TaShay was getting most of the attention from the camera crew. They had three different camera guys set up to snap pictures from different angles and on different film. One guy shot in black and white, another guy shot wide color angles, and the last guy shot close-ups and reaction shots.

There were ten models and two makeup artists representing all shades and nationalities from Asia to Africa, Europe to South America. We took our individual shots and a few shots all together in various pieces of white. But when it was TaShay's turn for her solo pictures, we all stood around and watched. I guess it had a lot to do with how well she worked the cameras and how the white outfit contrasted with her brown skin. I looked good in my contrast as well, but a young woman in white is a young woman in white. She drew more attention.

I leaned into Paula in the background. "Looks like you got a winner on your hands," I told her.

She smiled and said, "We were actually looking forward to meeting you last night."

"Yeah, I just didn't make it out," I told her. "I got lazy in my room."

"Oh, I know how that is, believe me. But you should have seen the attention TaShay got last night. She just took the place over."

I could imagine it. When white folks jump for you, they jump for real. Paula was starting her niece off in the right crowd.

EVERYONE WAS FINISHED with the photo shoot by close to seven that night. We had a group dinner to attend with our sponsors at nine at the Bennigan's restaurant that was near our hotel. Many of the models and sponsors had already met the night before, so I was one of the few new faces at dinner that night. We were all dressed casually in our own favorite colors.

I met with Michael Bradmore, a city official with the Healthy Environment and Body program in Chicago; Walter Clay, with the Non-

Smokers America Committee; James Polk, of the Walk and Breathe for Your Future campaign; and several other sponsors and officials who were all combining resources in a regional and national fight against lung cancer.

Kim was there as well, but she didn't seem too concerned about me that night. She was pretty much mingling with everyone. So I took her cue and sat back and relaxed. There was no sense in me being alarmed. She wasn't out to get me. She still had a job to do.

After a while, Paula's niece TaShay slid over next to me and sat in a vacated chair to my left. I saw her do it, but I was daydreaming, too. I don't know what I was thinking about. My mind just was not there. Sometimes you drift off in the moment of your life, you know.

"So, how do you feel about your life?" TaShay asked me.

Was she reading my mind or what? At first I just looked at her to make sure she had asked me that.

"Why do you ask?"

She shrugged. "I'm just getting into this modeling thing, but it feels like . . . I don't know. I get bored with it at times."

I smiled and looked across the room toward Paula. She probably had a lot to do with TaShay's boredom in modeling. They were too close for her.

I said, "So you mean to tell me you haven't done the wild and crazy after parties? You know, the hip-hop fashion shows and whatnot?"

I knew she hadn't. I just wanted to hear what she had to say about it.

She frowned immediately. "Are you kidding me? My aunt and mother won't let me anywhere near that stuff. They barely like me listening to it, let alone watch the videos. And you're asking about after parties. I wish. They won't let me go to the before parties."

"Well, what do you think about those videos as it relates to models?" I asked her.

She smiled. "Now I can't argue about that. I mean, they could definitely find more clothes to put on those girls."

"Okay, so if modeling is boring at this point, then what would you rather see yourself doing?" She could have been attending college somewhere.

"Acting," she answered. "I mean, I'm a natural at it."

Seemed like every pretty girl wanted to act, model, sing, or dance. Or maybe that came out because they knew I was around it all the time.

"Haven't you been in cameo movie roles?" she asked me.

I had, but that's all they were, cameo camera shots. It wasn't as if I had to memorize any lines or anything.

I nodded. I said, "Yeah, but I wasn't really acting. I mean, what is acting to you?"

I wanted to challenge her. Saying it and doing it were two different things.

She picked up on my challenge and went right into role-playing. She looked me in the eyes and said, "I can make people believe what they want to believe. That's why modeling is so boring to me. It's two dimensional. I want to do more. I want people to feel more. I want them to be infatuated with me. Can I do that just by taking pictures? I don't think so. I think I need to do it more with my voice, with my body, and with how I carry myself."

I was real calm and cool about it, but I had to look around the room to make sure no one was into our conversation, especially Paula and Kim. Once I saw that they were not paying that much attention, I had to ask TaShay how old she was again.

"How old are you again?" I started smiling before she even answered. She sounded much more mature than her age, and I was sure that Paula and her mother already knew it. In fact, I doubted I would have that much time alone with her before her aunt would break us up. I kept waiting for that to happen.

TaShay chuckled and said, "I wish I didn't have an age. I can't even drink as it is. Just two more years."

She could get a drink brought to her, though; plenty of them. And I'm sure she would accept a few of them if given the opportunity. Hell, I was tempted to give her a sip of my drink if she had asked me.

She said, "How old are you, if you don't mind telling me?"

I grinned. "I'm Jesus' age when he met the cross."

"Thirty-three."

I didn't expect her to answer correctly so quickly.

I said, "Obviously, I can't talk to you too much right here, but I'm assuming that your aunt and your mother don't know you as well as they think they do."

All she did was smile at me. She said, "I get older men, and they get me." Then she did her disappearing act and moved away again, leaving me with a tingle of vibration under the table.

Did she mean that figuratively or literally? I asked myself. I had to shake my head to deny my curiosity about her. *Leave her alone, Johnny. Leave her alone,* I told my big boy downstairs. And I took a sip of my drink.

A Crowded Room of Women

OR THE SATURDAY-NIGHT BANQUET, I had my penguin suit cleaned, pressed, and ready to go. Guys all looked the same at formally dressed affairs, so I jazzed my look up with a striking, lime green tie and a matching handkerchief. You also want to make sure you have a tight shave and a haircut in a dinner jacket. I had the shave down, but instead of a fresh haircut, I sharpened up my edges with my travel clippers.

"You're looking good, guy, looking good," I told myself in the mirror.

Right before I stepped out of the hotel room to head for the waiting limo, I got a call from Victoria.

"Hey, are you ready?" she asked me. She sounded ultra excited.

"Ahh, yeah, I'm good. So, who did you get to come with you?"

I was wondering if she had any black girlfriends she could have invited just to blend in a little more when I greeted them.

"Oh, I invited my girlfriend Jill. She's a tall blonde, green eyes, pretty nice-looking."

There goes that idea, I thought.

I joked and said, "Are you sure you want to bring a blond-haired girlfriend to this event? Aren't you concerned about her snapping up too much attention? And you say she's taller than you, too?"

It sounded like the wrong idea to me.

Victoria laughed it off. "I hope she does get some attention. I mean, Jill's pretty shy, so she always draws people to us that I end up having to talk to for the both of us. So it really works out well."

"Okay, if you say so. But she doesn't have to talk to take pictures. A lot of photographers like shy girls better."

"She doesn't like taking pictures either."

"Okay, well, I'll see you there in about an hour or so," I told her. There was no sense in prolonging the small talk.

"Okay, we'll see you there."

Victoria had picked up the tickets from the front desk of my hotel the day before. I didn't bother to meet up or try and hang out with her. There was just too much going on around me to sneak in time for her. The lung cancer group had kept me out until after two in the morning. I wasn't calling Victoria after that. I was feeling apprehensive about inviting her to the banquet and how the others would respond to her as it was.

When I arrived in the hotel lobby, I found that Paula and TaShay would be sharing the limo ride with me and a few of the other models who were ready.

"So what happens if one of us wants to go back to the hotel early? Do we all have to wait for the group or what?" Andrew Todd asked our driver. Andrew was the handsome white guy of the group.

I was sure he already knew the answer to his question. He was only showboating.

The driver, a short, round-bellied European immigrant, had to answer his question anyway. "No, you just let me know and I'll bring you back to the hotel."

I looked over at TaShay and smiled. She wore a white-and-black-striped zebra dress with matching shoes.

"Out to steal the attention again, huh?" I commented.

"That's what she does," Andrew responded before she did.

"You should always strive to make a statement," her aunt spoke up. Paula was wearing all white again, which complemented her niece.

She said, "And I like your lime green combo. It was a good choice."

"Yeah, he looks like a Christmas tree lightbulb," Andrew joked again, laughing at his own humor. I think he must have had some wine in his room before we left the hotel. He was buzzed already.

"Yeah, I like to stand out as much as TaShay does," I joked back to him.

"We will stand out," she commented with a grin.

Did she mean that individually or as a couple? I asked myself. *And is she referring to more than just the clothes?*

The girl really knew how to get to me, and she did it so cleverly. I began to wonder what she would think about me inviting Victoria to the banquet. It was the number-one concern on my mind when we arrived at The Millennium Ballroom, a huge place built from plate glass.

"Well, here we go," Paula said as we all began to climb out of the limo.

I had no idea how big the event was going to be. There were cameramen everywhere as soon as we stepped out of the limo and walked toward the entrance.

Kim was at the front to meet us, wearing a hot, red dress.

"Is everybody all right?" she asked us.

"What the heck is all of this?" I commented. Lights were steadily popping in my face. It was a red-carpet affair.

Kim said, "This is a big society event every year."

"Yeah, especially for those big-wig money guys," Andrew added.

I was about tired of listening to him, and I was hoping he wouldn't be anywhere near my table.

We all walked into the banquet with hundreds of people in attendance, and took more photos before meeting and greeting more people.

Escorts directed guests to their tables, a front-and-center host with a microphone made frequent announcements, and I found out that the models would be a part of the show once everyone had arrived at their tables and started on their meals.

"Shit, so they're gonna put us on the spot in here?" I asked Kim in private.

"Terrance, do you actually think these people are going to pay you guys thousands of dollars and not acknowledge who they paid for? Now you know better than that. That's all a part of modeling."

I knew she was right, I just didn't feel like going through the motions that evening. I wanted to lay back in the crowd a bit. However, that was not to happen.

"Mr. Terrance Mitchell," someone stated from my left. I turned and came face-to-face with Rachel from the Miami Hilton Hotel. She was wearing bright orange, and her face and hair were done up just right.

"Oh, hey, how are you doing?" I responded to her. I didn't know what else to say, other than asking her what the hell she was doing there. Was she stalking me now?

She smiled and said, "I see you didn't bother to answer any of my phone calls."

I asked her, "Did you leave any messages?"

"Yeah, I left two messages. All I was gonna tell you is that I was gonna be here. Some friends of mine told me they had selected you as one of the campaign models this year. I was gonna be in Chicago today anyway, so I decided to come."

"You paid to get in here?" I asked her. If she paid a hundred dollars for her plate, the general admission fee, then she was stalking me as far as I was concerned.

She answered, "No, my friends gave me tickets. They're involved in this event every year."

Obviously, I was not that well informed on the event. I hadn't bothered to read the lung cancer website Kim had told me to check up on. I mean, unless you or a loved one is dying of cancer, how often would you log onto a lung cancer website?

"Who are your friends?" I asked Rachel next. I was hoping they weren't anyone I knew or had talked to the night before while hanging out with the models and sponsors.

She blew the question off and said, "You don't know them."

I didn't want to get too involved with the conversation, but I was still curious about her connections there.

"How do you know I don't know them?"

"They would have told me they knew you."

"Where are they now?" I asked her.

"Why, you wanna meet them?"

I didn't, I was only skeptical of her legitimacy. But was she calling my bluff or what? I thought about it, and it wasn't worth it, so I left it alone.

"Nah, that's all right. I still have to find my table," I told her.

"What table are you seated at?"

None of your damn business, I felt like telling her. Our Miami conversation was over and done with.

I answered, "I still have to find out," and began to look around and away from her.

"Well, I'll see you later on," she told me. "Let me get back over to my friends." I guess she could see the hastiness in my eyes and in my reactions.

"All right," I told her with a nod, and I moved on.

As soon as I moved away, I caught TaShay's eyes and Kim's eyes, both spying me. I wondered what that meant. I didn't have time to think about it for long, though. Victoria walked in that next minute, and I froze. Why did she have to wear the exact same shade of green as my tie and handkerchief? I was ready to take it off immediately, but she found it humorous.

"Oh my God, look at this." She posed beside me so her tall, blond-hair friend could view our color coordination. Her friend was wearing all black, and she may have been tall and blond, but she wasn't that attractive. She had weak hair, bad skin, and everything. I guess Victoria knew what she was doing after all. Her girlfriend was no competition for her.

"Did you guys plan this?" she asked us, grinning.

"Absolutely not," Victoria answered her. Then she looked at me.

"But what does it mean that we did? Does it mean we think alike?"

I immediately wondered what other people would think about it, especially since I had invited her there. That made me hesitant to introduce her to anyone. I would need to explain our matching outfits to them all. Even if someone didn't ask, I knew they would have to think something about it. It was only natural. In fact, I would feel more comfortable around those who would ask. At least we could get it all out in the open and make a joke out of it.

I didn't get a chance to do that before a cameraman stepped up and took a picture of us standing there together.

"Oh, now that's classic," he told us as he snapped several quick shots. Victoria struck a pose for him and everything.

Shit! I thought to myself. I imagined that things would probably get worse there for me. Kim had met Victoria before at the airport, but I couldn't account for Rachel, TaShay, Paula, and the other black women in the room. We were not at all in the majority. Victoria and her friend fit in better than we did. I figured maybe that would help me out in the long run. At least she would feel comfortable if I left her alone in the crowd.

"Wow, this is quite something else here," she looked around and told me.

I was afraid to look with her. I didn't want to see who all were looking back at us.

Victoria was gorgeous that night, I'll give her that, I just had no idea how many attachments to various black women I would have in the room. It turned out I had more ties than I had previously expected, and that only increased my nervousness about inviting a couple of white girls.

"So, are we sitting at the same table?" Victoria asked me.

I looked again at her ticket stub. It read Table 43.

I shook my head. "I believe the models are all sitting at the reserved tables up front," I told her. That gave me a little bit of breathing room at least.

Right on cue, a female escort found me to guide me to my table.

"Ah, Mr. Terrance Mitchell?" she asked me with a smile. She was another attractive white woman wearing a black silk dress and high heels.

"Yes," I responded to her.

She said, "I'm sorry, I don't know how you got away from me, but I'm supposed to escort you to your table up front. My name is Darla."

I told her, "That was my mistake, Darla. I kind of drifted away from everyone else once I spotted a few folks I knew around the room."

I turned back to Victoria and started to introduce them.

"This is Victoria Mason, an up-and-coming mover and shaker in the marketing and entertainment field." I didn't know how else to introduce her.

"How are you?" the two women addressed each other.

"And this is her friend . . ."

"Jill," Victoria filled in for me.

"Right," I responded with a nod. "Well, I'll see you guys a little later once we get everything started in here."

"Oh, okay, well, we'll be here," Victoria promised me. "And remember, we're at Table Forty-three."

"I got it," I told her.

I moved behind my escort a few feet toward the direction of my table before I was stopped in my tracks again.

"Long time no see, Mr. Man."

I heard that "Mr. Man" quip and turned to my left. Only one woman called me that.

"Andrea," I addressed her. She looked good, only older in her gold designer dress. She had a matching gold flower in her hair.

"Surprised to see me here?" she asked me.

There was no hug, no handshake, no touch, just words and eyes between us.

"I knew we'd bump into each other sooner or later," I told her.

I was rather calm. With all the other women in the room, I'd forgotten all about her. Of course, I had a million questions I wanted to ask her now that she was there, if I would get any extra time to talk to her. So I planned to make that a priority, which meant that all my thoughts about moving on from her flew out the window.

"Ah, I'm sorry, but I really do need to get you to your table," my escort addressed me again. I guess she was already in hot water with the organizers by losing me in the first place. But it wasn't her fault. It wasn't as if I had waited around to be found or anything.

Andrea gave her a look that asked, *How dare you?* That was what I was used to from her.

She said, "Excuse me, we haven't seen each other in quite some time, and we have a little bit of catching up to do. So if you don't mind . . ."

"I'm only trying to do my job here," my escort explained.

I felt trapped. I wanted to make it over to my table if just to catch my breath for a minute. I also wanted to feel Andrea out and at least ask her a few of my many questions. And if I separated from her, I would need to keep my eyes on her to catch up with her before she had a chance to escape again.

"Just give me a minute," I said politely to my escort.

She nodded. "Okay." She couldn't force me to the table.

When I turned back to face Andrea, an older black woman wearing another green dress approached us. Her green was richer and darker than the green I wore. Her skin tone was richer and darker as well.

Andrea seemed to introduce her without even looking, as if she knew where the woman was by scent or something.

"This is my friend Brazil," she told me.

I looked at the woman who smiled readily. She had the same height and build as Andrea, but she was a little thicker in the body.

"Pleased to finally meet you," she told me.

Are you really? I asked myself. My mind began to race a thousand miles a minute. There was a lot going on for me in that place, and the plot was getting thicker by the minute. I started thinking about what Corey had told me about Andrea going the other way in her sexual preferences. I also wondered what she had said about me to her so-called friend. Was I the demon man who had turned her life upside down, or was it the other guy, the one she had married? Of course, had I not opened the door for her to get away, she would have never gotten married to him. Then again, how much could I hold myself responsible for the decisions Andrea made? I didn't tell her to get involved with the guy. That was her decision.

"Interesting name," I told her friend. I had to say something.

"For an interesting person," Brazil responded.

Whatever that meant, I wasn't trying to go there. I really just wanted to say a few private words to Andrea. We had a lot to catch up on.

I asked her, "Do you mind if I talk to you for just a second?"

I realized we were pressed for time, but so what? I felt it was urgent that I get a few answers out of her.

"What would you want to talk to me about? I'm not interested in a walk down Memory Lane, I merely wanted to say hi," she informed me.

It was the same old Andrea with her bullshit. She knew damn well she couldn't just say hi to me. I was still standing there in front of her friend and my escort, and I didn't want to cause a scene. That had never been my style. So I nodded my head and said, "Okay, I'll just see you around then," and walked away from her.

I decided I would play things her way. But inside I was dying. I wanted to find a way to ask her about that abortion situation my sister had brought up. In a way, I kind of felt like Andrea already knew that. I don't know why, but I just felt she knew. And now she was using my curiosity against me.

Damn I hated that girl!

I finally made it over to my table, and TaShay had a spot right next to me. I didn't feel comfortable with that, because I was no longer in the best of moods. There were too many relationships in the room.

Kim looked right into my eyes from the other side of the table. She shook her head and smirked. I guess she understood what kind of night I was about to have.

The host got to introducing the many sponsors and important money people in the room, but all I could think about were my own problems. People were introduced to speak about the importance of lung cancer organizations and the work they continued to do, but it all went in one ear and out the other. I just couldn't fucking concentrate.

That damn girl is the devil! I sat there and thought to myself about Andrea. I clapped hands, smiled, and laughed at the table, but it was all an act.

TaShay finally leaned into me from my left and asked me, "Where is your mind at right now?"

I guess she could read through the bullshit I was doing up in there. But she really didn't want to know where my mind was, nor was I willing to tell her. Then she rubbed her hand down my left thigh and squeezed my knee, with the coolness of a serial killer.

She nodded and said, "I understand."

This young girl was really asking for trouble. It was the wrong time of the night and the wrong mood for me to play her uncle. She didn't want to catch the wrath of my raw emotions up in a hotel bedroom somewhere. That was about the only thing that would calm me down. When all else fails, you find yourself a good piece of pussy and call it a day.

First I looked past TaShay toward her aunt Paula, who was busy grinning and applauding the speeches being given at the podium. Then I looked across the table to Kim. She caught me dead-eyed again. She smiled and looked away. But it wasn't an easy smile. It felt like she was a little bit jealous. Even TaShay caught it. So she straightened up and started clapping her hands like nothing happened.

Okay, this is crazy, I told myself. I had one, two, three, four, *five* women in that room who were all competing for pieces of me. One crossed wire and the whole neighborhood could explode.

I took a drink of water and tried to shake it off. I had been in many situations where several women were vying for my attentions, but it seemed different this time. In my younger years, I would map it all out and put them on a priority list. I told myself to do the same that night.

Stay cordial with TaShay, but let her know you're not going there. Have a much better talk with Kim about everything as soon as you get a chance. Introduce Victoria to one or two people, and point out others she should meet on her own. Ignore Rachel, because you don't want to have anything else to do with her. Then make sure you catch up to Andrea to ask her the questions that have been driving you nuts.

I was putting it all together in my mind. So by the time the host asked for the models to stand for recognition as he called out our names, I was back at peace with myself.

"Terrance Mitchell," the host called. I stood up, smiled, and turned to face the applauding crowd of guests while they flashed our picture individually and as a group on a large projector screen above the podium.

That'll get Andrea thinking about me again, I told myself after my towering image had been shown on the screen. However, so would the other women in the room.

We ate dinners of chicken or fish with fresh vegetables and potatoes, and they opened an area of the floor for dancing and more mingling. That's when I became nervous again.

TaShay went right after my hand like an aggressive schoolgirl. "You wanna dance?"

Did I even have a choice? They had an old-school, R&B DJ playing the jams of yesterday, kicking things off with the Philadelphia International Records classic, "Ain't No Stopping Us Now," from Gene McFadden and John Whitehead.

I slowed the young woman up with my hand and told her, "Hey, let me digest my food for a minute."

"Are you sure?"

"Yeah," I told her. "How about right after I make this trip to the bathroom?"

I made a swift exit from our table area, and by the time I had made it halfway to the restrooms, Victoria and Jill were in my face again.

"You really looked good up there," Victoria told me.

Her friend smiled in agreement. "Yeah."

I said, "Yeah, I know," just to get a laugh out of them. "But let me make this trip to the restroom, and I'll get right back to you," I told them.

I quickly moved on and noticed Andrea standing nearby with her friend Brazil. I worried they might be ready to leave early. Like a crazy man, I headed right for them before making it to the men's room.

"Hey, how did you get a name like Brazil, anyway?" I asked her friend to break the ice. I planned to play a game of hit and run. I wanted to get the information I needed from Andrea so I could move on with my night and with my life without letting her screw up my mood with all of her extra baggage.

Her friend smiled and answered, "My parents told me I was consummated in Brazil during their fourth anniversary."

I nodded. "Oh, so you had traveling parents."

"We were privileged, yes."

I guess she was an upwardly mobile, regal woman, too. She had those airs about her. But I didn't care. I just wanted to get back to Andrea.

I looked Andrea in her eyes again and said, "Just a few seconds if I may."

She changed the subject and said, "Your friends are looking for you."

I didn't have the time for those games. I didn't even look to see who she was referring to.

"Just a second. Please."

I wasn't really begging, I was just being polite.

Brazil said, "Obviously, Terrance, the second you ask for is maybe a second too much."

I had to ignore that, I really did. Because if I took it to heart and responded, the results would not get me closer to my goal.

Andrea asked her, "Are you ready?"

"If you are then let's go," her friend answered.

I was about ready to lose my mind in there. All I needed was one second from her to ask her one question in private, so that I could move on with my life. I needed closure.

To add insult to injury, Andrea commented, "Have a good night with your new friends, Terrance," as she walked away.

That BITCH! I thought. She was murdering me. I *know* she knew what I wanted to ask her. Why else would she be such an asshole about giving me one second? She had planted that lethal seed with my sister to explode whenever it exploded.

I finally looked across the room and saw not only Victoria and Jill waiting, but Rachel and her friends were not far away from them.

I took a deep breath and continued on my way to the restroom. Once inside the stall, thoughts about Andrea were ruining my state of mind. It was obvious she was going to make me work for any answers to my many questions. And it looked like Corey was right; she had changed her sexual preference.

I finished my business and went to wash my hands at the sink.

"I bet you got your hands full, huh, buddy?" an older white man commented.

He showed me his ring and said, "I miss those days."

He was referring to me being young, handsome, wealthy, and single.

I laughed and said, "Actually, the way I'm feeling right now, maybe it's better to have a woman guaranteed every once in awhile."

The guy looked at me and frowned. He said, "Guaranteed? Who in the hell told you that? At least you can shoot at different options when you're still out there. But when you got that committed ball and chain on ya' ankle, you're just sitting at the table waiting and hoping that there's any ripe food to eat that night. You know what I mean? It's the worst fucking feeling in the world. And you ask yourself, 'Who signed me up for this shit?' "

I laughed a little harder. This guy was a classic hard-liner. It was good to hear the honest-to-God truth from a committed man. I got tired of hearing that Hallmark shit from married guys. Everyone knew Hallmark cards were for women. Guys needed to tell the damn truth. Problem was, the truth wouldn't get you any play, so you couldn't tell it.

I marched out of that bathroom set on being reckless. Most women were not in the mood when they were pissed off, but as a man, I was ready to go into full dog mode. All I thought about was not being lonely at the end of the night. But I still had my limitations. I wouldn't choose to be with just any woman.

I looked for Victoria and her friend to introduce them to a few folks and find out as quickly as I could where her head was for the rest of the evening, but Rachel beat her to me.

"So, that's the kind of women you like, sticks and bones, model types?" she said to me.

I wasn't expecting that. She was coming on strong again with her bitter candor.

"Well, I'm around them all the time. What would you expect?" I asked her.

"White girls, too, huh?"

I hesitated. "No, not usually. I don't have a lot of experience with white women."

She said, "Looks like you're going to try one out tonight?"

I told her, "Look, there's mostly white folks in here. So I'm introducing a few people to a few people. They did invite us here. This isn't our affair."

"That doesn't mean you have to go the other way."

Over her left shoulder, I could see Victoria and Jill still waiting for me. That didn't look good. They were not working the crowd on their own at all. I thought the girl told me she was a wonder with people. How come she wasn't doing her thing without me?

I told Rachel, "I'm not going the other way. What do you care about it, anyway? I'm not your type, remember?"

She said, "Play it how you want to play it. I can't tell you what to do. But I will tell you this, you'd be surprised at how a *natural* woman could work it. So you keep that on your mind tonight," and she walked away from me with plenty of sass.

I didn't want to look back over at Victoria and her friend after that. I knew they saw everything, but how would they respond to it? Nevertheless, I had to make that journey back over to them. They were still waiting.

As soon as I approached them, Victoria attempted to let me off the hook.

"Look, ah, Terrance, I can see that you have a lot going on right now. So if you're not able to, you know, introduce us and show us around, I mean, I understand. I don't want to be a hindrance to you in any way where I'm just, you know, cramping your style or anything."

I was fine with it up until that point. The whole "cramping your style" line made me laugh. It also made me curious as to what she thought my style was.

I joked with her and repeated it, "Cramping my style, huh?"

She giggled. "I don't know, I just don't want to be a drag on your night."

I immediately began to wonder what Victoria's position would be on a more private party. All she could do is say she wasn't interested.

I asked her, "So what would you say if I wanted to leave here altogether?"

She looked confused by the question. "What, you're tired already?"

That was totally the wrong answer. That's why I didn't really deal with white women. They were going left and I was going right more than half of the time.

I said, "I'm tired of being pulled in a million directions by all of these different people, but I'm not ready to call it a night and crash or anything. I'm just ready to get out of here."

I could tell she wasn't ready to leave. She looked fully energized, and she had her friend behind her.

"Well, when are you gonna be back in Chicago?" she asked me.

Why? I was tempted to ask her. But there was no sense to it. She was a girl trying to find her way into the modeling, fashion, and acting industry, and I just wasn't the man to help her meet her goals.

I shook my head and had to level with her, because the charades were not going anywhere.

"Look, I'm sorry, but real life just isn't as simple as we all would like it to be. Now I know I promised you I would introduce you to some folks, but like you've already said, my head's really not into that right now. But at the end of the night, I'm still gonna want some company."

I stopped the conversation right there. I had said more than enough already. She got the point.

She nodded and said, "I understand. No hard feelings. So . . . I guess I'll just see you around then."

I felt terrible in a lot of ways. I had sent women away before to do something else, or someone else, as the case may be. But this white girl had me feeling overly guilty about it. That didn't settle well with me at all. Why was I giving her special treatment? I had to shake it off and do me.

"Yeah, you'll be all right," I told her.

I was being an asshole again to be alone and able to tackle whatever I had to tackle.

She looked at me with sadness in her eyes. "Okay, well, have a good night." Then she walked away and rejoined her friend.

Damn! That took a lot more out of me than I expected. I walked back in the direction of the dance floor where TaShay, Paula, Kim, and the other models and photographers were grouped.

TaShay was dancing up a storm and being the life of the party again. Everyone was loving her.

That girl's gonna have a heck of a future if she doesn't ruin it for herself, I pondered.

She spotted me and gave me all of her attention. Kim turned and eyed me herself. I motioned for her to walk over and chat.

Kim headed toward me and asked, "What's up?" She was still moving to the music, one of the many R. Kelly dance numbers.

I said, "I just want to talk to you."

Kim followed me back over to the table. "What's on your mind?" she asked me.

"Everything," I told her. "But first I just want to apologize . . ."

She held up her hand and shook her head to stop me. "I don't want you to do that. I need to apologize to you. I mean, it was real foul of me to impose on your life like that. You don't have kids for a reason, and I need to respect that."

"Yeah, but I didn't respond the right way," I told her.

"How were you supposed to respond? I'm the one who didn't think things through."

Looks like they were all letting me off the hook that night.

"So you don't feel, like, upset with me about it?"

"How could I be? It's your life, and your seed. You were right about that. I don't know what I was thinking."

I didn't know what else to say at that point. The discussion was over, so I changed the subject. "What do you think about TaShay as a model?"

"She definitely has what it takes to make it, I just don't know how long she can keep her head in it. She seems really distracted and young."

I looked over at TaShay again, enjoying herself on the dance floor, and her aunt was right there with her.

"You think Paula can reel her in and keep her focused?"

Kim grinned and answered decisively, "No. TaShay will be the only one who can stop or continue her career. She has already shown me that she's ready to make her own decisions, at least on a personal level. But she does seem to listen to her aunt and mother on the professional level. She knows what she needs to do."

I nodded. "Well . . . I'm thinking about getting out of here early tonight."

I still saw no reason to stick around too long. I had my pictures taken, said hi to two dozen people, put in my time, and I was now ready to go.

Kim looked past me and asked, "What do you plan to do about your two friends?"

I turned to see who she was referring to, but I already knew. Victoria and Jill continued to look lost in the crowd.

"Are they looking for you?"

I wasn't too hard to find. I was in plain view.

I shook my head. "Nah. I already told them I'm not staying long."

"Well, are they looking for you to say 'bye?"

I looked back at Victoria explaining something to Jill in the distance. Maybe she did want to have a few more words with me. But before I approached them again, I figured I'd ask Kim how she felt about them.

"What do you think . . ."

She cut me off again with a smile. "I already know. You've had a busy night tonight. And yes, I did see Andrea here briefly as well. But I told you that white girl was feeling you when I saw her at the airport."

I continued to deny it. "Nah, she's definitely all about getting the contacts she needs."

"Well, how come she isn't working the room to get them? Looks to me like she's waiting for something."

I took a breath and thought about it. I had already explained my position to her.

"I mean, if you invited her here, then go handle it," Kim advised me.

I started walking back toward Victoria and her friend without another word. All of a sudden, Rachel popped back up in the area. But I had things to do, so I planned to ignore her again.

"Are you okay in here?" I asked Victoria. She looked perplexed.

She said, "Actually, I'm not." Without a word, her friend Jill walked off, leaving Victoria and me for a private discussion. Once I saw that, I knew I was in trouble.

"Okay, what's the problem?"

I figured I would go about it like a medical doctor: examine the patient and prescribe the cure.

"Well, I was really looking forward to spending time with you here, and I think it's more than just meeting people. I mean, anyone can do that, but I wanted you to do it."

I opened my mouth to respond. I thought we had already agreed that I was not in the best frame of mind that night to be the introduction guy. But before I could speak, Victoria cut me off.

"Now, I understand that you have a lot going on, but I still want to be with you. And it's not fair for me to sit here and act like I don't. So I'm gonna have to be a little bit selfish and just tell you how I feel."

She was knocking me flat on my ass. I immediately thought back to what Kim had said when she first met and observed the girl: "These white girls don't play. They see what they want and they go right after it."

I don't know how true that was as a blanket statement about white women, I just looked at Victoria more as an East Coast girl who would say what she wanted when she needed to.

Well, I still didn't get a chance to respond to her yet.

She said, "And I don't know how it is with you and most of the women you deal with or whatever, but if you invited me here, then I expect to be able to talk to you. Or did you, like, invite everyone here with a whole bunch of tickets?"

I guess she wasn't letting me off the hook after all.

I finally answered, "No, I gave you the only tickets I had."

"Well . . ."

She was putting me back in dog mode, so I had to give it to her straight. She was asking me for it.

I said, "I told you earlier, when this night is over with, I want to leave with company."

She said, "I heard you."

"And you understand what I mean?"

"Of course I understand, I'm a grown woman."

I leaned back and said, "Well, excuse me." Then I figured I would lighten things up a bit. I said, "But I'm telling you now, I'm not planning on playing any late-night card games or anything when I say company."

Victoria started smiling. She said, "I think I can handle myself."

"But what about your friend?" I asked her.

"She knows how I feel. We've already discussed it. So she's gonna get her own cab."

I was impressed. She didn't even bring up anything about race. I guess she had been with black men before. Nevertheless, her bold decision was bound to put me in more trouble. How the hell was I supposed to get away from everyone else?

Without looking around, which would have made our intentions too obvious, I told Victoria, "Look, I need you to shake my hand, tell me that you've had a nice night and that you're leaving early, then find your girlfriend and walk out with her."

She followed my logic and asked me, "Then what?"

"When you get outside, you ask the limo drivers for the Swissôtel car for Terrance Mitchell, and then you wait for me there. I'll be out in less than ten minutes."

She nodded and said, "I can do that."

"Okay, let's do it then," I told her. "Let me see your acting skills."

She laughed and went right into it with her hand extended.

"Well, Terrance, I really had a great time here tonight, but I have to get up pretty early tomorrow morning, so I'm going ahead and leave now."

"Oh, okay. Well, I appreciate you coming out tonight. And you make sure to give me a call."

"I'll do that."

I walked away from her feeling giddy as a kid. I was going to tear fire to that girl, she just didn't know it yet. It was going to be a good night.

Rachel caressed my arm before I could make it back to my table.

"What are your plans for the rest of the night?" she asked me. She had a drink in her hand, and I suspected she had downed several others.

I told her, "Actually, I'm feeling a little exhausted right now. I'm just gonna go back and crash."

"Go back to where? What hotel do they have you staying in?"

I failed to name my hotel on purpose. I didn't want any surprises that night. Too many women knowing your hotel had gotten me into trouble before, several times.

I said, "It doesn't even matter. It's just a room that I'm gonna sleep in."

Rachel looked at me with glassy eyes and responded as if she hadn't even heard me. She said, "You don't have to do any work. All you have to do is lean back, and I'll do the rest."

Her strong advances didn't even sound tempting anymore. I didn't feel guilty about it either. The Johnson had spoken, and the Johnson wanted the cute-as-apple-pie white girl.

I shook my head and said, "Not tonight. I'ma have to pass."

"You gonna pass on these lips and this pussy? Why? You want that little white ho instead? She don't have enough for you."

I smiled and couldn't help it. I said, "Look, I told you earlier, I'm not here with a white woman. I came by myself, and I'm leaving by myself. Now let me get over here and tell all of these folks good-bye."

I walked away from her and didn't look back. Time was wasting. I approached Kim and let out a deep sigh.

She asked me, "So what happened?" She was still referring to Victoria and her friend Jill.

"She was a little peeved at me for not being able to, you know, introduce her to folks and whatnot. I mean, I just don't feel like it tonight."

Kim nodded and grinned, knowing my history. She said, "That poor girl had no idea that you'd be the last person walking around introducing people. Hell, you act like you're the only person alive in the world sometimes."

She was hinting at my selfishness again. I really didn't care anymore. I had to get out of there.

I said, "Yeah, well let me say my good-byes to everybody."

"Okay. But make sure you call me when you make it in."

So far so good, I thought to myself. I had knocked two down with two women to go; Paula and her insatiable niece.

I figured I would approach Paula first. It was the respectable thing to do. Besides, Paula would be the easier one to say good-bye to.

"Hey, ah, I'll see you next go 'round," I told her as soon as I approached them on the dance floor. She and her niece were still having a ball dancing.

Paula looked at me surprised. "You're leaving already?"

"Yeah, I've already put in my time," I told her.

She looked at her watch and said, "It's barely after eleven o'clock."

Actually it was closer to midnight than eleven, but I understood her point. The night was still young.

I said, "I'm not as young and energetic as I used to be. So I take my cues to rest when I get them. And right now I'm feeling a little bit exhausted."

She nodded. "Well, when are you gonna be back out on the West Coast?"

They lived out in the San Diego area.

"As a matter of fact, I have L.A. and then Oakland, back to back, in two weeks," I told her.

"Oh, well, let us know when you get out there."

"All right, I got your new numbers. I'll call you guys up," I told her. "Now let me go say 'bye to your niece."

I took a breath before I approached TaShay. Would I look the girl up later on or what? I knew I couldn't say good-bye to her as fast as I had with her aunt.

"Hey, I'll see you next go 'round, kid," I told her.

She immediately grabbed me into her and asked me, "What's your cell number?"

I froze for a second. Then I told myself, *What the hell,* and gave it to her.

She pulled out her cell phone right there in the open and logged my number in.

"Okay, I'ma call you, so expect my phone call."

Her game was straight crafty. She made it look like business, but I knew that it wasn't. I had just played that same game with Victoria.

I grinned, knowingly. "I bet you will," I responded.

That young girl had the hots for me. Or maybe that was just what she wanted me to believe. Who knows with young women sometimes. They seemed to change their minds a lot from what I had dealt with. One day they're totally into you, the next day they're just as passionate about another guy.

"Stay up late," she snuck out there as I began to walk away.

I froze for another second. *Stay up late? What the hell does that mean?* Was she planning on sneaking out to see me or just calling me?

I headed toward the door and said my final good-byes to some of the sponsors and admirers in the room. When I finally reached the limos outside, Victoria was nowhere to be found.

Then I spotted our limo driver.

"Ah, Mr. Mitchell, your lady friend is in the car straight ahead, sir," he told me.

He led me toward the limo parked at the front of the line of cars and quickly opened the door for me to climb in. Victoria was sitting inside smiling. She looked like an untouched lady with her hands folded in her lap.

As soon as the limo driver shut the door behind me, she asked, "Is everything clear?"

She seemed amazingly at peace with herself, all calm and civil.

"So far, so good," I answered. "But what about you? Is everything clear with you?"

She reached over to hold my left hand in her right. She nodded and said, "I'm good. I'm glad I'm still with you."

She had a sparkle in her dark eyes, looking everything in the world like a Hollywood romance movie.

I nodded back to her. "Okay, but I'm gonna make you bad before this night is over."

I didn't want everything getting too damn sentimental, because then I wouldn't want to touch the girl.

After my comment, she broke up laughing and remained loose.

She said, "I don't wanna be bad. I wanna be good to you."

The limo pulled out into the street, and we were off on our way to the Swissôtel. But Victoria was fucking up my mood with that good-girl shit. I didn't want a love story that night, I wanted some hot, wet pussy, no matter what color it was.

I told her, "Well, you're gonna be bad tonight," and I forced myself to lean toward her lips for a kiss. She accepted my advance and kissed me softly with an open mouth. And boy did her little tongue do nice work on mine. She teased me just enough to make me crazy curious about her. Then she pulled away and whispered, "Are you really gonna make me be bad tonight?"

Man, that white girl was ready to make me give it to her in the limo before we even made it back to the hotel.

"I only want you to do what you want to do . . . as long as it's bad."

She chuckled and said, "Okay."

Next thing I knew, she had slipped her hand away from mine so that she could massage the erection that had stiffened inside my pants.

"Is this bad enough?" she teased me.

"It's a start. I'm just curious to see how far you're planning to go with it."

She looked into my eyes all misty, and grinned. Then she bit her lower lip. "I guess we'll soon see."

No Peace, No Pleasure

VICTORIA AND I made it back to my hotel without getting too kinky inside the limo, and we stepped into the lobby, hand in hand, on the way to my suite for a night of fun-filled privacy.

"Hey, Terrance, perfect timing." It was Corey Sanders, standing right in front of me near the registration counter in a gray sweatsuit. "I've been trying to get in touch with you for two days. I was gonna leave you a message over here to call me."

It was the wrong time for me, and unfortunately for him, I was flying back out of town the next morning.

Corey looked to Victoria and nodded to her. "How are you doing?" She nodded back and said, "I'm fine."

I didn't want to say anything to him at all. I had a one-track mind on scoring, and I had been dodging Corey's phone calls on purpose. I even wondered how he knew where I was staying, though that information wasn't that hard to get. I never traveled in secret, and I usually took what accommodations my hosts would give me without much complaint. I wasn't high maintenance at all.

Anyway, Corey motioned for me to step aside in private. "Let me speak to you for just one minute, Terrance."

I was noticeably hesitant. "Not right now, man. I'll call you," I told him. I wanted to get on the move toward the elevators with Victoria.

"Just for a second, Terrance," Corey persisted.

I took a breath and looked to Victoria. "Wait for me over at the elevators." I didn't want her just standing there.

"Okay," she responded with a nod.

Corey grinned as soon as I faced him. "That's a good-looking white girl, man. Where you find her, at the cancer event?"

I couldn't remember if I had even told him the purpose of the event, but I felt as if I didn't want him to know anything at that point. He was really irritating me.

I cut to the chase and asked him, "So what's going on, man?"

He got excited. "Hey, did you bump into Andrea over there?"

I answered, "Yeah, but she didn't have much to say to me. But look, man, I'll tell you all of that over the phone. I gots to go."

I just started walking away from him. I had no more to say to the brother.

He noticed my urgency to leave and shook his head with a smile.

"I see. I guess I'll just see you around, man. Call me."

When I made it back over to Victoria at the elevators, she asked me, "What was that about?"

I shook it off and said, "I don't know. That guy . . ."

I didn't know what else to say about him. He seemed to be getting more peculiar by the minute, like he wanted an attachment to me of his own.

As soon as we stepped onto the arriving elevator, Victoria asked me, "Is he gay?"

At first I just laughed about it. I hadn't thought about that, but . . . I began to grimace in all seriousness. "Why would you say that?" I asked her.

She shrugged her shoulders. "I don't know, it's just the way he looked at you or whatever."

I was so busy trying to get away from him that I wasn't really paying attention to it. Nevertheless, I didn't want to spend too much time on that. I was with the preferred sex, and I wanted to get my mind back into it.

I said, "Well, if he is, then that's his problem," and I tugged her slightly into me. "Now where were we?" I asked her.

Victoria wrapped her arms around my waist and squeezed me. She chuckled and said, "You were telling me about all the bad things you were gonna make me do."

I corrected her and said, "No, that's all of the bad things that you *want* to do. Because I'm not gonna make you do anything that you won't allow.

"I want a woman to want me as much as I want her," I told her. "Sometimes I want them to want me more."

I was putting it on her strong. I didn't want her changing her mind all of a sudden, although I doubted that she would. It was nearly showtime.

Victoria told me, "I do want you," as soon as the elevator arrived at my floor.

"We'll see."

We stepped off the elevator and approached my suite. When I opened the door, my cell phone went off. I had the phone on vibrate and had ignored it for the majority of the night. However, Victoria heard the buzz of the vibration mode and smiled at me.

"I know you're not gonna answer that."

I grinned and said, "Of course not."

Inside the room, I turned a few of the lights on and noticed the hotel phone flashing red from left messages.

Victoria noticed it as well.

"It looks like you're a popular guy tonight."

"I guess so," I told her.

It wasn't anything new to me. I planned to ignore all of it.

She put her purse down on the dresser and walked through the spacious room. "Nice," she stated.

I sat on the king-size bed. "What did you expect? They generally try to show off for us."

"I see." She began to pull back the curtains of the full-view windows that overlooked Lake Michigan. "Nice view, too."

I didn't want to rush things, but I didn't want us to go cold either. So I waited a minute to see if she would approach me on her own. After a few minutes at the window, she did. She walked right over to the bed and stood between my legs.

"Well, you got me over here. Now what?"

I gripped her by the waist and pulled her closer to me.

"How long are you planning on keeping these clothes on?" I asked her.

She smiled. "Not long at all." Then she pulled the straps of her dress off of her shoulders.

I kissed her bare shoulder and worked my way down to her breast before her dress fell to the floor. Then I kissed her pert nipples. She cradled my head in her hands while I sucked them slowly.

"So I guess this answers my question," I told her.

She began to get into it with a slow rowing movement.

"What question is that?"

"You have been with black men before."

She chuckled and said, "What if you're the first one?"

I seriously doubted that. She was too comfortable with me. And she had been comfortable for the entire night, much more than I was.

I decided to play along with her anyway.

"The first one, huh?" I mumbled through kisses and soft sucks of her breasts. She wasn't as pale as I thought she would be. She had a nice color to her. Maybe she was mixed with Italian.

"Maybe," she responded. Then she pushed me back on the bed. I figured she would climb on top of me, but she didn't. She went after my pants instead.

"You want me to close my eyes now?" I asked her.

She unzipped my zipper and went right after me. "If you want."

I didn't even have time to prepare.

"Ooh," I responded to her soft lips and tongue. Her gentleness with me increased the pleasure tenfold. She knew how to work all the right spots.

"Is this bad?" she asked me.

I shook my head against the pillow and could barely speak. "Unt, unh."

As soon as I mumbled to her, she tightened up her lips on me.

"OHH." I jerked forward, responding to her increased pressure.

She curled up on me in the fetal position and continued to work. There was no more talking after that, only steady pleasing, until the damn phone rang and irritated me.

BRRRRUUUURRPPP . . . BRRRRUUUURRPPP . . .

"Fuck!" I cursed the phone and whoever was calling. I wanted to knock it off the hook, but I had to wait until it stopped ringing first.

BRRRRUUUURRPPP . . . BRRRRUUUURRPPP . . .

It was an outside call with a double ring.

BRRRRUUUURRPPP . . . BRRRRUUUURRPPP . . .

Victoria was pretty much ignoring it, but I wasn't. The phone was really bothering me.

BRRRRUUUURRPPP . . . BRRRRUUUURRPPP . . .

How many times is this shit gonna ring? I asked myself. That's when it stopped ringing.

I began to feel the heated intensity when my cell phone vibrated with another call. You could hear the buzz a little more in the silence.

Victoria finally took a pause and commented on it.

"Somebody else wants you, too."

She climbed up from me and tugged off the rest of her clothes, revealing her straight brown hair below. It wasn't a lot, but it was enough. She had nice curves on her, too. I was impressed with her whole package.

She looked at me watching her and asked, "Are you just gonna lay there or get naked with me?"

I guess I had started daydreaming. I leaned up to start undoing the rest of my clothes.

"You have any protection?" she asked me.

"Yup," I answered while I tugged off my shoes, socks, and shirt. Then the hotel phone rang again.

BRRRRUUUURRPPP . . . BRRRRUUUURRPPP . . .

At that point, I got really curious as to who was calling me. Whoever it was knew where I was staying, but I don't know if they knew my cell phone or not. Maybe it was two or three different callers, or the same one. I don't know.

BRRRRUUUURRPPP . . . BRRRRUUUURRPPP . . .

That was it! I said, "You know what, I need to find out who this is," and I approached the hotel phone while grabbing my cell phone at the same time. I wanted to read all of the calls I had ignored earlier on the cell, and see who was calling me at the hotel.

"Hello," I answered. I tried to make sure I held my emotions in check when I spoke. I didn't want to give anything away.

"Did I catch you in the middle of something?"

I froze and didn't bother to look at the rest of the cell phone numbers. It was Andrea calling.

"Did you just call a few minutes ago?" I asked her. It was the wrong damn question, too. It made it sound obvious that I had ignored the phone. Then I tried to cover it up.

"I had just missed it," I told her. But that didn't sound good for Victoria. It made the phone call sound more important than her, and she was still sitting there butt naked, waiting for me.

"That was me," Andrea answered. She was far more mature than when I knew her, that was for sure. She had this new poise that I had never seen her display. She had shown it to me earlier that night at the banquet.

But now I was in a new dilemma. I damn sure couldn't ask Andrea what I needed to ask her while Victoria was in the room with me.

I asked Andrea, "How did you know to call here?"

I was stalling while I tried to figure how to work everything out.

Andrea ignored my question. "So, what did you have to ask me earlier?" I guess she realized my hotel question was meaningless. It was easy for her to find out where we were staying. All she had to do was ask a few people who were at the event earlier.

I thought fast and came up with the only solution. I had to ask her without asking her.

I said, "Somebody told me that you gave them some information at the airport some years ago, and I wanted to follow up on the truth of it."

Andrea didn't budge. She said, "You have someone in the room with you?"

There was no sense in lying to her about it. I wasn't with her anymore and hadn't been with her for years.

"Yes, I have company." I had to make Victoria feel privileged to be with me again.

In the middle of my act, my cell phone went off in my right hand. I should have turned it off, but it was too late for that. I didn't even look at it.

Andrea said, "Stop talking in riddles. Ask me what you want to ask me."

I knew she knew what I wanted, I told myself. She was playing me like a flute.

"How 'bout you give me your number and I'll call you back at a better time?" I told her.

I had to get the hell out of it and get back to her. It was my only solution. Otherwise, I would ruin everything I hoped to have with Victoria. All the while, my cell phone continued to buzz in my right hand.

Andrea responded, "How 'bout I don't?"

I was stuck. I looked over at Victoria; she was staring into empty space thinking who knows what.

Okay, this is fucked up, I concluded. *Why did I even answer this damn phone? Asshole!*

I said, "Okay, well, you call me when you get a chance then." I was praying that Andrea would go along with it and hang up, but she didn't.

She said, "Wait a minute. You were practically killing yourself to talk to me earlier, now you're trying to hurry me off the phone."

"I told you I have company. Now either you give me a contact number where I can reach you, or I'll just talk to you whenever."

I was trying to make myself sound as cold, business-oriented, and distant as I could.

Andrea said, "Well, I'm not calling you back. So I guess it wasn't that important then."

She was killing me, but I refused to make an even bigger fool of myself by bringing up too much of my personal history in front of a two-day acquaintance.

I nodded my head with my left ear against the phone and said, "Okay. I'll just see you around then," and I hung up the receiver to save the rest of my night. I even turned my cell phone off, which I should have done earlier.

I looked over at Victoria, and she was still staring into space and thinking something. The groove had definitely been busted. But maybe if I turned the lights off . . .

I moved to switch off the lights, but as soon as I turned them off, Victoria moved toward her clothes, and started to put them on.

"What are you doing?" I asked her through the dark. I could see her in the moonlight that shone in from the opened curtains at the window.

She shook her head and didn't answer.

I took a breath and didn't bother to fight it.

Victoria finished dressing and grabbed her purse from the dresser. Then she finally spoke to me again. She couldn't even look me in the face when she spoke.

"You know, I tried to tell myself to just ignore it all and have a good time with you, but . . . I mean, how stupid can I be, Terrance?

"I mean, I really like you, but . . . I don't even really know you," she reasoned. "And that doesn't make any sense."

I didn't have any comment for her. I didn't know what the hell to say to the girl. I could have made up something, but I didn't really feel up to it. It had been a long damn night.

I said, "I understand."

Victoria didn't leave too fast though. It seemed that she was still struggling with her decision.

She shook her head again. "This is just . . . I don't believe this."

I walked over to comfort her in the dark. Maybe she was thinking about staying anyway.

"Look, you can just relax, have something to drink, and, you know . . ."

I was basically telling her she wasn't under any pressure, and it seemed to be working. She didn't move toward the door. I held her there, thinking about taking the hotel phone off the hook.

"Let me, ah, take this phone off the hook," I told her as I moved toward it. I had made it halfway there when the phone rang again.

BRRRRUUUURRPPP . . .

I didn't want to answer it like a fool a second time. I stopped and looked back to my bemused company. The whole situation was becoming ridiculous. Victoria smiled and shook her head again.

BRRRRUUUURRPPP . . .

I said, "After it stops ringing, I'm gonna take the phone off the hook. Okay?"

"It doesn't matter at this point. I'm just gonna go ahead and go," she told me.

"You don't look like you wanna go," I responded.

"Yeah, but it's the right thing to do."

"Not when you get back home and you wish you had stayed," I hinted.

BRRRRUUUURRPPP . . .

"If I do stay, tomorrow I'm gonna wish I had left."

I said, "So you're in a losing battle either way then. And if you need to pick between the two, then pick not being alone."

That hushed her up for a minute. Then she came back with, "I am alone. That's how I'm feeling right now. I'm not really with you. I know that now. We don't really know each other to be together. We're still strangers."

What could I really say to that? She was right. I took another breath as the phone continued to ring.

BRRRRUUUURRPPP . . .

"You still want me to call you . . . when I'm back in town?" I asked her.

She smiled again. "If you have time, sure, why not?"

I nodded. "Well, before you leave, let me at least hug you."

She stood there and waited for me. I walked over and hugged her with more than half of my clothes off. I squeezed her into me and she squeezed back.

"I apologize for all of this," I told her.

BRRRRUUUURRPPP . . .

"That's just your busy lifestyle. Some guys don't get any calls at all."

"Well, I guess I'm not in that category," I joked.

That was the last of the phone ringing. I hurried back over to take the receiver off the hook.

Victoria started to move toward the door before I could make my return to her.

"You're really gonna leave?" It was my last effort to get her to stay. I wasn't trying too hard though. I didn't want to look desperate. If she really wanted me, there would be another day.

She nodded and said, "Yeah, I'm gonna go ahead and go," and opened the door.

Before I let her leave, I asked her, "So, what was your full intention when you first met me?"

My question stopped her in her tracks. I wasn't trying to accuse her of anything, I was just asking for the facts.

"I wasn't expecting this, if that's what you're thinking."

"I'm not, but . . . I mean, I liked you like that," I told her. "I thought you were fabulous from the moment I saw you. But you seemed to be all about business."

"I am," she told me. "I'm usually very professional. But, you know . . ."

"Did I turn you on?"

She smiled and admitted it, "Yeah, you can say that."

"Good, because if I'm a professional model and I can't turn a woman on, then I'm losing my edge."

She put her hand against my chest at the door and assured me, "You're not losing your edge at all, but I really need to get to know you better first."

AFTER VICTORIA had left me there in my room, unsatisfied and horny, instead of me calling it a night and licking my wounds, I turned my cell phone back on and checked my missed calls and messages.

My mother and sister had called me; Danni had called me twice, Corey twice, Rachel twice, and TaShay called last. The other calls were insignificant, or at least at the moment.

I sat there and contemplated who to call back first. Corey and Rachel were out of the question. Danni I could call back at any time of night, because she was nocturnal. TaShay . . . I still had to think on that one. And my sister was an easier call than my mother, so I decided to start things off with Juanita. I wanted to say a few things to my sister about me bumping into Andrea out there in Chicago, and what she said to me.

"Hello?" my sister answered on a short ring.

"What are you, sitting right next to the phone?" I teased her.

"Oh, Terrance, thanks for calling me back."

She sounded excited to hear from me for a change. That made me curious as to what she wanted.

I said, "You wouldn't believe who I bumped into out here in Chicago tonight."

Juanita paused. "You didn't bring up anything about the pregnancy, did you? Please don't tell me you did that."

I said, "Well, that's the only thing that really mattered to me out here."

"So you did ask her?"

"Not directly, no."

"What do you mean, not directly?"

"Other people were around when I spoke to her. So I had to bring it up, you know, under code."

I said, "Now you know I was gonna talk to her about that eventually. It was only a matter of time until I caught up with her."

Juanita changed the subject. "Anyway, you know I don't usually ask you for anything, but this month I went a little over on my checkbook, and I have a couple of outstanding bills I need to take care of. So I was wondering if I could borrow two thousand dollars from you for a month."

I had given Juanita money a few times before, but she had never asked for much. However, I was skeptical of this whole "borrow" term she was using. That made me feel like she had something up her sleeve.

I said, "Don't you have other bills to pay after this? How are you gonna give me back two thousand dollars next month? You plan on hitting the lottery?"

Juanita worked as a manager at a department store, which only meant she was a little more responsible and had been working there longer than the other employees. But being the manager did not mean that she made that much more in income. At least not as a floor manager. So paying me back an extra two thousand dollars in a month was out of the question, unless she had money coming in from other sources.

"Okay, well, I need your help with things this month then," she stated.

I shook my head in my hotel room. Juanita must have really been in a bind, because she had to know what I was thinking. If she couldn't handle her checkbook now, what in the world did she expect to do as a single woman with a child?

I said, "You can see where this is going, can't you? I mean, you're intelligent enough to see where you're headed."

"Look, either you're gonna help me or you're not. Nothing else has anything to do with this," she snapped at me.

I said, "Well, do I have the right to say no, that's all I want to know?"

I wanted to establish the relationship to my sister and her unborn child in advance.

"If that's what you want to do, then just say the word," she told me.

"I'm just trying to understand where you're going with your life, Juanita, that's all."

She said, "You know what, I knew I shouldn't have called you about this. You don't care about anything but yourself."

"Is that not my right as well?" I asked her. "Who says I have to come to your rescue just because I'm your older brother? What if I didn't have it?"

"But you do have it!" she yelled through the phone at me. "And you have the right to remain selfish."

"Yeah, and so does this ballplayer you laid up with," I commented. I didn't even mean to go there.

Juanita said, "You know what, you're gonna get what you deserve one day. So just forget I even asked you for anything."

"I never said I wouldn't give it to you," I told her. "But I'm not gonna give it to you without talking about it, because I can see where you're headed. Next month it'll be another five hundred dollars. And then . . ."

My sister cut me off and said, "I have never asked you for anything in a row. But if you ever needed something from me, I wouldn't even hesitate. I wouldn't sit there and make you . . . I mean, this is already a tough situation for me to do as it is."

"And how do you think it's gonna get better when you go ahead and have a baby? That's all I'm saying. That's the same thing Mom is concerned about."

I said, "Did you ask her about this first?" I doubted if she had asked our mother for the same amount of money she was asking from me. Juanita probably only asked Mom for eight hundred or so. That thought only made me more curious about how much money my sister really needed.

"So what if I did?" she asked me.

"Okay, when we had this same conversation a couple a weeks ago, you pretty much told us that you were prepared to handle things on your own," I reminded her.

"I did not say that."

"You didn't?"

"No, I did not."

I reflected back, and I guess it was just me thinking out loud as a response to my mother's concerns. I had given Juanita the benefit of the doubt before she had even asked for it. I guess I just assumed that she would try and take care of her situation as a grown woman who had left the house years ago.

"Okay. Well . . ." I wasn't going to offer her the money myself. If she really needed it, she was going to have to ask for it again.

"So, are you gonna help me out or what?" she asked me again. I guess there was no shame to her game. She really needed the money.

"All right. I'll send you a check."

"Can you wire it to me tomorrow at Western Union?"

I paused. *Now why does she need it . . .* I stopped in mid-thought. There was no sense in starting a new argument about it. Either I was gonna give her the money when she needed it or not.

"Okay. I'll do it tomorrow as soon as I get back to Atlanta."

"Why don't you do it from Chicago?" she asked me.

"Because I'm not gonna mess around and miss my plane while looking around for a Western Union office in the morning, that's why."

"I'm sure the hotel people can tell you. You can have a taxi take you to Western Union first, and then go right to the airport."

The girl was asking for ice water in hell.

"Look, Juanita, I'm gonna get it to you when I get it to you. I'm not gonna be running around here looking for a Western Union in the morning. I'm gonna get my rest, and I'm gonna go straight to the airport to catch my plane."

My sister finally settled down and said, "Thank you. I appreciate it."

It didn't sound like it, but it was a done deal. I would wire her money as soon as I got back to Atlanta.

I hung up the phone with my sister and thought about calling my mother. They both kept late hours so I wasn't concerned about the

time. But before I could make up my mind to call her, my cell phone
went off again.

I looked down and read Rachel's 614 area code one more time.

I frowned and asked myself out loud, "What the hell is wrong with
this girl?"

I decided to answer it just to tell her ass off, but as soon as she spoke
on the line, she stated, "You're a coward."

"What?"

"You heard me. You gon' go right ahead and run away like a bitch,"
she said. "I knew I read you right the first time."

"You don't really know me like that," I responded to her.

"Yes I do. You're a bitch," she snapped. "And I bet you're a bitch
with all the women."

She sounded like she was drunker than earlier. I could hear her
friends laughing in the background.

She said, "You probably don't even like girls. Damn faggot."

It was insane to argue with that woman, so I planned not to.
Answering her call was a mistake.

"All right, well, have a nice life," I told her. I was ready to hang up.

She said, "Well, what is wrong with you?"

"What is wrong with *me*? You need to be asking yourself that question," I told her. "I'm not the one calling *you* disrespectful shit over the
phone."

Suddenly she quieted down and whispered to me, "Look, that was
just to get your damn attention. I know you're not a damn faggot."

I didn't even like her using that word. I was surely a heterosexual,
but I was never into bashing guys and girls who were not. To each his
own and her own.

I said, "You're still being disrespectful."

"How so?"

"Nobody wants to be called a faggot. That's rude."

"Well, what do you call them? Friends?"

"No, I call them gay," I answered. "But look, it's a little late right now,
and I was mainly answering your call to say that I was in for the night."

I was basically trying to tell her that the night was over with for me, but it was the wrong comment. She paused and asked, "Do you want any company?"

I chuckled at it. She was unbelievable. I said, "Company? Okay, let me get this right. First you curse me out and call me a coward and a faggot, now you want to give me company for the night."

"Oh, I didn't say nothing about the whole night. Maybe for a couple of hours or so, depending on how you rock it," she told me.

I just shook my head. This woman was determined, I'll give her that.

I joked and said, "I don't think I can handle you, actually."

"You don't have to handle me. Like I told you before, all you have to do is lean back," she reminded me.

I already had my lean back action that night, but Rachel didn't know that.

I shook off her desperate temptations and said, "Nah, I'm a little tired tonight."

"Would you be tired if that lil white girl had come over?" she questioned.

She was right on it. I was wide awake for Victoria, but I was lying about being tired to her.

I finally asked, "What exactly do you want from me?"

"I already told you what I want. I wanna put something on you."

Talk about determination. The next thing I knew, I said, "You can't even get in the building at this time of night."

It was nearing midnight, but that didn't mean anything. It was the weekend at a popular Chicago hotel. Of course she could get in.

She said, "The Swissôtel. Please. I know how to get where I want to go."

Okay, so what next? I asked myself. I couldn't believe I was even thinking about it.

"So, you want me to come over there or what?" she pressed me.

I figured it would beat getting into trouble with Paula's niece. But who said I had to call TaShay back either.

"Look, man, what are you afraid of?" Rachel asked me. "I'm not gonna hurt you."

I'm afraid of you expecting more out of this than a one-night stand, I thought to myself.

She had me searching for the right words to respond. Then she ran out of patience with me. "Well, when you make up your mind, you call me back and let me know. Okay?"

"All right," I mumbled to her.

"Don't just be saying that to say it."

She was hounding me like I was the girl.

"Let me have a few minutes to think about it," I commented.

"Okay, that's fair, and you just call me back then."

The night kept getting longer and longer. I didn't want to call Rachel back, but I was still horny. Sex was a lot more stable for me when I kept a woman. So, better times with Andrea popped into my mind again. Guys think of security, too, sometimes. Andrea was my security. Imagine having a fine mate to accompany you for travel, dinner, movies, plays, walks in the park, showers, and lazy days and nights in bed. Fresh memories of her were never far away, I had simply blocked them out through my time with other women. Nevertheless, Andrea couldn't force me to commit to her for the long haul, and now she was gone.

I shook my head and said, "Fuck it! She's gone." Out of desperation for a piece of anything, I decided to call Rachel anyway. I wanted to see how long she would take to get over to my hotel. Evidently, she already knew where I was staying. I guess everyone knew.

"You make up your mind yet?" she asked me when she picked up her line.

There was no small talk in this woman's game.

"How long will it take for you to get over here?"

I was going straight for the jugular myself.

"Twenty, twenty-five minutes."

I doubted she could get to me that soon, but at least she had her thoughts in line with mine on not wasting any time.

I said, "That's all? Are you sure?"

"What? Look, I'll be there then in ten minutes," she told me. "I'm right around the corner from you."

I was stunned. What could I say to that?

"Okay." That was about it.

"What room are you in?"

I gave her my suite number, hung up the phone, and was utterly confused.

"What did I just do?" I asked myself. "Did she just con me into that?"

A few minutes earlier, I didn't want anything to do with the girl. Now she was hurrying on her way over to my room for hot sex on a platter.

"Shit!" I cursed. It was too late for second thoughts, but just because she was on her way over didn't mean I had to do anything with her. Nevertheless, I straightened out the bed, the room, the bathroom, and tossed on a pair of blue jeans with my bright white T-shirt to prepare for her arrival.

Sure enough, in sixteen minutes, there was a knock on my door.

I took a breath and walked over to answer it. Before opening the door I looked through the peephole.

What the . . . I panicked. It wasn't Rachel out in the hallway. It was Victoria.

I quickly opened the door and asked her, "Did you forget something?" I wanted to give her whatever she forgot in a hurry and get her out of there before Rachel arrived.

Victoria smiled and said, "Actually, I didn't."

I had a fast decision to make. If I used too many words with her, we would be caught. If I tried to walk her back to the elevators or even allowed her to walk back on her own, we could still get caught.

Victoria went on to explain, "I got inside the cab, made it halfway home, and realized that you were right. I was missing you already."

That sealed my fate for the night. I allowed her back into the room and shut the door. I locked it and put the latch on. Rachel was just out of luck.

Once the decision had been made, I immediately turned my cell phone off, and then the lights. Victoria walked straight over to the hotel phone and took it off the hook herself. I guess she had enough of that.

"So we start all over again with more confusions," I commented to her.

She looked at me and shook her head. "There are no more confusions." She had made up her mind to go all the way with me no matter what.

I spoke in lowered tones, "This has been, and still is, a very long night." Then we heard the first knock at the door.

I looked into Victoria's eyes and put my index finger to my lips for silence.

"A lot of women want me tonight," I whispered to her, "but it looks like you're the one who gets me." Then I kissed her lips.

I figured we would make love in silence while Rachel tried to break the peace.

"Hello," Rachel called through the door after her knocks went unanswered.

"So I'm the lucky girl tonight?" Victoria mumbled through her smile. I went on to undress her in the silence of the dark room, and she undressed me.

"If you remember, you were here first," I told her.

"Terrance, are you in there?" Rachel continued from the hallway.

Victoria and I stripped naked and fondled each other in the privacy of the room.

"Great body," she whispered as she touched me.

"It better be. That's what I make my living with," I told her. "Yours ain't bad either."

Rachel got fed up at the door and stated, "If this motherfucker made me come all the way over here . . ."

I was quietly moving Victoria to the bed.

She asked me, "So, what if I had come ten minutes later?"

That was a tough question made easy. "You didn't," I told her. That's all I planned to say about it. I reached for my condoms and joined her on the bed.

BOOMP, BOOMP, BOOMP!

I don't know if it was the slow, silent, meticulous stroke, or the fact that another woman was locked outside the room, but the push in Victoria's pussy was spectacular. I couldn't keep a straight face. Every move sent a shock of enjoyment to my mug.

"Do you like it? I know I'm rather tight," she commented.

That only made it feel better. I had to increase my stroke a touch while still being mindful of the bedsprings.

"Yeah," I breathed into her face.

BOOM!

I ducked forward as if someone was shooting at me.

Rachel had kicked the damn door. "Fuckin' coward! Damn asshole is plain scared of this pussy," she spat through the door.

Victoria was caught between a smile and a grimace from my steady stroke.

Then she tried to talk. "She, she, she was . . . oh, oh, oh yes."

"She was what?" I asked.

Victoria shook her head with an open mouth and no longer cared. Nor did I care anymore about the bedsprings. It was feeling too good up in there.

"Are you glad . . . you came back?" I asked her.

"Yeeaah," she panted.

All of a sudden, her grip upon my lower back became more urgent.

"Is it deep enough?" I asked her.

She nodded to me. "Mmm, hmm."

"Will you let me do it again?"

"Mmm, hmmm."

"You sure?"

"Yesss."

When she said that, my muscles tightened up as sensations shot from my toes to the back of my spine. The juices were building up to something powerful.

"Oh, I'm ready. I'm ready," Victoria moaned. I believe we were past the whisper point, but I no longer heard Rachel at the door, so I didn't sweat it.

"You're ready for what?"

She squeezed her eyes shut until tears ran out of them.

"To cummmm," she moaned.

She shook like she was involved in an exorcism, and I became concerned for her health for a minute.

"Are you okay?"

She couldn't even speak. All she did was nod to me.

Well, I wasn't done yet. So I began to put it on her a little stronger, and Victoria responded to it.

"Unh, unh, unh, unnnh!"

She started shaking again, and gave the shakes to me. I felt like I was ready to push straight through her body. Then I lost control of my stroke and started going in crooked and sideways.

The concentrated nut hit me with a thud and squeezed out of me for what seemed like a full minute. That's a whole lot of nut. So I couldn't speak a word either. I bounced up and down on her body and grabbed a fistful of the sheets and a fistful of her hair.

This nut was so strong it felt like my ass cheeks were about to break. Was I that excited for this girl? Was her shit that good? Was it just the mood I was in that night, or what?

Victoria took a couple of breaths under my weight. She said, "That was so good. I need a shot of that instead of coffee in the morning."

I couldn't even laugh straight. I ran out of breath too quickly. I had a series of quick starts and stops.

"So . . . where do you go from here . . . back home to Atlanta?" Victoria asked me. She had to pause in between breaths herself.

I nodded to her. "Yup." I was about to say more but I stopped myself. How much information did she need? I guess I was already on the defensive.

"Will I see you again at the airport somewhere?"

I rolled off of her and continued to breathe.

"Are you assuming that I won't call you?" I asked her.

She turned to face me and placed her head on my chest.

"I don't know your M.O. yet. I don't even know if you've been with a white girl before," she teased me.

I chuckled at it. I said, "A few . . . but they were just romps in the hay for the hell of it. I don't even remember how we got there. We were pretty much like, 'Hey, let's try this out.' You know what I mean?"

"And what about this?" she asked me. "And us?"

I said, "Are you kidding me? Neither one of us will forget the details of this."

She started laughing against my chest.

"You can say that again. This is the craziest thing I've ever done," she told me.

"Yeah, right. You know you've had some more off-the-wall nights than this. This is just one of the top ten," I teased her.

"No, this is the top *one*," she insisted. "I've never been in situations where other girls are right there in my face or outside of the room. I mean, I've been around other disturbing phone calls, but . . . this here was just . . . crazy."

I ran my hand through her hair and bragged, "That's just how much you wanted me."

She chuckled at that twice before she commented on it. "Yeah, I guess you're right. But now what am I gonna do?"

"You continue doing you," I told her. I just didn't get how so many women felt they had to change their lives around just because they gave a guy some pussy. Act like you never gave it to him and make him want it again.

I said, "And you never did tell me if you've been with a black man before."

"Yeah, I have. But you knew that already," she stated.

"So, you're comfortable with it, huh?"

She said, "We're all human, you know. It's not like you're from outer space or anything. We all have the same emotions when we feel something for someone."

"And you feel something for me?"

It was a rhetorical question.

Victoria lifted her head to look into my eyes. "Actually, I hate your guts. And I don't even know you that well. So I have no idea what you did to me to make me feel this way. I guess it must have been something in the wine at the party."

I smiled. It wasn't the wine that did it at all.

I said, "You were feeling me before the party. But you do want to be a part of the lifestyle. I can tell that. So what did you date, basketball and football players?"

After a guy gets some, we get a little cocky sometimes and end up saying anything. But I was cocky most of the time.

Victoria looked at me and stated, "That is so stereotypical. And I'm offended by that. I dated one football player, and he turned out to be a jerk. Now he's playing in the NFL, and he's still a jerk. He even had the nerve to call me and tell me that he missed me after he married his old girlfriend. They have kids and everything now."

"So you didn't respond to him?" I was just curious about it.

"Not like he wanted me to. I told him to go back to his wife."

"Was she black?"

"She's mixed."

I nodded. "That's black in our book. So you would marry and have kids with a black guy?" I was still curious, just asking questions for the details.

Victoria looked into my eyes again. She said, "I don't get involved with guys who I wouldn't stay involved with. What's the point in that?"

"You would just be doing you, and having a good time, you know."

"Yeah, and even then, I would only get involved with a guy that I would see again."

I said, "Okay, so I'll have no problem hooking up with you again, huh?"

She laughed against my chest. "You better. Or I might just have to hunt you down and . . . make you do it."

Guilt-Ridden

ARLY THAT MORNING, I could just imagine how many phone calls I needed to make. Or did I really need to make them? Who did I owe a phone call to? I was a free-ass man. Nevertheless, it was only seven in the morning, and I was up wondering about everything, while Victoria was still sound asleep.

For whatever reason, I kept wondering what had happened to Rachel. Did she go off and find some other guy to spend her night with, or was she just after me? Why was she after me so much anyway? I figured it had a lot to do with my disinterest in her. A lot of women were turned on by that. I even felt that Victoria had fallen for my elusiveness. But what did I owe her now?

Shit! Why am I even thinking about this? I asked myself.

Honestly, it all came back down to Andrea. If that damn Corey hadn't told me how her life had changed for the worse on account of me, including my sister's information on an aborted child, and then meeting Andrea for myself with her so-called friend in tow, I would have continued to live my life without feeling confused about everything. But Andrea didn't look that bad to me. In fact, she looked good. So why was I still thinking about beating myself up over my actions?

Without waking Victoria, I turned my cell phone back on just to check my messages. Eight more calls had popped up; three from Rachel, another two from TaShay, and three from Danni.

When you got 'em good, you got 'em good, I thought to myself with a half-smile.

I figured I would call Danni first, as soon as Victoria was back on her way home.

When Victoria finally awoke, I had already taken a shower and was nearly done packing my clothes. It was close to ten o'clock, and time for me to start making my way to the airport.

She stretched and grinned at me from the bed. "Wow, you really wore me out last night. You have a lot of energy."

I grinned back at her. "What did you expect? A busy lifestyle needs energy."

"Yeah, it does, doesn't it?" She climbed out of bed and stretched again in her naked splendor. Victoria was put together really well. I didn't want to say it, but her tight body reminded me of *Playboy* magazine spreads, and that was a good thing.

"Well, I guess this is it . . . until next time," she commented.

She seemed optimistic and uncertain of herself at the same time. I could understand it though. For all she knew, it could have been strictly a one-night stand. Only time would tell if we would get together in the future.

I pinched her cheek and kissed her lips to settle her nerves.

"It'll happen. Have faith in it," I told her.

She paused when she looked at me. I guess she wanted to say something, but she was hesitant. Since I had to finish packing, I ignored it and went back to what I was doing.

"I just want an opportunity to make you happy," she said to my back. "I mean, I know you have a busy life and everything, but you seem really stressed right now. So if there's anything that I can do . . . anything . . ."

I turned to face her and nodded. She walked over and stood butt naked at the bathroom entrance, pouring her heart out to me before I left.

I teased her and said, "Anything?"

"Yeah, anything."

I nodded. "Okay. I'll think about that."

• • •

AS SOON AS I was in my taxi and heading to Chicago's O'Hare Airport, I got on the cell phone to call Danni.

"Where have you been?" she asked me. She didn't sound irritated. She sounded more concerned.

"Out of batteries," I answered.

"Your phone doesn't take batteries."

"You know what I mean."

"And you couldn't call me from your room?"

"I was too busy getting ready to leave. And you know how much hotels charge for their phones. It's ridiculous."

"Aren't they paying for your room?"

"So that means I just run up the phone bill for the hell of it?"

"Calling me is just for the hell of it?"

It was another cat-and-mouse game, but I didn't plan to sweat it. I planned to have a good day.

I changed the subject and asked, "How is your photo shoot going?"

She had a two-day gig.

"I'm about to get a change of makeup in the next few minutes," she told me. "But we had to go inside yesterday. It was overcast and then we had some rain. So we're gonna have to go back outside today."

"Okay, well, call me later on when you get another break period. I'm on my way to the airport to fly back to Atlanta. When are you getting back in?" I asked her.

"On Monday evening. They want to make sure we have another half-day to get everything they need from me."

"Okay, well, I'll see you Monday night then."

I wanted to keep the conversation short and sweet. I was basically calling just to check in on her.

She asked me, "You wanna pick me up at the airport? I didn't drive. I didn't feel like leaving my car over there."

I figured, *Why not?*

"Sure, I can do that, just give me the flight number and the time."

"Okay, I'll do that first thing tomorrow morning."

That wasn't bad at all. I hung up with Danni and felt relieved. Then I thought about calling my mother back. I didn't get a chance the night before.

When I called her, she was peeved at me as usual about not calling her in a timely manner. As soon as she came on the line, she said, "I'm not asking you for much, Terrance. All I'm asking is for you to recognize and abide by your mother. Is that too much to ask? Because if it is, then I just won't bother you anymore."

I smiled it off. I wasn't disturbed by it at all.

"That's not too much to ask, that's why I'm calling you bright and early this morning," I told her.

"You call ten o'clock in the morning 'bright and early'?"

I ignored it. "So what's going on? What's the latest news?" I asked her.

"Your sister has already started asking me for money. I mean, does she have any decency and self-respect left at all? Who raised this girl? It couldn't have been me."

It was a self-indictment.

I answered, "Yeah, I talked to her myself."

"And what did she say?"

"She said she needed help to make it through the month. So, how much did she ask you for?" I wanted to compare notes.

"Enough."

I nodded. "We'll all work it out."

"Not with my money we won't. So how much did she ask you for?"

"I don't believe she wants me to reveal that."

"What do you think, I'm gonna run right back and tell her?"

Yup, I acknowledged to myself with a chuckle. I said, "I refuse to answer that question."

I was nearing the airport terminal in my taxi.

"We can talk about this later, Mom. I have a plane to catch back to Atlanta now."

"Well, where are you?"

I didn't even want to say it. Chicago was too close to home for me not to stop by and visit, or at least from my mother's standpoint.

"It doesn't even matter at this point. I'm pulling up to the airport now."

"See, now that's the kind of disrespectful bullshit that both of you put me through after all I've done for the both of you. I ask you where you are, and you can't even give me a simple behind answer."

The cabdriver looked back to view my response from the earful my mother was giving me and he smiled.

I looked at him and shook my head.

I told my mother, "Chicago," just to prove what I already knew.

"Chicago? You mean to tell me you couldn't catch a train ride over here to Indiana to see your mother?"

I was reaching into my wallet to pay my driver his fare.

"This is not a pleasure trip," I told her.

That only made it worse. "I don't give a damn if you were in Chicago to see the president, you still could have scheduled time to see your mother. What do you have to return home to anyway? You don't have a day job. You don't have a wife and kids. So what stops you from coming over here to spend time with me?"

She had a point—from her perspective, but from mine, I figured, *For what? What in the world would we do after the first five minutes of my visit?*

Every time I visited home, things just seemed to stand still, and I didn't particularly like that. Then I would have a household of old neighborhood girlfriends jockeying to see who could tie me down, and they were no longer cute.

I was ready to enter the airport with my bags for my flight, and I saw only one way of ending the phone call with my mother on a good note.

"I'm gonna make plans to come home as soon as I get back to Atlanta," I told her.

"But you're already here. All you need to do is reschedule your flight."

I wasn't planning on doing that.

"Mom, I'm at the airport, and I'm catching my plane. Now, when I get back to Atlanta, I'll look at my schedule, and I'll make a definite date to fly into Gary to see you and then Juanita in Indianapolis."

I needed to look Juanita in her face anyway.

"Mmm, hmm," my mother grumbled, "and how long will that take?"

That meant she agreed to it, she just had to see me carry out the plans.

"I'll call you back later on tonight and let you know," I told her. "But I really have to go now."

"Mmm, hmm, tell me anything," she pouted.

I hung up with my mother and shook my head with a smile. Imagine her being with a man. Nothing ever seemed good enough.

I printed out my e-ticket, showed my boarding pass, made it through the security checkpoint, and headed to my gate for my flight to Atlanta.

In the middle of my walk to the gate, someone called my name from the sports bar and restaurant to my left.

I looked over and spotted Jerry White from my high school basketball days at West Gary. He was sitting on a bar stool with coffee on the counter. He had picked up a considerable amount of weight and had a full beard and thick mustache, but I still recognized his boyish face. The dark facial hair fit well with his deep brown skin tone. He looked like a throwback to the seventies when thick beards and mustaches were cool for black men.

I walked over to him with a little bit of time to kill. My gate was only a few feet away.

"Hey Jerry, long time no see, man."

We smacked palms like we were still members of the basketball team. I sat beside him on a bar stool.

He said, "I've been seeing your face everywhere, man—magazines, billboards, television. Who would ever think you would do that?"

I stopped him short and said, "You haven't seen me on any television ads yet." He was going a little overboard with that one.

"That's up next though, ain't it?" he assumed.

"Yeah, we'll see. So, what's been going on with you, man? I see you've been eating well."

He chuckled at it. "Still Terrance," he commented on my persistent candor. He said, "But yeah, that's about all I can say lately. I'm still eatin'."

The bartender asked me if I wanted anything. I told him a glass of water with ice in it.

"What have you been involved in lately?" I repeated to my old teammate.

Jerry shook his head. "Baby mommas for the most part. I got three of 'em now."

I was actually speaking in terms of career moves, not his personal life.

"Oh yeah?" I didn't know how to respond to his women issues. I wasn't expecting that.

He said, "You got any kids yet, man?"

"Nah," I told him.

He nodded. "Good. Because once you get 'em, there ain't no going back to just being you. You're a daddy whether you like it or not, and you damn sure have to pay the price for it."

He said, "It's just a crazy thing, man. Now I know the full extent of the sacrifices our parents went through to raise us."

The conversation was a little too depressing for me. I didn't know how to add anything to it.

I said, "It's a tough job, huh?" It was just a generic response on my part. Like I said, I didn't have a father, and I wasn't trying to be a father.

Jerry took a gulp of his drink. "It's much more than a fuckin' job. It's more like a lifelong poison. Sometimes it feels good to you, sometimes you wish you were dead—either you or them."

That was extreme. I said, "A poison? Come on, man, I thought kids were our greatest treasure." They just weren't the greatest treasure for me.

Jerry looked me in the eyes and said, "Let me tell you something, man. My third child was a girl. And I didn't even know her mother that well when she got pregnant. I found out when she was about two months in."

He said, "I was already in deep shit with my other two baby mommas. So I argued with this damn girl to the point of wanting to kill her, not to have this baby. I mean, I had my hands full as it was. And I swear to God, man, I don't know if it was me worrying about new child support payments or what, but I could feel the entire pregnancy draining the damn life out of me. And I didn't feel that way with my first two. But this last one, man . . ."

"Maybe it was because she was a girl instead of a boy," he suggested. "But after that, I went ahead and got myself a vasectomy."

"A vasectomy?" I repeated. That was more than extreme in my book. That was crazy! Why would he do that to himself instead of simply wearing a condom?

"Yeah, man. No more slip-ups for me," he told me.

"They were all slip-ups?" I asked him. I could see once or even twice, but three times . . .

He shook his head and took another gulp of his drink. "I know. I only have myself to blame. But sometimes you wanna feel it all. Those condoms take the feeling away for me, man."

I took a sip of my water. "Excuse me for asking you this, but have you ever once thought about staying with one woman, and putting her on birth control or something?"

I was asking him for the both of us. It sure made things a lot simpler if you remained with one woman and her one set of problems than multiple women and multiple sets of problems. But who was I to tell it? I was still collecting new women all over the country.

"I tried that before, man, but the girl didn't want to be on birth control. And then I would have to pay for it even if she did use it."

"Well, you're gonna have to pay the piper before or after anyway. It's a lot cheaper to pay before," I told him.

He said, "I know, man, I know. So now I'm in a three-woman, three-kid bind, and they're all trying to top one another."

I looked at him and asked, "All three of them?"

He nodded. "You would think that at least one of them would be sane, right? But nope."

I joked and said, "Well, you just have some bad-ass choices in women then."

He laughed it off. He said, "Anyway, man, I don't want to worry you with my problems. What's been going on in your life? Where are you living nowadays?"

I looked at my watch before I answered to make sure I was still on track.

"I live in Atlanta now. What about you?"

"Columbus. Gary got too hot for me. Then I went down to Columbus, Ohio, and it got hot. So what the hell is the difference? But Atlanta? Man, I hear they got all kind of women down there."

He was still thinking about women. I guess a vasectomy doesn't kill your appetite, it only kills your ability to reproduce.

I laughed and said, "I'm just hoping to stay out of the same trouble you got yourself into. But I understand it, man. I just don't understand the women sometimes. I mean, I know why we do what we do."

Jerry laughed and said, "Well, we tend to be a little opposite. First we do it to please ourselves, then later we do it to please them. But they do it to please us first, then they do it to please themselves. So in the long run, they're the ones who try to keep the shit going, while we're busy trying to finish it."

"Good point," I told him. "But I got to catch this plane."

"Hey, what's your number, man? We need to stay in touch."

I traded numbers with him before I headed to the gate.

"When is your flight?" I asked him.

He grinned. "My flight ain't for another two hours. I just got here super early to watch people with lives to live and places to go. It's therapeutic. It makes me know that I gotta keep it movin'."

I walked away from Jerry and felt sorry for him and cautious for myself. I made jokes about his situation to keep it loose, but ties to three women with children had to be hectic. I didn't even have an official girlfriend and I had problems juggling that, so I could just imagine the stress of three women with my kids.

Hell, I started thinking about thanking Andrea for not bringing a child into the world after meeting up with Jerry. But that was only his interpretation of things. Kids were still a joy to most people. What if Andrea had a beautiful baby girl for me? Would I call her a poison? I seriously doubted it.

I arrived in Atlanta, wired my sister money at Western Union, and made it back to my place to answer another seventeen messages on my office phone. One of the messages was from Nicole from Baltimore. I hadn't heard a peep from her since our crazy night in Atlanta two weeks ago, and I was glad I hadn't heard from her. She called and gave me a lecture about respecting a black woman. I had to reflect back to what we had gotten into such a fight about.

I remembered I didn't want to invite her over to my house because of Danni. Could I respect Danni and not respect Nicole? Or could I also be disrespecting Danni by having Nicole give me a blow job? It was all confusing to think about the rules and regulations of relationships. Who made up those rules anyway?

While I continued to relax at home, I got a call from Kim. She was thanking me for my participation in the cancer event.

"Hey, it's best to get paid for an event that actually means something," I told her.

"And I want to apologize again for our little incident," she said.

I knew that was coming. I was only waiting for her to say it. She was bringing up the artificial insemination again.

"Adopting keeps things simple," I suggested. "All you have to do is show the child plenty of love and loyalty."

Kim took a breath. "I'm still thinking about it all."

"Yeah, you do that," I told her.

"Well, you should have a more open mind about the possibilities in life, Terrance. It isn't all as cut and dry as we'd like to think."

I said, "I understand that."

"Do you, really? Anyway, enough about that, we'll just have to agree to disagree for the most part," she concluded. "And oh yeah, I did remember to get something else for you that you had asked me about."

"What's that?"

"I got Andrea's number last night," she told me. "Or do you have it already? I saw you talking to her."

I said, "Oh, thanks. Nah, I didn't get it. I was too busy running my mouth last night."

"You still want it?"

"Yeah. I didn't get a chance to talk to her like I needed to."

Kim paused. "Is it something pressing?"

"Nah, it's just closure. We stopped dealing with each other on a social level years ago."

She didn't need to know more than that.

"Okay, well, I have her home number and her cell phone number, but don't say you got it from me. I'm just doing this as a favor to a friend."

"Oh, yeah, I understand. I wouldn't do that anyway. So is she getting back into the modeling game now?"

"I'm not sure, but who knows. She may call us about work, she may not."

I got Andrea's numbers from Kim and smiled from ear to ear, with a touch of nervousness. I would call her and get down to the bottom of things.

"So what's next on your menu?" Kim asked me.

"I fly to L.A. in two weeks. So I have another nice break period until then."

"Yeah, Paula told me about that last night. And you know her niece has the hots for you."

I chuckled. "What's up with that?" I asked. "That girl knows I can't deal with her."

"Well, she wants what she wants," Kim joked.

I smiled to myself and thought, *Yeah, so does everybody.*

She said, "From what I hear, TaShay likes flirting with older men."

"Yeah, well, is that all she does with them?"

Kim laughed. "I seriously doubt it, but I guess it would depend on how often she's able to get out on her own. I believe Paula has a pretty tight leash on her."

"What about when she turns twenty-one, twenty-two?" I questioned.

"When she's all the way grown, she's all the way grown, just like any other woman. But what about your white girl, Victoria? Did you find out what you needed to with her? By the way, she looked good last night. Did you tell her to wear the same color you were wearing?"

"Absolutely not," I answered. "In fact, that put me on guard for a minute, thinking other people would believe that. So I tried to stay away from her."

Kim laughed hard at that. "It was just a wild coincidence, huh?"

"That's all it was," I assured her.

"And who was the other girl hounding you in the orange dress?"

Obviously, Kim hadn't let anything get by her, and she was letting me know as much.

"Actually, I just met that girl in Miami a few weeks ago, right before you called me about this event. So she found out her friends were going to the same banquet, and she got all excited about it. But I told her I would be on the busy side before she showed up. I mean, you can't please everybody."

"I see," Kim quipped.

Was she getting at something with that? I wanted to leave it alone, but I couldn't.

"Are you sure you don't have any hard feelings about me saying no?"

She took another breath. "Terrance, I told you, we don't have to go there or ever talk about that again. It's over with."

I wanted to believe her and move on, so I decided to let it go. It was the best thing for both of us.

WHEN I HUNG UP the phone with Kim, I wondered how long I would wait before I called Andrea. But since I didn't want the subject on my mind any longer, I figured calling her immediately would be the best thing.

I stood up from my black La-Z-Boy chair, stretched my muscles, walked around my spacious living room, and sat back down to make this all-important phone call to my old fling in Chicago.

I dialed her number on my office phone and took a breath to get right into it. The phone rang twice, and as soon as she picked up the line on the third ring, she told me, "Terrance, whoever gave you my number is getting fired immediately."

She caught me off-guard with that. I didn't know whether to laugh or to beg for reason.

"I don't want to take too much of your time, I just want to know if it was true or not," I commented.

"If what is true?"

She knew damn well what I was talking about, and I didn't have to speak in code anymore.

"If you were once pregnant with a child of mine," I asked her.

"What if I was? Can you change it? And would you have wanted me to have it?"

I nodded my head and swallowed hard on the reality. It was true. Andrea had never been good at lying. She wore her emotions on her sleeve.

I said, "So it is true?" just to confirm it.

"Is it? You tell me."

She still wanted to be difficult.

I said, "How come you never even told me."

"For what? You had made up your mind already that you didn't want to be with me."

"It wasn't that I didn't want to be with you, I just didn't want to be pushed into being so serious so soon."

"Yeah, well, I had some decisions of my own to make, and the last thing I wanted to have was a screaming and yelling relationship with my child's father, because that's where we were headed if I decided to take that road."

"And you never thought once of telling me?"

She said, "Of course I did. Then I thought about how you would respond to it. And I came to the conclusion that you would have thought I was trying to trap you. Which I wasn't, but that's how it would look to you. And I still wanted my career at the time anyway."

I said, "But you showed me that guy's ring," reminding her of how she tried to put pressure on me to take things more seriously. "You could have kept pushing for your career without him."

"But if I told you that I was pregnant . . ." She stopped mid-sentence. "And I surely couldn't go into a relationship with Jayson that way, so it was all for the best."

"But why did you tell my sister of all people? You should have known it would get back to me sooner or later."

I slipped up and put Juanita out there anyway.

Andrea said, "And look how long it took. But basically, if you were against it, you would have been happy with my decision, and if you were not, you would have felt how I wanted you to feel."

"And how is that, betrayed?"

She hesitated with her answer. "How did you think I felt?" she asked me.

It was a good point.

She said, "So, with you calling me about this now, what does that mean? Where are you trying to go with the information?"

I told her, "I just needed closure on whether it was true or not, that's all. So, what about that money-grubbing husband of yours, are you still with him?" I figured I may as well get all of the answers at once, while I still had her on the phone.

"I'm sure you already know the scoop on that. If you got my number, then you already know I'm not with him right now."

"Right now?" I questioned. Were they planning on getting back together?

She said, "Our divorce is still pending. There's a whole lot of money and property issues to be worked out, and he still has his two kids from previous relationships to factor in."

Andrea was being extremely civil for a change, and giving me far more information than I expected or deserved. Since I was on a roll, I asked her, "So now you've decided to spend more time with women?"

She chuckled at my insinuation. "Still the same Terrance," she told me. "You will say whatever's on your mind."

"And so do you."

"Well, yeah, I'm totally at peace with myself now, and I'm extremely satisfied. I don't have a whole bunch of drama in my life anymore, I'm not chasing things or trying to convince people, and I feel good."

That blew me away! No wonder she seemed all calm and collected. That lesbian shit turned me on a little, too. I could imagine rolling in the hay with Andrea and her new friend Brazil in a heartbeat.

I said, "Well . . . what do other people say about it?"

Andrea was an only child with an extended family that she didn't really deal with too much. She was one of those girls who got out of the house early and dealt with the world on her own terms.

"Who cares what they think? As long as they don't put their fuckin' hands on me, I'm good," she told me.

That was a piece of the Andrea that I was more familiar with, a volatile vixen.

I smiled and chuckled at it. Well, that answered all of my questions. I didn't know what else to say to her. I knew what I was thinking though.

"So, how long have you been involved with this woman?" I asked her.

"That's getting a little off the subject, Terrance. Now, you asked me your question, and I've answered it. In fact, I've given you more than enough answers. So be satisfied with that, because I'm not going into details about my private life. That's why it's called 'private.' "

She said, "But I will give you some advice, because I can see that you haven't changed much."

Why should I? I thought to myself. *I've always been satisfied with myself.*

She said, "If you're going to continue to deal with women like you do, then you better learn how to loosen up and give them more of what they want. Now I was pretty generous to you, so I got myself together and moved on, but some of these other girls may become more vengeful if you keep acting like you do toward them."

I was wondering how she knew.

"What makes you think that I . . ."

She cut me off and said, "Just like you knew some people around me at the cancer function last night, I knew some people around you. And from what I've heard and witnessed for myself, all I can say is that you need to watch yourself. And that's just one person to another."

She sounded like she genuinely cared about me.

I said, "Well, thank you. And you know I had a crazy dream about you, too."

"I'm sure you have," she responded. "But it's time for me to go ahead and go now. Nice talking to you, Terrance. Be good."

"Oh, yeah, you know I will."

" 'Bye now."

She wasn't giving me an opportunity to say much else.

I said, "Okay, I'll talk to you later."

That was it, she gave me a fast dial tone.

I looked at my phone and said, "Damn! That's how she treats me now?"

It's amazing how a woman you used to have the upper hand on can flip the script and have an upper hand on you. After the conversation with Andrea, that's exactly how I felt. She made me feel seven years younger than her instead of the other way around. I felt insignificant and childish.

I reminded myself that Andrea was only twenty-six years old. She seemed much older though. She had lived a full adult life already. And there she was giving me advice on how to live mine now. So how had I ruined hers? Had I turned her into a lesbian? Had she given up all hope in men because of me? What was the extent of my damage to her? And how much of that damage could be attributed to her husband? How had her husband, Jayson Walker, felt about his role in her life? Did he even care that she was no longer with him? Had he gotten over her and her relationship with me?

I never did get a chance to ask Andrea about her rumored miscarriage. Maybe that wasn't my business either.

"Give them more of what they want, huh?" I repeated to myself out loud. "Starting with whom?"

I felt like I had already been giving women what they wanted, or at least lately. But maybe not with all of them, and maybe not everything they wanted. Who can give a woman everything? They don't appreciate everything anyway. In fact, it seems like the more you give a woman, the more they want.

I thought about that and laughed. Some of us men were the same way.

Right on cue, I got another phone call on my cell from Rachel. I looked down and read her 614 area code once again on the screen. I took a breath and wondered, *Should I answer this girl and see what she wants?*

"Hell, I already know what she wants: she wants the royal Johnson," I said out loud with a chuckle. I was being put to the test immediately. Could I really decide on giving women what they want?

I went ahead and answered the call before the phone stopped ringing.

"So what, are you gonna curse me out again?" I asked Rachel as soon as I answered the line.

"For what? It don't seem to work."

I was actually impressed with her persistence. If you stay at it long enough . . .

"Are you still interested in me?" I asked her. I still didn't get it. How much did a woman want a guy to play hard to get? Only I wasn't playing, I really didn't want her.

"Why?"

I took another breath. I said, "That wouldn't be a bad thing."

"What wouldn't be a bad thing?"

I was basically talking out loud to myself.

"If I went ahead and tore you limb from limb," I answered.

"Yeah, I heard that shit from you before, and you disappeared on me."

"True, true, but the man is still alive, and you're still calling."

"I don't know why."

"Because you still haven't gotten what you want from me. And you're spoiled."

"Spoiled?"

"That's what I said. You really expect me to be what you need. So I guess you don't have that boyfriend anymore."

"Yeah, and I just go from one asshole to another."

Was she talking about me? "You're not calling me an asshole, are you?"

She said, "Well, if the shoe fits, then take a picture in it."

I know she's not thinking of me as her man, I told myself. Then I repeated my question. "So, you're no longer with him then?"

"You didn't care if I was with him when you met me, so why are you asking about it now?"

Good point. I didn't care. It was a late-night groove thing when I met her. Now she wasn't letting me go.

I stood up from my chair and walked over to the window in my living room. It was beginning to get dark outside. It was a peaceful feeling.

Yeah, I could probably do this, I continued to convince myself. *How bad would it be to just give in to a woman for a minute?*

I said, "All right, forget I asked. But we do have some unfinished business to take care of, right?"

"Yes we do," she responded. She wasn't shy about that at all.

I told her, "Well, I'm not gonna be back in the Chicago or Ohio area anytime soon, so how are we gonna do this?"

"Actually, I'm thinking about visiting a friend in Atlanta next week," she said to my surprise.

Here we go again, I thought. I didn't really need another woman on my home turf with Danni floating around. But had I not given Danni what she wanted and kept our relationship ultra loose, like in the beginning, I wouldn't have anything to worry about at home.

"What part of town does your friend stay on?"

"She stays on the Southside, but I'll probably get a hotel room downtown. I like having my own space, so I rarely stay with people when I travel."

I nodded with the phone in hand. "Okay, we'll see what we can get into then."

"Yeah, I just won't hold my breath for your ass, because I don't trust you now. Where were you last night anyway?" she asked me.

I paused. Did I need to tell her the truth or make up a convenient lie?

"I ended up hanging out late with old friends," I lied to her. There was no sense in making things more complicated with the truth.

Rachel said, "Why don't you just tell me what you really got into last night? I won't be hurt by it. It's not like you're my man or anything."

I was immediately conflicted. Did she want the raw truth, that I did my thing with the white girl she kept hinting about at the cancer dinner? Or did she want me to tell her a better lie?

A better lie would keep the opportunity open for Atlanta, but the truth, more than likely, would close the door on everything. However, I didn't feel like exposing too much of my personal business with the truth. And instead of telling her a better lie, I decided to stick with the first one.

I said, "I don't know who your friends are, you don't know who my friends are, and it's best we keep it that way."

"I didn't ask who your friends are, I just asked what you did last night," she responded.

"And I already told you," I answered. "Now the only thing else I can do is give you names and places, and that's only needed if I need an alibi in court for murder."

Rachel took a big breath and said, "We don't need all that extra drama."

"That's exactly my point," I told her.

She saw the painted picture and moved on. "So, if I come down there, you're not gonna hook up with your friends and blow me off again?"

"You would be my friend and I would spend time with you if you were here. I just can't promise how much time."

I wanted to get that out in the open as quickly as possible.

"Could you spend the night?" she asked me.

That could happen, as long as I had an alibi ready for Danni.

I said, "I should be able to, but we'll have to wait and see."

I didn't want to commit to the idea, but it was doable.

"Do you have any 'friends' in Atlanta that I need to know about?" she questioned.

There was no sense in lying about that one. That would have been too big of a lie that could come back and bite me in the ass, so I told her the truth.

"As a matter of fact, I do."

"Another model chick?"

"Yeah."

"Well, you tell her you were out with old friends like you just told me."

Imagine that? Rachel was scheming and making up her own lies for me. I guess she wanted me that bad.

I chuckled and said, "That's pretty scandalous."

"Look, I'm like this now; if men can do whatever they want and satisfy themselves with whoever they want to, then why can't I do the same thing? Nobody sees it as abnormal when a guy keeps calling a woman to get what he wants from her, so why should it be different for a woman?"

She was answering all of my questions with clarity. Rachel wanted me and she didn't care who knew about it.

She said, "So if you don't mind me saying it, I want some unconditional, no-strings-attached sex."

I grinned from ear to ear. "Okay." What else could I tell her?

"Now, you're not gonna disappear on me again, are you?"

She wanted my commitment to sex. Not that it had never happened to me before, but I don't remember it being mapped out that obviously. I couldn't stop from smiling. It was flattering to say the least. I even wondered if I should charge her a few hundred dollars for it. Wouldn't that be something? But I wasn't ready to turn into a gigolo. I still made a good living providing nothing but good face.

When I hung up with Rachel, I had a warm feeling about things. It was great to be that wanted. Then I thought about returning a call to TaShay. I hadn't spoken to her since the party. Since I was two for two on positive phone calls, I figured I would go for three for three and keep it moving.

"Hello," she answered on the first ring. When that happened it usually meant you were waiting for a call or already on a call.

"You're on the phone already?" I asked her.

"Who is this?"

She sounded bothered like a lot of young women did when they have too much going on in their lives.

"Terrance."

After hearing my name, she changed her tone. "Oh, hi. You finally called me back, huh?"

The question still stood. "Yeah, but are you on the other line? I can call back later," I told her. I didn't want to destroy the streak of my positive phone calls by being rushed.

She said, "Oh, no, wait a minute, let me clear that line."

I guess that established me as a priority. TaShay clicked over to the other line for a few seconds and returned to me.

"So, where were you last night? I tried to call you," she commented.

Since she was still under the drinking age, I had a total different approach for her.

Nonchalantly, I said, "I was off being a grown man somewhere."

She stopped and said, "Oh, it must have been nice then."

I immediately changed the subject back to her. "What were you doing?"

"Watching movies with my aunt. At first I was hanging out in the lobby," she answered.

"Out in the lobby? What were you doing there?"

She giggled. "Hoping to see somebody."

"What, Usher was in town and staying at the same hotel? What a coincidence."

She laughed and said, "I hardly would have been waiting for Usher. I mean, I like his music and he's cute and all that, but he's still like a little boy to me."

"He's like five years older than you, at least. He's not that young anymore. He's old enough to drink at least."

"Oh, you got jokes," she commented. "Well, I can get drinks when I need to. But anyway, Usher's still, you know, in that young crowd. He's young. All that pop and crunk music stuff is young to me. I like real R&B and soul music."

This young girl was indeed an old soul, but she still expressed her opinions like a brash youth.

I teased her. "You're more of an R. Kelly kind of girl, huh?"

She grunted, "Mmm, no comment there. He needs to . . . mmm."

I couldn't tell if that was good or bad, but it meant something.

I kept moving the subjects around. Young people like to keep it poppin', you know.

"So what's on your agenda for the rest of the month?" I asked her.

"Why, aren't you coming out to the West Coast in a couple of weeks?"

"Yeah, but I was talking about *your* schedule."

"Oh, well, I don't have anything coming— Oh, yes, I do," she stopped and corrected herself. "I'm shooting a fashion spread for *Vibe* magazine."

"Oh, *Vibe*, that's good. Is it an entire spread or just a page?"

"Whatever it is, I'll take it," she answered.

Then I decided to tease her again. "But isn't *Vibe* kind of young, too? That's Usher's prime audience."

"Yeah, it is, isn't it."

"You should be pushing for *Essence*, or getting involved with the Ebony Fashion Fair."

"Oh, we are. But in the meantime—"

I cut her off and said, "This *Vibe* spread was not your aunt's idea, was it?" I was quite sure that Paula knew better than that.

TaShay answered, "Oh, no, she doesn't want me to do it. I just figured it would be fun to get a little funky in the clothes. *Vibe* gets funky with it. A lot of the other magazines look stuffy to me."

Yeah, she was still young all right. Fashion modeling wasn't about how the clothes looked as much as it was about the perception that people had of you while in the clothes. Funky in *Vibe* could also mean urban, and not mainstream to the main brands, which could lock TaShay out of a more lucrative modeling career.

I said, "Did you fight your aunt for this *Vibe* spread?" I just couldn't see Paula going for it. *Vibe* was very much a part of the video culture they were trying so hard to steer TaShay away from.

"Well, I tried to explain to her that I need to be seen by as many people as possible, and not by just one particular crowd of people," she explained to me.

I said, "You can do that through ads. You get her to pitch you to Rocawear, Baby Phat, and all of those guys for clothing ads, that way you're getting paid more to do it, and you get more of a premiere spot with an ad.

"Less is more, and in your case, less is also best," I told her. "In an ad, you would be pushed more as an individual, and you're actually being pushed by a brand. That's the major difference between regular models and supermodels. Supermodels get the brand names behind them."

TaShay got real quiet on me. I didn't like the sound of that. I didn't want to come off like an overbearing father figure or anything, I was just expressing what I knew about the fashion, modeling, and magazine industries. So at the end of all of that, I backed off and said, "But that's just my opinion. You could very well be right. Hip-hop is controlling everything now. It's the new wave of the future."

She chuckled and said, "Thank you for trying to contradict yourself, but I can take good advice when I hear it. I'm not that fragile. I'm not that weak at all."

"Well, you know, you got mighty quiet over there, so I was trying to make sure I didn't scare you away with too much daddy talk," I told her.

"Daddy talk?" she asked me.

"Well, maybe that's the wrong word, but you know what I'm trying to say."

She laughed. "Yeah, I know, but . . . daddy talk? That just sounds . . . that's crazy."

"Aw now, it don't sound that bad. Stop overreacting."

"So, deep down inside, you want to be my daddy, or you just want me to call you daddy?"

She was having a good time working that one. What exactly was I saying? Was it a Freudian slip?

"Okay, here we go," I told her.

"You're the one who said it."

"Anyway, I was just calling because I didn't get a chance to talk to you before leaving Chicago."

"Well, we're still here. We're leaving tomorrow," she told me.

"Oh yeah? Where's your aunt right now? Is she right next to you?"

"No, she's in the workout room."

"And you're not?"

"Not right now. I don't want to work out too much. You start looking too masculine."

"Yeah, you're right," I told her. "So you're up in the room watching TV and eating room service."

"Wow, you know me so well already. That's good!"

"Actually, you've been munching in my ear from the moment you answered the phone. And with all of that dramatic music and explosions coming from the television, it has to be a movie."

She laughed. "I'm sorry. You caught me right in the middle—or not even, really. I just started this movie when my food arrived."

"Well, go ahead and enjoy your food and your movie. I don't want to hold you up. I'll talk to you later."

"How much later?"

"I can't say if it'll be today, but it will be soon," I told her.

"Good, because I really like talking to you, so you make sure you call before you come out to L.A., and right after you touch down at LAX."

"I thought you guys live in San Diego?"

"We do, but L.A. is only a few hours in a car from us."

"Oh, okay." I had been in fashion shows in both places, but I couldn't remember how far apart they were. I said, "Well, go on back to what you were doing. I'll catch up to you."

"Hey."

"Yeah," I answered.

"Thanks for calling me back and schooling me on the industry. I mean, I know my aunt means well for my career and everything, but it's real good to hear it from someone else in the business for a change. You know, a different perspective."

"Don't even mention it," I told her. "I'll help you out in whatever way I can."

"Cool. I'm gonna hold you to that."

"I expect it," I told her.

After I hung up with TaShay I was back on my own time. Leisure was really afforded to the wealthy. I wasn't filthy rich by any means, but I was comfortable. So I took my time to relax and enjoy my place, nice and boring—the way I liked it. There was no reason to feel guilty about that. I had a good life.

Turned Out

I HAD A PRETTY EVEN WEEK, hanging out with Danni, returning phone calls to Victoria and Judi, and setting up travel plans to
visit my mother in Indiana for a few days. Then the end of the
week came with Rachel calling me back to remind me of her visit to
Atlanta that weekend. She hadn't called me all week, so I had basically
forgotten about it. But then on late Thursday night, I get this phone
call from her.

"I'll be getting into Atlanta tomorrow at four-thirty PM. I'm staying
at the Marriott Marquis downtown."

"The Marriott Marquis?" I asked her.

"Yeah, I have a friend who works there who hooked me up with a
discount for the weekend."

How many friends in different cities did she have?

I said, "Okay."

She asked me. "You wouldn't have time to pick me up at the airport, would you?"

All of a sudden, I began to wish I was out of town on another
photo shoot somewhere. There were times when my schedule was a
lot more packed than others, and other times when my schedule was
open. I was pretty much open, which gave me a whole lot of free time
on my hands. Danni was still flying in and out, but she would still be
home in Atlanta that weekend.

I told Rachel, "Let's just keep it simple and have you catch a taxi like you normally would. Since you haven't called me all this week, I hadn't set up time to see you yet, especially as early as tomorrow afternoon."

"Well, I got real busy this week at work so I could leave early on Friday, but I had already told you that I was coming."

She actually told me there was a possibility that she would come; we had never confirmed anything.

Anyway, it was too late for the back-and-forth confusions, so I told her, "We'll work it out. I know where you are and I know your number."

"Okay now, don't bullshit me again," she warned me.

I ended the phone call with Rachel and immediately thought about ways of becoming absent from Danni that weekend. She had become comfortable in my presence. I guess that's what happens when you give a woman what she wants.

"Now, I'll need to go over there and spend time with her tonight to smooth things over for the weekend," I advised myself.

However, when I called her up, Danni wasn't in the mood for having company.

"I don't feel like that tonight," she told me.

I said, "We don't have to do anything, I just figured I'd relax with you."

"Good, because my period just came on this morning. But you know what, I really just feel like being by myself tonight. Don't be mad."

Interesting, I thought to myself. Was I already beginning to bore her? I doubted it, but you never know. Nevertheless, she was giving me a free missing-in-action pass for the weekend. So not only would I give her Thursday night to herself, but Friday, Saturday, and Sunday, too, while I finally got around to pleasing Rachel.

"Oh, I'm not mad. I'm cool with it," I told her. "I mean, I understand. You got a whole lot of emotions that get involved with that."

"Now that don't mean you're free to go buck wild on me tonight with some other woman. I know how guys get down when you can't have what you want," she stated.

I chuckled. "Actually, it seems like you like sex more than I do. So maybe this is a little harder for you than it is for me."

"Wait a minute, are you trying to call me a nympho? Because you don't want me to shut shit down. I can do that you know."

That was the fear many men had about keeping only one woman; she could control your sex life. So a loyal man became dependent upon keeping her happy in life, satisfied with his performance, or just plain obedient to his needs and desires. Sometimes it took a combination of all three of those things, or so I've heard from my married friends and the relationship experts.

"I'm not calling you that," I backed off and told Danni. I wanted no part of the love games. I wanted to keep everything simple.

"So, what are you saying then?" she asked me.

It was as if she was trying to instigate a fight. I didn't mean anything by it. It was only a joke.

I paused and said, "You know what, I'm not trying to go where you're trying to take me. So I'll just call you back next week or something when you're feeling a little better."

"Next week?"

"Doesn't it take that long?"

"That doesn't mean you can't call me."

"All right, I'll call you sooner then," I told her. I was ready to get the hell off the phone at that point. Our conversation was going nowhere good.

She said, "You can call me tomorrow. I just don't feel like having company tonight. I mean, I'm not sick or anything, I'm just a little cranky and tired of having these cramps and shit, that's all."

It's funny how when you get closer to a woman she starts bringing up things you rarely had to deal with before. When Danni was still insecure and trying hard to please me, it was like she never had a period. But now that she was confident in her relationship with me, all this other bullshit came out. Am I supposed to be attracted to that?

I said, "All right, will do," just to get off of the phone with her.

"Are you sure you're not upset with me, because you sound a little bit irritated?" she asked again.

"Do you want me to be upset with you? I said I wasn't, so let's just leave it alone."

She finally toned down. "Okay. Call me tomorrow."

In your fucking dreams! I told myself. That was exactly why you couldn't give a woman what she wanted. They started acting like real bitches as soon as they felt like they had the upper hand. Or maybe that was just Danni.

"All right, she just asked for it," I mumbled to myself. I felt much more relaxed about entertaining Rachel after that. Danni had terrible timing to act a fool.

I ALWAYS LIKED taking women away from downtown Atlanta, because I had no idea who I would bump into, including Danni and her friends. Since Rachel loved Italian food, I drove her out to an Italian spot in Marietta, where I had shot a local men's clothing store ad. Danni lived on the opposite side of town in Buckhead, so I was safe.

Rachel wore all shiny black, from head to toe, which was in stark contrast to my colorful outfit. I wore dark brown leather shoes, blue jeans, a yellow button up shirt, and no tie with my cashmere sports jacket.

"Well, from an outfit standpoint, we don't look like we're together at all," I teased her.

"We do look good together, though," she commented.

I didn't add anything to that, I just smiled at her across our dark table.

She looked around and said, "This is a very interesting place. But it's so dark in here that a girl may think that a guy was trying to hide her."

I said, "If you're enjoying that guy's company, then does it really matter?"

"You don't want a guy to feel ashamed of you," she commented.

"Is that how you feel? I just thought this was a very good private restaurant away from any drama of the city."

She shrugged her shoulders and dug into her salad and the bread that had been brought to the table. "Would you bring your model girls over here?" she mumbled through her food.

She was beginning to fuck up the mood before the night had even gotten started.

I spoke my part and told her, "Quit while you're ahead and just enjoy the night." I had been around Rachel enough to know that you didn't hold anything back with her; you tell her exactly what's on your mind or get eaten alive.

"So, are you saying I only get one night with you?"

What the hell was wrong with women? I was trying my best to give Rachel what she wanted, and she was making it very hard for me.

I answered, "If I don't like how this night goes, then yeah."

She stared at me. "Is that how it goes with your model women, too?"

I took a breath and said, "Hey, Rachel, why don't you stop talking about everyone else and everything else, and enjoy your date while you're having it. Because all you're doing right now is airing out your own insecurities."

She nodded to me and finally got my point. Or at least I hoped she did.

We received our food without any further incidents or disagreements and began to enjoy our meals.

"Well, the food is good," she told me halfway into her lasagna.

I grinned. "Everything's gonna be good."

I didn't even bring my cell phone with me. This was Rachel's night with no outside disturbances.

Finally, I got the kind of response that I expected from her.

She grinned back at me and said, "We're gonna soon find out. So let's order our desserts and take them with us."

I raised my brow in wonder. "You're planning on using it later?"

She chuckled. "You'll find out. Let's just take it with us."

I didn't know what I was expected to do with New York cheese-cake, but Rachel's lemon meringue pie had whipped cream to do plenty with.

We left the restaurant with our desserts and headed back to her hotel in downtown Atlanta. Rachel looked across at me from the passenger seat. "I finally get to put something on you, huh?"

I had met her only a month ago, but it seemed like we'd known each other longer. We had been around each other in three different cities already.

"I just hope I don't disappoint you," I told her.

"Oh, I won't let you do that. The only way you can disappoint me is if you have a tiny dick that I can't really work with."

I don't know if her frankness was turning me on or off at that point. All I can say is that I was thrown off-guard by it.

"Do you always tell a guy what you're gonna do to him in advance?" I asked her.

She looked me over and frowned. "I haven't told you what I'm gonna do to you yet."

It sure felt like she had. She had me feeling like another plate of food. I was about to be marinated, seasoned, cooked well done, and sprinkled with salt and pepper.

We pulled up to the valet at the hotel, and I was actually feeling excited. What did this woman plan to do to me? She had me mad curious.

I had never been in Atlanta's Marriott Marquis before. It was pretty elaborate with a giant-size lobby that went up to the top floor. They even had glass elevators where you could look out at everything on your way up. A lot of celebrities stayed there. I was impressed. Rachel had friends with good taste.

I smiled on the elevator with her. "How many celebrities have you seen in here so far?"

"You mean besides you?"

"I'm way low on the pecking order in this city, honey."

"Not in my book you're not, so stop talking about yourself like that. You're a gorgeous man. A lot of other so-called celebrities are ugly."

She had a point, but without my good looks, I had no fame at all. My looks were my fame. I don't know if that made me more self-conscious about my appearance or not. Was I more concerned about it than other celebrities? I guess I had to be. Then again, I didn't really see myself as a celebrity. I was a model, no more no less.

When we arrived at the seventeenth floor, Rachel grabbed my free hand and led me off the elevator. I carried our bag of desserts in the other hand.

I teased her and said, "You want me to close my eyes and act like I'm blindfolded now."

She had me feeling like a curious woman. What was I about to get myself into? Could I trust her? Did I need to be on guard? Or should I have blind faith in her showing me a great time?

Rachel laughed at my suggestion and led me to room seventeen-twelve.

She said, "You don't have to close your eyes . . . not yet, but it'll be a good idea once I get you out of them clothes."

I was getting hard with anticipation as she opened the door with her plastic key card. The room was nice, with comfortable furniture and a king-size bed. I had been in better show-off places, but it was still nice being Rachel's guest.

I nodded my approval. "Nice room."

"I like treating myself when I travel," she told me.

"I see."

No sooner was I inside the room facing her then she ran her left hand across my crotch.

"Mmm, I see somebody's excited. That's a good thing."

She slid her hands around my waist and up my back, pulling herself close enough to kiss me on the lips.

"Mmm, this is gonna be good."

"Are you sure?" I continued to tease her.

"I'm gonna make sure," she answered.

She pulled off my jacket and went straight for the buttons on my shirt. She got my shirt open at the top, just enough to kiss my chest. Then she slid her hand back down to massage my hard dick.

"Looks like you know what you're doing," I told her.

"I'm not even started yet."

She pushed me over to the bed and eased me down on it. "Don't close your eyes. I want your eyes wide open for this," she told me.

I chuckled and kept my eyes open. What did she plan to do to me?

I let her strip my clothes off before she stripped her own. And boy did she have a heart attack body. You talk about curves; Rachel had curves in places I didn't know you could have curves, and it all looked extra soft on her.

Yeah, she's gonna tear me up, I told myself. I laid across that king-size bed feeling like a sacrificial lamb. Then her cell phone went off in her purse. How ironic?

I smirked and asked her, "Are you gonna get that?"

She looked at me and answered, "Hell no. I ain't Superwoman. So unless somebody wants me to fly out the window and save the world right this minute, which ain't possible, then there's nothing I can do for them right now."

I laughed. I needed to think about that myself next time I ended up in a phone jam.

Rachel walked over to our bag of desserts and pulled out her slice of lemon meringue pie.

I asked her, "Now what are you gonna do with that?"

She scooped up the pie in her right hand and smashed it together in her left. Then she walked toward me on the bed.

"You know what? You're starting to ask too many damn questions. Now just relax. I'm not gonna hurt you."

She smeared some of the pie on both my nipples, some on my lower torso, and then a giant glob of it on my dick, before she spread my legs and smacked some of it near my asshole.

"Whoa, whoa, wait a minute. What are you doing with that?"

I moved to stop her, but before I could make it, she attacked my hard-on with her mouth.

"Mmm, mmm, mmm . . ."

She shocked me with it and froze my nerves. All of a sudden, I couldn't move. I couldn't talk; all I could do was squeeze my eyes shut, grimace, and twist my neck left, right, and sideways while she devoured me. I must have looked like Stevie Wonder playing the most passionate song of his career on a grand piano.

"Mmm, mmm, mmm . . ."

She was working the knob like a jackhammer. I fell back with my head sinking into the pillow and imagined myself in Alaska with the Eskimos. For some reason, the sensation was chilling to me. Then it got as hot as Africa as Rachel slowed her pace.

"Mmmmm, mmmmm . . ."

I started lifting up my hips and ass like levitation in a magic trick. Then I reached to grab her head to steady my explosion.

Rachel squeezed my hands with hers to stop me, while she continued to work wonders with her mouth.

"Mmmpt, mmm," she grunted.

She lifted her mouth from me for just a second. "Trust me, I got you. I know what you want." Then she circled my nipple with one or her fingers.

I was just about ready to blast off to the moon when she went back to her business down below with long, slow, and blissful sucks.

"Mmmmm, mmmmm . . ."

I guess she could feel what was about to happen. She sped up the pace in perfect rhythm and started bringing it up out of me.

"Mmm hmmm, mmm hmmm, mmm hmmm . . ."

Boy, I got to shaking up and down in that bed like I was being electrocuted for triple murder. When my gigantic nut arrived, I howled like a wolf.

"WHOOOOOOOOOOOOOOO . . ."

Rachel took it all in like a suction machine.

"Mmmmmmmmm..."

I couldn't see how she could do it without choking and dying, but she did. The next thing I knew, the room was spinning around in circles, and I felt as if I was ready to faint.

That's when Rachel snuck me and started licking around my asshole. I tried to jerk away from her, but I was too damn weak to stop her. She grabbed my legs with her full arm strength and started to attack my ass with her insanity. I guess that was her whole game plan, to take me there. It felt like a wet feather was licking out my asshole.

Oh shit, she's nasty! She's fucking nasty! I told myself. Yet I was helpless to stop her. I was too spent from her lemon meringue blow job. As much as I tried to squeeze my ass cheeks together to keep her tongue away, she continued her pursuit until I gave it up.

I'm not gonna kiss her ever again in her life! I told myself. *I am not fucking kissing her!*

Once she drove me crazy, she came back up for air and attacked my chest, sucking hard on my nipples.

Just don't go near my lips, girl. Don't go near my lips, I warned her in my mind.

I raised my hands up to my neck to protect myself just in case she tried to go any higher, but she didn't. She went back down, licking my torso, and then into my pubic hairs before she toyed with my dick to make it hard again.

Then she started fondling around in her purse.

"What, what are you, what are you doing?" I stuttered.

"I'm getting out a condom. It's my turn now. We're not done yet. We got a long way to go."

Oh God! I prayed. *She's gonna kill me in here!*

She slid one of her ultrathin condoms over my new erection and eased herself down on me.

"Oh, Tee, this is nice and long and thick. I can work with this," she told me as she worked herself up.

She grabbed both of my hands and placed them on her huge titties. "Come on, work 'em, daddy, work 'em. Put your sweet lips on 'em. Suck 'em good," she told me while she rode up and down. "Suck 'em good, daddy, suck 'em good."

I rose up as if I was hypnotized and did what she asked me to do. I put my lips and tongue on those beautiful round melons and sucked them individually, then I pushed them together and sucked and licked them as a pair.

Rachel grabbed my head into her brown melons and damn near suffocated me.

"Yes, daddy, yes! Suck 'em, daddy!"

That daddy shit sounded so real that I began to wonder where it came from. But I wasn't gonna ask, at least not while she was bouncing up and down like a madwoman on my dick.

"Unnh, unnh, unnh, unnh . . ."

She was tearing my ass up all right. I don't know how I was taking it, but she was sure feeling good.

Then she stopped bouncing up and down and started swishing her body sideways, like she was trying to rub me out or scratch a deep itch inside of her pussy.

"Oooh, oooh, oooh . . ." she moaned hysterically, while smashing her big-boned body into my chiseled frame.

Then she dropped her load and went bananas on me. She shook me around under her weight and came all over my helpless balls.

"AAAAAHHHHHHH, DADDY! YOU FUCK GOOD! YOU FUCK GOOD!"

I had barely done anything. All I tried to do was hold my weight underneath her.

When she was finished with her sloppy, monstrous, and noisy nut, she climbed off of the wood and fell down beside me in the bed. Then she raised her ass up to the ceiling.

"Hit me from behind, daddy, come on. Come on." She was begging me for it.

I was ready to ask her what was up with all this daddy shit, but her heat was too strong to stop the action. So I climbed behind her and poked my way back in.

"Give it to me hard, Terrance. Give it to me hard."

I backed up my hips and pounded into her with rapid and forceful strokes just like she asked me to.

"Unnh, unnh, unnh, unnh . . ."

I was a lot more conscious of my surroundings while I was in control from the back. I started thinking about the people in the room next door.

Either they're enjoying the hell out of this freak show, or they're about to call the front desk on us for disturbing their peace; that is, if they're even in their room, I told myself.

It was too late to stop or to slow things down. I could feel my second nut approaching. That's when I started talking shit.

"You want it like that, huh? You want it like that?"

"Mmm hmmmm," she muttered into the pillow. "Yeaaaah! I want it! I want it!"

"You gon' get it, too! You gon' get it good!"

I was spanking that wet ass like it had been suspended from grade school, and talking shit while I did it. I had her mumbling in tongues I was hitting it so hard.

"Yea-yea-yea-yuh-yuh-yuh . . ."

I gripped up on those curvy brown hips and stroked her as deep as I could get until my legs started to cramp up.

"Ah," I responded to the cramp in my right thigh. At the same time, my nut was building, so I couldn't stop.

I grabbed my thigh with both hands and kept stroking. I was supposed to be in great shape, or at least I thought I was, until I fucked with this girl.

"Don't stop, daddy, don't stop," she begged me. I didn't but I caught a cramp in my left leg right as the nut came.

"Ah, ah, ah!"

I was screaming for three reasons; both of my legs were killing me, and the nut was tremendous.

Rachel was so excited she started shaking and bouncing her ass into my pelvis.

I was done at that point. I took Johnny out of the fire and rolled over on the bed to try and shake the pain out of my legs.

"What's wrong?" Rachel asked me.

"I got cramps in both my damn legs. They're killing me!"

She tried to work them out with her hands. It felt good, too. It seemed like her hands and fingers were stronger than mine at applying the needed pressure, or maybe she just had more energy than me at the moment.

Once my legs were relaxed again, I was scared to move them.

"Are they okay now?" Rachel asked me. She seemed all caring and motherly after the great sex.

I thought, *Wow! Look at the change in this woman.* I needed to give women what they wanted more often if that was the case.

I took a few deep breaths to recuperate. Rachel got up and went to the bathroom. She ran water in the sink while I closed my eyes on the bed and just . . . breathed. I was about ready for the afterworld.

Rachel walked back out from the bathroom and wrapped a warm wet face cloth around my balls to pull the soiled condom off.

"That felt great," I told her with my eyes still closed. "Where you learn all these tricks from?"

She laughed. "Just living life, baby, just living life." Then she laid down beside me and began to rub my chest.

She chuckled out of the blue and said, "That's all I wanted to do to you."

I assumed she was talking about the great sex we had just finished. I had no idea in the world when I first met her outside the elevators in Miami that she could put something on me like that. And I had been ignoring the damn girl.

She asked me, "Was it worth your precious time, Mr. Terrance Mitchell?"

I just smiled. I didn't have the energy to do much else. That girl had worn tire tracks into my ass like a truck had just run over me.

She said, "And here's a few words of wisdom for you. A lot of women in this day and age don't want a bunch of bullshit when it comes to sex. If you want to get it on with them, then act like it. If you don't, then don't play the game. 'Cause see, we all gotta fuck somebody, and we all want to. So when a woman act like she don't, she either don't want it from you, or you just don't know how to get it."

New Tricks and Treats

RACHEL BARELY allowed me to sleep that night. She kept waking me up for new rounds of over-the-top freakiness. All I know is that I planned to take an extralong shower in the morning to make sure I washed all of her inner freak out of my system. I can't say that it was a bad night though. I can't say that at all. She had raised the bar to new heights in sexuality.

I was pretty satisfied in just getting a girl to the bedroom before Rachel, and a solid blow job came along with nearly half of my dates. But Rachel's level of passion and shamelessness was indeed something to think about.

I went over to her hotel room again that Saturday night for another lesson of uncut nastiness. When it was all over, she headed back home to Columbus, Ohio, on Sunday afternoon, and left me thinking about her words of wisdom to me:

A lot of women in this day and age don't want a bunch of bullshit when it comes to sex. If you want to get it on with them, then act like it. If you don't, then don't play the game. 'Cause see, we all gotta fuck somebody, and we all want to. So when a woman act like she don't, she either don't want it from you, or you just don't know how to get it.

They were some strong-ass words. I mean, I realized all of that before, but to have it put so plainly from another woman was mind-boggling. Rachel sounded like a female pimp.

I sat up in my place watching TV that Sunday night and giggled my ass off. I wondered how many other women had inner freaks in them as strong as Rachel's. I didn't plan to do all of the things that she had done to me, but I surely admired her technique. She knew what worked and how to work it. At the same time, I had to think long and hard about whether I would keep a freak like that as my woman. I didn't even want to kiss Rachel when it was over . . . but I missed her. What did that mean? Did it mean I was willing to keep dealing with her as long as she never kissed me? Hell, if she kissed me before, then that was shit on my lips from the last guy.

Then again, that was all ridiculous. The girl brushed her teeth and washed out her mouth. I saw her do it. It's not as if she would eat a guy's asshole out and then go kiss the next guy right afterward. Or would she?

She had told me I was special. "Your body's so perfect and clean and beautiful," she told me. She couldn't have been lying about that. It was all true. I couldn't get paid what I demanded as a model with a sloppy, dirty, ugly body. So maybe it was me who had unleashed that ultimate freak in her. I wasn't too certain about any of it, but I was pretty clear about one thing: the girl had me impressed and inspired.

I wanted to talk to all of my women with new zeal and cockiness after that. So I called Danni up that week and told her, "You may still be on your cycle, but I'm not. So if you're serious about taking care of your man, and you want him to remain loyal to you, then you would take care of him no matter what."

She said, "Excuse me. I am not your whore, and I don't play that."

Now this is coming from the same girl who fucked me on a moving elevator. Who the hell was she kidding? I guess it's really true, you make a girl your main item, and she immediately climbs up on a damn pedestal.

I said, "You see that, Danyel? We can't be no serious couple. It hasn't even been a month yet, and already you're telling me what you're not gonna do."

"Yeah, you don't start telling me what I'm supposed to do," she snapped back at me. "You wouldn't have tried that before. You were Mr. Cool about everything. That's why I liked you. But now all of a sudden, you got rules and regulations and shit."

I said, "What the hell are you talking about? Are you getting me confused with someone else? I don't have any rules and regulations for you. I let you come and go as you please. I just don't like how you did me the other night."

"Well, get over it. That's how I act sometimes when I'm on my period."

"Well, I didn't know that shit before, did I? I could say the same thing about you changing up on me. But I knew your ass was crazy from the start," I told her. "I just thought you were sane with me."

"Whatever." She didn't want to hear it.

I said, "Okay, I said my piece. That's all I wanted to do. I'll get out of your hair now."

"Whatever," she repeated.

"Is that all you have to say? 'Whatever'?"

She said, "I know I'm not coming over there to suck your dick tonight, that's all I know."

I stopped and thought for a minute. We didn't have to end things on a bad note. It was all about how you went about things. So I joked with her and said, "I could just drive over to your place and get my dick sucked over there then. How about that?"

That only made Danni more incensed. She said, "What? Motherfucker, you must have bumped your damn head somewhere! You don't talk to me like that. Who the fuck you think you are?"

"I'm the same nice guy who picked your skinny ass up from the airport last weekend. What, you forgot about that? Now you done climbed up on your high horse to treat me like you treat everybody else. Well, fuck it then! I don't need a two-faced, Olive Oyl and Popeye chick like that."

She said, "Evidently, you liked it. You had your tongue all up in

Olive Oyl's skinny pussy. And you damn sure ain't no fucking Popeye, because I've had much bigger."

"And you begged them other jackhammers to be your one-man show too, huh?" I asked her.

"Maybe I did."

"And maybe they all did the right thing by turning your crazy ass down, too," I told her. "You don't know what the hell you want, girl! And almost had me going for some sucker shit. Well, I ain't playing that game no more. I'm going back to doin' me."

"You do whatever you need to do," she told me.

"All right. Say no more." And she hung up on me.

I wasn't expecting a conversation like that. However, Danni had undergone a drastic change on me. My guess was that she didn't want to be in a real relationship in the first place, so arguing with me was her way of getting out of it. I only made it easier for her with my new attitude. But hell, she was gonna kick me to the curb sooner or later anyway if she had it in her mind to do so. At least I could now leave with my dignity in tact.

Then I went ahead and called Victoria with more cockiness on my mind. Rachel had me on a roll.

"Hey, Terrance, how are you doing?" Victoria asked me. She recognized my Atlanta number.

"I'm just calling to see if you missed me," I told her.

She said, "Of course I do. I miss you every day now."

"You don't call me every day."

She paused. "You would allow me to?"

"I couldn't stop you."

"But would you want me to do that? I mean, because I could, but I just figured that you would want to have your space, you know."

"Shit, I'm a two-hour plane ride away. I have all of the space I need," I told her.

She chuckled and said, "Well, yeah, I guess you're right about that."

I said, "I miss your cute face, that's why I called you."

I could imagine her blushing through the phone.

"Oh, well . . . thank you."

"I would thank you if I was over there. I'd take everything off and bless you. Would you like me to be there?"

"Of course. Anytime, any day."

"So, what would you say if I was in Chicago right now?"

She giggled. "I would say that I needed a shower before you come over."

"Why, you go to bed dirty?"

"Well, no, I just didn't take a shower yet."

"Well, if I come over, you're just gonna get dirty anyway. So what's the use in taking a shower?"

She laughed again. "Well, wait a minute, wait a minute, you're actually here in Chicago? Oh my God, you didn't even tell me you were coming. Well, let me get in the shower then. I look a mess."

I laughed myself and said, "Hold your horses, girl, I'm not in Chicago yet. I just wanted to see how excited you would get."

"Aww, don't do that to me, Terrance."

"Why, your other boyfriend is in town?"

"My other boyfriend? Who's that?"

"Whatever guy you were thinking about before I jumped in the way."

"Well, whoever that was is long gone now, because I only think about one person, and that one person is you."

She sounded like a Hallmark card, but that wasn't a bad thing. It was genuine.

"That's nice," I told her.

"It's also true."

I said, "I know."

She chuckled and asked me, "How do you know?"

"You mean, you would lie to me already?" I insinuated.

"No, no, I would never lie to you."

I repeated that. "You would never lie to me. You mean that?"

"Yeah. What would I have to lie to you about?"

The girl sounded too good to be true.

"Well, you couldn't exactly tell me who you got dirty with earlier."

She said, "Yes I could. I was with my friend Miriam, working out at the gym. And when I got back in I got lazy, so I've been lying around the house watching TV before I finally take my shower. But if you were actually here, like you said you were, then I would have jumped right up and gotten in the shower in a heartbeat."

I corrected her. "I didn't say I was there, I asked you 'what if' I was there."

"Oh, yeah, you did, and got me all excited for nothing."

"So, there's no other white guy or anyone who can get even close to you, huh?"

I could have had Victoria laughing all night. I guess a lot of the things I said to her tickled her funny bone.

"Actually, to tell you the truth, I get a kick out of turning guys down for my man. I mean, it just makes it, you know, that much more special for him."

"Yeah, so you can be a total freak for your man, right? I understand. You unleash it all on one guy."

She laughed again, confirming it. "That's the way it should be, right?"

I said, "So, if you chose me, you'll do anything I tell you to do? Is that it?"

"Well, yeah," she answered with a pause. "And I already have chosen you."

"So, what's up with the hesitation? It sounded like you were unsure."

"Well, I mean, you always want to do everything for your man, but once you've been burned, you get a little bit scared each time."

"That's life, Victoria. I mean, there's reason for me to be afraid every time I get on an airplane. That damn thing may not land in one piece."

"Don't say that," she told me. "I'd rather hate you than to have something like that happen. I would rather be on that plane with you then."

I heard what she said, and thought, *DAMN! This white girl can't be real.*

I asked her, "You really mean that? That's like saying you would die for me?" *And you still hardly know me,* I told myself.

She said, "That's just the way I am. That's why I get so afraid whenever I'm involved with someone."

"Well, what happened to living life for just you?" I questioned.

"I still do that. I haven't stopped pursuing my dreams."

I said, "But what if I told you not to go for it, and to help me book more of my modeling gigs? What would you say to that?"

"Well, first of all; I would be honored to help you book more modeling jobs, and I would be getting the needed experience in the business that way. An inside position is always better than an outside position. But why would you tell me not to go for my own dreams? I think I would be able to do both."

I was only testing her temperament, and so far, she was passing my tests with flying colors.

I said, "It was just another hypothetical, but this is not; I'll be transferring planes from Atlanta to Chicago and from Chicago to Los Angeles on Friday morning. But if I fly earlier, and stay over in Chicago the night before, then I'll have time to see you. That is, if you'll have me," I added.

She got excited again. "Yeah, of course I would. So you would fly in on Thursday night?"

"And I'll book a hotel room for us at the airport, that way I don't have to get caught inside the city in the morning," I told her.

"Yeah, that's a good idea, because the traffic in the morning would be murder."

"But what about you getting back to work in the morning?" I asked her.

"Oh, don't worry about that, I'll get there."

The rest was on me. I thought about it and said, "Okay, well, let's make that happen then. You book the room at a nice airport hotel, and I'll pay for it when I arrive."

"Okay. Is there anything else you want me to do, or something special you would like for me to bring?"

She was tempting me, so I came right out with, "Yeah, you can pick me up at the airport with no panties or bra on. That's what models do."

She laughed. "Oh, is that what they do? Well, I think I can do that."

"Do you *think* you can, or do you *know* you can?"

"I know I can."

"Good. That's all I want."

"Well, you got it . . . unless you want more," she teased me.

That white girl was working her magic.

I smiled and said, "Of course I want more, but I'll save that for when I get out there."

When I hung up with Victoria, I immediately thought back to Danni.

"Now you see how easy this white girl made everything?" I said out loud. All Victoria wanted was an opportunity to please me, and I found myself perfectly fine with that. Why make things hard on myself if I didn't have to?

I got to thinking again, while still in my adventurous zone, about who else I could call and tempt. As outlandish as it may seem, I came up with Andrea. I wondered if I could tempt her into allowing me back into her world. I had been thinking about it already. In fact, I had fantasized about it; a threesome with Andrea and her new friend. How crazy was that?

Nah, she would never go for that, I told myself. Nevertheless, we still needed closure, so I had to try something with her.

I got back on the phone to call Andrea, feeling nervous about it. I had no idea what I would say to her. I would just have to wing it and see what happens.

"What can I do for you, Terrance?" she answered.

I said, "I haven't been able to get you off my mind. I keep thinking that a lot of the things you've been through is all my fault."

"Get over it," she told me. "I've moved on; you need to move on, too."

"I wish it were that easy," I responded. "But now I'm having these awkward dreams about you and Brazil."

I actually said that shit. I had lost my mind.

She asked, "Me and Brazil? And what exactly did you dream about us?"

I said, "Well, what exactly is your relationship with her?"

"Why?"

"I mean, is she like a *girlfriend* girlfriend, or just a girlfriend?"

I sounded silly, but I had to establish my train of thought with her first.

Andrea started to chuckle, forecasting where I was going with it, I'm sure.

She said, "Terrance, do you think you're the only man who has thought some shit like that? Men are always trying to nose in on something. But our relationship is not some damn freak show. It's a genuine, caring, and respectable relationship. And I'm offended that you're even trying me like that."

It didn't sound like she was offended. She was too calm. Or maybe that was more of her new attitude. I was expecting her to flip like a typical black woman, the Andrea I used to know. Or maybe I really didn't know her anymore.

"I'm just being honest with you," I told her.

"Well, I hope you don't think that means anything to me, because it doesn't," she said. "I don't owe you anything, and you don't owe me anything, so we can just leave it at that. In fact, I don't even need to answer your phone calls anymore."

She was being real hard-lined about it.

I told her, "That doesn't mean I'm gonna stop thinking about it."

"Well, we all think about things we'll never have a chance to do. I still think about modeling."

"And you can still do that," I told her. "You still have the look. Who said we'll never have a chance to do it?" I continued to tempt her.

"Terrance, that's the farthest thing from my mind right now," she stated. "And you would be the last person to experience something like that from us. Or maybe second to last."

"So, you still do hold a grudge against me," I responded. I figured her biggest grudge was now her estranged husband, Jayson Walker.

"Look, I just wouldn't go there with you."

"But you would with someone else? I mean, at least you know me."

I was trying my best to break her down. For some reason the idea of a threesome no longer seemed crazy to me. At least we were talking about it.

She said, "You know what, this conversation has gone on long enough. You have a nice night."

"Do you ever even think about me at all?" I asked her instead of hanging up.

"Why?"

"I'm just asking."

"For what purpose?"

I know she had thought about me, she just didn't want to admit it. She had to think about me. It was only natural. We were very close at one time.

I told her, "I miss your sexual energy, that's why these dreams keep coming. At the same time, I guess my mind is accepting that you're a little different now."

"A little different now?" she asked.

"You know what I'm talking about."

"You know what, it wasn't even my place to tell you that," she responded in reference to her new relationship.

"But you did, and I'm thinking that you did it for a reason. You still miss me," I tried to convince her.

"That is hardly the case," she told me.

I said, "You know it is. You can't lie to yourself."

Andrea broke down and asked me, "Okay, what are you trying to do here? Are you trying to get me involved in something? Is that it? Because that's not gonna happen."

I took Rachel's advice and went for broke with the truth.

I said, "Yeah, I'm willing to experience something new with you."

"And what makes you think I want any part of that?" she asked me.

Because you're still on the phone with me, I told myself. But instead of saying that, I answered, "You still hold on to me. You never wanted to marry that Jayson guy. He was just a way of trying to punish me, and you ended up punishing yourself with him."

I didn't want to go into detail about Corey telling me about a miscarriage. That may have been too painful for her.

She took a breath, and I jumped on her while reading the opportunity to do so.

"Did your friend ever like men?"

I had to do at least a little research on Brazil.

Andrea took too long to answer.

I said, "She did, didn't she? She probably still has curiosities about us."

I was pulling out every thought I had about it.

Andrea said, "I don't believe you. I don't believe you're sitting here . . ." She stopped and told me, "You haven't changed a bit. You're still trying to get what you want."

I didn't know how long I could go back and forth with her. I just wanted to put the idea in her head, the rest would be up to her and her friend.

Quit while you're ahead, I told myself.

I said, "Okay. But I want you to know that I have changed a little. I'm thinking about what you told me, to give a woman more of what she wants, no matter what it is."

"Well, you need to do that with a woman who cares."

I said, "You still care, you know you do. But I'll let you go. You know my number now."

"I won't be calling you," she stated.

"As long as you know what it is, I'm satisfied with that."

• • •

WHEN I HUNG UP with Andrea I felt optimistic for some reason. I guess I felt that way because I was able to state my case to her. It was crazy, but I had done it, and there was no going back.

I grinned and asked myself, "What the hell am I doing?" I felt like a mischievous kid. It was as if I had just started having sex and was trying to go after every girl in the neighborhood. Rachel had really turned me on to the possibilities. I was ready to try anything with anyone.

In the Closet

I WASN'T EXPECTING DANNI to call me back after our last argument, but she did. She called me on my house phone right as I was leaving for the airport to catch my day-early flight to Chicago. I was packing the last few items in my suitcase.

She said, "I realize that I was wrong in our little argument or whatever, so I'm calling to make it up to you now."

It was a week from Thursday when she was first on her period. I guess she was off it now, but it was too late to make it up, at least on that night.

I said, "Okay, so you can admit when you're wrong, huh?"

She took a breath and said, "Please don't make this any harder than what it already is."

Imagine that. The girl called me up to apologize and yet she still had attitude.

I zipped up my carry-on bag for the airport and was ready to split.

"Well, we can talk about it when I get back," I told her.

"You don't want to see me before you leave?"

"No. We'll just talk when I get back."

"Well, what are you gonna do tonight? You leave in the morning, right? I figured I'd come over and spend some time with you."

I actually held the phone away from my ear and looked at it. She had to be bullshitting me.

I said, "So that's it, huh? You got bored with me treating you with some respect, so now that I tell your ass off, you call me back with some makeup shit."

"Terrance, I rarely do this shit, okay. When I fuckin' walk, I walk. So consider yourself privileged that I'm even calling back, let alone trying to make up with you. Now I said I was wrong already, but I'm not calling you to beg."

Yes she was. She would beg if I made her. She was already begging if you asked me. I was just ready to catch my plane.

"All right, well, we'll talk about it when I get back," I repeated to her.

"Why do you keep saying that?" she asked me. "What do you have planned for tonight?"

"I'm leaving tonight," I broke down and told her.

"For where? I thought you flew out to L.A. tomorrow morning."

"Yeah, well, things changed. I'm flying out there tonight now. So I'll call you when I get back."

"You'll call me when you get back? Who do you plan on being out there with? You can't call me while you're there?"

Was I really supposed to answer that?

"Look, you're gonna make me late for my plane," I commented instead.

"I'll just call you on your cell phone then."

Danni hung up without another word. Then my cell phone went off from my hip.

I checked my suitcase once more to make sure I had everything I needed. I walked out the door with my bag. There was no sense in answering Danni's phone call until I made it to my car and was headed for the airport.

However, once I hit the road, I got a call from Corey. I hadn't spoken to him since Chicago. How ironic was that with me flying back out to Chicago that same night?

"Long time no hear from," I told him. I actually enjoyed my peace of mind away from Corey. He had become the bearer of bad news, particularly with information about Andrea. Turned out, Andrea wasn't in dire straits after all. Things had definitely changed for her though, and she was getting used to living in her new skin.

Corey said, "You know my number, man. Why I always have to call you first?"

I immediately thought back to Victoria asking me if Corey was gay. I smiled it off again, still doubting it. I told him, "Don't get all sensitive, man." I was planning on using specific language to see how he responded to it.

"I'm not getting sensitive, I'm just stating the facts. I mean, you came out here to Chicago and didn't even share a drink or two, man. I thought we were friends."

"I told you how busy my schedule was going to be."

"And what part of your schedule included hooking up with the white girl I caught you with? I didn't think you would even go that way, man."

"Go what way? You mean with a white girl? Are we still into restrictions in the twenty-first century? I mean, admit it, man, you saw her. My white girl is fine."

"Oh, she's your white girl now."

"Yeah," I told him. "I'm claiming her."

I was singing her praises on purpose, just to see where Corey wanted to go with it.

He said, "So, what about your love for the brothers and sisters? Is that out the window now?"

Brothers and sisters? I thought to myself. Was he trying to combine the two terms to send me a signal? He even had a nerve to sound militant with it.

I said, "I haven't lost love for anybody. I think I'm expanding the love if anything."

He said, "Well, expand some my way and stop acting like a stranger in town."

Stop acting like a stranger, huh? I pondered. That was generally a woman's term, but guys could use it, too, I guess. Maybe I was over-analyzing while trying to find something.

I told him, "Well, I have to get ready to go into a meeting in a few minutes, man." I was getting closer to the airport and it was none of his business that I was flying back to Chicago for the night.

"Well, anyway, I just wanted to let you know I'll be back in Atlanta next week," he hurried to tell me. "So I'll be calling you, man. Look out for me."

"I'll do that."

I GOT INTO CHICAGO at 9:39 that evening. Victoria was supposed to meet me at the baggage claim and ground transportation so we could ride a shuttle bus over to the airport hotel. That was the plan, and I was eager to see what she would wear for me.

So I got off the plane with my one carry-on bag and headed toward the baggage claim area. Right before I reached the escalators for baggage claim, someone called out my name.

"Terrance."

I turned and faced Andrea's friend Brazil. I guess she was out of town when I talked to Andrea a few days earlier, tempting her with a threesome. Meeting Brazil there at the airport immediately made me wonder if Andrea had talked to her about our conversation. So I felt a little bit uneasy.

"Oh, hey, how are you doing?"

She grinned. "I heard you talked to Andrea recently."

That made me even more uneasy.

"Ah, yeah, I did."

Brazil nodded. Now that I could focus on her without any distractions, she looked better than I thought she did when I first met her, even in the basic gray sweats she was wearing. I was in blue jeans, white T-shirt, a sports jacket, and the comfortable brown leather shoes that I usually wore for travel.

"So, how's it going? You have another event in town this weekend?" she asked me.

I locked in and focused on her beautiful brown lips. They had the perfect size and plumpness.

"Ah, no, I'm just staying over for the night. I'm actually on my way out to L.A. tomorrow."

I wondered if she was thinking the same thing I was thinking, only Victoria would be in the way of things. In fact, I didn't even want Brazil to see me with Victoria. I didn't want to spoil anything for the future.

So instead of walking forward toward baggage claim, I stopped and stood there.

"Where are you flying back in from?" I asked her. It was none of my business, but I didn't know what else to ask at the moment.

"I have family in Kansas City."

"Oh, Kansas City. Is that where you're from?"

She looked me in the eyes and said, "I was an army brat. I've lived everywhere."

"So, what does that mean, you don't have a home turf?"

"Chicago," she told me, "it's my adopted city now."

I nodded back to her. "Big choice. Few cities in America are bigger." After that, we just stood there awkwardly for a minute.

"Are you walking to baggage claim?" she finally asked me.

I said, "Yeah, but I just forgot, I wanna buy some good coffee and hit the restroom before I leave. But tell Andrea I said hi."

Brazil smiled. I wondered if she realized I was bullshitting. At least she was being cordial with me. She didn't have to speak to me at all.

"Okay, well, I'll tell Andrea I saw you."

"Yeah, you do that," I told her, and I walked off toward an airport coffee shop. Then I wondered if Brazil knew what Victoria looked like from the cancer dinner at The Millennium Ballroom.

Even if she does, that doesn't mean she can link her to me, I thought to myself as I walked away.

I walked off to the restroom to force myself to piss, before ordering coffee and an apple pastry. I was stalling for time to make sure Brazil had cleared the area. I gave myself ten minutes, while sipping my coffee and munching on my pastry before I began a slow walk toward baggage claim and ground transportation again.

When I arrived, I looked first for Brazil, and then for Victoria. Brazil was nowhere to be found, but Victoria was in plain view, wearing a sky blue dress with matching colored heels and purse. Her hair was combed out long with full, dark body. She spotted me and smiled, glowing like a virgin.

"Hey, Terrance," she called to me.

Among the weary, nighttime travelers, Victoria stood out like a lightbulb.

"Hey," I spoke back to her.

As we approached each other, I thought about the hug that was forthcoming. How comfortable would I feel about that out in public?

Well, Victoria wrapped her arms around me with no shame and squeezed me hard. Then she whispered into my ear.

"I did what you told me to. Wanna test and see?"

Boy, my dick was ready to jump out of my pants and pound her right there in the airport, but I had to keep my cool.

I chuckled and said, "Nah, not here. But I'll be testing you soon enough."

She said, "I can't wait," and went to grab my bag.

"I got that, I'm good," I told her. "You just walk with me and look pretty."

She smiled and asked, "Are you sure? I mean, I don't mind it."

She was really eager to please me, even while wearing her clingy dress and heels.

"Yeah, I'm positive. So, which way is the shuttle?"

"This way."

I followed her out of the airport terminal, watching everyone who watched us. We were generating a lot of attention, and I didn't even have a limo out there waiting. Fortunately, the hotel shuttle pulled up right as we made it to the stop. I jumped on after Victoria and put my bag up on the luggage rack before sitting down next to her. There was no one on the shuttle but us, so I felt open to flirt again.

"How was your flight?" she asked me.

"Not as good as it's gonna get," I told her. Then I checked for her panty line along the hips of her dress.

She chuckled and asked me, "Did you find anything?"

"Not yet," I told her.

"You won't. I have another surprise for you, too."

She gently took my hand and rubbed it across her braless titties.

"You feel that?"

I just laughed. Victoria was following instructions well, and I couldn't wait to get her to the room.

"So, what does the room look like?" I asked her.

"It's nice and comfortable; office space, king-size bed, separate shower and bath, airport view, nonsmoking."

I grinned. "Sounds like you work there."

"I'm just very detail-oriented. It's part of my job."

"I see."

We pulled up to the hotel and hopped off the shuttle bus.

"You all have a good night now," the elderly driver told us.

Victoria beat me to the response. "Same to you."

"What floor are we on?" I asked her as we entered the hotel lobby.

"The eighth."

All of a sudden, she reached over to my cell phone on my hip and pulled it out to see if it was on.

"Oh, it's off."

"Yeah, I never turned it back on after getting off the airplane."

"Good thinking. We don't want a repeat of the last time."

"No, we don't," I agreed.

It was a pretty decent hotel, but I wasn't there to sightsee. We walked straight to the elevators.

Victoria was ready to ride the first one up with an older white couple, but I stopped her. When the elevator doors closed, I said, "We want our own elevator. I still need to check you."

She chuckled. "Okay."

We got on our own elevator up, and I immediately dropped to my knees in front of her and leaned under to look up her dress while pulling it away from her naked body.

"Oh my God!" she responded, embarrassed.

"Don't you pee on me while I'm under here," I told her.

She broke up in laughter.

I said, "It smells good under here, too."

"It better," she told me.

"What you spray under here?"

Before she could answer, I slid my index finger up into her cream spot. She closed her eyes and jerked forward, liking it.

"I think I want you to keep this dress on once we get to the room. You got a problem with that?" I asked her.

Before she could answer, I fingered her cream spot again.

"Uunh, no," she moaned and jerked forward a second time.

We reached our floor where I immediately climbed back to my feet.

"You okay?" I teased.

She looked at me and said, "No, I'm not okay. Somebody's gonna have to finish what they just started."

I smiled and followed her to the room, where she took out the key from her purse and opened the door. I walked inside and noticed that she had already pulled back the covers. I also noticed that she had taken the phones off the hook.

I pointed at it and smiled. "Nobody even knows I'm here."

"I don't care," she told me. "The phones are off. Period!"

I walked over to face her in her light blue dress and gave her a good feel all over with my hands.

"I see what you did with the bed, but we may not use it too much," I told her.

She looked at me and smiled. "The shower?"

I looked in the opposite direction. "How about the closet?"

She grinned. "The closet? That's rather kinky."

"Yeah, and I want you to keep your heels on, too."

"You think we can both fit in there?"

"We'll make it fit."

At first she was hesitant. Then she agreed to it. "Okay, if you say so."

I walked over and opened the closet door to make sure there was enough room inside. First I had to remove the ironing board, the iron, and the hangers. Victoria helped me to empty it out.

"Okay, now, you want to be an actress, right?" I asked her.

She looked at me curiously with her mouth open.

"Okay, yeah."

"So I want you to act like you're not feeling me and you're definitely not feeling the closet, but little by little you give in to it."

She was grinning with twinkles in her eyes.

"That's original. I think I can do that."

"Good." I pulled out a stack of condoms from my suitcase to take with me.

I turned off the lights and said, "Allison, you don't mind if I turn the lights off, do you? It's kind of bright in here."

Victoria went right into her role. "Actually, I do mind." She turned the lights back on. "What would Roger think if he came back here and found us in the dark, Mike. I don't think that's a good idea. And I don't want to give my man the wrong impression about me. I'm a good girl."

"Nobody said you wasn't a good girl. But are you feeling guilty about the lights being off, is that it?" I asked her and clicked them back off.

She tried to reach again for the lights, but I caressed her arm and pulled it away.

"Allison, you just don't know how sexy you are," I told her.

She said, "I do know, and so does Roger."

"Look, I'm tired of hearing about that guy. He's not here right now, and what he don't know won't hurt him."

I finally started to pull her toward the closet.

"What are you doing?" she asked me.

"This is where we need to keep it, right inside this closet."

"I'm not going inside that closet with you. What is wrong with you?"

She tried to pull away, but I wouldn't let her.

"Come on, he won't know, just a couple of minutes."

"No, what are you . . . No."

I pulled her inside the closet anyway. I whispered, "Be quiet, the people next door may hear you."

"I don't care. I don't want to be in here with you," she whispered back to me. "How would you feel if somebody did this to your woman?"

"That's why I don't have a woman," I told her. I spun her around to bend her over.

"Stop it. What are you doing?" she whispered, facing me again.

I pulled my pants and drawers down to slide a condom over my erection.

"I don't know why you're doing that. You're not getting anything," she told me.

I turned her back around and pulled her dress up.

"Would you stop it. This is not right," she told me.

I don't know if I watched too many dramatic American movies about racial tensions or what, but my heart started to race as if it was all real. I was actually thinking about stopping myself, but I didn't.

I spread her legs just enough to guide myself in.

"Please, don't do this. Don't do this, Mike. I'm a good girl. I'm a good girl."

Man, she sounded too fucking real for comfort. I felt like I was about to get myself lynched, but I was already inside of her, and I couldn't stop myself from stroking. It felt too good. So I had to cut the acting shit out before it disturbed my groove.

"That's enough acting, Victoria," I told her. "No more. I don't want to get in trouble with the klan."

She tried to laugh, but she couldn't. It felt too good to her, too.

"Okay, Terrance," she moaned. "Okay," she repeated, while I slammed her from behind. I had her dress pulled up and her heels still on inside the closet, just like I wanted. I had one hand on her lower back and the other massaging her titties.

You talk about a rush of cum building up, it felt like I was ready to send her through the closet wall in a few more strokes. I lost all of my coordination and had Victoria speaking in gibberish:

"Unh, ah, hunh, euw, ah, euw, unh, ah, hunh . . ."

"Are you ready for this?" I asked her. "Are you ready?"

"Yea, yuh, ye, ye . . ." she whimpered.

I said, "Okay . . . I'ma take it out . . . I want you on your knees . . . you take it in . . ."

She said, "Okay . . . okay . . ."

So I pulled out, took the condom off, and I was still vibrating like a dog in heat when Victoria turned to face me and dropped to her knees.

"Do me, baby," I told her. "Do me good."

She sucked me back and forth about three times, and that was all that was needed. I grabbed the closet pole above my head, prepared to break it in half like a superhero in an action movie. Tears rolled out of my eyes and down my blissful face.

"Oooooohhh . . ." I moaned. But Victoria didn't stop there, she kept on sucking me even after I had emptied myself out to her. Usually, my dick was too sensitive to touch after I nutted, but she did this move where she sucked and licked just enough for me to know that she was there, but not enough to go overboard. I guess she had prior experience with a sensitive dick and had learned how to treat it.

To my surprise, she had me hard again.

"Oh, shit," I responded to it. "How'd you do that?"

"You just have to suck it softer." That's what she did, too. She sucked me soft and slow inside the closet until I was ready to explode a second time.

"Oh, shit," I told her and ran my hands through her hair. "Oh . . . oh . . . OH . . ."

This second nut felt as if it would be as strong as the first one. Could Victoria take down two solid nuts in less than ten minutes? I was amazed!

I started jerking around again and grabbing at the closet pole, and she swallowed down my second nut.

"Aw, you gon' get me addicted," I told her.

She said, "Good, that's what I want. I want you hooked on me."

By that time, our eyes had adapted to the dark of the closet, and I could read her face enough to know that she was serious.

"That's what you want, huh?" I asked her.

She said, "Yeah, that's what I want."

WHEN WE CLIMBED out of that closet, I was spent, but Victoria wasn't. I made it over to the bed and stretched out on it to rest. Victoria washed up and rinsed her mouth out in the bathroom. Then she took her dress and heels off and crawled up in bed beside me, butt naked and still horny. Her breath smelled like peppermint.

"What do you have, some gum?" I asked her.

"No, a peppermint," she answered. "You want one?"

I shook my head and answered, "Water. I feel dried out."

She hopped up and got me a glass of water. I took a few sips of it and laid back again. Victoria leaned over and sucked lightly on my nipples with her peppermint tongue and lips.

I smiled and asked her, "I guess I won't get a chance to sleep tonight, will I?"

She chuckled but didn't answer me. Then she commented, "I've been waiting all week for this."

I grinned. I guess Victoria planned to get all of what she had waited for.

The Mansion

WITH THE TWO-HOUR time difference from Chicago to L.A., I made it out to LAX international airport before noon and was tired as hell. Victoria had worked me through half the night. I think I bust around five nuts in less than twelve hours. I didn't know I was still capable of doing that in my older years. But that was what the girl wanted, so when everything was said and done, she walked away satisfied and wide open for more.

Out in L.A., I had a photo shoot in Santa Monica. Some old industry friends of mine had called me out there to shoot some restaurant scenes as a waiter at a place called the Pacific Grille, and for good money, too. To tell you the truth, though, I couldn't understand that one. I figured there had to be tons of gorgeous guys out in L.A. to pose as waiters at a much cheaper price. But sometimes old relationships were willing to pay your bills. It was a scratch your back now, scratch my back later kind of deal. And why would I decline or complain about a paid-for trip to L.A.?

I made it to the baggage claim area where I was supposed to meet my escort, who was to take me to the hotel and to my destinations. I would be out in L.A. for just the weekend, with a return flight to Atlanta on Monday morning.

"Hey, Terrance," a young white guy walked up and greeted me. He was a blond kid in his early twenties, wearing a turquoise T-shirt, blue jeans, and Nikes. He reminded me of the legendary James Dean. He just had that superstar look about him.

I told him, "You don't look like an escort to me, man. Where's the old guys and old ladies?"

He smiled and extended his hand for a shake. "There're a lot of different kinds of escorts, you know."

"Yeah, and you must be the other kind. What do you play, a bad-boy actor to the old, rich women out here?" I teased him.

I had just finished role-playing with Victoria the night before, so the idea wasn't far-fetched at all to me.

He said, "I see you're a fast thinker. That's what the boss said about you."

The boss he was referring to was Marcus Vissel, an old, established photographer who had traded in his camera for a bigger piece of the pie, agency contracts. Even though I declined to sign with the Vissel Model Agency, Marcus continued to be loyal to me. I had been one of the first African-American males he had shot in the early nineties to establish a prosperous and ongoing career. In fact, I was one of the first models he had shopped for new business. I just refused to play the exclusivity game. Those agency contracts were like marriages, and the divorces were just as tragic. Some agencies were able to make and break careers, and I didn't want anyone controlling my life that strongly.

"So, what's your name, James? What do they call you?" I asked my escort.

"Billy Wollimer. And ah, James Dean, yeah, he's my idol."

"So, I guess everybody says that you look like him, huh?"

"Yeah, I love that," he told me.

I followed him over to the parking lot area where we approached a yellow Lamborghini. Only in L.A. and Miami did they do that. They were the biggest two show-off towns for exotic cars.

"I see the boss sent you out here to pick me up in style," I commented. I was impressed.

Billy said, "That's how Mr. Vissel likes to do things now."

We climbed inside the yellow Lamborghini with all-black leather interior, and hit the road. However, the Westin Hotel was only a short trip away from the airport. So I found myself climbing back out of the Lamborghini at the hotel entrance only minutes after I had climbed in.

Billy told me, "The boss said to check you into the hotel and drive you over to the mansion ASAP."

He hopped out of the car with me and tossed the keys to the valet. "We'll only be a few minutes, we're just checking in."

I could already tell that I was going to like this trip. My old photographer friend was giving me the four-star treatment.

I checked into the hotel, received my key, let the bellboys take my bag up to the room, and I hit the road with Billy in the Lamborghini.

As soon as we were on our way, I remembered to call TaShay on her cell phone to let her know that I had arrived.

"Okay, where are you staying?" she immediately asked me.

I didn't want to give her all of that information. I was still leery about how I wanted to treat her.

"I'm staying near the airport," I answered.

"Yeah, but at what hotel?"

I guess staying away from her wasn't gonna work too well. I didn't want to seem too difficult or distant with her, so I just gave her the hotel information.

"The Westin."

"Oh, I know where that is."

"You stayed there before?" I asked her.

"I wish. Some of us haven't made it to the big time yet. But I've been past there plenty of times. I mean, it's right on the way to the airport."

"Yeah, I guess it is."

She said, "Well, here's the plan. Me and my girlfriend Tan are gonna drive up after she gets off of work, and then we'll meet up with you around nine or so to go crash a couple of parties."

I asked her, "Are you sure you young guys wanna hang out with me? I might bust your groove at these parties you wanna go to."

I still wasn't into parties like that. Billy overheard me from behind the wheel and chuckled.

TaShay said, "Please, California is not like the East Coast. We all party out here together. You'll be just fine. But I have to go now, so I'll call you back in a few. Okay?"

I looked over at Billy who was still smiling.

"Okay."

As soon as I hung up the phone with her, Billy asked me, "Is she hot?"

I started laughing. "She's extremely hot, like a perfect cup of expensive, brown coffee."

He nodded and continued to grin. "Wait till you see the new models Mr. Vissel has at the mansion."

For a minute there, he made it sound as if we were going to the Playboy Mansion. That made me curious.

"So, Marcus has models all around his mansion estate, like Hugh Hefner and Playboy?"

Billy continued to smile. "I'll just let you see it, and you can see for yourself."

California was one of those places where you could drive right up on the rich and famous without much to it. They were so used to stars and stardom in that area that it all seemed normal. So we drove up to Marcus Vissel's mansion among Bentleys, Rolls-Royces, Mercedes, Maseratis, Ferraris, various limousines, including several photography vans that were all parked around the circular driveway. The mansion was set nearly a hundred yards off the main road, but it was still in plain view. There weren't any gates to keep you off the property or anything.

"I see the boss is doing quite well for himself," I commented to Billy.

He smiled again and tossed the keys to the valet. There were about five guys in their early twenties dressed in white shirts, black ties, gold vests, black pants, and black shoes, who were parking all the cars at the front of the mansion.

We approached the front door, which had a huge Roman archway. "Well, here we go," Billy told me before we walked in.

I had nothing else to say until I saw what he was talking about.

We entered the mansion of high ceilings, striking colors, artwork, hardwood floors, and plenty of inspirational sculptures spread about. There was an immediate carnival atmosphere going on. Male and female models were working every part of several downstairs rooms, with photographers snapping their pictures for high fashion. They also worked the T-shaped staircase that led upstairs. And there were spectators everywhere, watching whatever photo shoot and models they wanted to watch. It looked as if the fashion world was on display for Mr. Vissel's wealthy invited guests.

I looked at Billy and asked him, "What's this, a fashion shoot showcase? There's a photo shoot going on all over the house, huh?"

He grinned and said, "This is just the front end of the house. Mr. Vissel wants to talk to you in the back."

I said hi to a few of the cameramen and models I recognized before following Billy around to a side door that led us through a long, outside walkway toward the back of the mansion.

"There's a lot of new ideas that the boss came up with to create this atmosphere for modeling and fashion, but I'll let him explain it all to you himself. He wouldn't have it any other way."

As we walked, two Filipina models approached us in designer dresses, purses, shades, and heels. They were all decked out and ready for their shoots. They even had their makeup ready.

Billy stopped both of them and introduced me.

"This is Terrance Mitchell, one of the first models Mr. Vissel credits for helping to start his agency."

"Hi," they both spoke to me.

They were both tall, slim, olive-toned, with long dark hair, and both strikingly beautiful.

I nodded to them. "How are you two doing today?"

"Good right now, but the day is just beginning, so ask us again later on," the shorter and slightly browner of the two answered.

Billy told me, "Mr. Vissel calls them Tapioca and Cream."

"Who's Tapioca?" I asked.

The shorter one smiled. "That would be me."

I liked her already. She looked like a Filipina movie star.

"Make sure I catch up with you two ladies later," I told them.

"Okay, Billy knows how to find us."

"All right, I'll see you later then."

When we continued on our way, Billy commented, "They are just some of the exotic women we have here. We have beautiful models from Hawaii, Japan, Brazil, Italy, Mexico, Colombia . . ." He shook his head and continued to grin. "It's just amazing, man. I love being here."

"What, you stay here all the time?" I asked him.

"Just about. I mean, why go anywhere else?"

"Well, how many rooms does this place have?"

"Twenty-nine rooms and six wings," he answered. "Then there's the guest house at the back behind the pool. That's where we're going now. Mr. Vissel's conducting several interviews today."

I couldn't wait to see him. Marcus had always been full of ideas. It looked like he had finally developed a few that were worthwhile.

When we arrived at the pool area, there were more men and women models in swimsuits taking fun-in-the-sun shots in and out of the extralarge pool. The pool had five sections; a feet dipping area, an adult-size slide, a waterfall area, a shallow end, and a deep end. Around the pool was more than enough poolside furniture for tanning and more pictures.

At center court in the pool area, sitting under a beach umbrella table, was Marcus Vissel. He was wearing dark shades, a white tennis shirt, white shorts, and white tennis shoes and speaking to an attractive female reporter. He looked good and tanned, with a full head of thick, dark hair that contained specks of gray. He was in his mid-fifties and still hip.

As soon as we neared him, Billy raised his hand to get his attention. Marcus acknowledged our presence with a nod.

He said, "In fact, let me introduce you to Terrance Mitchell, one of the first guys I began to pitch to friends of mine in the fashion industry as a top model prospect in the African-American community."

He was pulling me right into the interview. The reporter looked at me and said, "Hi."

She was a blond-haired white woman who looked like she could pass for a model herself.

Mr. Vissel said, "This is Janice Littlejohn. She's doing a piece on me for *Esquire* magazine. Say a few words to her for the article."

I smiled, but I didn't know what to say. Marcus was putting me on the spot. I said, "I thank Mr. Vissel for taking a chance on me years ago when I was just a college student with a handsome face and a still developing body."

The reporter nodded and recorded my comment on tape.

She asked me, "So, what do you think about the Model Mansion and all of his ideas for the fashion world?"

Since I wasn't totally informed about everything, I said the only thing that made sense.

"Well, Marcus always had great ideas, ever since I first met him, so it was only a matter of time before we saw some of those ideas come to fruition."

Marcus nodded to her and said, "Janice, if you'll excuse me for a minute, I'll be right back out."

"Oh, no problem. I'll just sit here and enjoy the view," she told him.

Marcus stood up and looked at me through his dark sunshades. "Terrance, follow me into the guesthouse," he told me.

Billy put a hand on my shoulder and said, "I'll see you later on, man."

I followed behind Mr. Vissel, feeling like the man of the hour.

When we got inside the guesthouse, he led me to a quiet study with a small library and closed the door behind us. We sat in comfortable wooden chairs next to a long wooden desk, where Marcus took off his sunshades and looked me in the eyes with compassion.

"How's life been treating you, Terrance? How's business?"

I nodded. "It's still paying the bills."

He just stared at me. He said, "Is that all you want to do with your life, pay the bills? What about your goals and aspirations?"

I really didn't have any aspirations anymore. I just liked keeping my life simple. I shook my head and said, "I don't need or want any extra stress in my life, so I just like to maintain what I have."

He nodded to me. "Are you still single?"

"Yeah," I told him.

"Any kids yet?"

"Nope."

"You still don't have a family?"

"Nope."

He nodded again. "Perfect," he commented. "That's why I called you out here to have this chat."

I grimaced. "So, there's no real shoot at the Santa Monica restaurant tomorrow?"

"Yeah, there's still a shoot for tomorrow. I'm shooting that one myself. I just had some other things I wanted to chat with you about while you're out here."

"Okay. Shoot."

He said, "You really could make a lot more money if you remained with one agency. But I respect your independence. A lot of models would never last as long as you have on their own, but things are changing, Terrance. Things are really changing."

I said, "I see. I really like what you have going on here. So you just use your own premises to shoot models, clothes, scenes, spreads, the whole nine?"

"And everything's paid for, and everything's for sale," he told me with a boyish grin.

"Everything?" I asked him curiously.

He said, "The pretty girls, the pretty boys, the clothes, accessories, pictures, you name it, as long as the price is right."

"So, they're not really models then," I commented. "This is more like an exotic brothel."

He said, "It's all a brothel anyway. The world is a brothel. We're all selling ourselves for something."

I had used that philosophy in Miami with Judi, but I didn't think of taking it to the extent of calling the world a brothel.

I asked him, "Ain't that illegal?"

"Not if you're doing it the right way. How can you stop an American citizen from paying for what they want. Or an international citizen for that matter."

I wasn't expecting that to come from Mr. Vissel. After all, he was a photographer, a visual artist who models trusted.

I said, "How did you even . . ."

He cut me off before I could get my full question out.

"It was simple," he told me. "I'd get around wealthy admirers of my work, and they would always bring up how wonderful it would be to go out with a few of the models that I would shoot.

"On the flip side, I would have models who would overextend their budgets and beg me for advances," he told me. "So I simply put the two together. And like I said, I don't know anything about it. We deal only with adults here. Underage or immature models are not included in the program."

I said, "But how would you stop an underage model from getting involved with that? You know how much guys like the young ones."

I had been in the business long enough to know that there were plenty of older guys dying to reclaim their youth through alliances with much younger women. The idea was even more prevalent internationally.

Marcus answered, "Easy, you don't shoot them, you don't sign them, you don't let them on the premises. That solves that problem."

"So, you don't deal with underage models at all anymore?"

"Well, I can have one of my photographers shoot them, sure, just not here."

I nodded and grinned. I said, "So, this really is like the Playboy Mansion."

Mr. Vissel didn't flinch. He boasted, "It's better. We have men and women, legitimate models, high-end fashion, better photography, and it's much more exclusive."

I said, "But you're here doing an article for *Esquire* magazine. Isn't that going to bring too much attention?"

I was sorry I said anything to the reporter without knowing his plans. Did I really want to be a part of his propaganda? No. Hell no!

"They're doing an article on the uniqueness of opening up the modeling world to those who are fascinated by it. It's like virtual reality and fantasy football. You get to be closer to it. Nothing else exists here."

I said, "But all they have to do is send in an undercover agent posing as a rich man, or even a woman for that matter, and everything falls apart."

I just didn't see a long-term future in the idea. Sure, it all looked good while it lasted, but it was also a time bomb, waiting for the wrong people to make the wrong moves.

He said, "We don't solicit to anyone here. They say what they want to buy on their own. That's the difference. To break the law, you have to solicit, and we absolutely don't."

"And all of the models are in on it?" I asked him.

"They all have the right to decline, just like they do in the real world," he answered. "The rules of general life still apply. Models have always been suspect."

I thought about it all and shook my head. There was a level of trust between a photographer and a model that went unspoken, particularly with a male photographer and a female model. If a model looked her part, then naturally, many men would want her. But for a photographer to actually aid in pimping her . . .

Before I could finish my thoughts, Marcus repeated, "The world is changing, my friend. We're in a world now where thousands of single and divorced women have as much money as the men. They didn't have it like that during the first sexual revolution in the sixties. But now they do."

Marcus didn't have a wife or children either. I had been suspect of his sexuality over the years. However, I had been around him and enough gorgeous women to at least believe that he was straight. Or he could have been bisexual. Hell, he could have suspected the same about me.

Finally, I said, "You don't expect me to go for this, do you? I'm not under any financial constraints. I make sure to keep my life simple enough to stay away from all of that."

He put a hand on my shoulder and said, "I'm just introducing you to the idea, my friend. You've always been one to make your own decisions. So I'll only open the opportunity for you to stay at the mansion if you want, and to participate in whatever you would like, as long as you remember to remain safe and sound with it. I tell everyone that. You only have one life to live in this world, so always protect the family jewels."

I listened and nodded to him. "Sexual revolution, huh?" I had been thinking about that myself. Maybe I was a little behind the times. In all my years of being around beautiful women, I hadn't even been in a threesome yet.

Mr. Vissel nodded back to me. He said, "That's what we're in right now, a new sexual revolution. It's almost anything goes; older women, younger men, celebrities and groupies, athletes and businesswomen. Now we had a lot of that before, but now the money is much greater. And you got a lot of women now who are willing to pay for entertainment services with the guys they see in magazines."

He said, "So I'm just getting you up to speed on the new world order, my friend. It's out here for the taking."

I thought about what had just gone on a week ago between me and Rachel in Atlanta and smiled. I couldn't deny the talk of a new sexual revolution, I just wasn't a major participant in it.

Mr. Vissel stood from his chair and said, "Well, let me get back to this interview. But you just think about things, no pressure, just thinking.

"There's a lot of money out here in sex," he told me. "Sex is economy and depression proof. There's nothing in the world that will get a man or woman up for the task of the day like a good piece of dick or pussy. And no matter how much I tried to fight it over the years, it always came back to the basics; sex and money makes the world go 'round."

He smiled and put his shades back on. Before he walked out of the room, he turned and asked me, "Are you still in contact with ah . . . what was her name?" He stopped and rose his hand to his temple to think about it.

"Andrea?" he asked me.

I was startled by it, but I kept my cool. I wanted to know what he would say about her without being biased. So I told him, "That girl has been missing for years." It was the truth. I had only recently bumped into her again.

He nodded. He said, "She's a beautiful girl; showed up here in tears years ago, just trying to make anything happen for herself. I felt sorry for her. But she met a few people and got back on her feet. We called her The Goddess back then. All of the rich guys wanted her. She even hooked up with one of my favorite girls here and they became real close before they both left us for good."

He said, "I wish them well," and that was it. He walked out of the room to leave me there to ponder everything.

Brazil, I thought to myself. Andrea had met her at Mr. Vissel's place. And if they had met each other there, I'm sure that nothing I could have said to her would have been out of the ordinary. She had been turned out already.

"The Goddess, huh?" I repeated out loud. I was shocked, but there was no denying it. Andrea fit the bill; she was a gorgeous woman who had sadly never made the cut as a model.

I thought again and immediately checked my cell phone messages.

Sure enough, among other calls, Andrea had left me a message: "I didn't know you were gonna be in Chicago tonight. Call me back when you get this."

I stopped the message and realized that I could have had my first threesome in Chicago that night. Now I knew that she and Brazil had talked about it, but I didn't feel excited about it anymore. I felt guilty and ashamed for Andrea. Had I officially made her my woman and taken care of her years ago . . .

But who's to say she wouldn't't still have been searching while she was with me? I asked myself. Andrea was simply insatiable. I couldn't have stopped her from feeling incomplete. That was just how she was.

I must have sat there for ten minutes still thinking about it. I couldn't move. Andrea falling into high-end prostitution was worse to me than her failed marriage, miscarriage, and abortion. Neither child had made it to the world, but she was alive, and selling herself to whoever had the money. How was I supposed to take that? I don't believe Mr. Vissel knew how much I still thought about her.

Damn, I mumbled to myself. Andrea's revelation had taken a lot out of me. The information of her recent past was punishing me in every way.

"Hey, what's going on? Why are you still sitting here?" Billy popped his head into the room and asked me.

I shook it off. "I was just thinking, man. There's a lot to think about in this place."

He laughed and said, "Tell me about it. But hey, more women are out there now, man. I think you wanna see this. If you think Tapioca and Cream are hot, wait till you see the Brazilians. Their bodies are just . . ." He couldn't even get his words together. "Man!"

"How many of them are there?" I asked him.

"Five."

I wasn't really interested in entertaining, but I didn't want to seem like a glum party pooper either.

"So, what exactly are we supposed to do with these women? I mean, are they models or what?"

Billy looked at me before he answered. "Well, they are models, but a lot of them are still in training, you know. But the way it works is this: if a photographer shoots a girl and takes her pictures to some of the designers who like her, then she gets upgraded immediately. So, it's almost like a minor league baseball system for all of them."

I said, "And how does this thing work monetarily?"

"Well, everybody pays a membership fee, or gets a frequent-visitor pass, and everything that leaves here has to be paid for. And we own all photography copyrights."

I listened and picked up on it. "So, all of the models get paid from percentages of the membership fees?"

"Yeah, and then they get extra if they do anything else."

"Like tips, huh?" I joked with a smile.

"A lot of people can only dream about the tips these girls get," Billy told me.

"What about the guys, they're in business here, too, right?"

He nodded as if it pained him. "Yeah, but realistically, us guys are never gonna have it like the girls. I mean, I do pretty well, but then when I compare it to what the girls are able to do . . ."

Enough said. Modeling and prostitution had always been more lucrative for women. Guys made their big money in corporate business, sports, and all other forms of entertainment. Then they go out and pay women to perform for them.

I said, "So why would I be interested in this if the women are making all the money? I may as well keep doing what I've been doing."

"Well, you know how women are, they're inconsistent. First they want to be here, then they don't. And they're always coming back and forth after makeups and breakups with their significant others. I mean, you know how that goes. What guy wants to see his woman being looked at and hit on all day while she's shooting pictures? So this atmosphere is definitely not for everyone."

I nodded to him. I then stood up to leave. "Okay, let's go see these Brazilians."

Billy got excited like a teenager with a brand-new car. He said, "I'm dying to see which one you think is the hottest."

I just grinned and walked out behind him.

When I viewed the Brazilian women surrounding the pool area, I seriously wondered if *Sports Illustrated* would be interested. Mr. Vissel's ideas became full blown with those Brazilians modeling exotic swimsuits. On one end, I was proud that all five of them were beautiful women of color, but then I was saddened in knowing that they would all be up for sale afterward. There was a certain respectable protection that went along with a snobbish supermodel. There was an understanding that only a few chosen guys could get anywhere close to them. But Marcus was making it possible for any geek with a bank account who could pay the membership fee to walk into the mansion and sweep a dream girl off her feet for the night.

I leaned and whispered to Billy, "How often do the prettiest girls in here say yes to a guy?"

He looked at me and answered, "Some of them never say yes. You have a few girls in here who only show up to work with the best photographers, and model in some of the top designer clothes."

He said, "They look at it as strictly business, and they stay focused on what they came to get out of it."

That made me feel a little better about the idea. It wasn't mandatory that a girl sell herself, it was only an option.

I looked back over at Mr. Vissel, and he was still enjoying his interview under the umbrella table with the woman from *Esquire* magazine.

Billy said, "These interviews are a way of attracting more members who can afford to be here."

He sure knew a lot about the operation. I guess his young, boyishness didn't stop him from knowing what he needed to know.

He asked me, "So, which one do you think is the hottest?"

I looked again at the Brazilians and answered, "The one in the sunflower swimsuit with the mole on her cheek."

Billy responded, "Exactly! I mean, what is it about those moles that make them so damn sexy?"

"They're small," I told him. "But if they were as big as major pimples, you'd feel differently about them."

He laughed and admitted it. "Yeah, you're right about that. A big zit on a girl's face is the ultimate turn-off."

I grinned. I guess Billy was young after all.

AFTER A WHILE I became more comfortable in the carnival atmosphere, but that still didn't mean I would agree to stay there. By the time it got close to six o'clock, I was about ready to go.

"Are you gonna try and hook up with anyone before you go?" Billy asked me. He said, "Your date is on the house, compliments of Mr. Vissel. You still want Tapioca and Cream, or you want the Brazilian with the mole and a friend?"

I looked at him and asked, "I thought you told me it's up to them."

"It is, but they still have to be able to hang out with you to make up their minds."

"So they would just go out on a date with me to see if they want to deal with me or not?"

"Basically, yeah. If they do they do, and if they don't they don't."

"What about them protecting themselves? You could be dealing with a maniac."

"Well, we haven't had any maniacs yet. We've had a couple of guys who left their wives for models, a couple more who became obsessive, and a few more who are no longer allowed on the mansion grounds because of a lack of satisfactory payments, but other than those few bad apples, Mr. Vissel's been managing quite well."

I nodded to him. "I'll think about it and call you on it before the night is over."

"No rush, man. Some of these girls stay up all night looking for something to do. They'll be here."

We began to make our way back through the crowd, and I noticed more male celebrities and athletes around the place, watching. I won't name any names, but I looked at Billy and asked him, "How normal is this?" referring to the presence of the popular high-rollers.

"Oh, this is very normal. It's Friday. Friday through Sunday are the best. But the girls I told you about who are strictly business, they usually come Monday through Wednesday to avoid the temptations. They just want to take the best pictures they can take."

"Has it worked?"

He shrugged. "Well, you're a professional model, right. And from what I've seen, it has all to do with what the designers are looking for, not so much with how you carry herself or your reputation. I mean, you could be a perfect angel, but if no one is buying your image, then what use are you to the designers?"

I nodded. "That's true."

We made our way back to the front door and retrieved the Lamborghini. As we cruised back to the airport area, I was just itching to call Andrea back. It was after eight o'clock Chicago time, so I knew I could catch her before a party or whatever. However, I didn't want to talk to her in front of Billy, so I had to wait until I reached the hotel room for privacy.

When we reached the Westin Hotel, Billy asked me, "So, what do you want to do? You wanna go hang out with a few of the models or what?"

I passed on it. "Nah, I'm still feeling a little jet lag, so I need to rest. Then I'm supposed to hook up with the niece of an old friend of mine later on. They'll be on their way up from San Diego."

"Well, have them come out with us. We'll make it into a big party."

That was the last thing I would do with TaShay, being as curious as she was. Mr. Vissel and his people were not something she needed to even know about.

"Nah, that's all right, but I'll let you know if we get bored."

"Yeah, you do that," Billy told me.

I got back to the room and immediately called Chicago to track down Andrea and Brazil. I had more than a few questions to ask them, but I had to slow down and remain poised. I had been the one to send Andrea scrambling to find herself, so I had to remain aware of that.

"Are you still in Chicago?" she answered the phone and asked me. She actually sounded pleased to hear from me.

"What if I am?"

"Are you?"

"I wish I were," I told her.

I leaned back on my comfortable king-size bed and relaxed.

"Why?" she asked me.

I said, "I saw Brazil at the airport last night, and I started thinking about you guys all over again."

"Well, how come you didn't tell me you would be here. You should have called last night."

"What would have happened if I called last night?" I questioned. "Is it the same thing that will happen on Monday when I'm on my way back to Atlanta?" I hinted.

"Is that what you want?" she asked me.

"Does that mean you're willing?"

We were playing a cat-and-mouse game.

"Maybe."

"Did you tell Brazil what I was thinking?"

"Of course."

"So, the idea wasn't repellent to you then."

"Like I said, you're not the first man to be intrigued by two women who are girlfriends."

"I know that's right," I told her. "So, where did you meet Brazil again? I was thinking when I saw her at the airport last night that she has model looks herself. Did she ever used to model?"

I figured I would take it real slow and confirm what I felt I needed to without a direct attack.

"Yeah, she did a little something."

"For men's magazines?"

"Why would you say that?"

"Well, she still has more body than most fashion models."

"And more body automatically makes you a men's magazine tease?"

"Usually," I answered. "Was she?"

"You could say something like that."

I chuckled. "I'm surprised you didn't tell me it's none of my business again."

"It's really not, but she doesn't seem to mind it."

"Yeah, she's pretty cool with me. She seemed cool last night, but I didn't know that from when we first met."

"She's always protective of me when she first meets people."

"So, you guys meet a lot of people together? You know, usually a girlfriend couple keeps things to themselves," I assumed.

"Why, because you figure we have something to hide?"

"You tell me. Do you?"

She paused for a moment. I wasn't going to say anything to alarm her. I wanted to take it slow and easy with her. I had all night to get to the truth.

"Where are you right now?" she asked. Andrea had a habit of doing that whenever she didn't want to answer something; she would just change the subject.

"I'm on anther photo shoot out in the Bay Area."

"San Francisco?"

"Yeah."

"I love that city," she told me. "Now I'm thinking about going to Tampa Bay for a boat party."

"A boat party? Who invited you?" I asked her.

"Some friends of friends."

I had never been on a Tampa Bay boat party before, but I had heard about them. It made me curious. I wouldn't mind a boat party myself. I had been on a riverboat party before in Pittsburgh, Pennsylvania, but that was about it. I hadn't even tried the riverboats in Cleveland, only a state away from home.

"Well, let me know how it is when you get back," I told Andrea. "I might want to go on the next one."

"Okay. So, you're gonna be back in Chicago on Monday?"

"I could be, and all I have to do is take a Tuesday-morning flight back out to Atlanta. But that's if I have a reason to stay in Chicago," I hinted.

"Why did you stay in Chicago last night?" she asked me.

"So I could get out to L.A. sooner without killing myself."

"L.A.?" she asked me. "I thought you said you were in San Fran."

"Yeah, my mistake, I'm tripping. I guess I'm always thinking of L.A. when I fly west, just like you normally have to fly out of Chicago or Dallas–Fort Worth when you're flying from the East Coast.

"When was the last time you've been out here on the West Coast?" I asked her. I took a breath and kept my cool after my slipup.

"I'm always back and forth," she told me.

"What about Brazil?"

"What about her?"

"Does she travel a lot, too?"

"I'll let you ask her that on Monday."

I paused. "So, you're telling me that you guys will give me a reason to stay the night."

"If that's what you want," she answered.

Now I figured the truth would come out in time. There was no sense in forcing it over the phone. I was still curious about a three-some anyway.

I said, "Okay, I'll make that happen then."

"Well, stay safe in San Fran and call me when you get here on Monday."

Just like that, Andrea was off the phone, and I was pretty much set for my first experience with two women, though I still didn't know how I felt about it. I just laid there and held the cell phone in my hand for a moment. Then I decided to call TaShay to see where she was with her friend. I still had a couple of days and nights out in L.A. to assess my feelings before I faced Andrea in Chicago. There was no sense in me stressing. I had to take my mind off of it and enjoy myself in L.A.

So I called TaShay and got her on the first ring.

"Hey, we're on our way," she told me. "And my girlfriend had the nerve to ask me if you looked as good in real life as you do in pictures."

I smiled. *Girls will be girls,* I thought. "So what did you tell her?"

"I told her ass, 'Hell yeah!' Then she started talking about male models being gay and shit."

It was a total change of pace from the conversation with Andrea. I could hear TaShay's girlfriend laughing and carrying on in the background.

"Why would you tell him that?" she whined loud enough for me to hear her.

"Because you did say that, and he's not gay."

I could already see what kind of night I would have with them. It was time to get my vitamins out, and that scared the hell out of me.

"How old is your girlfriend?" I asked.

"Oh, she's twenty-two, and she's a hot bitch; black and Japanese," she said. "You know how Kimora Lee Simmons looks? Well, my girl Tan makes her look like the ugly duckling in the family."

They Got Me

I TOLD TASHAY and her friend that I didn't have any transportation, so they were headed straight to the hotel to pick me up. That was better than having Billy chauffeur me around in a yellow Lamborghini and drive the girls into insanity. I didn't need all that attention, nor did I want Billy around me to influence anything. I planned to keep a cool, adult head around the girls and keep them safe. Billy would have been as wild as they were, or worse.

I didn't even know what to wear around the girls, so I kept it basic: a clean white T-shirt, blue jeans, my comfortable brown leather shoes, and a sports jacket. The catch for me was always the cologne. I traveled with at least five different scents at all times. I didn't wear the Cool Water much, but since the girls were young, I figured I'd splash on the old, Snoop Doggy Dogg brand.

By the time the girls arrived at the hotel, I was already waiting outside for them at the front entrance, while getting myself plenty of attention from the Angelenos. I loved when pretty women stared; it always made me feel up to the task of romance.

"Excuse me, do you play football for the Chargers?" a smiling Latina woman asked me. Her two friends were milling around in the background. I guess she was the bold one sent to do their dirty work.

"No, but thanks for the compliment. I did play some basketball in high school, but that's about it. I make my living taking pictures now," I told her.

"Taking pictures? You're a model or something?"

"Yeah. We all gotta make our money some way."

She continued to smile. "Well, it must be nice, man."

"Yeah, it's real nice; nice and big," I told her.

She looked at me in shock and started laughing. Then she waved herself.

"Oooh, man, too hot for me."

"What did he say?" her two girlfriends stepped up and asked her.

"He said everything is nice . . . and big."

They screamed out laughing and got a chuckle out of me.

Before anything else could happen with the Latinas, TaShay and her friend Tan pulled up in front of me in a dark Honda Civic.

"We didn't keep you waiting too long, did we?" TaShay asked me through the window.

I raised my index finger and thumb and told her, "Just a little bit."

She looked at me and grinned. "That's all I want, too."

Her friend Tan broke out laughing from the driver's side of the car. I couldn't see her that good yet, but she sure laughed hard. She laughed like she had no shame.

I said, "What are you laughing at? Get on out the car and let me see what you look like."

"What?" Tan responded. "He don't know me like that."

I could see what kind of broad she was, and if I didn't straighten her ass out immediately, it would be a long night for all of us. So I walked around to the driver's side of the car and just stared into her face for a minute. And damn if she didn't look good. Her face was much thinner than Kimora Lee Simmons's; she was golden brown, with extra dark eyes, and her hair was either dyed light or naturally light. However, she had a rough edge about her. I could read it in those fierce eyes of hers. I don't think she liked guys that much. She liked girls, girls she could bug out with and overrule.

Instead of saying anything confrontational, I nodded my head and told her, "Yeah, you look good," and that was it. I planned to freeze her out for awhile and see how she responded to that.

She caught me off-guard when she responded, "Yeah, you look good, too, but that don't mean you can boss me around."

I joked and asked her, "You wanna boss me around?"

She said, "That's the only way I get down."

Her bold comment made TaShay laugh. I imagined that both of them together would be something else to handle.

I said, "Okay, so, where are we off to?"

"TaShay knows all of that. Ask her. I'm just the driver."

"Is that all you're gonna do tonight?" I teased her.

She looked me up and down and said, "We'll see."

"What I got to do with it?" I asked her.

She made it appear as if her decisions depended on me.

"You don't have nothing to do with it," she snapped at me.

I figured I needed to quit while I was ahead with that girl. But before I did, I stated, "I hope somebody gives you what you're needing."

TaShay laughed so hard she had to stick her face out the window for more air. Even Tan was forced to laugh. It was a perfect comeback line, but I wasn't trying to score any cool points with it, I was just letting the girl know I was no amateur.

I walked back around to TaShay's side of the car to climb in.

She said, "You wanna sit up front, so you can stretch your legs out?"

I thought about Tan. "Are you sure your friend wants me sitting next to her?"

Tan said, "You can sit up front. I won't bite you."

She said she won't bite, huh? I thought about it . . . and left it alone. "Okay, I'll sit up front then," I commented, staying on the safe side.

TaShay climbed into the backseat and let me take the front.

"Bitch, you could have just gotten out of the car instead of kicking me," Tan cursed her. I couldn't believe that girl. She really needed it bad, a long, stiff one to calm her down.

TaShay didn't even respond to her.

Before I climbed into the passenger seat up front, I looked back to my Latina sisters. "I'll see you guys around," I told them.

"Okay," the ringleader spoke up again. "You have a good time tonight."

"Oh, I will," I told her, and I climbed into the Honda Civic.

Tan looked at me and said, "You're an all-out ladies' man, huh?"

"Who told you that?"

She smiled and grunted, "Hmmph," before she looked away from me and drove off.

I felt a bit old hanging out with two college-aged girls. Not that I didn't date young women, but most of the younger women I dated acted older than their age. I figured TaShay could hang with an older crowd, too, but definitely not while she had Tan around. I wondered what TaShay's aunt and mother thought of the girl.

Before I knew it, we were flying up Interstate 10 for West Hollywood.

"So, where are we going?" I turned and asked TaShay in the back.

"There's this new club called The Palace off Santa Monica that I wanted to go to."

"What do you have, a fake ID?" I asked her.

"Of course she does," Tan answered me.

"Is that the only place you want to go?"

"Not if it's boring," Tan answered again.

If I bothered her in the beginning, she was definitely giving me payback. It seemed as if TaShay was allowing her to irritate me on purpose, just to see how much of it I could stand.

I leaned back and relaxed without another word, and listened to their selection of music to stay out of trouble. The rapper 50 Cent was the new popular choice of music in town.

"You think he looks good?" TaShay asked Tan.

"I mean, who really cares?" Tan commented. "If he gets money like that now, then that's all the girls will care about."

I couldn't help it. I asked, "What about you?"

Tan smiled and said, "I like the money, too."

I nodded. "So, if a guy has the right amount of cash, he's good-looking regardless?"

"No, I didn't say that. I said nobody's gonna care what he looks like."

"Okay, but would you have kids with him?" TaShay butted in.

"If you're in to him like that."

"She's talking about you," I stated.

Tan grinned and answered, "I wouldn't, no. I have pretty girl genes to protect."

TaShay laughed from the back.

I said, "That's interesting. But you would do him for the money?"

"I mean, how many girls wouldn't? Let's take a poll," she asked me.

I said, "But what if he wanted to boss you around and tell you how to do it?"

"Oh, well, we would have problems with that."

I wondered how serious she was about staying in control, and I was interested in testing her willpower on that. I also wondered how she had slipped past Paula's radar. Did she play a good girl around TaShay's family or what?

WE ARRIVED at the West Hollywood nightclub slightly after ten, and there was already a line outside.

"Oh, shit, this place is poppin' off early!" TaShay commented.

I looked at the line of twenty-somethings eagerly waiting to get in, and I was immediately turned off by it. I hadn't been made to wait in line for a party in years. I was a special invited guest at most of the parties I went to.

"You think you can introduce yourself to the guys at the front door and get us in ahead of this line?" TaShay asked me. We drove around the corner from the club in search of a parking spot.

I didn't want to try anything extra to get us in if the end result would be a failure. At the same time, I would look insignificant if I didn't at least attempt something. So I came up with a plan.

"I'll see what I can do," I answered them.

We found our parking spot halfway down the block and climbed out of the car to walk back to the club. When they stepped out, both girls were dressed casually in blue jeans, attention-getting tops, high heels, and small purses. In fact, we all looked good together and that strengthened my simple plan.

As we walked back to the club, I noticed that the girls walked slow on purpose to whisper comments and giggle behind my back. I could only imagine what they were giggling about.

Yeah, they're asking for it, I told myself.

When we rounded the corner and got closer to the club, TaShay asked me again, "So, what are you gonna do?"

"Wait on the side for a minute while I talk to the guys at the door," I told her.

"Okay."

As soon as we approached the front entrance, I walked up beside one of the three bouncers dressed in all black. I said, "I'm in a bind here, brother."

He looked at me and asked, "What's the problem?"

"You see these two models over here?" I moved just enough so he could see past me.

He peeped them both and nodded. With their heels on, TaShay and Tan both had the towering height of runway models.

"Yeah," the bouncer told me.

"Well, they're not used to waiting in line, and most places they go to have cut lines. So I was willing to offer a hundred dollars for the three of us to walk on in, or they'll choose to go someplace else, because I know they don't want to wait."

He nodded to me again. "Hold on." He stepped away from me to talk to the other guys. The other bouncer looked toward my girls before one of them slid inside the club for a minute. When he returned, he gave the first bouncer the OK, and he walked back over to inform me.

"All right, come on."

I looked toward TaShay and Tan, gave them a hand motion, and that was it. We all flowed into the club ahead of the line.

Once we were in, Tan said, "It's good to be the king."

I just grinned at her. I figured she would pay me back later, and with interest.

This place was a large room with several elevations for VIP. Disco lights were everywhere, flashing bright colors into your eyes. It was multicultural like Miami, with all ages. The VIP elevations were already occupied by athletes, movie stars, and people who were known for spending big money.

Tan looked up to the VIP elevations in envy. There were six elevations; four small, two large. They were all in clear view with gates and guards at the entrances.

"How do we get up there?" Tan asked me. I knew it was coming. I was just about ready to tell her ass that I was no king, and that I was only in there to please them. Then I thought about what Andrea had told me again: *If you're gonna continue to deal with women like you do, then you gotta learn how to loosen up and give them more of what they want.*

So I took a deep breath and told her, "I'll be right back." I walked back over to the entrance and asked the girls behind the money counter, "How much is a VIP band?"

"Twenty-five for the yellow and fifty for the orange," they told me.

"What's the difference?"

"The yellow bands are only for the two large areas, but the orange bands can get you on the four exclusive areas."

I shook my head and smiled while pulling out my wallet again. Parties had always been a racket to me. All you had to do was use someone's vanity against them, and they would pay all kinds of money. Fortunately, money wasn't an issue for me.

"The exclusive areas are only as space is available," she continued. "So once they get crowded, we can't guarantee you any room up there."

That wasn't an issue either. We were there early and they still had room. So I went ahead and paid a hundred fifty dollars for three orange VIP bands and returned to the party.

Tan saw the orange bands in my hand before I even reached them. "It's good to be the king," she repeated.

TaShay was excited about it as well. "Thanks," she told me.

They pulled me right along to the entrance of the VIP area. We showed the guards our orange bands and made our way up a spiraling staircase to the elevated area that overlooked the rest of the nightclub. We were about fifteen feet high. The ceiling of the place must have been around forty feet.

"Wow, this is it!" TaShay exclaimed.

I had seen better, but each nightclub had it's own unique flavor to it. They even had a bar on the elevated area.

TaShay and Tan got to ordering drinks and dancing immediately. Their favorite guy, 50 Cent was back on.

"We gon' party like it's your birthday . . ."

As long as they were having a good time, I figured I would just relax and enjoy the setting.

"Excuse me, aren't you a model?" a woman asked me. She looked Indian to me, in silky brown skin and thick dark hair. All she needed was a dot on her forehead and the shimmering clothes.

I said, "Yeah, you read a lot of magazines?"

"I love magazines," she told me. "I'm working on putting one together now for East Indian design. Our idea is to put everyone in East Indian clothes to cross them over."

She pulled out a business card in a flash and handed it to me.

"My name is Donjha."

Her business card had colorful Indian designs twisting and twirling around the edges. She was a design assistant at *Influence* magazine.

I nodded to her. Then I stood beside her and asked, "Do you think these two girls have the winning look to help cross over some of your Indian designs?"

Donjha followed my eyes to TaShay and Tan. She spotted them and smiled, nodding to me excitedly.

"Yeah, they're hot."

I looked them over for myself, dancing only a few feet away from me, and they did look hot. They both had that winning appeal on the dance floor. Other people were watching them dance as well.

Just out of curiosity, I asked Donjha, "If you could only chose one, which one would you choose?"

She frowned at me and shook her head. She said, "They're different, but they're complementary. And they have the same size. That's great. I would use both of them.

"Are you modeling with them?" she asked me.

"I modeled with one, but I just met the other."

"Well, we could use all of you. Just give me a call on Monday and I could introduce you to the editor. She's real cool. Her name is Sarah."

I had to be frank with her about all of that. I wasn't a successful model for nothing.

I said, "Well, you know, I don't really model on the start-up levels anymore. And I would have to talk to their people about them."

Donjha looked at me and smiled. "We already know what the prices are. We want to go after nothing but the best."

She went on to name-drop several supermodels, some of whom I recognized, and some I didn't. But she was losing my interest. Name-dropping only counted with me if she was using known photographers or fashion designers.

"Just call me on Monday, and we'll talk," she told me. That was the right move, let the editor talk to me about their rates; everything else was just hot air.

As soon as Donjha moved on, TaShay danced over to me with an apple martini in her hand. She asked me, "What was that about? Someone hitting on you already?" she teased.

I shook my head. "Nah, she was all about business." I showed her the business card. "She wanted all of us to model for her magazine."

TaShay eyed me and said, "That would be fun. All of us together, huh?"

I had already thought about the possibility of a threesome with TaShay and her friend. I thought about that from the moment I talked to her on the phone earlier, but I was still trying to push the idea to the back of my mind. I didn't want to go there.

I said, "Well, I don't model without the bills being paid. So, I'll just have someone call and see what they're talking about."

TaShay grabbed my hand and said, "We're not here for business anyway. Let's dance."

She pulled me on the dance floor to a new song from Ashanti, and she and Tan sandwiched me with reckless grinding.

"You're the envy of every man in here now," Tan spoke into my right ear.

They started freaking me something good. That led me to believe that they had experienced it all before. They worked together too good for it to be spontaneous. They knew exactly what they were doing.

By the third hour and the fourth drink, the place was jam-packed with A-list celebrities breaking out from a back room off the main dance floor; Jamie Foxx, Shaq, Lindsay Lohan, Paris Hilton. No wonder the prices were so high.

I mean, this place was rocking! The club was in an all-out frenzy, but I was worn out and ready to leave.

"Where are they coming from?" Tan questioned of the big stars. They weren't up in our section.

"It must be another VIP area down there," TaShay answered.

They both looked at me. "How do we get in there?"

That one was beyond my reach. There were VIPs, and then there were superstars. I didn't want to embarrass myself with my ranking, so it was time to go.

I said, "Hey, let's ask and then get on out of here. I still have a photo shoot tomorrow."

Tan looked at me and said, "You wanna leave? It's just getting started now."

This girl had been getting attention all night long, and she still wanted more. I knew I couldn't argue with her without starting a fight, so I talked to TaShay in private about it.

I said, "Look, I know you guys came to party all night and all of that, so I might just take a taxi out of here." I knew TaShay wasn't as starstruck as Tan was, so it was her move.

She grabbed my arms and said, "No, you're not taking a taxi." She was a little tipsy, too. They were both tipsy. I was only buzzed.

TaShay stepped on my feet with her heels and whispered, "We can have our own party."

I said, "I don't think Tan is up for leaving, and she's the one who drove us here."

I just wanted to get the hell out of there before the girl started going mad for the bigger fish and pissing me off. I never liked that pecking-order shit unless I was the one doing the pecking.

"She'll leave," TaShay assured me. "Let me go talk to her."

She broke away from me and squeezed through the crowd toward Tan. I waited there for her and thought about the both of them again. Did I want to get involved, or did I want to send them both home?

I looked around at all the game players in the club and figured, *If I don't get involved with them, there are plenty of guys in here who will.*

Just give them what they want, I told myself again.

TaShay came back holding Tan's hand. "She just wants to meet a few people, then she'll be ready to go."

I looked at Tan, who may have been more than tipsy, and she winked at me.

This girl is ready to get in any kind of trouble she can get into, I told myself. I still didn't want to be embarrassed by her drunken assertion, so I planned to stay clear of them while they went star searching.

I said, "All right, well you guys stay safe and sound, and I'll be waiting for you near the entrance."

I surely wasn't planning on standing around while they squeezed, and pushed, and begged to get near Jamie Foxx and crew. I even heard that Will Smith was in the building. Shit, a guy has to have his own pride, you know.

I was standing there minding my own business when a familiar face walked up to greet me.

"Long time no see, stranger."

"Hey, how are you doing?" I asked her. It was Shauna Eubanks, the first California woman I ever slept with. I met her on my first trip out to L.A. in the early nineties. Shauna was a budding model herself back then, and she still looked tight and good. A lot of folks my age had gotten loose around the belly, but she had kept it all together and was wearing a red, mid-thigh skirt to prove it. In fact, I met her through Marcus Vissel.

She said, "I've been doing my thing, I can't complain. But you know I have two kids now."

It seemed like everyone was throwing that in my face just to say that I was getting old and useless or something. Or maybe that was just how I perceived it.

I joked and said, "They're not mine are they?"

I caught her off-guard with that. She chuckled and said, "Hey, man, you don't want to play that game. Do you have any kids?"

"Not that I know of," I told her.

She eyed me and asked, "You're still loose like that?"

I shook it all off and said, "Nah, I'm just bullshitting. I'm still out here in full career mode. In fact, Marcus flew me out."

She gave me the eye again. "Have you been over to his mansion?"

I smiled at her. "I was over there earlier today."

She smiled back and said, "Things have changed a lot, haven't they?"

I thought about it before I spoke. I said, "Not really. If you think about it, we've always been hos and we've always had opportunities. People just respond to it differently when they get older."

She laughed and said, "You know what, that's so true. Now let me get back over to this man before he starts thinking I'm ready to fuck you over here for old time's sake. And you're right, ain't a damn thing changed."

She said, "Well, I just wanted to stop over and say hi to you."

I nodded to her. "Thanks."

"So, who are you in here with, yourself?" she asked me before she left.

I grinned and answered, "Trouble." I wanted to remind myself as much.

Shauna laughed. "Well, you need to stay out of that." And she faded back into the party.

TaShay and Tan appeared soon after.

I asked them, "Did you get it all out of your system."

"Fuck them motherfuckers," Tan spat. "They ain't no-fuckin'-body."

I figured it was the alcohol talking. She definitely wasn't driving me anywhere.

TaShay grinned and said, "We couldn't get past the guards."

Of course you couldn't, I thought. There was too many people in there. The stars would have gotten mobbed if security didn't do what they were supposed to do.

"So, are we ready to go now?" I asked them.

TaShay nodded.

Tan said, "You're driving."

"I already know," I told her.

"How you know?" she asked me while we headed for the door.

"I wasn't gonna let you drive."

She looked at me and said, "Well, how are we getting home then?"

"Somebody's gonna have to sober up," I told her. "I know I'm not driving down to San Diego tonight."

"Nobody's driving to San Diego tonight," TaShay told the both of us. We were back outside the club on the pavement. Neither one of them could walk straight. Tan even started walking in the wrong direction.

I said, "The car is this way."

"Oh, shit, yeah," she mumbled.

TaShay started to laugh at her.

"What are you laughing at, bitch! You're drunk, too?"

"Not as drunk as you are."

It must have taken us half an hour just to get back to the car.

As soon as we all climbed in, I adjusted the seat behind the wheel to drive. TaShay sat in the passenger seat, and Tan crashed in the back.

"So, where are we going now?" Tan asked me.

TaShay answered, "I already told you where we're going, girl."

"Well, he didn't even invite us yet."

Obviously, they had a conversation in reference to me.

TaShay looked in my face and said, "Terrance, are you gonna invite us to stay with you for a minute?"

I started the car with the intention of driving back to my hotel. I had left my cell phone in the room on purpose to keep myself away from too many bothersome distractions. But at that moment, I began to wonder when or if TaShay's aunt or mother would call her on her cell phone about her whereabouts. She was still only nineteen.

I asked her, "How long can you stay out?"

"Um, I'm over Tan's house tonight," she answered with a chuckle.

Tan heard that and fell out laughing from the backseat.

"You ain't over my damn house."

I said, "In other words, you two are just out on the town for the night."

"Basically," Tan answered.

TaShay reached over and squeezed my right thigh. "We just need to lay down for a couple of hours, that's all."

Tan was silent for a change.

I nodded my head, thinking everything over as I began to drive. What could I say? If I really didn't feel comfortable with things, I guess I could get them their own room. But how would TaShay respond to that? I could see that she wanted to tempt me.

I said, "I'll see if I can get an extra room there for you guys to crash in, and you can leave in the morning."

Tan responded, "What? You don't want us in your room? That's a first. Guys usually try to break their arms off to get to us, and fail at it.

But she wanted this. She had me drive all the way to L.A. for it, and this is how you treat her?"

Tan was running her drunken mouth all over the place. But TaShay got silent. She removed her hand from my thigh and looked away from me.

"Okay," she mumbled.

Damn! I thought to myself. *Here we go again. She wants something that I don't want.*

I went back and forth about the idea for the entire drive to the hotel, and Tan was still busy running her mouth.

"If he don't want it, he don't want it," she commented. "You can't force a man to take what he don't want."

"Would you shut up?" TaShay finally snapped at her. We were pulling up to the parking lot of the hotel.

Tan shouted, "Girl, don't fuckin' get mad at me because he don't wanna do shit! It ain't my damn fault!"

I had no idea the city of San Diego could raise such an unruly girl. The next thing I knew, they were ready to get in each other's faces inside the car. I rushed to park in an open space as quickly as possible so I could get them out of the car and separate then.

I grabbed TaShay as soon as we all jumped out.

"She's been acting like an asshole all night," she shouted about her friend.

I looked her in her eyes to calm her down. I said, "Wait a minute. What happened to the mature girl that I met in Chicago? Now all of this extracurricular hostility is crazy. You are both here, you are both drunk, and you both need to rest. Now I don't even trust putting you in a separate room," I told them both.

"Well, you can give me my keys and I can drive back home then," Tan commented. She could barely stand up straight.

I said, "Okay. Let me see you walk a straight line."

She actually tried it, too. She was walking sideways like a broken steering wheel. TaShay watched her friend and started laughing.

"Her ass can't drive nowhere."

"Yes I can, too."

I shook my head and took the girl's hand. I had TaShay in my left, and Tan in my right.

"Let's go," I told them.

"Why, you don't want us?" Tan responded.

I shook my head again with no comment. I had to get those girls out of Dodge as quickly as possible. It would have been insane for me to take them anywhere near the front desk. They would have called the cops on us all. So I got them inside the hotel through the side door with my room key, and we made it straight to the elevators on the way to my room.

"I gotta pee so fuckin' bad," Tan said out of the blue.

I was convinced; the girl was crazy. I picked up the pace with them as soon as we made it to my floor, and I rushed them to the room to stop Tan from having an accident. That would have been the last straw for me.

I opened the door, and she nearly fell into the bathroom to make it.

"Oh my God!" she expressed as she relieved herself. I even had to close the bathroom door behind her.

TaShay laughed and fell out on the bed. "I gotta go next," she told me.

It was gonna be another very long night. I could see it. They were making me extratired already.

As soon as Tan walked out from the bathroom, she asked me, "Did they give you a minibar in here?"

"You don't need anymore to drink," I told her.

She looked at me and frowned. "I'm not talking about that. I just need a candy bar or something."

"Do they have all-night room service here?" TaShay asked me as she stood from the bed.

"No," I answered her.

"Damn, I could eat a steak right now," she stated before she walked into the bathroom.

"Yeah, she could eat a steak all right, a man steak," Tan joked.

"I heard that," TaShay responded from inside the bathroom. At least she had closed the door behind her.

Tan helped herself to a Snickers from the minibar.

"Oh, you don't mind, do you?" she asked me after the fact.

"No, go right ahead," I told her. "Take all you want."

"Oh, you got jokes," she responded as she chomped into it.

When TaShay walked back out from the bathroom, we were all there and wondering what was next.

"Are there any more Snickers?" TaShay asked her friend.

Tan chuckled with her mouth full, and she pointed to me.

"There he go right there. Go unwrap him."

TaShay got silly and actually went after my clothes.

She said, "You gon' stop me?"

I got curious. Just how far was she willing to go?

I said, "What if I don't?"

Tan got big eyes and said, "Oh, shit, is that a challenge? I know he just didn't challenge you to take his clothes off."

"That's what it sounds like, don't it?" TaShay added.

First she went under my shirt to display my six-pack.

"Oh, shit," Tan repeated. She moved closer to get a closer look.

TaShay went ahead and took my sports jacket and T-shirt off.

"Oh, my God! Now I see what you were talking about," Tan stated.

TaShay laughed and went after my pants. That's when I hesitated. I guess she wasn't afraid, but I was. Because if she took my pants off and felt my dick . . .

"Aw, he bluffed. He ain't serious," Tan commented. She was having a good time just giving the blow by blow.

I looked at her and said, "I don't see you with any of your clothes off, either one of you."

Tan said, "Oh, it ain't nothing but a thing to me. I was raised to be proud of my body." She started taking off her clothes on the spot. Not to be undone, TaShay started taking off her clothes.

"I'm always taking my clothes off for work," she commented.

In just a few minutes, both beautiful girls were standing butt naked in front of me. All I could think about was, *Nineteen and twenty-two. Nineteen and twenty-two.* But they surely had me looking.

Tan said, "Okay, so, what are you gonna do? You just gonna stand there with your pants on?"

I looked at TaShay, and all she did was smile at me. She said, "I am so horny right now. Just let us see it. It's not small, is it?"

Tan said, "Hell no it ain't small. You can't see that bulge in his pants? He's as horny as we are, in here trying to fake it."

I asked, "You're both feeling it?"

Tan answered, "Yeah."

TaShay nodded and grinned.

What the hell was I about to get myself into now? I couldn't make a decision on it, so TaShay took things into her own hands and went after my pants again.

I grabbed her hands and told her, "Wait a minute."

Tan got impatient and pushed me down on the bed.

"Get him 'Shay."

They both jumped on top of me with none of their clothes on.

"Hey, hey, hey-hey," I muttered. Things were getting out of hand.

Before I could stop her, Tan kissed and sucked my right nipple, and TaShay kissed and sucked my left.

"Oh, shit!" I reacted. I never had both of my nipples kissed and sucked at the same time. Then they both worked my crotch with their hands.

"You know you like this shit, so don't even try to stop us," Tan told me.

"For real," TaShay added. She slid her left hand inside my pants to squeeze me.

"Yeah, it is big," she told her friend.

Tan slid her hands down for her own squeeze.

"Oh, yeah, we gon' have fun with this."

"How often have you done this?" I asked them. They were working me like pros again.

"We haven't, we just talked about it a lot," TaShay answered.

Tan ripped my pants wide open and started pulling them down with my drawers. While she did that, TaShay continued to kiss and lick and suck my chest.

I asked, "You haven't done this before?" I didn't want to be the one who turned them out.

Tan said, "You talk too much. I know how to shut you up though."

She had her hand firmly on my shaft. Then she went down on it with her mouth and came back up. Her suck was so sudden and explosive that I jerked like a chicken with his head cut off.

"OH!"

"Hold him down up there 'Shay."

"I got him."

TaShay climbed up my chest and attacked my lips with hers.

"Mmmm," she moaned while she kissed me. "Thank you, big daddy."

Tan worked my lower head with another explosive suck, causing me to jerk forward again. However, TaShay had her full weight against me, holding me down. Then she climbed completely on top of me.

She whispered in my ear, "You can cum in me. I'm on birth control."

What was she talking about? I was only kissing her. I wanted to respond and tell her she was nuts, but I couldn't because Tan was sucking my dick too good. All I could do was shake my head and mumble, "Mmmt-mmm. Naw."

TaShay kissed my neck and sucked on my ear.

"Mmm-hmm," she mumbled back.

I'm in there thinking, *This shit is crazy! They're both crazy!*

Tan started saying "This . . . mother . . . fucker . . . is . . . big" in between her sucks.

TaShay started grinding on my torso while she continued to kiss me.

"Put it inside me when it's ready, Tan," she told her friend. "Put it inside me."

"Mmmt-mmm, put a condom on me," I told her.

"I don't need it . . . I'm clean," TaShay insisted between her kisses. "You can do it . . . do it . . . please." All the while, she was grinding me. I could feel her moist pussy against my body.

I was about ready to lift up and push TaShay off of me with her crazy talk, but then I could feel the first explosion rising from Tan's work below.

"He's . . . about . . . to cum," she said in between sucks again.

"Put it in me," TaShay told her. She started bouncing up and down on my body as she felt me growing tense from Tan's pleasure.

I could feel Tan's fingers bending me back toward TaShay's sweet, wet hole, and guiding me in.

"Don't do that," I told her. I didn't want to throw her completely off of me, but she was asking for it. I wasn't going to go raw and come inside of her. That was insane. I had always been protected, except for a few slipups.

But then I was hit by the first strong nut from Tan's lips and tongue. Both girls managed to lower TaShay's body on me. She straddled me high and Tan straddled me low. My dick extended inside of TaShay's young, hot body and exploded.

"Yeah, yeah, yeah, yeah . . ." she moaned.

Tan hugged and fondled her titties, kissing and caressing her from behind.

I jerked into her beautiful brown body like a train wreck and twisted my face into a million knots.

"Thank you, thank you, thank you!" TaShay cried into my face. "I needed that so bad."

What the hell was she talking about? Why would a nineteen-year-old, perfectly healthy girl, with a bright future ahead of her need something like that? I thought sexual healing was only for guys? What in the world was she healing from?

"Shit, I want some of that next," Tan expressed. "I did all of the work, and you got all the glory. But was it good, girl?"

"Yes, yes, yes," TaShay answered her. She fell across my chest after we had completed our crash landing.

I didn't know what to think, let alone what to say to them.

They got me, I started to panic. *They just got me.*

I felt like I was at their mercy, a damned fool. Then Tan leaned over and sealed me with a kiss.

"Did you like that?" she asked me.

I tried to move to get up, but the weight of both of them pinned me down. *I'm stronger than this,* I told myself. But maybe I didn't really want to move. The recklessness of their youth had overtaken me.

"I want mine next," Tan repeated. "And I'm greedy. So I hope you got a lot more of that."

It was too late to feel guilty. So I cupped Tan's head of long, thick hair into my arm and French-kissed her in the mouth.

"Now you want to be with me, huh?" I asked her.

She chuckled. "I always did. We both did. I just play a good game of hard-to-get. I wanted to see how bad you wanted it from me."

TaShay laughed into my chest and said, "Don't worry, Terrance. We won't tell anyone. Just do it to us again."

Tan smiled and said, "Yeah, fuck us until the sun rises."

Anything Goes

I BARELY GOT A CHANCE to recuperate before they were both working me again. Tan kissed my lips while TaShay sucked, licked, and kissed my chest. I felt guilty and I liked it at the same time. How could a man turn down two gorgeous young women in the heat of passion? It was an impossible predicament to be involved in.

"Somebody get a warm rag and wipe me down at least," I told them. I felt extra slimy.

TaShay giggled before she went into the bathroom to wash herself down. I left it up to her to take care of me as well, while Tan continued to kiss me and grind her naked body against mine.

"I want you to hit me from the back when you're ready," she told me.

TaShay returned with a warm rag to wipe off the mess we had made.

"Is that better?" she asked me.

I nodded. "Yeah, much better."

Once they had worked me enough, I found myself regaining my energy.

"Hold on," I told them both. I climbed to my feet from the bed and went to pull out my condoms from my luggage. I wasn't going to allow them to have me raw again.

Before I climbed back into the bed with them, I stared at them for a minute. They were both exotic young women, lying side by side in bed, and waiting for me. It seemed like the oldest sin in the Bible. Lust. And I was falling for it.

I asked them, "Have you ever kissed each other?"

They looked at each other and started to giggle.

"You promise not to tell?" Tan asked me. Then she caressed TaShay's chin and they kissed each other with open mouths.

"I can't tell anybody about any of this," I told them. My lips were sealed.

They began to face each other and feel on each other while I stood there and watched. They were so gentle and seductive that it turned me on; flat stomachs, flawless skin, and perfect curves. It was all beautiful.

Before I knew it, I was standing there rock hard again.

"So you want me to hit it from the back, right?" I asked Tan.

"Mmm-hmm," she mumbled, while she continued to kiss, suck, and touch TaShay's body.

Tan rolled TaShay over on her back and began to lick her body toward her pussy. While she did it, her nice, round ass moved closer to me.

"Go ahead, from the back," she looked back and told me.

I was standing there aroused and hypnotized by the two girls pleasing each other. I had seen porno movies before, but I had never actually been in the room with two naked women working each other. I had always had private affairs with the women I dealt with.

I looked again, and Tan's ass was right there in my face at the edge of the bed, while she ate TaShay out.

TaShay had her head back in the pillow with her eyes closed and her knees up. She reached down and ran her left hand through Tan's hair, while she sucked the finger on her right hand to make it moist, before she fondled her right titty with it.

Tan ate TaShay out and caressed her left titty with her right hand, while she fingered her pussy with her left hand.

Damn, these girls are freaks, I told myself. I was still standing there in suspended animation. I couldn't move. I didn't know what to feel or what to do.

Tan stopped licking TaShay's pussy and asked me, "What are you waiting for? Fuck me from behind!"

I shook off my daze and jumped to it. I pushed my dick into Tan's pussy and grabbed her smooth hips with both hands. I stroked her real slow so as not to disturb the groove she had with TaShay. I didn't want to ram her head into TaShay's pussy. So each stroke was a long, slow push, and a long, slow pull.

I guess Tan liked it that way, because she began to work her ass into my pelvis in wild circles. The more she worked her ass, the more I stroked her from behind. The two girls began to moan simultaneously as we formed a link chain of pleasure; TaShay spread-eagle on her back at the top, Tan with her ass out and face down in the middle, and me standing from behind.

"Harder, fuck her harder!" TaShay told me.

"Mmm-hmm," Tan mumbled with her mouth full.

What could I do? It felt good to me, so I fucked her harder. And instead of Tan's head crashing into TaShay's pussy and hurting her, TaShay seemed to like it.

"Oooh, yeah, unh, unh, unh . . ."

That only made me more excited, so I started ramming Tan like an absolute madman. TaShay gripped her head with both hands between her legs to steady her. Once I saw her do that, I became a little nervous.

"Can she breathe?" I asked TaShay. It looked as if we were ready to suffocate her.

Tan mumbled "Mmm-hmm, mmm-hmm" while I continued to pound her from the back, and she ate TaShay's pussy in the front.

TaShay began to go crazy in the bed with her legs shaking. She had the whole bed shaking.

"You ready to cum up there?" I asked TaShay.

"Yeeaaahhh," she moaned.

"Mmmm-hmmm," Tan moaned between her legs.

That made me ready. It was insane.

"Ooh, shit!" I told them. I lost control of my stroke, and it felt like a heat wave was about to hit me. At the same time, Tan tightened up her ass cheeks.

"MMMMMM!" she moaned as her ass began to shake inside of my grip.

TaShay went right after her, "EUUUUUUWW!"

Then I went, "AAHHHH!" The nut was so strong and good, it felt as if I was ready to snap Tan in two from my grip. Fortunately, I didn't.

I pulled out of her and took a deep breath. Tan crawled back up on the bed and crashed in TaShay's arms. I looked at them hugged up on the bed and wanted a piece of the love, so I climbed in bed next to Tan and tossed my right leg over hers.

There was satisfied silence for a minute. Then out of the blue, Tan started laughing.

"I'm in trouble now, y'all," she commented. Hearing that, I became nervous and was afraid to speak.

TaShay chuckled and caught her breath before she asked her friend, "Why?"

Tan answered, "Because I might want this shit every day now. I've never felt this exhausted after sex."

I exhaled and relaxed. I asked her, "Is it a good exhaustion?"

Tan smacked my thigh and said, "Hell yeah, it was good. Why would I want to do it every day if it wasn't good?"

"Okay," I told her. I was glad we were still safe.

Then TaShay said, "Terrance?" and she waited for me to respond to her.

"Yeah," I answered.

"Are you glad you did this with us now? Because at first, you acted like you didn't want to."

"Yeah, he was gonna get us separate rooms and shit," Tan commented. She laughed and added, "But we were still gonna have our fun. He just wouldn't have had any."

I grinned, but I still didn't know what to say about it. It was definitely a new experience for me. I didn't know if I was supposed to feel
good about having sex with them. I still wanted to know if I was the
first. Somehow, that would have made a world of difference to me.

I said, "And you say you two have never done this before?"

Tan answered, "We've been with ourselves before, but we never
included a man in it."

"It was my idea to include you," TaShay told me.

I asked, "But why me?"

"Duuhhh, because she likes your ass, that's why?" Tan teased me.
"And now I see why. You got it going on."

I was flattered, but I still was confused about how I felt about it.

"So, you haven't answered the question," TaShay pressed me.

I figured, *What the hell? I don't want to disappoint the girl. What's done
is done.*

So I told her, "Yeah . . . I'm glad we did it."

"Now was that so hard to say?" Tan asked me. "Shit, you act like
you don't like pretty pussy. You know how many guys would pay us to
do this shit? And you got us for free."

"Well, we're not any damn whores, either," TaShay informed her
friend. "I keep telling you to stop thinking like that."

"Okay, well, we're just pretty freaks then, but not whores," Tan
commented.

TaShay paused and said, "Yeah." Then she laughed like a schoolgirl.

I laid there with them and asked myself, *Is this what they wanted?* . . .
I guess it was.

I WAS TOTALLY out of it by the time I made my ride for the photo
shoot in Santa Monica that morning. Billy came to pick me up in a red
Ferrari Spider.

He smiled and said, "How do you like this one?"

I was too tired to get too excited about it. I guess Mr. Vissel was using all of his toys in an attempt to impress me.

I nodded. "It's nice."

"That's all? The girls lose their minds for this car," Billy told me.

I hopped into the saddle brown leather interior and leaned back in the passenger seat.

Billy asked me, "So, what did you do last night? Those two girls were looking for you, man."

"What two girls?" I asked him.

It was slightly after seven in the morning. I had only gotten two hours of sleep, and TaShay and Tan were still inside the room sleeping. They had nowhere urgent to go but back home.

Billy answered, "Tapioca and Cream."

He was referring to the two Filipina women I had briefly met at Mr. Vissel's mansion. For some reason, the pet names sounded ridiculous that morning.

I asked Billy, "What are their real names?"

He looked at me and was puzzled. "You know what? I don't even know their real names, I just call them what the boss calls them. But anyway," he told me, "they were definitely asking for you last night. Did you receive any of my messages on your cell phone?"

I snapped my fingers. I had left my cell phone in the hotel room again.

"As a matter of fact, I still don't have it with me," I told him. "I accidentally left it on the charger last night."

Billy made an immediate U-turn to head back to the hotel. We had not quite made the freeway yet.

I said, "Nah, man, we don't have to get it. Let's just go to the shoot."

He looked at me in disbelief. "Are you sure? I mean, you're gonna be there for hours, man. You know how these photo shoots are. That's why I'm in no rush to get you there. They'll still be setting up the lighting."

"Thanks for thinking about me," I told him. "But I'm cool with no phone. It makes my day a lot more peaceful."

Billy nodded and made another U-turn as if we were above the L.A. traffic laws. He was just a carefree kid.

I asked him, "So, what did Tapioca and Cream want from me?" As sick as it was, I was already thinking of another threesome.

Billy smiled. "They just wanted to hang out . . . and do whatever. I mean, hey, what would you do with them?"

"What do they have a reputation for?" I asked him.

He shook his head and shrugged his shoulders. "Tell you the truth, I don't know too much about them. They show up and take a lot of pictures, and they love to flirt, but I don't really know about them hanging out with anyone," he told me.

I nodded and closed my eyes. I figured I could get a little more rest on the way to the shoot, and I would deal with the Filipinas later. Maybe I was just having a lucky streak, or maybe they were all freaks, I didn't know. But I was surely willing to find out.

WE ARRIVED at the Pacific Grille off Santa Monica Boulevard for the photo shoot a good half-hour late, and I was right on time. The lights were all set up, and the other young models were dressed, with makeup, and ready to go. They were all wearing white server jackets against a dark restaurant setting, so the photos would all display plenty of contrast and pop. That place was all old style with dark mahogany wood and candles.

"Hey, over here, Terrance," Marcus Vissel called me.

He was sitting with an elderly white man at a table near the kitchen area. I walked over to them and Marcus introduced me to his old friend.

"Terrance, this is Peter Hausted, part-owner and manager of the Pacific Grille. He's been running this place as a family business for the past thirty years. Our whole plan now is to take this operation national. So we want to place a few ads in national magazines, call up a few editor friends of mine for write-ups, and scout our first locations for other restaurants—Miami, New York, Chicago, Atlanta, and maybe Dallas."

I guess Mr. Vissel was taking the term *boss* seriously. He was a pure artist when I first met him. It was all about his camera. Now he had a lot of new business ventures in mind.

I reached out and shook Mr. Hausted's frail hand. He was a small wiry man with fuzzy gray hair, eyebrows, mustache, and beard. He looked strict, too, a no-nonsense kind of guy.

"How are you doin', Terrance?" he asked me. "Do they ever call you Terry?"

I didn't even want to answer that question, but since it was asked, I told him, "I prefer Terrance. Terry sounds feminine to me," I explained.

The old man smiled. "If you don't know that you're a man by now, then a name's not gonna make any difference. I grew up in Brooklyn sixty years ago with a guy named Marcy. He was the toughest son-of-a-gun I ever knew."

I joked and said, "Yeah, probably because he didn't want people teasing him about his name."

Peter laughed and said, "You're right, he didn't."

I changed into my white clothes and had my makeup done before I was ready to shoot. As I watched the other guys, I wondered immediately if Peter Hausted had paid any attention to them. Seemed like I was the only masculine guy in the room. It had been that way in the business with a lot of the male models. But like I said, I didn't hang out much with them anyway. I would take my pictures, make my money, and then leave with a woman. Now I was thinking about leaving with two.

As Marcus snapped my pictures like old times around the restaurant, I wondered if any women would be featured.

"So, this place doesn't have any female waitresses?"

Marcus said, "That'll come later. First we want to get the big-money spenders. Then we'll come back down to the average guys."

I thought about that for a minute.

"Are you saying that the average guys respond more to women than big spenders do?"

Marcus continued to snap his shots while I worked my poses.

He answered, "Absolutely. Big-money spenders are used to the male fraternity. It's like a golf course. You're not looking for women out there. You're looking for other rich men. You wanna strike deals. But the nine-to-five guys are always looking for beer and pussy."

Mr. Vissel was putting a lot on my brains. I was thinking about pussy myself, even while he shot my pictures.

I finally smiled and joked to him, "So, you don't think about it anymore? You just use it for everyone else?"

Marcus laughed with me. He said, "Sure I do, I'm still an artist. Artists love pussy. But I'm trying to figure out the life strategies of the other guys. I'm trying to figure us all out."

"So, all of this is like a big picture to you, huh? And you're trying to focus your camera on it all?"

"Exactly," he told me. "I'm working on my next masterpiece. That's why I'm trying to include you in it. I'm trying to include all of my good friends."

I nodded to him. "Thanks. I'm learning a lot out here."

We shot for seven hours, inside and outside of the restaurant with plenty of breaks in between before our day was done. Before I left with Billy, Marcus pulled me aside again and asked me, "Have you given it any thought yet?"

There was so much to think about that I had no idea what specific thought he was referring to.

"Think about what?" I asked him.

He shook his head. "This here restaurant business is totally separate. It's something I have to learn. But the illusion of the high life and fantasy sex, I've already mastered. Sex is selling like never before, Terrance. And you better believe it. You're still a great-looking guy, so you need to take advantage of that."

I grinned and said, "How, by being an American gigolo?"

Mr. Vissel was not amused. He kept a straight face and said, "You figure it out for yourself, however you want to be involved in it. Just remember not to let it control you, you always want to control it."

I nodded to him again. "Okay. I got you."

He nodded back. "I hope you do."

I DROVE BACK into the California sun with Billy in the red Ferrari. It was late afternoon by then, on a Saturday, and everyone was loving our ride.

"What kind of car do you drive at home?" Billy asked me.

"A Mercedes CL Coupe, AMG model."

He nodded. "Is it black?"

"Yeah."

"That's the only color that looks good in Mercedes. They make awesome cars, but the paint jobs are really lousy.

"So, where do you wanna go now?" he asked me.

"First I have to get that phone back from my hotel room," I told him. I had to call TaShay to see if she and her friend Tan had made it back to San Diego safely. They should have been home by then.

"Okay, back to the Westin we go," Billy commented.

When I retrieved my phone from the room, I found that I had fourteen messages, but half of them were repeat calls.

"That's why I don't keep this damn phone on me," I hissed. If I answered every phone call, I would rarely have any peace.

I checked my messages from all of the recent connections in my life, and some new folks. There was Victoria, Judi, Danni, Rachel, TaShay, Kim, my mother, sister, new modeling dates, and Michelle from San Francisco.

"Michelle from San Francisco?" I wondered out loud. She didn't leave any specific message, she just told me to call her. I barely spent much time with the girl. I remember her being a very secluded woman. She worked for a San Francisco bank, went to work, to the libraries, the bookstores, and then back home to read. I met her at a party that one of her girlfriends forced her to attend.

Michelle was a pretty girl, but she wasn't much fun to be with. I guess she was calling me to shoot the breeze for old time's sake, but I had no interest in calling her back.

I hustled back out to the car with Billy, and we hung out for two wild nights in L.A. We never did catch back up to the Filipina girls from the mansion, but we had enough fun with a few other girls. I didn't have another threesome, but I did get laid on both Saturday and Sunday nights. I was pretty satisfied with that. That made four nights in a row with five different women. I had never done that before.

Monday morning, I was on my way to face Andrea again in Chicago. If I had another threesome with Andrea and Brazil, that would make five nights in a row with seven different women. That was crazy, but I'm sure there were other men who had been busier than that. I guess it just depended on how many women wanted you and how many of those women you allowed yourself to have.

I got off the plane in Chicago in the early afternoon and called Andrea from the terminal immediately. There was no sense in me staying there if nothing was up. Then again, I could have called Victoria back. However, Andrea answered her phone and was very receptive of me.

"Where are you? Are you in Chicago already? How was San Francisco?"

I was glad she reminded me of my lie. I most likely would have slipped up again about being in L.A. instead of San Fran had she not said anything about it. I just didn't want her to know that I was in L.A., and with Mr. Vissel at his busy mansion. I didn't know how Andrea would feel about me knowing her situation there, but how long could she keep that sort of thing under wraps anyway, especially knowing that I had a history with Marcus? I had been the one to introduce her to him.

I answered, "Yeah, I'm back in Chicago. Are you two both still in town?"

I had one thing on my mind. I wanted to see if Andrea and Brazil could outdo TaShay and Tan. There was no stopping my train ride. I was a man on a mission.

"Yeah, we're both here. Why?" Andrea questioned me.

I thought it had already been established. I had a fantasy I wanted to fulfill with the both of them.

"I thought it was already . . . spelled out," I responded to her with a pause. Was I being too eager? Did I need to just let it happen instead of pushing for it? I had no idea what TaShay and Tan had in store for me. I mean, they had hinted at it a few times, but it was never a sure thing until it happened.

"How much is that experience worth to you?" Andrea asked me next.

I ran her question through my mind. *How much is it worth to me? Is she trying to get me to pay for it?* I asked myself. After all, she had met Brazil under the conditions of Mr. Vissel's prostitution idea. Maybe they were now in business for themselves.

I said, "What do you mean, 'How much is it worth to me?' I mean, it's a fantasy."

If she was trying to talk money, then I was going to allow her to bring it up on her own.

"Well, fantasies sometimes have a price tag."

"What are you trying to say?"

Andrea sighed. "You know what? This entire conversation is a mistake. We don't have anything going on here."

I guess I was making the sell too hard for her.

I asked, "We don't? Well, what did Brazil say about it? She seemed pretty friendly to me when I bumped into her here last week. I mean, I'd love to hear her thoughts on it."

There was a long pause before Andrea responded to me. "You don't have a history with Brazil, so that's not the problem. But you do have a history with me."

I saw her point. It was a little awkward for both of us, but I still wanted it. More than anything, I still wanted a connection to Andrea.

I was willing to accept it however she would allow. Everything else I was doing I considered experimental, but having Andrea back in my life was a real goal. So I backed off of the threesome idea.

I said, "You're right, maybe we should just deal with each other."

"Anyway, Brazil is not a random woman," Andrea explained.

I no longer cared about Brazil. I just wanted Andrea back. My mind was focused back on her and her alone. I would do whatever she wanted to have her back. I wanted to make things up to her.

I said, "We don't need Brazil, just me and you again."

I sounded desperate but I didn't care. My real emotions were getting the best of me. Andrea was the end of the line for me. I understood that now. All of my thoughts and actions pointed in the same direction. I needed stability. I was only getting more reckless without her, and everything else would continue to be meaningless sex. My friend Judi had it right all along.

I asked Andrea, "Are you still married to what's-his-face? Was there a divorce settlement between you two or what?" I figured I needed to know more about her legal marriage.

"We're still working on that, but I don't think I entered the marriage in the right way to begin with, and we didn't have any kids."

"You signed pre-nup papers?" I didn't really care about that part of it. I just figured I'd ask while we were still on the subject.

She took another breath and answered, "Yes, but I'm still fighting that on the grounds of a situation that occurred due to the stress of the marriage."

I figured she was referring to her miscarriage now. But I wasn't going to bring that up if she wasn't. I didn't want to let her know that I knew. I was willing to throw it all out the window to have her back. We all had history and flaws, even painful ones. None of us was perfect.

Out of the blue, Andrea told me, "Hold on," before she put Brazil on the phone. I didn't even get a chance to tell her not to.

"Terrance, this is Brazil. Of course, Andrea told me about your fantasy, but the reality is, you're in a position to be a part of what we do based on your ability to help us pay our bills. Now it's nothing personal, and we both like you and all, but reality is what it is. You understand us?" she asked me.

I paused. I said, "But that sounds like . . ."

Brazil cut me off and said, "I understand you just had a photo shoot in San Francisco. Now, did you get paid for it? Because I'm assuming that you taking these pictures will eventually fulfill someone else's fantasy, a fantasy for which a company is willing to pay and market nationally."

Her point was well taken; we were all selling something or being sold. But I didn't want to deal with her anymore. I wanted to talk to Andrea again. My fantasy idea was over. I had already had a threesome, and now I just wanted my girl Andrea back.

"Can I speak to Andrea?" I asked Brazil civilly. I didn't want to hear what she was pitching.

Brazil played the go-between again and said, "She wants me to do the talking now."

I asked her, "Is this a normal thing for you two?" I didn't know what else to say. But as soon as I asked her the question, I realized that I should have left it alone. I didn't want to go there. They were not young experimentalists like TaShay and Tan claimed to be. I was assuming that Andrea and Brazil were seasoned, and I didn't want to get involved with them like that. It was destroying my individual history with Andrea. But ultimately, what did Andrea want?

Brazil answered, "It's brand-new," and left it at that.

"It's brand-new?" I repeated. "What do you mean . . ."

She said, "Look, either you want what you want or you don't."

I thought about it in more detail. I had spent up to three hundred dollars in party funds for TaShay and Tan in L.A., and now I was being asked to cough up whatever amount in Chicago for Andrea and Brazil. But the money was still not the issue, I just didn't want to be paying for sex. I wanted real emotions and some form of commitment back. And I couldn't believe it myself.

Brazil said, "Look at it this way; how often do you pay for a date and gifts for a woman you really care about to treat you how you want to be treated in return? Then think about how much you would have to do to get that woman to share you in bed with another woman, if she would even be willing to do that.

"She may even cut you loose for asking," she suggested. "You catch my drift? So just put it all in proper perspective."

Obviously, their decision had been made. I would pay them for a threesome experience, or I would have nothing. Brazil would not even put Andrea back on the phone with me. She was all about business. So my fantasy was now getting in the way of a real relationship.

I asked her, "So, where would you guys like to go out for dinner tonight?"

Sexaholic

I MET ANDREA AND BRAZIL at another dark Italian restaurant in downtown Chicago. It was their choice, and it seemed that we all liked Italian food in a dark setting as a kind of foreplay to hot sex. If I happened to bump into Victoria or any of her friends there, then it was all business. And in actuality, it was. Brazil and Andrea had made it that way, and I was forced to accept it.

We were all very tactful in our dinner conversation, and both women were elegant in their dress. We decided that we would all go back to my hotel room at the airport.

Andrea looked across the table and hinted, "It's been a long time since we enjoyed each other, Terrance."

I looked into her familiar dark brown eyes, and was trapped, but Brazil was in the way of our privacy.

I said, "It has, hasn't it?"

Brazil noticed our connection and remained silent as she ate.

I began to wonder how different things could have been had I vowed to marry Andrea years ago. I'm sure she had spent time thinking about it as well. She may have even been thinking about it simultaneously with me at the table, but Brazil was in the way of either one of us voicing it.

"I guess life is a long journey," I commented. "Who knows where it will take us."

"Indeed," Brazil spoke up.

Her interruption redirected my thoughts. There was no sense in thinking about the past anymore, we were all there for the present and for the future. Or not really the future, just the present. I doubted I had any future with both of them. I would only try my hardest to push Brazil out of the way.

"So, how was the weather out in San Fran?" she asked me. I don't know if her intention was to break my concentration from Andrea or what, but she was beginning to irritate me.

"Sunny as usual," I told her. "It doesn't change much out there."

I found it ironic that I had made up a trip about San Francisco to keep them from thinking about our shared associations in L.A., just for an old San Francisco fling to contact me. It would have been crazy had they all known each other. The thought did pop into my mind. Stranger things have happened. But I let it stand as just a coincidence.

"So, getting back to us, how do you two really feel about it?" I asked them both. It looked as if I had no way out.

"What, a threesome?" Brazil stated nonchalantly. She said, "We're grown women."

"How do you feel about it?" Andrea asked me.

I wanted to tell her I didn't want to do it anymore. I wanted to tell her that I wanted us back together again. But instead, I backed down and said, "I still can't believe you both agreed to it."

"Why not? You asked for it, didn't you?" Brazil stated. "Why would you ask for something you didn't believe you could have?"

She had a point, and I had another opportunity to end it. But what did Andrea want? I still didn't know. She was letting Brazil do all the talking. So I asked her, "What do you think, Andrea?"

I was looking for a way out. But it was all up to her now.

Brazil and I both looked at Andrea, and she nodded to us.

"I wanna do it," she answered. That was it. She had sealed the deal. So I agreed to pay them what they asked, two thousand dollars on a "friendship bargain" was what Brazil had called it. She said their normal rate could be as much as twenty thousand depending on the client. You believe that?

ANDREA DROVE US back out to my airport hotel in near silence behind the wheel of their copper-toned Nissan Altima. We listened to the radio instead of talking. Alicia Keys was on. She was singing about real love, old-school style. And her song only made me feel more meaningless.

"What do you think about her?" Brazil asked me. She sat in the passenger seat and I sat in the back.

I nodded. "She's a talented girl with a bright future ahead of her."

"You think she's attractive?"

"Of course," I answered.

Brazil looked at Andrea and grinned. I didn't know what that exchange was all about, and I didn't care. I was only thinking about our predicament.

We arrived at the hotel and headed straight for the elevators, where I began to feel apprehensive.

How old is this girl Brazil, anyway? Is that even her real name? I asked myself. She didn't act like a woman in her twenties, that was for sure. But it's funny how I didn't ask many questions about Tan. I didn't know her either. However, I got to learn a little bit about her at the party.

When an elevator opened to take us up to my floor, we walked in and stood alone. As soon as the doors closed for our privacy, Brazil pushed Andrea up against me and began to kiss her softly on the lips, while sandwiching Andrea between us.

It all happened too fast for me. Brazil made the decision to include me by grabbing my arms and placing both of my hands on her surprisingly soft ass. Her ass felt like round Jell-o, and just as I had suspected, she wore no panties.

She looked me in my eyes and said, "Get what you want from this, baby. Don't hold nothing back."

That caught my attention. Just that fast, Brazil had me curious again and into it.

We made it to the room, and Brazil started to squeeze my dick through my pants while Andrea caressed my ass before I could even open the door. Hell, I was rock hard already, and I was no longer apprehensive about including Brazil. I was ready to tear her soft, Jell-o ass apart.

When I opened the door with my key and walked into the room behind them, they pinned me up against the door and went after my pants and shirt. They were just as aggressive as TaShay and Tan had been, maybe more so. I guess that's how women got down in threesomes, I don't know. I had limited experience with it.

"You get him high, I'll get him low," Brazil ordered. She was definitely the ringleader.

They both pulled their dresses over their heads right there at the door and stepped out of their shoes to stand butt naked before me. Andrea kissed my lips while she tugged and pulled at my clothes to get me naked with them.

"You're about to get your fantasy," she told me with a grin.

Once they had stripped me from my clothes and tossed them into a pile on the floor with theirs, I grabbed Andrea by the back of her head and kissed her hard. I hadn't felt her smooth head of silky hair in years. She had cut it down shorter since then, but it still felt like soft feathers in my fingers.

Damn I missed this girl, I told myself. Brazil dropped to her knees and began to play with the naked head of my dick, but I was still paying more attention to Andrea. I wanted to feel if she was as soft and moist as she used to be. I wanted to touch, and kiss, and eat her, like I used to. Running my hands through her hair and kissing her brought it all back to me.

"I know," Andrea whispered to me. "I missed you, too."

At that moment, Brazil sucked around the edges of my head. The edges of the head are the most sensitive part of a guy's dick. That made me curl and grab Andrea into me.

"She got you, baby. She gon' take real good care of you," Andrea assured me.

Brazil did it again and made me jerk back against the door.

BOOM!

I said, "Shouldn't we get away from this door? We might make too much noise over here."

Brazil laughed and actually pulled me toward the bed by my dick.

"Whoa, whoa, that's a sensitive tool there," I told her.

Andrea followed close behind, kissing my shoulders, neck, and back.

"She's not gonna hurt you. We know what we're doing."

"I hope so," I told her.

We made it over to the bed where Brazil pulled me on top of her. She pushed me forward and onto my hands and knees, where she ended up underneath me. Then Andrea climbed to the top of the bed above Brazil and put her juicy platter right smack in my face, with her legs wide open.

She grabbed me by the top of my head and told me, "Come get what you want," while pushing my face in between her sweet spot. While I slid my tongue around Andrea's edges, up and down, and in and out of her treasure, Brazil continued to suck me off.

Andrea massaged my neck and shoulders as she slowly worked her pelvis into my open mouth.

She's still soft and sweet, I told myself. *She still got it.*

Brazil worked me enough to put a little extra spice on my tongue for Andrea. I started bouncing up and down and tensing up as my arms and legs began to shake from the pleasure.

"Ahhh," Andrea moaned. She started squeezing my shoulders harder. "Put a condom on him, girl," she told Brazil. "Put a condom on him."

I was glad to see she wasn't as crazy as TaShay had been. Going raw was dangerous for plenty of reasons, especially with our history. So Brazil slid from underneath me, climbed off of the bed, pulled out a condom from her small purse, and came back to slide it down my shaft.

When she was finished, Andrea pulled me forward by my arms and grabbed my dick to slide it into her soft wetness.

"Ooh, bring it home to me, baby. Bring it home to me."

I started to stroke Andrea for the first time in years, only for Brazil to climb on top of my back and hold on tight for the ride. She kissed and licked the back of my neck and bit softly on my earlobes, while she rubbed my chest with her soft, moist hands. But I was concerned about our combined pressure on Andrea.

"Wait, is this too heavy? . . . Is it too heavy?" I asked her in between strokes.

"No . . . I'm good . . . I'm good," she moaned in her response.

So I continued to pour it on her.

Brazil gave me compliments from behind.

"Ooh, you workin' it, Mister, you workin' it."

Then she went and stuck a wet finger in my asshole.

I jerked back and said, "Hey, stop that!"

I was already too far along to stop or to slow down my stroke. So Brazil poked me in the ass anyway. The irritation forced me to stroke Andrea faster and harder to get it over with, while I squeezed my ass cheeks tight to keep Brazil's wet finger out.

"Do it, baby, do it! Show 'er what you been holdin' back! Show it to her!" Brazil pressed me.

That woman was crazy, but it all worked. Andrea tightened up and let loose right before I did. Brazil held onto my back for dear life and sucked my earlobe.

Andrea moaned, "Oooh, Terrance, Terrance, Terrance!"

She sounded like she was crying, as if I had broken something inside of her. I felt heat pouring through my body like the condom had popped. So I became nervous and couldn't wait to pull out to make sure the rubber was still on and in one piece. All the while, Brazil continued to kiss my back and grind my ass like a gay man.

I pulled back from her and said, "Hold on, hold on," so I could withdraw from Andrea and check the condom.

I pulled out and looked down, and it was still in one piece.

Whew! That was close! I told myself. I didn't need any more complications with Andrea. Although I had missed the sex, I didn't quite know where we were headed. Getting her pregnant again without more direction would have been insane.

Brazil finally slid from my back and joined Andrea in bed for a cuddle.

"Are you okay, baby?" she asked her. Andrea looked exhausted and sweated out. Her wet hair was a mess all over her head. I hadn't even noticed how much I was sweating until I looked down at my chest. With Brazil riding me like she did, three lustful bodies had definitely built up too much heat. No wonder I felt such a strong heat flash.

"I'm okay," Andrea told her lady friend between breaths. She was still trying to suck up enough air to recuperate.

I looked down at the two of them naked in bed, and I realized that the only thing I had going for me in romance over the caring, gentle touch of a woman was a big, bad dick. My dick meant everything. And if a girl didn't want one, then what else did she want from a man; his wallet? Well, they had gotten both.

I actually sat there and thought about that. A good dick and money was all every woman wanted, then they could all crawl up and hug each other for love and support. I sat there and thought about all kinds of crazy shit like that. What if I got both of those women pregnant at the same time? Could that actually happen? Could my sperm be strong enough to impregnate two women with one big nut? Could I fuck every set of girlfriends in America? Could they all be turned out for the right dick and the right dollar? Like Rachel had told me, they all had to fuck somebody, unless they weren't fucking at all.

Brazil finally broke me out of my daze when she asked me, "What in the world are you thinking about?"

I guess she could read the confusion on my face.

I responded "Fucking you from the back" with no hesitation. A cocky man will say just about anything.

Andrea started a slow laugh and kept going with it.

Brazil shook her head and said, "You see how good pussy goes to a man's head. He probably thinks he can fuck every woman in the world now."

She was right, I was thinking that. So I started to grin. I could fuck every girl I went after. That's what they all wanted, to be captured and fucked by a guy who meant it. You just had to bring the freak out of them first.

Plenty of Options

I TIGHTENED UP BRAZIL, played a few more rounds of bedroom kinkiness, and fell asleep with both women in bed. In the morning, they showered, dressed, and left me.

After they were gone, I sat up in bed until close to noon, which was late for me. I had been going to sleep late and getting up early for the past few days, and it had taken its toll on me. I needed the extra rest. But all I could think about while I rested was how differently I felt about Andrea. I couldn't trust her to be my woman anymore. Who was I kidding? Her whole lifestyle had changed. That left me with a feeling of emptiness. My quest for her was gone and replaced by nothing.

When I was finally up and about, I saw no reason to return to Atlanta so soon. I wasn't crazy about crawling back to Danni anymore either. So I called my mother to see if she still wanted me to drop by and visit her in Indiana.

She said, "What? Boy, you didn't give me a warning or anything. I thought you said you were gonna call me first."

"I am calling you," I told her. "I'm calling you now."

"Yeah, on the same damn day you're supposed to come. That's not enough time to let me know. I don't even get off until seven."

"I'll just come by and get the key from you then," I told her.

"No, I might just try to get off early. What time are you gonna be here?"

"I'd say after three o'clock or so. I can catch the train around one."

Gary, Indiana, was nowhere from Chicago.

"Well, I can't get off that early," my mother told me.

"You don't have to. Matter of fact, if you don't want me to have the key, then I'll just go around and visit old friends until you get home. Everybody says I never look them up anymore."

"You don't."

"Well, I got a good life to live. What can I say? I'm busy."

"That don't mean you can't visit your old friends, Terrance."

I nodded. I said, "Well, okay, let me start getting myself together. It's gonna be twelve o'clock soon, and I still have to make it downtown to the train station."

I hung up with my mother and gathered my things at the hotel. I had to take a good, long shower and get moving.

I MADE IT TO the Chicago train station by one o'clock and bought a round-trip ticket to Gary. I had to return to Chicago to fly back out to Atlanta. If I stayed over in Chicago another night, maybe I would call up Victoria for round three. I don't know. I was capable of doing anything. I was a free man.

You would think I would be tired of sex after five nights of it in a row, but I wasn't. I was getting along like a well-oiled machine. Even on the train ride I looked around at a few of the women and fantasized about taking one or two of them into the bathroom for a quickie.

I sat there in my seat and just shook my head. Having a threesome with Andrea was the worse thing I could have done to myself. I thought of every woman as a freak after that. Deep down inside, every one of them could be turned out. That's what I was thinking, and it was terrible. I mean, I had always been after sex from a woman, like any other guy. It was only natural. But I rarely thought of them all as freaks.

A tall sister in a dark blue business suit and wire-rimmed glasses walked by and froze above my seat. She had clear, dark brown skin and her hair pulled back in a ponytail.

She said, "I know I know you from somewhere."

I nodded to her. "Either from magazines or from billboards," I told her.

She snapped her fingers and said, "You're a model."

"Yeah, what are you?" I asked her. There was an empty seat beside me next to the window. I asked, "You wanna sit down?"

She hesitated. "I really shouldn't."

She was right. I had the wrong thoughts for her in mind.

"Why not, it's just a seat," I told her anyway. It was like I couldn't stop myself. I was on a devilish roll, I really was.

She said, "No, I was just, you know, saying hi."

"All right, well, hi to you, too, then."

She smiled and got to stepping. "Okay, well, 'bye."

I nodded again and let her go without further discussion. You can't have them all. I was glad she turned me down. But I knew I would have more opportunities in Gary; it was my home turf. The old neighborhood girls loved me there.

I made it to Gary safe and sound, and without taking a woman into the bathroom stall like I thought of doing. I arrived in the city and got a taxi to take me to my old stomping grounds on the West side. I climbed out of the car with my wheeled luggage and actually started walking the streets of Gary in search of old friends and memories.

I hadn't been back out on the streets in years. Modeling was a very sheltered lifestyle if you manage to keep your money right, and I had. So the return to real life in the streets was refreshing.

The streets of Gary weren't as crowded as when I was growing up there in the seventies and eighties. Seemed like the new generations were inside kids as opposed to outside kids like we were. That was a fact. Generation X and Y, as the American media called them, had more internet, television, computer games, and virtual reality addictions than we would have ever stood for in my day. After a while, it was just time to get back to real life, you know, and interact with real people. That's how I felt while back on the streets. I was back to real life for a change, with street trash and normal people walking around.

I walked past a new neighborhood grocery store on West Avenue and watched a young mother strolling out with groceries that filled the back of her baby carriage. She was wearing all pink from her boots, to her pants, to her T-shirt, and her visor hat.

Then she turned and started walking in my direction. I stared into her baby carriage to see what the baby looked like. The floral colors the baby wore told me that she was a girl. She wore a minihat as well, so I couldn't confirm anything from the hair. She did wear little gold earrings though. The baby was cute, too, with smallish eyes, round cheeks and her right-hand thumb in her mouth. In fact, I was paying so much attention to the daughter, that I didn't look back up to the young mother.

All of a sudden, the mother said, "Terrance? Terrance Mitchell?"

I looked up into her face and noticed that she wasn't so young after all. She looked good though. I guess she looked younger from a distance in her coordinating outfit. But I still couldn't place her.

I stared into her face as she and her daughter stared into mine. I was trying my hardest to recognize her and to come up with a name, but I couldn't.

She said, "I'm Theresa, Quinton's little sister."

I still didn't recognize her. I went to high school with Quinton Dixon and hung out on his block as a teen, but I didn't remember . . .

"Wait a minute, you had to be like, five, six years old, running around on the porch and the lawn like a tomboy," I recalled.

She smiled and her face lit up like a Christmas tree. "Yeah, that's me."

She was so young at the time, I wondered how she even remembered me.

"You can remember me from that age?" I asked her.

She laughed and said, "No, but Quinton and them would show me your old pictures and stuff and talk about how you look different now in your modeling career, and I would just laugh at them."

That made sense. I nodded and asked her, "Well, how is Quinton doing?"

She shook her head. "He's gone, man. He got shot and killed three years ago, right before I got pregnant with my daughter."

She didn't even flinch when she said it.

I took a breath and asked her, "You all right?"

She blew it off. "That was years ago, man. I mean, you gotta get over it and move on. But that stopped me from dealing with my baby's father. He's in jail now."

"What, he had something to do with Quinton's death?" I asked her.

She nodded. "You know, man, they was out there selling that stuff. So I told my baby's father I wouldn't tolerate that shit no more. But he didn't wanna listen. So he ran out there with his other women or whatever, and he finally got his behind locked up."

That was all normal in Gary. After my senior year of high school, we had overtaken Washington, D.C., as the number-one place in America for a young black man to be sent to the cemetery with a bullet hole in him. That was a part of the streets that I was not happy to return to.

"So, how are you making out?" I asked Theresa. "And what's her little name."

She smiled into her baby's face and said, "Kiearra. She just turned two a couple of weeks ago."

"She can't walk?" I asked. Why was she in a stroller at two?

Theresa laughed and said, "Yeah, she can walk. She's just slow sometimes, so I put her in the stroller when I'm in a rush."

"Oh. And how's the rest of the family?"

Quinton had a big extended family with plenty of cousins.

Theresa answered, "Everybody's doing their own thing now. It's best that way. I mean, when you try to help too many family members out, you just end up with a lot more stress than you need. So I just decided to keep everything simple, find my own little place, keep my job and day care right, and do what I gotta do."

Amen to that! She had the right idea. I understood just what she was talking about. I had the same philosophy; out of sight is out of mind, and the less you help, the less they think about getting help from you.

"So, how long are you in town for?" she asked me. "I see you got your luggage and everything out here."

I laughed. "Yeah, I just figured I'd crash at my mother's tonight instead of at a hotel."

Theresa looked puzzled. "She doesn't live over here anymore, does she?"

"Nah, she's out in the suburbs now, but I just wanted to come back and walk around out here to see the old neighborhood, you know."

Theresa nodded. "Okay, well, you look good." Then she smiled. "I guess so, right, with you being a big-time model now and everything. So, you're leaving tomorrow then?" she repeated.

"Either tomorrow or Thursday," I told her.

She paused for a second. "Well, give me a call, you know, if you decide to stay longer. Today was my day off from work, too. I work downtown now, so I probably wouldn't even have seen you."

"Probably not," I admitted.

"So take my number down," she told me. I guess she must have been around twenty-three, but she appeared eighteen, nineteen from a distance. You had to get up close to see the serious concerns of life in her eyes and read how old she was. But when she smiled, she looked like a teenager again.

I took out my cell phone and punched her number in. Then she reached out and touched my hand. "Don't be afraid to call me before you leave, all right. I'm up late most of the time."

"Doing what?" I asked her for the hell of it.

She shrugged. "Watching TV. I got nothing better to do." She squeezed my wrist and said, "So call me."

"Okay," I told her.

I tried my hardest not to look back when we went our separate ways. Old neighborhood girls were always asking me to call them, every time I came back home.

Speaking of old neighborhood women, my mother invited one of her favorite neighborhood daughters over to the house to eat with us that night.

I said, "Why did you do that, Mom? You're gonna play matchmaker while I'm trying to eat."

My mother continued preparing her meal of boiled chicken, corn, greens, and potatoes at the stove. She was forever the busybody and was still in pretty good shape to prove it. She wore the apron, the cooking gloves, and everything.

She said, "I just wanted you two to compliment each other on how you're both doing. Geneva's going to law school now."

"Mom, you know how many lawyers and professional women I know?" It was no big deal to me. But I usually tried to stay away from those kinds of women. I guess, since I was a model, they tried to treat me like a plaything who needed a real job. So I never really liked their attitudes.

"Well, she's right here from Indiana, and we need to support each other when we make it," my mother explained.

She was always trying to show me off to somebody, and since it was her house—that I helped her with the down payment on—she could invite over whoever she wanted. I would just have to deal with it. That's why I never enjoy staying home that long. If I stayed for a week, my mother would introduce me to five different women. I was amazed sometimes that she even knew so many young people. I guess that came from running her mouth to everyone's parents.

The Geneva Pitts that I remembered was a bashful yellow girl with curly light brown hair, who reminded me of a television kid you would see on *The Cosby Show*. She was the oldest daughter of one of my mother's old friends. Geneva was Ms. Goody Two-shoes all the way, another grown-up Raven-Symoné, and I was not attracted to that at all.

She arrived at my mother's house at ten after seven, and my mother gave me a final warning.

"Now Terrance, you treat her nice and with respect. Don't you be in here ignoring her."

I had been forced to tune out some of my mother's overzealous company before, but I was a little too old for that now.

I told her, "I'll be on my best behavior, Mom." Then I planned to get back to my regular life.

My mother walked to the front door to let Geneva in while I waited in the kitchen area.

"Oh, I like the dress. That's very nice," I heard her compliment Geneva as they made their way through the house and toward the kitchen.

"Thank you. You know, a girl's gotta do what she can to try and stay on top of the fashion world."

I grinned. They were forcing me to think about the dress before I even saw it. So as soon as Geneva walked into the kitchen behind my mother, I checked her out from head to toe.

Her hair was still light brown, curly, and at shoulder length. The dress she wore was off-white and knitted, hugging every curve on her fit body, and stopping at mid-thigh. And her boots were brown suede. She also wore a pearl necklace with matching earrings. My mother hadn't said anything about that. I guess she left that out to surprise me with. I'm sure she realized I was listening to her every word. My mother spoke too loudly for you not to listen.

Geneva stuck out her hand to me and said, "Hi, Terrance."

I extended my hand to receive hers.

"I see you're all grown up now," I told her.

"It was going to happen eventually, right?"

The dinner meeting was awkward for both of us. The sooner we got it over with, the better. So I pulled a chair from the kitchen table and offered her a seat.

"You wanna sit down?"

"Sure."

My mother stood behind the stove and watched for chemistry between us, but I was just being a gentleman.

Geneva took a seat and looked around.

"Cozy kitchen," she commented. My mother had decorations and oxygen plants hanging from everywhere. It made her feel like she was never alone.

I sat to the right of Geneva and asked her, "So, you're going into law school now."

She perked up and said, "Yes, I am. It's a big step for me."

"What kind of law?"

"Business law. I wanna go where the money is."

I nodded. I said, "Is that your reason for wanting to be a lawyer?"

"Oh, no, of course not. But if I'm gonna be in law school, then I want to be able to help small business owners to protect themselves, and get them a much bigger share of the deals that are being made out here."

I nodded. I could see my mother smiling in my periphery. I guess she figured it was a good answer.

Geneva asked me, "What about you? What do you have up your sleeve for when you're no longer modeling?"

I guess everyone assumed that you couldn't make an extensive living from modeling. I didn't want to argue about it myself, so I decided to make jokes.

"Well, I guess I could look to marry a female lawyer in a couple of years, and just handle the kids at the house."

Geneva smiled at it, but my mother didn't think it was funny. I could see her frowning at me over my shoulder.

"That sounds like a plan. So you already have your lawyer picked out?" Geneva joked back to me.

"Actually, I don't think she's passed the bar exam yet, but I'm pretty confident she will."

Geneva shook her head and started laughing. I really didn't care if

she liked me one way or the other. I was just entertaining myself. I
knew where I stood in life, and I had a couple of healthy nest eggs to
fall back on.

"Terrance, help me to set the food out on the table," my mother
stated.

It was perfect timing to break up my sarcasm with her company. I
knew that's how my mother was reading it. So I stood up to help her
bring the food to the table.

"I can help, too," Geneva offered.

"No, you're a guest, so you just relax," my mother told her.

"Are you sure?"

"She's sure," I answered for her.

After setting the food on the table, we all sat and piled up our plates
with my mother's home-cooked meal, including buttered biscuits. In
the middle of us eating and doing basic small talk, I looked Geneva in
her face and asked her, "You got a man?"

She grinned and shook her head. My mother stared me down to
see what my angle was. I guess my question was too blunt and out in
the open to be taken seriously.

"Why not?" I asked. "I mean, you're an attractive girl with your
head on straight. There should be plenty of guys knocking on your
door."

Dinner wasn't going the way my mother had intended.

She snapped, "Why would you ask her that? Do you have a
woman? There should be plenty of women knocking down your
door, too."

Geneva answered, "Well, a lot of guys can knock, but that doesn't
mean you have to answer the door if it's not the right one."

I nodded to her. "That's exactly how I feel about it. You know, you
don't answer your door, but in the meantime, you go knocking on a
couple doors yourself when you need it. You know what I mean?"

Geneva smiled again.

My mother caught my drift and said, "I know one thing, all that
damn knocking on doors don't make no damn sense. That's why we

have so many young people with problems now. You learn to stay in your damn house with your husband or wife, and you leave them other doors alone."

I didn't know who my mother was to talk. I guess she was preaching from what she wanted and not from what she ever done. There was no husband or wife in our family, just door knocking, however discreetly. But I didn't want to say anything to my mother about that in front of Geneva. I figured I'd allow her to voice her family values. Then again, my mother's conservative views allowed me another opportunity to toy with her company.

I asked Geneva, "So, is that what you do, you stay at home and let nobody in your door?"

"Now cut it out, Terrance!" my mother shouted across the table at me.

"Mom, she's a grown woman. I know she's your friend's daughter and everything, but you invited her over here by herself this time because she's grown."

"Well, that doesn't mean you have to sit in here and ask her these filthy questions. That's just plain disrespectful. And right over the dinner table."

Geneva didn't say a word. When dinner was over, I got a chance to talk to her alone outside, on the porch.

She smiled at me and shook her head again. "You're bad. You're just so bad."

"And you're good. You're just so good," I told her.

She looked at me and said, "How do you know?"

I stopped and thought about it. I really didn't know. Geneva could have been a down low freak, too. I didn't put it past any woman.

I asked her, "Are you any good?"

She broke out laughing. My question had a double meaning to it.

She answered, "I'm not gonna say, but I know what you are. I can see that right now. You're bad."

"And that's good, right? A good girl and a good guy don't match. You need a little edge in your life."

"I don't think so," she told me. "We don't have anywhere to go but one place. And fortunately, I don't make my decisions like that anymore."

"But you used to, huh?" I asked her.

She smiled and shook her head again. "I'm not gonna go there."

My mother walked out of the house and asked me, "Are you still bothering her?" She was getting right in the way. I wanted to break Geneva down and uncover the freak in her, but my mother wouldn't let me.

"I'm not bothering her, she likes me," I told my mother. "You can't tell when a woman likes a man. It's not when they have great conversations at a dinner table, it's when they have great conversations away from the dinner table."

I was just making up some bullshit to humor myself.

Geneva took it seriously though. She said, "I disagree. I think a good couple can have great conversations anywhere."

"I'm sure a good couple can," I told her. "I like to talk anywhere myself."

I gave Geneva a look and was still going at it with her.

She grinned and said, "I'm sure you do like to talk. You showed me that tonight."

"Nah, I didn't show you anything yet," I told her.

"You didn't show her what?" my mother asked me

She was way out in left field with no glove to catch the ball with.

"Nothing, Mom, nothing at all."

I really wanted her to leave so I could continue flirting with Geneva, but it wasn't gonna happen.

"Well, let me get ready to get on out of here," Geneva began to tell us. She looked at my mother and held her hands. "Thanks for the great dinner, Ms. Mitchell."

All of sudden, I didn't want to see the girl go.

"What do you have, an early class tomorrow or something?" I asked her. It was only after ten.

"I have to work in the morning," she answered.

I nodded. I guess I had to let her go then. "Okay."

I was ready to ask her how I could call her, but my mother had her information already, and if I ever really wanted it, I figured I could get it through my mom.

"Until next time," I told Geneva.

"Next time when you know how to act," my mother barked at me.

Geneva looked at me and nodded. It looked as if she wanted to say something else but was hesitant.

"Well, let me walk you to the car," I offered. My mother had disturbed us before I could really get Geneva going. And she was still frowning at me, but she couldn't stop a guy from walking a girl to her car at night.

When we approached the curb where Geneva's blue Volkswagen Jetta was parked, I whispered, "So, how do I get your number without my mother seeing us?"

She laughed and said, "When you're serious about doing more than knocking on doors, your mother knows how to get in touch with me."

"But someone might get in your house before then. I want to make sure I can keep them out," I joked with her.

She looked at me and asked, "And you can just be friends with me?"

I didn't like the sound of that shit. Once a woman put you in the friend department, it was hard as hell to get back out. So I was tempted to pass.

"Ahhh . . ."

She said, "I understand. You're probably not used to being friends with women throwing themselves at you all the time."

"Who told you that?"

"It's obvious," she responded. "But look, I'm really going to be all about my studies for the next few years, so . . ."

I knew it. I should have left that damn girl alone before I started. Now I was looking like I had the hots for her, and she was turning me down cold.

I said, "Well, can I ask you a question before you leave?"

"Sure."

"What did you think about meeting me before you came over here today?"

"Well, to tell you the truth, at first I just thought about telling your mother I was busy. But I didn't want to lie to her. So I told myself, 'How bad could it be to eat dinner with her and her son?' "

I thought about that and grinned. My mother had cramped my style. I nodded and said, "Thanks. That's why you never allow your mother to invite a woman over to meet you. You're at a disadvantage before you even speak to the girl."

"No, because if it wasn't for her, then I wouldn't even have thought about you," Geneva argued. "But don't forget you're the one who doesn't want to be friends first."

"I'm fine with friends first, but friends only and forever is a little limiting," I told her.

She said, "I would hope that we could be friends forever, even if it turned into more than friendship. Why can't a woman be friends with a man she's involved with? I mean, is that a crime or something? Why do so many guys fight that idea?"

I asked her, "Is that how you're looking for your next man?"

"As a matter fact, it is. And if a guy can't be friends with me first, well then . . ."

I said, "But just because a guy says okay to that, that doesn't mean he's gonna automatically move past friendship, right?"

"No, it doesn't."

"Okay, well, I'll think about it then."

She was hesitant to leave. I think I caught her off-guard with my response to her. But if I had to wait to be more than friends, then she had to wait to be friends.

I said, "Okay, well, my mother has your information, right? I'll just have to get it from her then. If I'm serious, right?" I asked her.

Geneva nodded and decided to move on. "Yeah."

When she drove off, I returned to the porch.

My mother asked me, "So, what do you think about her? I know you're attracted to the girl because you kept talking that filthy talk, but what do you think about her in a relationship?"

I stopped and thought about it. I really couldn't read the girl. I would have to be around her more and in a different setting.

I said, "I don't know yet. I mean, she could be the real thing, and then again, she could just be faking."

My mother said, "She is the real thing. She's a good girl. I can tell what's what. So you need to really think about her. She's gonna be making her own money, too."

I wasn't thinking about her money. I rarely thought about that from a woman. I always had my own solid income. But I was thinking about whether she had any freak in her body or not.

I know one thing's for sure, I told myself, *I don't want boring sex for the rest of my life. So if a woman's not willing to let me test the goods before hand, then all bets are off.*

"So, how long are you gonna stay in Indiana?" my mother asked me.

"Just for a day or two," I answered. "I have to get back to Atlanta before the weekend. I'm running out of clean clothes. I've been in Chicago and out in L.A. since last Thursday night."

My mother frowned and said, "You could just go buy some new clothes then. Go spend a hundred dollars at Wal-Mart."

I ignored her. "Mom, I need to borrow your car tonight."

"Where are you going?"

"I bumped into some old friends earlier. They want to shoot some pool and drink a few beers downtown," I lied to my mother. She didn't really want to know where I was going.

She got the keys and said, "You bring my car back in one piece, too."

AS SOON AS I hit the road in my mother's silver Lincoln, I called up Theresa to see how serious she was about watching TV all night. It would be after eleven by the time I could get over there. You could call it her lucky night if she was willing, and she had Geneva to thank for getting me curious and horny. I was just uncertain about whether I wanted to go through with doing my high school friend's little sister.

"What, you're on your way over here?" she asked me. She sounded surprised by it.

"Not if I'm not wanted," I told her. I didn't want to sound too eager. It was a lucky night for her, not for me. I was still trying to decide if I wanted to do it or not.

She said, "Oh, you're wanted. I just put my daughter to bed, too. Man, you called at the perfect time."

Shit, she sounded like a guy. I knew it was on with her.

I said, "Well, since you know I'm coming, I need you to do me a favor."

After talking to Geneva's goody goody ass, I needed to get my freak back on.

Theresa asked me, "What's that?"

"Don't wear nothing too complicated. Less is best," I told her.

She laughed. "I know that's right. Let me take my clothes off right now then."

I had a pocketful of condoms, and I planned to use them. I was a bad man indeed. So I made it back over to the old neighborhood, and it was more people out at night than it was during the daytime.

Shit! It looked like ten people would see me walk up to Theresa's front door. At least she had her own place. Then I thought about who else she could have been dealing with. Was she the untouchable girl, or could anybody get it?

At least she only has one kid, I told myself. *But she could have a second one from me if I'm not careful.*

I thought about bumping into Jerry White at the airport, and his revelation about three baby mommas all came back to me.

Do I really need to do this? I asked myself as I sat there in the car at the curb. I looked up toward her house and saw Theresa peek out the window. At the same time, a group of four of the people who were outside moved farther up the street, and two others walked inside their homes.

Okay, it's down to four people. It's now or never! I told myself. I decided to go for broke and climbed out of the car.

Theresa opened her front door as soon as I began to walk up toward her house. I walked straight ahead and never looked back. As soon as I made it inside, she quickly closed and locked the door behind me. She seemed to be as concerned about the perception as I was.

"I don't have a lot of people coming over to my house at night," she told me. I guess I was an exception, but I didn't comment on it. I looked around and was impressed. Her home was clean, furnished, carpeted, decorated, and all in order. I had the wrong perceptions about her just because she was still there in the 'hood.

She was wearing a silky pink nightgown and pink slippers. Without her hat on and her tall boots, she looked extra young again. She had a small head with short hair.

I joked and said, "I guess I don't have to ask what your favorite color is."

She chuckled at it. "Oh, all this pink. It's just my color for the year. I tend to pick theme colors each year," she told me. "So next year I might buy a whole lot of beige."

I took a seat on her multicolored couch and didn't know what to do. I had lost my hard-on and natural aggression thinking about whether I should or shouldn't. Theresa seemed just as cautious.

She said, "Umm . . . I have a confession to make."

That made my heart race a little faster. What was she about to say? "What's that?" I asked her.

She said, "I'm a little nervous about this. I mean, I know what I was thinking when I saw you today. But once I gave you my number, I said, 'He ain't gon' call.' So when you called, I got a little bit excited. But now . . . I mean . . . I don't really get down like this."

I couldn't believe it. I was about to get turned down again. So I just started smiling. I guess it was good for me. My streak was over.

I said, "The first thing I thought about was your brother."

She said, "I know, right? Seems like he's watching us or something."

"Maybe," I told her. However, she didn't appear to have any clothes on under her pink nightgown.

I said, "So, you weren't nervous about gettin' naked though, huh?"

"Oh, naw, I'm proud of my body. I had my daughter and went up to a hundred and sixty pounds, then I got right back down to one-eighteen." She even lifted her stuff up and showed me her flat stomach. That was the wrong thing to do. After I saw how tight her body was, I wanted to dig into her right there on her living room floor. She even had a diamond ring in her navel.

"That's ah . . . pretty tight," I told her. All of a sudden, I could feel my pants getting tight again.

I asked her, "Can I see that again?"

She looked and smiled at me. "I don't think I should," she told me. Then she said, "You let me see what you got. You're the model, right? I'm just a regular girl."

We were going down the wrong road of temptation. Both of us.

I stood up from the sofa and showed her my chest and abs anyway.

I said, "So, we're gonna do a striptease here?"

She smiled and said nothing. Then she turned away. "I shouldn't even be thinking this way," she confessed.

"It's too late now," I told her. "I thought the same thing when you flashed me."

"You thought what?"

"Damn, she got a tight body," I told her. "I want a piece of that."

She grinned and shook her head slowly. "I need some bad, too."

"You need some what?"

She looked at the tight crotch area of my jeans.

It was crazy, but I was ready to do another one.

Theresa looked away again and seemed bashful.

I told her, "Don't be ashamed of how you feel. It gets the best of all of us."

She shook her head again and kept her distance from me.

I looked like a damn fool standing there. But I had made up my mind. I wanted more action.

I asked her, "When was the last time you had any?"

"It's been too long," she told me.

"Well, you gon' start counting from zero again after tonight," I told her boldly. Fuck it, I was ready for her.

"Is that right?" she asked me.

"Only if you allow it. But if you don't allow it . . . I mean, it's all up to you."

Theresa was laboring in her decision to do anything with me, and I was becoming anxious. So I pushed up on her and placed my dick on her ass through my jeans and her pink nightgown. And I know she could feel how hard I was. I was already throbbing for her.

"What are you doing?" she asked me.

"I'm letting you get to know what it feels like."

She didn't push me away, so I started to pump her slowly from behind.

"You gon' start something," she told me.

"Good."

She reached back with her right hand and grabbed my crotch. So I reached around with my left hand and started to finger her pussy. She wasn't wearing any panties.

She started to get into it, rowing forward from my touch.

"You got a condom?" she asked me.

"Several."

"So, I guess my brother is gonna have to be mad at us."

"I guess so," I told her, because if I got myself started, I surely wasn't stopping.

She said, "Come on," and took my hand to lead me upstairs. I followed her up to her master bedroom in her three-bedroom home, and I dropped my clothes in a pile on the floor next to her bed.

She had a high wooden bed with a burgundy quilt, matching

sheets, pillowcases, and throw pillows. Against the wall in front of her bed was an arch-shaped mirror attached to a long wooden dresser that matched her bed frame. She had a tall wooden dresser against the wall to the left of the bed, in between her two windows. On the bed were various stuffed animals that she pushed off for me. I was impressed again. I expected less.

"Nice place you have here," I complimented her.

"I try."

"Looks like you're doing more than that. You're succeeding."

"Thank you."

I stood there butt naked at the foot of her bed while she pulled her sheets and quilt back.

"You want me to climb in and put a condom on?" I asked her.

She nodded. "Yeah, you do that. I'll go check my daughter right quick."

I took out my first condom, slid it down my shaft, and climbed into Theresa's comfortable high bed to wait for her.

She walked back in from checking up on her daughter and closed her bedroom door, leaving a slight crack.

"Is she all right?" I asked her.

She nodded again. "Yeah." Then she climbed into bed with me while still wearing her pink nightgown. She straddled me and leaned over to kiss my chest.

"You have a beautiful body, too," she told me.

I said, "It's a job."

She immediately grabbed my dick and slid it into her. It wasn't a perfect fit either. She was a bit tight.

"Mmm," she grunted, "this is gonna hurt a little bit." She slid my erect manhood inside of her anyway. Then she began to ride me real slowly.

She asked me, "You get to do a lot of pretty girls, don't you? So I'm just another one."

I was paying more attention to her slow stroke. She was doing a pretty good job of it.

I asked her, "Does that bother you?"

She shrugged. "I guess you take it if you can get it," she commented. "Just keep yourself safe, that's all I can say."

With her talking to me and stroking me at the same time, it threw off my rhythm. I didn't know when to brace myself for the pleasure, it just kind of snuck up on me.

"Oooh, shit, you, ooh," I responded to her, jerking forward. She had some tight pussy, too. Her sweet cave was as fit as her body, so I could feel every slow pull on my dick.

She balanced herself against my stomach and moved in small, up and down circles that were killing me. I leaned up and sucked her shapely titties. She had the kind of titties that didn't need a push-up bra. They were already up.

As soon as I began to suck on her chest, she cradled my head like a baby and fingered over my short-cut hair.

"Mmm," she moaned, and continued to stroke me with her body.

I thought about how peaceful it was. There we were in the silent dark of her bedroom, slow fucking, while all kinds of chaos awaited in the streets. No wonder sex was so powerful and addictive. It was an oasis of humanity; man and woman enjoying the explosive forces of their natural bodies in every city, town, and private home.

I started thinking that I was glad I had decided to go through with it. Everybody needed love, or the feelings of love. There was no race, class, or gender to separate those feelings. Maybe guys thought about sex more physically than women, and women thought about it more emotionally than men, but it was what it was, and it needed to be available to all of us. So I closed my eyes and enjoyed Theresa's ride in peaceful silence.

Back to Chaos

I SAT UP IN Theresa's bed, still thinking about the peaceful therapy of good sex. We had completed a couple of rounds, and had used a couple of condoms already. Theresa leaned over beside me and looked into my face.

"What are you thinking about?" she asked me.

I paused for a minute. "Sex," I told her. I was totally relaxed by it.

"What about it?"

"It's just what the doctor ordered."

She laughed and fell back down. "Tell me about it."

Then we were silent again.

"So . . . when am I going to see you again?" she asked me. That's when the reality of life smacks you back in the face.

Instead of answering her question, I asked her, "Have you ever thought about how great it would be to just lie in bed all night with no time on the clock? I mean, like, the clock never moves, you know. So instead of it being three in the morning, and almost time for me to go, it's still midnight, and going nowhere."

"Hmm," she grunted. "How would you feel about that? You're the one who has to go."

I said, "I feel great right now."

"Mmm-hmm, right now, is the key word," she told me. "Everybody feels good right after they just had sex. But how do they feel about it the next day?"

"First of all, everybody doesn't feel good right after sex. Sometimes the shit ain't no good," I told her.

"Well, you know what I mean, after good sex then. But without real meaning to it, it's only sex."

"Is that how you feel? You're telling me that you didn't need this tonight? You would rather have meaning or no sex at all?"

She stopped and thought about it. "You need both," she answered. "That's when it's the best."

I nodded. I could see her point. Meaning was the concern that Geneva had expressed to me earlier. Had there been any real meaning for dealing with me outside of just fucking, I could have been with her that night instead of Theresa. But Theresa needed companionship more than Geneva, so I ended up with her. It was that simple. No more, no less. And at the end of the night I felt sorry for Theresa, sorry that I would never stay.

"WHAT TIME did you get back in here this morning?" my mother asked me. I was sleeping in her cozy guest room. I had no idea what time it was when she asked me that, but I knew she had to go to work by eight-thirty, so I assumed it was sometime after eight.

"I don't know," I mumbled. "I guess around five-thirty or so."

"Well, nothing stays open that late around here on a Tuesday, so you weren't out with your friends all night."

I didn't respond to that, and my mother didn't wait around for a response. She gathered her keys and left for work, and I went back to sleep.

When I was back up for the day, it was nearly twelve o'clock and my mother's home phone was ringing. I figured she had an answering service, so I just let it ring. The phone call wasn't for me. But then the call stopped, and when it started ringing all over again, I went ahead and answered it.

"Hello."

"Geneva said you could have her phone number to call her," my mother told me.

"Yeah, she told me that last night."

"Why didn't you take it then? I told you she's a good girl. You need someone to take you off these streets. I know what kind of trouble you can get into out there."

"Are you on lunch break?" I asked her. She was getting rather personal in her conversation with me from work.

"You know, you got a way of always dodging questions, Terrance," she commented.

"Of course I do," I told her. "I get it from you all."

"Well, I'm gonna give you Geneva's number right now. So take out your cell phone and put her number in."

I went ahead and took the girl's number, but I wasn't planning on calling her any time soon. I was the wrong guy to be thinking about settling down, and I had half a dozen other phone numbers that were more pressing than hers. Geneva was no Andrea, and we had no history together.

My mother asked me, "So, when are you leaving for Atlanta again?"

Honestly, I didn't see any reason in staying in Gary long. I still hadn't seen many of my old friends, but so what? They weren't going to cry over not seeing me. We could all wait until the next time.

"What time you get off work tonight?" I asked her. "Same time?"

"No, since I cut out of here early yesterday, I promised to work a little later tonight."

I said, "I might get out of here today then." I expected to get an earful over that, but I didn't.

My mother grunted, "Mmm-hmm, I figured that. Once you stayed out late last night, I knew you would want to leave today. The old hit-and-run move. But if it was Geneva, she'd make you stay."

My mother sure had a lot of faith in that girl.

I said, "Mom, has it ever crossed your mind that she may not even like me?"

"Good, I'm glad she doesn't. A man needs to learn how to work for something. But she likes you enough to give you her number."

I didn't have anything else to say. I thought about asking her about my sister to get the subject off of me, but that would have started another long conversation, and I didn't want to be on the phone that long.

I said, "Well, we'll see what happens, Mom. We'll see."

As soon as I hung up the phone with my mother, my cell phone rang from my hip. I looked down at the number and saw that it was Theresa calling me.

Should I answer this? I thought to myself. I felt we had a peaceful night together, so I hoped she wasn't calling to ruin it. Sometimes you just had to let things be. However, I answered her phone call just to make sure everything was okay.

She said, "I hate to bother you, but you still haven't answered my question from this morning. Am I going to see you again?"

I paused. Her phone call wasn't that bad, but I had to wait and see how far she would go with it. There were no fairy tales for me to tell her, so I just stuck to the truth.

"Theresa, we already know the answer to that. If I'm here, and we both have the time and the desire to see each other again, then we will. But if I'm not here, and you're not where I'm at . . ."

"All right, I just wanted to see what you were gonna say. So thanks for being honest," she told me.

"We're both adults here," I explained. "So there's no sense in me lying about it."

She said, "Sometimes we want the lie, but the lie fucks us up for later. So thanks for not fucking us up."

I noticed her language and asked her, "Are you at work right now?"

She laughed at me. "I'm on my lunch break. I wouldn't talk like this on the job, or get into my business like that."

"Oh, okay," I told her. "I was about to ask what kind of job you had."

"Hmm," she mumbled. "There's a lot we don't know about each other."

I thought about her comment and felt bad again. The truth was, I didn't want to know that much about her. We had a good night together, we knew each other from the old neighborhood, her older brother was my friend, and she had some nice, tight pussy. I mean, it was a terrible thought, but that was about all I needed to know about her.

I told her, "We'll have time for that. But right now, I was just about to start packing up to hit the road again."

"You're leaving already?" she asked me. She had urgency in her voice.

I said, "You know, once you get used to traveling, it becomes normal to leave. That's just my lifestyle. It's been that way for years now."

I was telling her the absolute truth.

She said, "Oh. Okay." She sounded disappointed. I wanted no part of that. She was bringing my energy down.

"Well, let me go ahead and finish up what I was doing," I told her. "You have a good day at work today."

"I never said that I was finished talking to you." That was the next thing that came out of her mouth.

I looked at my cell phone and shook my head. That was exactly the kind of woman I wanted to avoid.

Maybe I shouldn't have gone over there last night after all, I thought.

"All right, well, I'ma let you go ahead and go," she finally told me.

"Thanks," I mumbled. "And you have a good day," I repeated.

"Yeah, you, too."

When I clicked off the line, I vowed that she would never hear from me again, and I meant it. More contact with her would only lead to more pain.

"Let me get the hell out of here," I said out loud. I went back to my mother's guest room and started packing up in a hurry. I didn't have that much to pack, so I was done and ready to go in no time. I called a taxi to take me back to the train station for my return to Chicago. Instead of calling my mother and telling her that I was leaving, I took the cop-out approach and wrote her a nice letter to leave on the kitchen table where I knew she would find it.

During the train ride back to Chicago, all I did was think about my life. My freedom was the sweetest joy in the world. I figured I really had to love a girl to get married. I had to love a woman more than I loved being free, and I doubted if that would ever happen. At the same time, all of my bed hopping still felt meaningless. What was it all for?

I must have been thinking real hard about my life, because I made it to Chicago quicker than a finger snap. I jumped in another cab and headed straight for the airport.

On my way to Chicago's O'Hare International, I started thinking about Andrea again. Finally, she was just another woman to me, and a freak at that.

She still got some soft pussy, though, I thought to myself with a grin. Would I still do her? Of course I would. But I no longer felt guilty about her. She would find a way to get along with her life, and it looked like she would be fighting to make Mr. Walker pay for it. It served him right for taking her from me in the first place. Now life had ruined her, and I felt ruined right along with her. But I would have to live with it.

WHEN I ARRIVED BACK at my place in Atlanta, I tried my best to ignore the world for at least a day or two to recuperate from everything. I was really worn down, but that damn Corey Sanders blew up my cell and my home phone until I finally answered his calls on Thursday evening.

He said, "You remember I told you I was coming to Atlanta? I'm in town, man. I'm staying at the Hyatt downtown on Peachtree."

I wanted to hang up on his ass and tell him not to call me. I needed rest from swinging, but Corey wasn't trying to hear it.

"I got these two ladies in Atlanta now, man. They're both fine and they're down for anything. And I do mean, anything," he told me.

I just started laughing. The last thing I needed in the world was another matchmaker. Nor did I need any more sex for a while. When was enough enough?

I finally said, "Corey, do you actually believe that I need you to introduce me to any women here in Atlanta? I mean, come on."

"Well, it's not just about you, man. I just figured you wanted to hang out with me, and if women are what you need to feel comfortable, then I was gonna get that for you."

I said, "Yeah, but we can meet women whenever. And I'm not feeling that right now."

He said, "Terrance, trust me on this, man. These two girls are fine with a capital F."

I shook my head over the phone. Corey just wasn't getting it. I didn't care how fine these women were. I needed to rest from it all.

"Corey . . ."

"You promised me, man. Now come on," he pleaded.

I still couldn't understand why he was so adamant about hanging out with me. There had to be plenty of folks who were a lot more successful that he could hang out with in Atlanta. He did security for the stars.

I figured the only way I could make the situation work for me was if I went along with his double date idea and became extra boring. Maybe if I showed up with no personality or interest, the women would decide that I was not worth their time, and Corey would move on to hang out with the next man of stature with women. There were plenty of them to go around. I guess the difference was that I had been the only fool willing to respond to him. Or maybe I wasn't. Maybe Corey had propositioned other guys through their past histories together as well.

I said, "All right, all right, I'll go, man. But I'm warning you now . . ."

I stopped myself in mid-sentence. If I warned him that I was tired and didn't feel up to entertaining in advance, then maybe he would chalk up my whole plan of boredom as just one of those nights and still bug me about hanging out.

"You're warning me of what?" he asked me.

"Nothing. Let me just go ahead and throw something on. Where do you want me to meet you?"

"Oh, I'll just pick you up at your place. It's doesn't really matter to me."

It mattered to me though. He didn't need to know where I lived, if he didn't know it already. I couldn't put too much past this guy. I needed to get rid of him once and for all. I guess a social turn off would have to do.

I said, "Well, where do you have in mind to take these girls?"

He paused. "Actually, man, we could just eat and talk and drink at my hotel. We don't have to take 'em nowhere if we don't want to."

"So these girls are real low maintenance, huh?"

"They just want to have good company, man, that's all. What's wrong with that?"

I said, "All right, let me get dressed and I'll just meet you at the Hyatt then." There was no sense in prolonging the issue. I wanted to get his eagerness over with.

I hung up the phone and thought about the most boring outfit I could wear. It's funny how I put on nice clothes to make a living, but in my actual life, I typically dressed casually. Well, what if I showed up overdressed this time? Would that turn them all off or on?

"Women tend to dislike stuffy men," I reasoned. So I went ahead and got stuffy in a dark blue suit, dark tie, and dark shoes.

I showed up at the lobby of the Hyatt Hotel, looking as if I was about to attend a gala affair. Corey looked me over and started laughing. He was wearing my usual gear: blue jeans, comfortable shoes, a basic tee, and a sports jacket. It looked as if we was trying to steal my casual style.

He said, "Hey, man, I thought I told you we were just gonna hang out over here at the hotel. You look good, though, I'll give you that. You making me feel underdressed now."

"Well, what are they wearing?" I asked him about the women.

He continued to chuckle at me. He said, "I doubt if they show up looking anything like you. You're gonna be the star of the night."

I laughed it off with him. But inside, I knew the girls would think I was too much. Maybe I'd create a whole conceited attitude to match. Women hated that, too. I would look the part and play the part and get dissed. I couldn't wait. I even brought my cell phone with me to let it ring, and I planned on answering every single phone call, as if they were all important.

Corey and I sat down at the bar in the lobby area and immediately ordered drinks. After our orders were filled and we took our first sips, Corey said, "You know what I told you, right?"

I frowned at him. "What you told me about what?"

He leaned closer to me. "These girls, man, will do about anything."

I said, "Oh, yeah," and took another sip of my drink. He had no idea what I had in store for them. But I know one thing, it seemed like he was sitting a lot closer to me than I felt comfortable with.

When these women showed up, we were on our second and third drinks already.

"Hey, how you doin'?" Corey stood up and greeted them.

I looked them over, and they weren't bad. In fact, they reminded me of a meatier, less attractive version of Andrea and Brazil. They were both wearing colorful skirt and dress outfits like older women who hung out in bars were prone to do. Only they weren't that old-looking.

Corey introduced us all.

"Yeah, this is Janice and Selena, and this is my friend Terrance, the model."

We shook hands, exchanged nods, and greeted one another before we found a four-seat table to sit in. Janice was Brazil, and Selena was Andrea. I was tripping that way, while sizing them up for the night.

"Are you coming from an earlier event or something?" Janice asked me. I could tell she was going to be the talker. I could see it in her curious face.

I said, "No, I just like to make a good impression when I meet a group of nice ladies, so I went ahead and put on my Sunday best."

Selena grinned with double dimples and said, "Well, it ain't Sunday."

I figured she would have looked a lot better if her face was clearer. I asked her, "And how old are you?"

"Old enough," she told me.

I said, "Well, there are a few products that I could write down for you that would give you much smoother skin if you're interested. I mean, I'm just ah, passing on some of the things I've learned about keeping clear and smooth skin in the fashion and modeling industry."

They all looked at me in shock. I expected it from them.

"So, what are you trying to say?" Janice asked me.

"He's saying she needs to clear her skin up," Corey responded for me. I didn't expect that.

I said, "But she still has more attraction in a modeling sense than you would have," I told Janice.

Selena began to smile, but Janice gave me the evil eye. Even Corey looked confused.

Janice said, "So, you're just one of those conceited, rude-ass motherfuckers, huh?"

"I don't use that kind of language to express myself with either," I told her.

She said, "I don't give a fuck what you do to express yourself . . . faggot."

That one came out of left field. I kept my cool with her and said, "Is that the lie you've been told about male models, because I'm not a gay man. I simply prefer women of a higher caliber."

"From what I hear, you don't like women at all," Janice responded.

What in the world was she talking about? Was my suit and tie look making her believe I was gay? That wasn't the impression that I was aiming for.

I looked at Corey to see what his response would be. He looked at me for a hot second and looked away. Did he think I was gay, too? He knew better than that.

I lost my cool and told Janice, "So if I fucked you in the ass, would that prove that I liked women?"

"I thought you said you don't use that kind of language," she told me. "And a gay man *would* fuck a woman in the ass. That just shows how you're used to doing it."

"And what about you two lesbians?" I shot back. "I guess you both get off eating each other's pussy," I assumed distastefully. I was just saying wild shit.

"Well, which one is the man and woman for you two?" she asked me.

I didn't even look at Corey for that. Either this woman was playing a better game than me at throwing me for a loop, or I was definitely barking up the wrong tree with my scheme.

I said, "You sure got a lot of mouth sitting over there. Now I'm wondering how much of my dick I can fit in it."

The next thing I knew, Corey and Selena were laughing as if it was all a game. I didn't think it was funny though. Even Janice began to crack a smile.

She said, "I can swallow a lot more than you think."

Was it all a part of their game plan on me? I was as confused as ever.

Corey said, "Well, let's all go on up to the room and see what's what then."

Janice stood up from our table. She said, "Shit, I ain't afraid of him. Bring the shit on."

Had I missed something? It appeared that my foul mouth had turned the bitch on. Selena stood up, too, along with Corey. I was the only one still seated.

"Well, come on, Brooks Brothers. You the one talking all that shit. Let me see you peel off that tight-ass Superman suit and give me what you got."

I began to look around at the other tables to see if anyone had heard us. I was sure they had heard some of it, but they were mostly white folks who would rather ignore the embarrassment of it all.

All of a sudden, all eyes were on me.

I said, "So, now you wanna get my suit all messed up from messing around with you."

I was basically stalling. My game plan had failed, and theirs was working wonders. They were all ready to venture up to the room and get wild. It felt like that was what they wanted all along. I had been the fool.

Janice said, "You won't get your damn suit messed up. I'm gonna be the one on my knees."

Corey started shaking his head and was grinning from ear to ear. He said, "I told you how they were, man."

He was saying it right to their faces. I had the feeling they were hookers or something. I mean, how obvious could we get? I couldn't budge.

Corey said, "Come on, Terrance, let's rock and roll wit' it."

With them just standing around and waiting for me, people started to look curiously in our direction, so I finally stood up to make my way over to the elevators. I didn't want to continue drawing so much attention to us.

Janice kept talking smack on our way up the elevators to the room.

"Now we'll see what your tight faggot ass got to prove."

I didn't even have any damn condoms. I just knew my plan was foolproof. For once, my cell phone wasn't even ringing.

Come on, somebody fucking call me! I panicked. I was ready to make a call on my own in a minute.

"Why you so quiet now?" Selena asked me with a grin. We were getting off on the sixteenth floor.

This is fucking ridiculous! I told myself. I was ready to say *Fuck it all!* and break the hell out of there, but I didn't.

We made it to Corey's room, and he had double beds. Had this motherfucker been planning a tag-team match? I assumed . . . Hell, I didn't know what I assumed. I just didn't expect to be in that situation that night.

I sat down on the long dresser cabinet and began to scramble in my mind for a last-ditch opportunity to get the hell out of there. Before I knew it, Corey and Selena were already taking their clothes off with no foreplay or anything.

I had to look away to stop from seeing the man's ass.

"What's wrong now?" Janice asked me. She walked over close and began to grab at my clothes.

I grabbed her hands to stop her. I said, "I don't even have any condoms with me."

"I got condoms."

Selena said, "We all have condoms in here. Are you crazy?"

Hookers would have condoms.

I asked them, "Are you two hookers or what? I mean, you just seem a little too eager for grown women. Is Corey paying you for this?"

It was my last chance to turn them off, but all it seemed to do was irritate Corey.

He said, "Man, you sound like the bitch. You talked about putting your dick in her mouth, now do it. You need a dick in your ass to get you started?"

He was approaching me with his dick out as he spoke.

I was incensed! What was he trying to say? And where was he going with this?

I stood up from the dresser and said, "What?"

He said, "You heard me. Do I have to bend you over to get this shit started up in here? Is that how you like it? You gotta be forced to do it?"

The girls began laughing and backed away to watch a confrontation between us.

I was frozen for a minute, while trying to figure out if this was really happening. I guess I was waiting to wake up from the dream, or the nightmare, because it was all crazy.

Corey stripped himself fully naked and walked over to make sure the door was locked and latched. My heart started racing in my chest. The man was bigger than me, and I was going to have to fight his ass to the death if he was serious.

He started walking back toward me. "Now we gon' see what's up. I've been thinking about this for a while now," he revealed to me.

Janice and Selena looked turned on by it. They were both giggling and fondling each other, while stripping from their own clothes.

Janice joked and sang, *"Somebody's gonna get his assss took . . ."*

That shit woke me up from my daze. It was not a joke in there. So I rushed at Corey and pushed him into the wall with a thump.

BOOM!

Somehow he grabbed me by my arms and pulled me into him, kissing me on the mouth.

"You want it rough, huh?" he said, and started grabbing at my tailored clothes.

Finally, my stupid-ass cell phone rang. It was too late to pay attention to it at that point. I was in a fight for my manhood.

I yelled, "You sick motherfucker!" and struggled to get my arms loose while he continued to try and kiss me.

"Is this how y'all usually get down?" Selena asked. These women still looked as if it was a game. I don't know what Corey had told them, but they must have really believed him.

I went wild and head-butted him in the mouth.

"ARRGH, ARRGH, ARRGH!" I grunted, head-butting him again and again. I had busted his lip open but he still wouldn't let me go.

"Damn, he's really fucking fighting him," Janice stated. I guess it finally dawned on her that I wasn't fucking playing.

"Bitch, I'm not gay!" I screamed at her.

Corey said, "Yes, you are, I heard about you. I heard all about you."

He tried to spin me around while I continued to struggle with him. I got my right hand free and pummeled him in his face with my balled fist.

"Get the fuck off of me!" I yelled as I punched him. I got my left hand free and beat him with both hands. "You motherfucker!"

Selena said, "Damn, this is serious."

I don't know how tough of a man Corey was, but I had him curled up in a ball on the floor, while I kicked and stomped his head into the wall.

"You know you want it, man," he insisted. "I heard about you."

Janice said, "Well, you must have heard the wrong shit, because he just kicked your ass instead of fucking it."

I was still confused and in need of answers. My hands and clothing were a bloody mess. I stopped stomping his head into the wall and screamed, "Who told you that bullshit? Andrea told you I was fucking gay? That bitch told you that lie?" I yelled at him.

He whimpered, "They all told me at this mansion in L.A. They said everybody was doing it. That's how they got me to do it. They said you were doing it, too."

I was shocked. Was Marcus Vissel spreading false rumors about everyone he worked with at this mansion of his to turn people out? How crazy was that?

"They said a lot of celebrity folk were down with it. It was like a Roman society," Corey continued. He started running off known names in Hollywood that I would not repeat.

Janice heard some of the names and responded, "Get the fuck out of here. Are you serious?"

Corey cried, "I saw some of them there with my own eyes. They have other places out in California where they do it, too."

This big security agent was beaten bloody and crying in a ball, like a butt-naked baby. And he was uncovering everything.

I screamed, "Just because they were there don't mean they're all fucking each other! You went for that stupid shit!"

He said, "They are. I even fucked a couple of them."

"Oh my God," Selena responded to it. But she didn't sound disgusted like I was by it; the slut looked turned on. "Which ones did you fuck?" she asked him.

I didn't want to hear shit else about it. I had to get the hell out of there to regroup and to change my clothes. I was there at Mr. Vissel's mansion, and at various other spots in L.A., but I surely wasn't fucking another man, and no man was fucking me.

I looked back at Corey and his two, freaky consignors. I said, "You motherfuckers are all crazy," and I stormed out the door.

"Fuck you!" I heard one of them shout as I left. It was probably Janice.

I made my way to the elevators thinking a mile a minute. It was just after eleven o'clock, so I could call Marcus in L.A. and it would be only after eight. Then I would call Andrea back in Chicago and reveal what I knew about the secrets of the mansion. I guess she still wasn't out of my life after all.

"Fuck!" I cursed myself on the elevator. I wasn't going to make any phone calls until I got the hell out of there. If someone saw me with all that blood on my clothes, they might report me to security for an assault. I even had to wipe the blood from my hands onto my suit to stop from smearing it over everything else I touched.

I got off the elevator at the garage level below the hotel and felt safe and sound as I made it to my car without notice. Had I gotten off at the lobby floor, I surely would have been busted by a crowd of hotel guests and workers.

I climbed into my car and started stripping down my bloodied clothes, beginning with my tie.

"Now what the hell do I tell the cleaners?" I asked myself.

It was an Yves Saint Laurent suit that needed delicate care. But I guess I would have to wash it myself or throw it away. I was too ashamed to even have to lie about the events of the night. I just wanted to forget about it. How hard would that be?

I drove out of the parking garage, hit the street, and headed back toward home still stunned and confused.

I looked down to start making urgent phone calls to L.A. and

Chicago, but the phone rang right as I began to dial. It was my sister.

She rushed onto the line and said, "Terrance, that asshole just tried to choke me to death to kill me and the baby!"

I asked her, "Who are you talking about?"

"The asshole who got me pregnant. He hates me, Terrance! He hates me!" Juanita screamed hysterically into the phone.

"'Where are you?" I asked her.

"I'm just driving away from his house."

"You know where he lives?" For the life of me, I assumed that Juanita was one of this guy's playthings that never made it to his home. A lot of players didn't allow women to know where they lived. I know I didn't. You did your business at their house or at the hotel, and you left it there.

Juanita shouted, "Of course I know where he lives! What kind of question is that? I'm not some hotel whore!"

I didn't know what else to say to my sister. I had just escaped a life crisis of my own. How ironic. Juanita had me thinking what my mother was up to. She hadn't spoken to me since I left the house with my little note for her. Could we all have been involved in crises at the same time? I don't know why I was thinking that, but it was on my mind.

Juanita said, "He had another woman at his house, and he told me he didn't ever want to see me again, and that I should leave him the fuck alone and forget where he lives."

I took a deep breath while I drove. Nothing I had to say to my sister was going to make her feel any better. This basketball guy had already told her to get an abortion. We all did. But she was still trying to force the guy into caring for her and this unborn baby. That was what the situation was to me. Whether I was her brother or not, I was still a man who sided with the other man. He didn't want a kid out of their relationship. He only wanted some pussy.

My sister could eventually get an unwarranted child support settlement out of him, but outside of that, I didn't see where her situation would get any better. In fact, I didn't feel like she deserved a settlement. They had sex together, and she had gotten pregnant by him, but they had options to come to a sane conclusion. However, Juanita's decision was forcing them both to act insane. It would be the wrong decision made for the rest of her life. But she refused to listen to reason.

I asked her, "Are you still dead set on having this baby?"

My sister didn't answer me immediately. There was an extralong pause. She finally said, "I don't know anymore, and I can't think about that right now."

"No, you need to think about it right now," I insisted. "Because the same feelings you have right now are what you're gonna be dealing with for the rest of your life."

I said, "It's never gonna get any better than this, Juanita. You need to understand that now. This is not a soap opera. Nobody can change the episode and make this guy come back to you. There is no happily ever after in this shit. Do you understand that?"

"Well, if he felt that way, then he shouldn't have gotten me pregnant," she whined.

I couldn't believe my sister. She sounded like a spoiled teenager, and I was not in the mood for sympathy. She was twenty-eight years old. I know she had better sense then that.

I shouted, "You sound like a damn fool, Juanita! How the hell is this man gonna get you pregnant without you lying down with him? You don't let this guy take control of your life. And you don't let an unborn child do it either!"

I said, "This is still *your* life, and if you allow this situation to dictate how you live the rest of it, then that's on you. But you're not getting sympathy from me, so don't call me with this shit no more!"

My sister hung up on me just like I expected her to. She just caught me at the wrong damn time. I had a bunch of anger still running through my system from what had happened to me that night. I still had my own stressed-out phone calls to make. But then I thought back to my sister. What if she got too disturbed to drive home?

I got nervous and called her back. The first three times she didn't answer the phone. When she answered my fourth call, she cried, "Look, if you're gonna treat me just like he does, then I don't ever need to talk to you again. You fucking men are all the same!"

"Actually, I was calling you back to see if you were all right," I told her.

She asked me, "Why, because I'm your little sister? What if I was just a regular woman? Would you call me back if I was just one of your many girlfriends?"

She had me there. But I had explained that to her weeks ago.

I said, "I already told you how selfish I am. We both know that already. But you fail to realize that there are men out there who are not selfish. So why get involved with us?"

"Because that's all I fucking know is selfish-ass men!" she yelled through the phone at me. She said, "When was our father ever around? I've never even had a fucking hug from my father! Not even one hug!"

Damn! What could I say to that? I was stunned. But how long would the fatherless thing continue to hurt her? So I said the only logical thing that came to mind.

"That's why you should have an abortion," I told her. "All you're about to do is continue the cycle. You're about to bring another fatherless child into the world when you haven't even healed from your own pain. You can't see that?"

She broke down and started crying louder. "You don't care what I feel. You don't care about my feelings at all. I need somebody to love me. My baby will love me."

Oh my God! I thought to myself. I was sorry I called the girl back. She was insane.

I said, "Juanita, don't you see that's the same mistake that every other girl makes. That child is gonna want more love than you can offer, just like you want more love than what Mom could give us."

"She gave *you* love. Mom still loves you," my sister argued through her tears.

I had to pull over and park. I was just a block away from my place, but I had to stop and shake my head. It was a crazy-ass night.

"She loves you—"

"No, she doesn't," my sister cut me off before I could finish. "She's always loved you more."

How could I ever end a conversation like that? Juanita had always believed our mother loved me more. I actually had to think about it. I was the firstborn, the only son, I was mostly out of sight and out of mind on my own adventures, and I had done quite well for myself without ever finishing college. Juanita was the second born, a girl who needed a lot of attention and maintenance, and she had graduated from college and still couldn't keep her life or income in order. Now she was bringing an unwanted child into the world without marriage or stability, a child that only she wanted, but we would all be forced to pay for.

Again, how could I ever end a conversation like that?

Party Over

I WAS ON THE PHONE with my sister for nearly an hour, ignoring five other phone calls, while we reminisced on our childhood in Gary, Indiana. It hadn't been that bad. We agreed that we had both made it to adulthood with opportunities to go to college, I just had no idea how many scars we had picked up and carried with us along the way.

Juanita said, "At the end of the day, it's just better being a guy. That's all there is to it. All you have to do is just pick up your clothes and leave."

I wanted to dispute that with some profound statement about the advantages of being a woman, if just to make my sister feel better, but I felt they would sound hollow. Truth was, I was glad I was a man. Juanita was right; all I had to do was keep women at a distance, while staying focused on my career, and I had my whole life in front of me. But could a woman stay focused just the same without being in love with a man?

I thought about the successful female models I had been around over the years. Many of them had done quite well at keeping men at bay. Although they rarely had to worry about chasing a man. And some of them had long-standing boyfriends who were more than thrilled to be involved with them.

Ultimately, I told my sister, "You might just have to let this father-hood thing go and just treat a man like your brother. You know, you fight with him, you make up, and you never get pregnant by him."

Juanita at least chuckled at it. Then she said, "But I want a family of my own, Tee. I'm almost thirty now."

"Well then, get married first," I told her. "If you get married first, then at least you know that the man is willing to confess his love and loyalty to you. That's the way family structures have lasted for many thousands of years. And don't tell me nothing about what's going on now with so many women raising children themselves, because if you didn't care about having a man in your life, you wouldn't be pregnant, and you wouldn't be calling me right now to complain about the nigga."

Juanita chuckled again. I didn't mean to disrespect my fellow broth-ers with the use of the word, I just understood how violently our women felt about us whenever we failed to do what they wanted us to do. I was a nigga to many women myself, just because I wanted some milk and not the cow.

When my phone buzzed from the other line again, Juanita told me, "I don't want to hold you up anymore. I feel a little better now, and I'm almost back home, so thanks for talking to me and hearing me out."

Nevertheless, I was still concerned about the final decision on her pregnancy.

I said, "Okay, but I'm still gonna be honest with you before I hang up this phone, Juanita."

She beat me to the punch. "I'll think about, Terrance. Okay? I'll think about it."

There wasn't much to think about in my book; no marriage, no kid. It was a simple one-two punch to me. But I wasn't a woman, and I still couldn't understand a lot of the decisions they made.

I said "Okay" but I still felt uncertain when I hung up the phone with her.

I hope she does the right thing, I told myself. I clicked over the line and caught a call from Florida just in time. It was Judi calling me.

She said, "I haven't talked to you in a minute. What have you been up to?"

I asked her, "Are you still celibate?"

"Yes, I am," she told me.

"Well, that might not be a bad idea after all," I stated.

"Why, what did you do?"

Judi was the right person for me to talk to at the right time.

I said, "What didn't I do? This last past week has been . . . Damn, where do I start?"

I had been tempted out of this world after Judi had preached celibacy to me only a short while back. I had gone in the opposite direction.

"Mmm-hmm," she grunted. "The beast can catch you out there. So what did you do? I won't pass judgment. I've been through plenty myself."

I asked her, "Just by chance, have you ever been out to Marcus Vissel's mansion in California?"

"Yes I have," she told me, "and if you're asking me that, then I guess I don't have to say much more about it."

I paused and thought about it. "Is that why you had a change of heart about sex?"

"It's one of the reasons, yes. It was all part of the process of me reevaluating who I am, what my worth is, and what more I could be doing to reach my maximum potential instead of selling my mind, soul, and body so cheaply."

"Tell me about it," I told her. "I even had a guy try to physically assault me thinking that I would be willing to fuck him. And you know I'm not going anywhere near that shit as much as I love women," I stated.

"You mean as much as you lust for women," Judi corrected me. "But I've seen it all, Terrance. That's why I'm no longer moved by it. You can't get to where you're trying to go on your back."

But do I give up sex entirely? I pondered.

I asked her, "So, what do you do when you have that itch?"

She joked and said, "I go to a doctor. But no, seriously, you just have to pray through it. Ask for strength, and then you go find something else to do."

Her weeks of abstinence had turned into months and still counting. I guess she was succeeding. I still didn't know if I could do it, but after the incident with Corey Sanders and the freaky week I had, I was definitely in need of reevaluation. What were my own priorities?

Judi asked me that question right on cue. "Terrance, what do you really want out of life? Have you ever asked yourself that question, or recently?"

"My life is pretty good. I don't think about wanting too many things," I told her.

"And you can continue to live like that? I mean, what's your motivation?"

That question was a lot easier for me. I answered, "Easy living and good travel. I don't ask for much. And I pretty much get that."

"What about from a woman?"

"Well, you know what I want from a woman," I told her with a grin. "But it always seems like as soon as you get a little bit too close to them, they start changing all the rules. That just happened to me a few weeks ago. Next thing I knew, I'm fucking everybody, and two girls at a time. I never did that before."

She paused for a minute. Then she said, "So, you're obviously in with the wrong crowd of people then. Maybe you need to change your scenery."

"To what, hanging out with celibates who practice yoga and eat fruit all day? I mean, this is my crowd. I just have to get back in control of it," I told her.

Judi sighed. "You're still fighting me, Terrance, but I'm not your enemy. I'm sure you've already met your enemy."

I looked over at the bloody clothes I had tossed onto the passenger seat and knew that she was right.

I joked and said, "So if I came down there and spent a few weeks or so with you, then I know I would be doing the right thing, huh?"

"It's not all about you coming down here to see me. You have to live the right way wherever you are," she responded. "That's like folks going to church on Sunday while sinning Monday through Saturday. They need to live by the way of God every day if they're going to claim it. I mean, I'm not calling myself or anyone else perfect, but at least be consistent."

"They are consistent, consistent in going to church on Sunday," I joked. Keeping things lighthearted was the only way for me to maintain my cool sometimes.

Before Judi could respond, my cell phone started warning me of a low battery.

"Hey, Judi, you know what. I'm gonna have to call you back in a few once I get back in the house. I need to recharge this phone."

"Oh, well, do what you have to do, and just call me when you're ready. I'll be here."

"Good. I'll call you back later on tonight then."

She said, "Terrance, do you realize what time it is?"

I looked at my car clock; it was twelve thirty-eight.

I answered, "It's nearly a quarter till one in the morning. Why?"

"When are you planing on calling back, before three?"

"Well, why are you calling me this late?" I asked her.

"Actually, I was just calling to leave you another message to call me when you got the chance to. But I guess you've been busy running wild out in the streets."

"Yeah, well let me get in off the streets before my battery runs out."

"Okay, I'll talk to you."

I hung up my cell phone, restarted my Mercedes, and finished driving home. When I made it in, I began to recharge my cell and thought about who I wanted to call to curse out first, Marcus Vessel in L.A. or Andrea in Chicago. And again, the phone rang while I held it in my hand, this time it was my home phone.

"Hello," I answered.

"Terrance, this is Paula Robinson in San Diego. I need to talk to you about my niece TaShay."

I was totally caught off-guard by it. Paula sounded extra professional and measured as if she had practiced keeping her cool before she called me. Did TaShay tell her aunt something? And did she know how late it was on the East Coast?

"Yeah, what's going on with her?" I asked. I wanted to sound alarmed and innocent. She wasn't getting any confessions out of me. But my heart was racing just from being asked about her. What if TaShay really wasn't on any kind of birth control and I had gotten her pregnant?

Paula asked me, "Did she and her friend Taniva drive up to see you when you were out here in L.A. last weekend?"

My heart jumped through my white T-shirt. I had to be very cautious with everything I said.

"Is she in some kind of trouble?" I asked Paula slowly.

"Well, I have a few questions on my mind about her and Tan last weekend that still don't quite add up, so I'm trying to get down to the bottom of this."

"And she told you that they were with me?"

I wasn't saying that they were or that they wasn't until I heard all the facts.

Paula said, "I didn't believe her when she told me that, that's why I'm calling you."

I said, "So, what's going on? Did something happen to them?"

I never did find out how long TaShay remained with Tan before she returned home. They could have gone anywhere and done anything while they were still together.

"Well, I don't quite know how to say this, but I feel that she's been out here on the wild side with this girl Tan, and she's been giving me all kinds of alibis as to where they were, so I'm just trying to dot my I's and cross my T's."

It didn't sound like she suspected me, so I could either leave TaShay out to dry, or I could help her out with a story of my own.

I said, "Am I allowed to be honest here?"

Paula paused. "Yes, of course."

"Okay, well, they did make their rounds with me on Friday night," I admitted. "We went to this club called The Palace in West Hollywood, where both girls got away from me and returned drunk. So I became concerned about them driving back home to San Diego in that condition, and I put them up at my hotel. But I had an early-morning photo shoot that Saturday morning in Santa Monica, and I left my cell phone in my room charging, where I wasn't able to check on the girls before they checked out of the hotel and left for San Diego.

"But now you're saying that they got in trouble on what night?" I asked carefully. I still didn't know what Paula knew, but I was assuming that TaShay hadn't told on me. I figured she was using the fact that Paula would never suspect me of anything, so I was going for broke with that assumption.

"How did TaShay even get in the club?" she asked me.

"Well, I believe she has a fake ID of some sort, because I don't remember there being a problem with her age at the door."

TaShay getting in hot water for a fake ID and alcohol was definitely better than any sex acts.

Her aunt said, "Okay, so Friday night is accounted for. Now I have to see about Saturday and Sunday nights. And I'm sorry about this, Terrance."

"Oh, it's no problem. So, how'd you come to your conclusions on them?" I asked her.

"I've just been told a few things by people I know in San Diego. And I don't think I want TaShay around this girl Taniva anymore. A bad reputation like that could ruin her career before she even gets started."

I said, "I understand. And you're right, of the two of them, Tan was a lot more loaded than TaShay the night that they were out with me."

I couldn't defend both of them. That would have been suspect. So TaShay would have to lose Tan to protect her modeling career. Or if they had a strong enough bond, they would continue to be friends anyway. But I had to give her aunt something to run with to cut TaShay some slack. Simply speaking, Tan would have to become the scapegoat.

Paula said, "Well, again, I apologize for calling you this late and asking, but I had a heated conversation with my niece today, and I needed to know what I needed to know."

"Yes, you do," I told her.

When we hung up, my heart was still pounding in my chest, and I had to take several deep breaths to calm myself down.

"Shit!" I cursed out loud to relieve more of the tension. "Never a-fuckin'-gain," I told myself. "What the hell was I thinking?"

I don't know who else, or what else those girls had done or gotten themselves into, but I was already thinking about protecting myself as much as possible. I had to come up with a workable response for everything.

All of a sudden, the incident with Corey was the last thing on my mind. I was thinking about leaving everyone alone—no Corey or Andrea, no Danni or Theresa, no TaShay or Tan, no Rachel or Victoria, and definitely no more of Marcus Vissel. The man and all of his ties had turned into the devil. Surely, I couldn't blame Marcus for all of the decisions that I made and the people that I had dealt with, but as Judi had said, it all added up together, and it was all wrong. I would have to distance myself from all of that. It was all about personal survival now. Fortunately, I had enough money stashed away to even change my career if I needed to. All I had to do was pick another profession.

I went through all the recent messages on my cell phone and home phone to see who I would ignore and who I would call back.

Danni had been blowing up both my phones with messages explaining her erratic behavior since the day I left for L.A.

She said, "I know I can get used to a normal relationship. It's just that I've been so used to expecting the worst out of men, that I always brace myself for the bullshit, whether it's coming or not."

As I had told my sister earlier that night, if you treat your man like family, then you can always find a civil way to stay close to him no matter what the issues are. But I didn't trust Danni to stay close to me at all. When the going gets tough, Danni was the kind of woman who would have no problem disappearing. She was the female version of me, and she was only calling me back to explain things because I had cut her ass loose first. I only wondered how long she would continue to call me if I failed to respond to her in the time frame that she wanted me.

Dealing with Danni was like setting an alarm clock. How many seconds, minutes, and hours would you get before she went off. She couldn't change just by saying it. She would need years of work and trust to change, and I wasn't the patient man that she needed to help her work through it. I was an alarm clock my damn self. I had my own issues to work out.

Rachel had called a few times, too, with more of her bold temptations.

"Let me know when you're ready to see me again. I still have a few tricks I haven't shown you yet, you delicious ass man you."

There was no way in hell I would deal with her again. She had opened up my closed mind in ways that I still had to think about. I mean, how kinky did a man want to be with his main woman versus his freakfests? Was there that much of a difference? Should there be? Maybe Rachel represented the sexual freedom and experimentation that you could hold as an option to spice up a committed relationship. But I didn't need anymore up close and personal lessons from her. I think I would rather watch some porno movies for ideas instead.

I moved on and listened to a message from Victoria. I really felt sorry for her. She was just a white girl caught up in the middle of things. I wasn't the kind of black man to forsake everything for the illusion of two to three mixed kids and a picket fence with a man-pleasing white woman. Victoria had all the signs of a woman who would forgive me over and over again. She showed me that on our first night together in Chicago. But . . . I just couldn't see myself going there. I listened to her message anyway.

"Hey, this is Victoria, I've been thinking about you." She laughed and said, "I have a couple of role-playing ideas of my own now, if they don't scare you away. But anyway, I miss you, and I'm here for you. Whatever you need, just think of me. Okay? Call me. 'Bye."

I sat there and listened to her message three times. I really wondered if black women realized the seductive appeal of a white woman. The illusion was so sweet that it was hypnotic in a way. All you had to do was find a white girl who liked you, and they would take it from there.

Whatever you need, just think of me.

Wow! She meant that shit, too. It was hard to turn down. Even when you did turn a white girl down, you would still think about her. She was the get-away-from-it-all girl. They represented peace from the struggle. I just didn't know how much peace I wanted in my life. I guess I was used to at least a little bit of turbulence. I didn't know if I would still feel alive with a white girl. It seemed like you were a living zombie once you went over there. You had food with no taste to it; no spices, no special recipes, but plenty of dessert. Everything was just too cool for comfort.

Anyway, Victoria would be missed.

I listened to a few other phone calls from women who I hadn't dealt with in a while, who were just calling me up on a whim. And there was a call from Michelle out in San Francisco again.

"Terrance, I really hate to bother you like this, but we really need to talk about something. So please call me when you get a chance. It's Michelle again."

She sounded patient, determined, and urgent, but with tact. She didn't want to alarm me with the nature of her phone call, but there was obviously something on her plate that wasn't going to go away.

By that time, it was close to two in the morning, and I was still wide awake. It would be close to eleven in San Francisco. I figured a grown woman would still be up to accept phone calls before eleven. Especially if it was urgent, so I went ahead and called her back.

"Hello," she answered.

"This is Terrance calling you back," I told her. I wanted to sound as calm and reserved as she had sounded in her messages to me.

"Oh, hi," she responded. It seemed as if I had caught her off-guard.

"Did I catch you at a bad time?"

"No, I just . . . Well, how have you been? Still busy modeling?"

We were headed for the small talk before we got to the beef.

I said, "Yeah, I'm still modeling. And I'm still a good-looking man," I joked. Even if I was cutting back on my activities with women, I still wanted to sound like myself in a first phone call in years with her.

She chuckled at it. "I would think that you would be. I still see some of your ads here and there when I'm flipping through the magazines or whatever."

"Are you looking for me?" I asked her.

She chuckled again. "Well, I guess you can't help it. Once you see people you know in magazine ads, you get used to seeing them there, and I guess you start to expect it."

I nodded, but I was quickly running out of patience. I wanted to get to the beef.

I said, "So, what's been going on with you?"

I really wanted to ask her what she wanted from me and cut to the chase. But I told myself to chill and let it happen naturally. She would get to it.

"Well, I've been pretty much taking care of myself. I have a new job with a bigger bank . . ."

I cut her off and asked, "Does that mean bigger money?"

"Yes, a little bit."

It all started to come back to me. Michelle was always the understated, practical woman, and I had felt overanxious with her. Things with her just seemed a little too . . . unrealistic, I guess the word would be. I mean, Michelle was fine; smooth reddish-brown skin, tall and curvy, brown curly hair, long legs, dark insatiable eyes. All of that, but her personality was as dry as a bag of airplane peanuts. She gave me the urge to want to shake her and say, "Wake up and come to life, woman!"

I remember when I first hooked up with her. The other guys at the party were amazed. "She actually likes you," they told me. But after I had been around her for awhile, I didn't see anything special about her. I would have given her back in a heartbeat. Walking around with her was like being with a ghost, an unseen spirit or something. Her emotions were that reserved.

Anyway, I got back to the present with her.

"What else is going on?" I asked. Little by little, she would tell me what she wanted. That was just her way.

"I've been, ah, staying busy. I have a new home. I have a daughter now. We work out at the gym together."

I stopped her and asked, "You have a daughter now? When did that happen? You got married recently?"

"No, no marriage, just my daughter and me. In fact, I haven't been with a man in years."

"What about the father?"

I was just having a basic conversation with her, you know. I understood her pace, and I was wide awake, so I began to relax with it. She would tell me what she needed to when she was ready.

"He's the last man I had sex with," she told me.

I said, "Oh yeah? So what happened with him?"

I just expected women to move on with their lives after me. I didn't own any of them, and I didn't want to. So I had no jealousies about it. Andrea's moving on was the only one that bothered me.

There was this awkward silence after my last question to Michelle. She said, "Actually, I don't think my daughter's father knows."

"He doesn't know? Why not? I mean, how old is your daughter?"

"She turned three in the spring."

All of a sudden, I stopped and starting counting back. I had been dealing with Michelle around that time; three to four years ago.

Maybe it was even five years. I remember it was well after my breakup with Andrea. But it didn't last long. None of my relationships lasted that long. My thing with Andrea was just more intense.

I said, "Are you trying to tell me something?" My heart started racing inside my chest again. What kind of fucking night was I having? It just never seemed to end.

"Well, I just want you to meet her," Michelle responded to me. "I'll pay for your airline ticket, hotel room and everything."

I said, "You want me to meet her? For what?"

There was an awkward silence again.

"I'm not trying to make this difficult," she told me. "I just want you to meet her, and that'll be it."

"That'll be it? Are you trying to see if I'm the father?"

I couldn't believe this shit! She was doing it smooth, too, even offering to pay for my plane ticket and hotel.

I asked her, "Why wouldn't you say something about that years ago? That's crazy! You wait for three years to bring this up?"

"Actually, it's been four years."

"Whatever! Why didn't you bring it up then?"

Boy, she was getting me on the wrong damn night. But no night or day would have been good for something like that.

"If you don't want to see her, then I understand," she told me. But she still didn't answer my question.

I said, "But why would you wait like this?"

I reflected again on one of the nights we had sex. Michelle got so wet and excited that the condom slid off inside of her. I was nervous for a bit, but she had told me afterward that everything was okay. Condoms had slid off inside of women before. It was a nuisance, but no one had ever gotten pregnant from it. It had always captured the semen before it slipped.

Michelle answered, "Well, I just . . . time just got away from me, and before long I felt connected to her."

"You felt connected to her? And you didn't even bother to tell the father? Well, why do it now?"

At least my sister was giving the guy an opportunity to fight it, and to let her know how things were gonna be. But to not even be told that a woman is pregnant by you is the ultimate sucker punch.

"Because she's been asking about her daddy," Michelle answered me.

I froze. I just held the phone and froze. My lifestyle had finally caught up with me. Then I tried to shake it off in denial.

She might not even be mine, I told myself.

"And you say that I'm the last man you had sex with? Four years ago? And you expect me to believe that?" I questioned.

As wet as she had gotten in sex, there was no way she could hold out that long without being turned on again.

She said, "I've only had three men in my life, and you were the third."

"That's crazy," I told her. She was another crazy woman having a baby on her own.

"Maybe, but it's the truth," she told me.

"So, what are you holding out for?" I asked her. "Four years?"

She said, "I just want a simple life."

"Well, this ain't simple at all," I told her. "How could this be simple?"

She paused before she responded to me. She said, "I won't send you any pictures. You have to see her for yourself. And if you don't want to . . . then we'll just leave you alone."

Motherfucker! I couldn't believe it! It was the ultimate setup. I hung up that phone with Michelle and just sat there in my living room, while staring out the window at the Atlanta skyline downtown. I didn't need to listen to any more messages after that one. I was done for the night.

"I'm not getting involved in this shit," I snapped to myself. "If she waited this long, then she can keep waiting."

I stood up and walked to my kitchen to pour a glass of orange juice from the refrigerator. I drank it down and poured another glass. I drank the second glass down and poured a third. Then I started thinking about my sister.

I've never even had a hug from my father. Not one hug.

"Shit!" I cursed. There was no way I could stop myself from at least seeing the girl. We still would have to take a paternity test, because I'm nobody's fool. But like Michelle said, she would be paying for my ticket. Maybe I could get her to pay for the paternity test to boot. Then I thought about the daughter and continued to shake my head. I mumbled, "I don't even know her name."

A New Beginning

I T TOOK ME ABOUT three minutes before I decided to call Michelle back.

"Hello," she answered again.

That's how tactful the girl was. She would answer hello even though she knew damn well who it was. She was the kind of woman who would stick to her script no matter what. She was unbreakable.

I said, "Let's do it. When do you want me out there?"

"Can you come next weekend?"

"That's when it's best for you?"

"Yes."

"Did you say anything to her about her father?"

"I told her I hope she likes him."

I said, "Well, I don't think you should introduce me to her as anything more than your friend. Because we haven't proven any of this yet."

"That's exactly what I planned to do," she told me.

"Good. And by the way, what's the girl's name?"

"Her name is Briana."

Her name rolled into my right ear and I liked it immediately. It was soft and simple, a pretty girl's name. I didn't want to like it. I wanted Michelle to tell me an ugly name, or something hard to pronounce. I was preparing myself not to like anything about any of it, and I was already losing.

The next thing I knew, I asked Michelle, "What's her middle name?"

"Marlon."

"Marlin? Like the Florida baseball team?"

"Yeah, but with an *o*," she told me. Michelle liked baseball. She had a younger brother who played for the Houston Astros. She had played softball through high school herself. She even thought about playing in college at Berkeley.

"Briana Marlon Deveraux," I said altogether. It didn't sound bad. Michelle had one of those French last names pronounced *Dev-er-row* from Louisiana, where her family was from.

She said, "Yeah, that's it."

I played with the name in my head for a minute. *Briana Marlon. Briana Deveraux. Briana Marlon Mitchell. Briana Marlon Deveraux Mitchell.* Then I asked myself, *What the hell am I doing?* I needed to get off the phone.

"Okay, well, you set it all up and I'll be there to meet her."

"All right. And Terrance?"

She waited for me to answer. "Yeah."

"Thank you."

Yeah, whatever, I thought to myself. But instead of saying that to Michelle, I mumbled, "Okay," and felt like a big wuss. This woman was out to try and change my entire life, and yet she was passing it off as just a meeting.

When I hung up with her the second time, all kinds of possibilities ran through my mind, and it was past two o'clock in the morning.

What if she is my daughter? I asked myself. *What will I do after that?*

I was already thinking about relocating to Oakland or San Jose, if it was true. I liked those areas, but not necessarily San Francisco. San Fran was more Michelle's kind of place, high-cultured society. It was the New York of the West Coast, but I was never a big fan of New York. I liked more open space and room to roam.

Atlanta? I didn't mind leaving Atlanta. I only slept there. I spent most of my time on the road.

But imagine that. I was willing to change my scenery without even knowing if the girl was mine yet.

"Shit!" I cursed myself again. "Who's out there holding a voodoo doll on me? This is crazy!"

Then again, raising a daughter gave me a purpose. I wouldn't have chosen it, but it looked like it was choosing me.

I HAD ANOTHER DREAM about my current situation over that weekend. I couldn't make out the exact features of the little brown girl who was holding my hand, all I knew is that she had ponytails and was wearing all pink, like Theresa in Gary.

"Come on, Daddy, come on," she told me in a singsong. She rocked my right hand back and forth with her left.

I looked to the other side of me, and Michelle was holding my left hand and grinning. The dream was short, but that's all I needed to remember. I woke up and shook my head again. The damage had been done. Nothing else was important to me. All I thought about was my trip to San Fran to meet up with Michelle again after four years, and to meet the daughter she claimed was mine.

Just as I had planned, I ignored phone calls from everyone but my mother and sister. I even failed to return calls on new modeling jobs. I didn't need to take all of them.

My mother called me early that next week and asked me, "Have you called Geneva Pitts yet?"

"No," I answered, "and I don't plan to."

"Well, why not, Terrance? What's wrong with her? She's pretty enough for you, isn't she?"

Truth was, I didn't feel like starting over with anyone. Geneva made things seem way too hard, and I didn't feel up to it, especially after the recent events in my life. I needed to focus on just one thing for a change.

I said, "Mom, if you're calling to do the matchmaker thing again, then I'm gonna have to cut our conversation short."

"Are you saying you're gonna hang up on me?"

"I'm saying I have other things on my mind right now."

"Like what, knocking on more doors?" She was loving that line and kept using it. She said, "Terrance, there is no future in that lifestyle. You're thirty-three years old now."

"I know how old I am. And I'm thinking about that every day now."

"Are you really?"

"Yes I am." I was telling her the truth. Thinking about a possible daughter I had never met before made me reevaluate a lot of things.

"Well, I'm not gonna keep you long. I'm just calling to check up on you. I haven't talked to you since you left me that little letter on the kitchen table last week."

I smiled. "So, you read it."

"Of course I read it, but I was giving you enough time to talk to Geneva before I called you."

"Well, don't hold your breath on that," I told her. "But I may have another surprise for you soon," I hinted.

My mother said, "I don't need any more surprises. Now what are you gonna surprise me with?"

"If I told you, then it wouldn't be a surprise."

"We'll see. All right, well, let me go on back to work before these people take away my retirement. These corporate folks are mean nowadays."

My mother was always running her mouth about something. She sure had a lot of character though. I imagined her around Michelle's reserved shell and doubted if my mother would ever like her. She would immediately think the woman was hiding something. And how could I blame my mother? Michelle had been hiding a daughter for three years. Or not really hiding, she just didn't say anything about it.

However, I didn't feel upset about it anymore. I just had to see the girl. I wanted to see what she looked like. Did she look like me? Did she look like her mother? Was she a perfect mix between the two of us? Or did she look totally like another man's daughter?

Speaking of another man's daughter, once I hung up the phone with my mother, I thought about calling Kim and my sister Juanita. My mother had gotten me started. I hadn't been on the phone for days. I just refused to answer it anymore. The phone had pretty much been an addiction for me for years. I was always having a battle with it. Turn it on or turn it off? Answer it or don't answer? Call her back or leave her alone? For years!

Well, I hadn't talked to Kim O'Bannon about her situation again at all. I wondered if she still wanted to have a baby without a husband or father. And how would she feel about another woman beating her to the punch with a child from my seed? Of course, I would never bring that up to her until everything was proven. But Kim would find out eventually. Everyone would have to find out. I didn't plan on doing what Michelle had done. Moving in silence may have been her way of doing things, but it wasn't mine.

So I made my phone call to Kim at her Chicago office. I knew I probably couldn't talk to her about babies and fathers and sperm banks while she was still on the job, but I could at least set it in her mind to talk to me about it after work that day.

"The Right Connection," someone answered the phone at her office.

I stumbled in confusion. "Aaahh, is this still the office of Kim O'Bannon?"

"Yes, I'm sorry. Everyone's getting confused by the new company name," I was told by the receptionist. It wasn't as if Kim had the same woman answering the phone there. There seemed to be a lot of turnover in young college interns at her office, particularly when it came to screening and directing her phone calls.

"Who may I say is calling?"

"Terrance Mitchell."

"Oh, okay. I heard her mention your name a few times. I'll see if she's available."

Kim jumped right on the line.

She said, "I was just thinking about you. I have a new job for you down in Houston."

That was ironic. I had been thinking about Michelle's brother Sean playing baseball for the Houston Astros again. They had just been on TV against the Atlanta Braves over the weekend. It's funny how a coincidence continues to pop up once the subject is on your radar. I'm sure the Astros had played the Braves plenty of times since I lived in Atlanta, but I had no reason to think much about it before.

Anyway, I asked Kim when I needed to be in Houston.

"Next month."

"Early or late?"

"Late."

I said, "Okay. I have a few things I need to work out before then. That'll probably be the next job I take."

She joked and asked me, "What if I got an offer for you for a hundred thousand dollars for next week?"

"I'll be there next week," I joked back to her. I had never been paid that much money for one job. There were very few male supermodels in that six-figure range. Women had a lot more designer clothes, magazines, runway shows, and opportunities to make that kind of money, but the most I ever made in one pop was a seventy-five-thousand-dollar weekend years ago in the prime of my career. That was when Andrea was around.

I said, "Anyway, you can book me for Houston. But I was actually calling you for something else."

"Oh yeah, what's that?"

"Well, I know you can't talk to me about it while you're still at the office, but I wanted to have another conversation with you about the whole baby situation. I just wanted to talk to you about it."

She said, "Oh, well, we'll talk. Yeah, I'll call you up later about that."

"That's what I figured," I told her. "And you can call anytime. I'll be here."

"Just kicking back today, hunh?"

I mumbled, "Yeah, I need to."

"All right, well, I'll call you later then."

I hung up with Kim and thought about calling Juanita at her job as well, just so I could get her mind right for a conversation that night. But when you are a manager in a department store, unless there was no one in the building, you seemed to be pretty busy working out all of the sales problems. It was hard to imagine my sister being the problem solver from what I knew about her personal life, that was for sure.

I was anxious to talk to her about my situation, in code language of course, so I went ahead and gave her a ring to set it up for later.

As soon as my sister answered her cell phone, she said, "You know I'm at the job, right?"

"Yeah, I just wanted you to know that I'll be calling you later on to talk to you," I told her.

She immediately jumped to conclusions concerning the purpose of my phone call. "Yeah, well, I'm leaning toward doing what you said now, but I'll talk to you about it later."

She was referring to getting an abortion, and she sounded positive about it.

I asked her, "You are?" That surprised me. I guess I wasn't thinking about it anymore. If Michelle could have a child on her own, then why couldn't my sister? Then again, those two women were miles apart in personality. Michelle was organized in every way to handle raising a child by herself, but Juanita . . . Maybe having a child without help would force her to make changes, but I doubted it. My sister never had a problem when it came to leaning on her family, and I didn't expect her to shy away from that anytime soon.

She said, "That's what you want to talk about, right?"

It was, but it wasn't. And if Briana Marlon Deveraux was indeed my child, then my sister having an abortion would look very hypocritical. Man, I didn't know what to think about anything anymore. The situation with Michelle had sucked me into a mental hurricane. I was just trying to find solid ground somewhere.

This has been one crazy-ass summer, I told myself. Ever since I received that phone call from Corey Sanders to meet him for drinks, things just unraveled. Him creating the leak of information about Andrea had led to everything that had gone haywire in my life, including having nightmares and dreams about women and fatherhood.

I told my sister, "We'll just, ah, talk about it later."

I hung up with her and I was itching for the rest of that day to talk to somebody about my concerns. I got a few more phone calls, but they weren't from people I wanted to talk to. TaShay called to thank me for covering for her with her aunt, and to apologize for getting involved with me, but I just decided to leave that alone. She was too young for me to be dealing with.

I did want to call Victoria back though. I didn't want her thinking badly about black men on account of me. Not saying that she would toss all black men in the same boat. She hadn't done it yet, I just didn't want to be the one who sent her overboard. Nevertheless, if I called her after concluding my situation with Michelle, I would have a concrete excuse not to deal with her anymore. In fact, Briana would give me a solid reason not to deal with a lot of women, if she was mine.

But Victoria's been through that shit before with a black man, I reminded myself. She had lost her last black man to a former girlfriend, marriage, and children, so how would she feel about losing me under similar circumstances? It would pretty much make her look like a twice loser.

I finally told myself, "Wait a minute, I don't owe her anything." I didn't treat her badly. I didn't force her into anything. I didn't mislead her. We simply had a couple of fun nights together, that's all.

In fact, "I don't owe any of these women anything," I insisted.

I guess I was going through relationship withdrawal, so I stayed in my confused shell. Of course, that didn't mean I wasn't curious about what they thought of me. So I listened to another phone message left from Danni.

"You are a weak motherfucker, you know that. Why can't you just

face me like a man? Why you gotta dodge me like a punk? Be a man!"
she challenged me.

I just laughed at it. I understood Danyel's position. She would be
pissed off until she got the last say. Well, I had news for her, she would
just have to get over herself. She was only giving me more reason to
pack up and leave Atlanta.

I thought about calling Judi back, too, but I didn't feel like talking
to her for too long. Her conversations were laboring. I wasn't interested in talking about the right thing, living life the right way, making
the right decisions for all the right reasons, and all that other crap with
her anymore. The fact was, Judi's life was on hold while she struggled
to figure herself out. I didn't look at her as being in a better situation
than anyone else, really. You didn't become a better player by sitting
on the bench and refusing to enter the playing field.

Celibacy was a cop-out for people. You didn't like the results of
what you were doing, so you quit. Whatever happened to learning
from your mistakes and playing a better game?

Michelle is pretty much celibate, too, though, if she's telling me the truth,
I thought to myself. *She's been holding out for four years! Will she let me
fuck her though, since I was the last?*

I grinned and started laughing out loud. I was a damn mess. That
kind of thinking was what got me in trouble in the first place. I just
didn't know which way was up anymore.

To kill time before Kim and my sister could call me back, I slid a
movie in my DVD player; *The Brothers*, starring Morris Chestnut,
D. L. Hughley, Bill Bellamy, and Shemar Moore. It's crazy how on
point a movie could be if you watch it at the right time. I thought
about every single issue in that movie. The only issue they didn't
cover was the baby's daddy from an estranged relationship deal. That
one was new to me, too.

Finally, it was after seven, and Kim was calling me back. I was anxious to talk to her.

"Hey, what it is, girl? What it is?" I answered.

Kim paused. "Aaahh, are you okay?"

"Yeah, I'm good, or trying to be good," I told her.

She said, "You sound a little bit hyper to me. But anyway, I talked to a few different doctors and parenting counselors, and you know, I've just been adding up all of my options. Why do you ask?"

All of a sudden, the subjects of my life seemed to revolve around parent, child, and nuclear family issues. Imagine that? Just a week ago, I was a sexaholic, screwing a different woman a different way every single night.

I asked Kim, "Are you still considering picking a certain man, or doing the random sperm bank thing? I mean, I guess by picking the right man you could at least influence a little of what the child would look like."

"Well, yeah, but some of the doctors were concerned about my weight with the whole thing. And I mean, I don't get that, because I see plenty of women my size who have children."

"Yeah, but do plenty of women your size go to have artificial insemination? They can't stop the other women from getting pregnant," I told her.

She said, "I guess they can't, can they? But anyway, some of the doctors advised me to adjust my diet and lose up to thirty pounds. They said I would gain about fifty during pregnancy.

"So, over the last few weeks, I've been thinking about adopting again as an option. Not to say that I wouldn't want to change my diet and lose some pounds, because I'm still deciding on that. But you know, picking up another fifty pounds in pregnancy would be . . . Whew!"

I chuckled. "That's all a part of getting pregnant, Kim. You had to have known that. You're carrying a developing body inside of you."

I said, "But let's say you got pregnant, right, in a regular relationship with a guy that you stopped seeing; would you go ahead and have the baby anyway and not tell him?"

Kim cut straight through the bullshit and asked me, "Somebody filed a paternity suit against you?"

"Nah," I told her, "I'm just bringing the issue up."

"Terrance, if you need to talk to me about this, then we need to talk straight. Now you know this is not going to go anywhere. So what's going on?"

Looked like I had let the cat out the bag. I said, "I don't have a paternity suit, but I do have a woman who says that the child is mine. So I'm going out there to investigate it this weekend."

"What do you mean, investigate it?"

"Well, she wants me to meet the child and all of that to see."

"Are you gonna take a blood test?"

"Of course."

Kim paused and said, "Mmmph."

"Ain't that ironic?" I asked her. "And this went down four years ago."

"And she's just getting in touch with you now?"

"Yup."

"Mmmph," Kim grunted again. "And the plot thickens. So, how do you feel about it? I know you're pissed off."

"Yeah, but what can I do about it now? If it's mine, it's here."

"Well, what do you feel about the woman? And stop saying 'it.' Is the baby a boy or a girl?"

"A girl," I told her.

"What's her name?"

Kim was really getting into it.

I said, "Kim, the main issue here is whether this is right or wrong."

"Who's to say?" she asked me. "I bet if you asked that child if it was right, she'd rather be alive than aborted."

"Kim, the girl can't even think that complicated."

"Yes, she can, too. And she can also respond to not being wanted."

It sounded as if I was losing the battle. How quickly I had forgotten that Kim would rather side with life than death on the abortion issue.

I said, "Well, I can see where this is going. And just to let you know, I'm not flying out there to cuss the woman out or anything. I'm already at peace with it. We just have to go through the figuring-out process."

"So, do you think she's yours?"

"There's a possibility."

"Is the mother a loose woman?"

"Nope, not hardly," I answered. "But you could never put a couple of one-night stands past a woman either."

"I know that's right," Kim agreed. "We're only human. But what are you gonna do if she is yours?"

"I'm gonna deal with it. But first, you know, I have to see what everything looks like."

"Well, good luck with that," she told me.

"Thanks."

After I hung up the phone with Kim, I didn't know if I wanted to talk to my sister anymore. How different would her opinions be? And how guilty would I feel about talking to her after knowing that I had asked her to do what Michelle had not done. But I would have told Michelle the same thing if I was given the chance. She had taken things into her own hands. How would my sister view that?

I didn't get a chance to make up my mind whether to talk to my sister or not because she called me that next minute, and I decided to pick it up.

She said, "Yeah, like I was saying earlier, I think that, umm . . . well, I'm just not ready for this. I mean, if he's not gonna be, you know, involved in it, then . . . I mean, it doesn't make any sense to do it."

I didn't want to say anything. I just listened. But once I thought that she was finished, I asked her, "What if he decided to be involved?" I was speaking more so for myself.

Juanita answered, "You know, like you said, I have to stop fooling myself, Tee. I mean, that's not gonna happen. He obviously doesn't want anything to do with me now. So I have to pretty much pick up my pieces and just move on."

"When you plan on getting it done?" I asked her.

"Umm, I'll just make an appointment for next week sometime."

That didn't sound too definite to me.

"Are you sure?" I asked. That would be the last time I would ask her about it.

"I mean . . . I don't know."

That's what it sounded like. My sister didn't have a clue what she wanted to do. I assumed that she would be the same after she had the baby. So she would have to figure that answer out for herself soon. Real soon. But I wouldn't make any more judgments or comparisons on her until I had settled my own situation.

I said, "Juanita, nobody can push you to do what you don't want to do, but understand that it goes both ways. You can't expect to push anyone else to do what they don't want to do either. So all of the guilt trips and tantrums and all of that, it won't mean anything."

"I know," my sister responded. But I don't believe she did. When you've known someone all your life, you know what they're gonna do before they do sometimes. And as soon as things failed to go well for my sister and her child, she would make sure that everybody knew about it.

I took a deep breath and said, "Well, you're a grown woman now, and you have your own family tree to establish, and so do I."

"What's that supposed to mean?" she asked me.

I wanted to keep it real simple and end our phone call in peace. I had a good idea about what I needed to do in my situation, and I didn't need my sister's confusions to throw me off track, so there was no longer a need to seek her opinion.

I answered, "Once you do what you decide to do, and that family legacy starts with that first independent child, it has nothing to do with me or mom or your father anymore. That's your tree, and it stops or continues with the decisions you make. The same goes for me."

I couldn't make it any more simple than that. It was time to move on. And Juanita didn't respond to it. I guess she still had a whole lot of thinking to do.

I said, "Okay, well, I have a few other things to take care of, so I'm gonna go ahead and go."

"Terrance?" my sister addressed me. "You really don't think I should have this baby?"

What in the world? I was tired of even thinking about it. Men and women just had different views on it. Then again, if there were no women who believed in abortion, it would never have become legal. Somebody believed in it.

I told my sister, "I will no longer answer that question. You do what you're gonna do, and you be prepared to pay the price for it."

"That's all you have to say about it?" she asked me.

"Yup, that's it," I told her.

When I got off the phone with her, I felt relieved.

"God help the man who ends up with her," I told myself. It was a terrible thing to say about your own flesh and blood, but I really meant it. Juanita was still an unstable woman.

FRIDAY MORNING, I was all packed up and ready to fly to San Francisco for the weekend.

"Well, here we go," I mumbled as I walked out of my place with my luggage in hand. There was no turning back. I felt as if a new life awaited me, and I hadn't even seen Michelle's daughter yet.

I made it to the Atlanta airport on time, checked my bag, made it through security, and as soon as I arrived at the gate to wait for my plane to board, I got a call on my cell phone. It was the last person I expected to hear from.

I looked at the phone and read the Chicago area code and cell number.

Andrea! I thought. *What does she want now?*

My cell phone rang a second time and I still didn't answer it.

Do I need the kind of closure where I tell her that it's over with forever? I asked myself. *Or do I just ignore the phone call and go on with my life?*

My cell phone rang a third time.

Finally, I shook off the temptation. Andrea was only a distraction now. I had to remain focused on where I was going. So I let the phone ring, and when it stopped, I turned it off, and I forced myself not to look back?

"Excuse me, I hate to bother you, but aren't you a model?"

I turned to my right and faced another attractive woman, dark brown, smooth skin, ponytail, tall, shapely, and still young. I could see where she was going to go before I even opened my mouth. She wanted to ask me about modeling, so I decided to run with my assumptions.

"Modeling is a business of people who choose you, or don't choose you," I told her. "You really have little control over it. All you can do is be as best prepared for it as you can."

She looked at me confused. "O-kay. How did you know what I wanted to ask you?"

I said, "Easy, you look like you wanna be a model."

She smiled and nodded. "Yeah, I do. But what about agency contacts? I mean, you have to get inside the game first, right? That's what everybody tells me; I need representation."

I went ahead and gave her Kim's number in Chicago, and a few other agency contacts that I used. It would be all on her after that. If they liked her, they liked her, and if they didn't, then it was back to the drawing board.

I said, "You also want to find a connected photographer to take great pictures of you. Ask them who they've worked with before, and what their honest opinions are of you."

"Thank you," she told me. "So, how do you like it?"

I didn't feel like having another conversation about modeling and stuff, I just wanted to catch my plane to San Francisco. And I wasn't interested in flirting with the young woman either.

I told her, "I don't mean to be rude or anything, but I'm really just trying to focus on my trip."

I explained it as nicely as I could, and the young woman responded accordingly.

"Oh, I'm sorry. Well, thanks for the information, and have a good flight."

"Thank you," I told her.

When I boarded the plane, first class, I sat in my window seat and took a deep breath. I began to feel like Michelle was fattening me up for the kill. She even planned to pick me up at the airport. I was hesitant about that part. I thought that maybe I would need time to digest everything after I had gotten off the plane. But it was already set, Michelle and Briana would be there at the luggage claim area to pick me up.

I had all kinds of nervous thoughts and illusions while on that plane ride from Atlanta, and I couldn't seem to stop myself.

What if she's extra big now and not as pretty as she used to be? She did say she was working out in the gym. Is she trying to work off extra pounds? I wondered. It had been four years since I had been with Michelle. A lot of things could change in four years. But I hadn't been with Andrea for six years, and she was still great looking.

But Andrea was a model, or trying to be one, I argued. You don't have to stay in shape at a bank.

I had to stop and transfer at Dallas–Fort Worth for the second leg of the flight. And on that second flight, my wild thoughts only intensified.

What if this little girl is a brat? She could be spoiled to death and unruly. But she's only three years old, I argued to myself. *Yeah, but three years old is still old enough to rip up some shit.*

I pulled out a copy of *Travel* magazine from the pouch on the seat in front of me to try and preoccupy my mind with the articles and photographs. And it worked, I made it through the rest of the flight in peace.

But once we landed and pulled up to the gate, my thoughts started up all over again.

What if this little girl doesn't even like me? I asked myself. Would I feel like a failure before I even got a chance to know her?

So what? She may not be mine anyway, I argued.

It was all an insane process. And since Michelle flew me in first class, I was the fifth person off the plane. I couldn't even stall for time.

"Thank you for flying with us," the flight attendant in dark blue told me as I stepped off the plane. I nodded and smiled at her, paying attention to every detail.

I headed up the bridge and toward the baggage claim area on a sunny San Francisco day. It was after two o'clock in the afternoon. I would be there for the rest of the day, Saturday, and Sunday. My return flight to Atlanta was bright and early Monday morning.

I made it to the baggage claim area and rode the escalator down to the bottom floor. I was all eyes and heart, looking for my two hosts. And in the middle of the floor, Michelle actually had her daughter holding up a sign with Terrance Mitchell written on it. Briana stood out with no less than five colors in her outfit: blue, yellow, orange, red, and green. Even her mini bucket hat was multicolored. She looked like a display right out of a children's clothing store.

Standing tall next to her was her mother, in burnt orange heels and an orange, cream, and yellow summer dress. She had a perfect hour-glass shape, with short-cut hair. She looked sharp and efficient, and was clearly a professional woman. She had a stance of organized authority. My eyes were glued on her. She had much more presence than I remembered. Maybe it was because she was waiting for me at the airport. Maybe the short hair did it. Or maybe it was something in the water that I drank on the plane.

"Here he is, Briana," she told her daughter with a tap on her left shoulder. At that moment, Briana was not looking in my direction. There were too many people walking out at the same time. But then she turned her gaze and locked in on me. When my eyes met hers, I was done; my heart fluttered, my knees got weak, my mouth felt dry. I felt this rush of energy take over my body. It was the weirdest feeling I had ever experienced in my life. There was nothing I could compare it to. A thousand butterflies were all flapping their wings under my skin. I felt as if I was going to fly away somewhere.

Looking into Briana's eyes was like staring into a mirror, only someone had made my face smaller, browner, and prettier and had decorated me in a little girl's outfit. Then she smiled at me.

SHIT! I was thinking. My chest felt like it was ready to explode. I
didn't feel like I was breathing correctly. I mean, I just wanted to reach
down and lift that girl into the air and plant a thousand kisses on her
face while spinning her around in crazy circles until we laughed with
glee. But I probably would have scared her and made her cry if I did
some shit like that. I was a stranger to her, so I had to keep my cool.

"Well, how are you doing?" I looked down and asked her.

She bashfully looked away. "Fi-i-ine," she answered me.

It sounded like her first words to me lasted for an entire sentence,
but it was only one word.

I told her, "I'm feeling fine, too. I just have to pop my ears."

She looked up at my ears and smiled in wonder. "Pop your ears?
You mean from the airplane?"

Whoa! I didn't expect all of that. What exactly were three-year-olds
capable of?

"So, you've been on an airplane before, too?" I asked her.

She nodded to me. "Yeah."

I could see her curly dark hair slipping out from under the edges of
her hat. She had long sideburns like her mother.

"Was it scary?"

She shook her head. "No. Well, but only a little bit."

"When we were landing, that first big hit on the ground startled
her," Michelle told me.

I was all into the girl. "Where were you flying to?" I asked her.

"La, umm . . . Louisiana."

I could have stayed in that airport with her all day.

"How many bags do you have?" Michelle asked me.

"Just one."

"What does it look like?"

"It's black with wheels on it."

I got the picture. It was time to get a move on and grab my luggage.
Briana would be with us all day.

I stood up tall and straight and began to look for the baggage claim
belt that my luggage would roll out on. Michelle beat me to it.

"It's number three."

"Thanks," I told her.

When we walked over to baggage claim area three, I was itching to take Briana's hand in mine, but I didn't.

She pointed to the first black bag with wheels that she saw on the belt.

"Is that one it?"

I looked and smiled.

"No, that's not it," I told her.

She waited for the next black bag with wheels.

"Is that one it?"

I could see where that was going. She would ask me about every black bag with wheels until we found mine, and I would answer her every single time anyway, and spoil her, just because I was new.

I had checked my luggage so I could keep my hands free to think about things. I also wanted to stall at the airport to feel things out like we were doing before we left. I had planned it all that way on purpose. I figured I needed a slight buffer period before jumping in their car with them.

"Here it comes," I told Briana as soon as I recognized my bag on the belt.

She clapped her hands and did a couple of jumps in the air like a mini cheerleader.

"Oh, she's adorable," an older white woman commented. She looked at me and Michelle and added, "You all are gorgeous."

All we could do was stand there and smile. It was an awkward moment, but it was true. I was a professional model, Michelle looked like a model, and Briana was the child. I mean, I still had to take a paternity test to make absolutely certain, but it was pretty obvious to me. Briana Marlon Deveraux was my daughter, and she had modeling chops already. You put us together in a picture, and I was the dad. It was just that simple. She had the eyes, the facial structure, the smile lines . . . No wonder Michelle wanted me to see her. She didn't even want an argument from me, and she wasn't going to get one.

I grabbed my bag off the belt and followed them to the parking lot area. I led my luggage, and Michelle led Briana.

"Where are you from?" my daughter asked me.

"Gary, Indiana," I told her.

"Indiana? Is that far away?"

She had great diction for a three-year-old, or at least I thought so.

"It's far enough."

"Is it far like Louisiana?"

"Yup, it's about the same distance. Only Indiana is north and Louisiana is south."

Michelle smiled at me and said, "Watch out, she'll talk you to death."

I smiled back and said, "Yeah, she reminds me of . . ." and I stopped myself.

Michelle looked me right in the eyes and didn't say anything.

I looked away and mumbled, "My mother." I didn't say it loud enough for my daughter to hear me, but I'm sure Michelle knew. But she had never even met my mother, nor had I met her family. I only knew her brother from her talking about him. Sean had just gotten called up from the minor leagues when I first met her. I guess we had a whole lot of introductions to do.

We made it into the parking lot and stopped at a teal blue, S-model Jaguar, where Michelle popped the trunk.

I looked at her and asked, "This is your car?" It looked too masculine for a woman. I mean, Jaguars had pretty curves and everything, but they also had very masculine muscle.

She smiled. "I like Jaguars."

"The real ones, or just the cars?" I joked with her.

"The car-r-rs," Briana butted in. She had this way of extending certain words that was as cute as ever.

I tossed my bag into the trunk, and we all climbed into the car. Briana had a child's seat in the back passenger side. I sat in front of her and started to adjust the seat, but I found that I didn't need to. I had plenty of leg room up front.

I looked at Michelle and asked her, "What tall guy's been sitting over here?"

She grinned at me from behind the wheel and began to back us out.

"I adjusted the seat for you once we arrived at the airport."

"I see," I told her.

Briana said, "Are we gonna show him all of our favorite places, Mommy?"

Man, just hearing that little girl's voice was sending chills up my spine.

"So, you hang out with your mother a lot, huh?" I turned from my seat and asked her.

"Yup. We go everywhere."

She's three years old! I kept telling myself. I hadn't been around kids like that in years. My professional life was totally with adults. I didn't even deal with a lot of women who had kids.

I looked at Michelle and placed my hand over hers on her wooden, Jaguar stick shift. And I nodded to her.

She looked me in my eyes again. She was surely a fine woman, but she had more business savvy than most women I knew. She had that don't-bother-me-with-me-no-bullshit look that scared most of the men who liked her. Her eyes had calculation written all over them. The bank was a perfect place for her. And she looked very comfortable over the wheel of her Jaguar, too.

She kept a calm tone and said, "Let's wait to make sure."

She got what I was telling her. Briana was our daughter. I accepted it. But she was right, I couldn't allow my emotions to get in the way of the process.

Figure It All Out

ONCE I GOT PAST the daughter part, I had to focus on dealing with the mother.

It was after ten o'clock Friday night when Michelle drove me back to the Sheraton Hotel downtown to drop me off. I had checked in earlier, and she had secured a nice suite for me. She was really treating me well. We enjoyed ourselves all over the city, with more to come on Saturday and Sunday.

"So, what time do we get started tomorrow?" I asked her. We sat in the car at the hotel's entrance. Briana was sound asleep in her car seat after enjoying a late restaurant dinner with ice cream for dessert.

"We can do breakfast by nine, and then get over to the zoo early before it gets hot and crowded," Michelle answered.

I had agreed to do everything they wanted once the day went well. If the day hadn't gone well, I had the option to do fewer things. That was how Michelle had worked the plans out with me.

When it was time to climb out of the car, I just went ahead and did it. Any hesitation would have made things awkward. But I still wanted to talk to her about everything.

I reached my right hand up to my ear and said, "Call me in the room when you get in."

She nodded. "Okay. And thanks again for agreeing to do this."

She made it sound like it was a privilege. On one hand, the old me would have liked that. Michelle was acknowledging that my time was valuable. But on the other hand, it made it seem as if my time was too valuable to spend a fun weekend with my daughter. I had to deal with that, but it was too long of a conversation to have while standing outside of the car.

"Just, ah, call me up when you get in," I repeated. I figured I'd work everything out with her over the phone.

She nodded again. "Okay."

As she drove off with our daughter, I walked through the lobby of the hotel feeling lonely. I felt like I should have been with them. Why the hell was I by myself at a hotel?

Because they don't know you like that, I told myself. *You have to earn their trust and act like you want to be part of their lives.*

I was pretty much telling myself how it had to be. Becoming a hit-and-run dad would always make me feel disconnected. Or could I actually get used to that?

I rode the elevator up to my floor, and when I walked into my room, I pounced on the comfortable, king-size bed like I had done a thousand times when I traveled for work. Then I looked up at the ceiling and wondered what Michelle's bedroom looked like. What did her house look like? What did Briana's room look like? I wanted to be a part of that, or at least see it while I was out there. Hell, I just wanted to feel included . . . in everything. Was that even fair for me to think? I was still a stranger.

I sat up and pondered everything until Michelle called me on the hotel phone after eleven.

"So, how do you feel about the day?" I asked her.

"It went good, real good."

"How do you feel right now?"

"Thankful."

Michelle gave you so little of herself that you always wondered how sincere she was. She was giving me one-word answers and everything. That was the part of her that I remember disliking. She needed more life in her.

I said, "That's all you felt about it? You're thankful? I mean, I felt all kinds of things."

She said, "Well, it's not as if you planned or wanted to be here. So, I'm still a little . . . tentative. I mean, a week ago you didn't even know about Briana."

She had a point. "Well, I know about her now," I told her. "And why haven't you been involved with a new man since then? I mean, I'm sorry to tell you, but four years sounds hard for me to believe."

It was time for grown-up talk. I figured I needed to be as frank with Michelle as possible. We had a lot of serious ground to cover.

"Well, I was pregnant for the first year; breast-feeding for most of the second; getting myself back into shape during the third; and contemplating on the fourth," she told me.

That sounded reasonable enough. But of course, I needed to know more.

"Contemplating what?" I asked her.

"Calling her father."

That answer stopped me in my tracks. It sounded like she still had feelings for me. I found that amazing.

"And you're just . . . I mean . . . who took care of Briana while you went back to work?"

She had thrown off my whole train of thought with her straight answers. So I just started making it up as we went along.

She said, "I hired a good nanny, and I found a good day care. And it's not like I travel all the time like you do. I like it here in San Francisco. So we've just been here, doing it."

Yeah, San Francisco was the kind of place where you could go on about your business without folks bothering you. It was a wealthy family's playground. But you definitely had to have money to stay out there.

I nodded. Michelle was an impressive woman. She had found her way to live without getting all caught up. She had a fatherless child and still wasn't caught up. In fact, she was doing quite well for herself from what I could see.

I asked her, "Did you want to have a baby when I met you?" I still needed to understand that part of it.

"As a family, sure, but not how it happened. Then I read the signs from you, and I knew that I couldn't count on anything," she told me. "At the same time, I wondered what it would take for me to get through it on my own. So, I just became more focused."

Amazing! I didn't know what else to say. I felt like I wanted to help her just because she had done so well at helping herself. Hell, she didn't even need me. Or did she?

"But I'm still hesitant to let you do too much now, even if you would want to, because my daughter is very regulated." So she gets used to things. And I wouldn't want anyone to come into her life that she can't . . ."

"That she can't be involved with on a regular basis," I filled in for her. I had already thought about that myself.

"Exactly," Michelle agreed. "So I take the time to thank you, because I don't expect it, and I won't allow my daughter to expect it."

"So, what are you saying, that I can be a part-time dad? I mean, what kind of father would you want me to be?"

I pretty much had it set in my mind that I was Briana's father before I went anywhere near a paternity test. So I was already jumping the gun on things, and I needed to know if I was expected to be in or out of my daughter's life.

Michelle told me, "If you want to be a real father then you already know how it's supposed to be."

She caught me off-guard with that response as well. I had to give her all the credit in the world for being frank. There was no sugarcoating the father issue in her book.

I said, "But you didn't even let me know that I was a father." I wasn't all wrong. Like she said, I had no idea.

"You were still too young to deal with it," she explained.

"And you weren't?"

"Obviously not."

This is how she was talking to me. She made me feel like a boy. And you know what? The shit turned me on. Michelle was giving me the facts with poise and no emotional attitude. She was worlds apart from the women I had been dealing with. And she didn't know it yet, but I was even willing to get involved with her again. Maybe a strong, organized, self-sufficient woman was just what I needed. But I didn't want a celibate woman or a mother of my child who I couldn't touch. What had she been holding on to for four years?

I said, "Okay, so if I'm a father to my daughter, and I'm doing it every day, and she's your daughter, too, then what's my relationship to you?"

That was the million-dollar question that we needed to answer.

She said, "Well, I'm not here to beg. And my process may be a little slower than everybody else's on sex, but I'm still a woman, and I have thought about my daughter's father in that way."

"Do you still think about him in that way now?"

She said, "Yes. Of course."

Man, my head got big as hell when that woman told me that—both of them. She had me speechless and sitting there grinning. There's nothing in the world like massaging a man's ego by letting him know that he's still sexy to you.

She said, "But the same thing goes for me that goes for my daughter. That's where she gets it from."

I joked and said, "So, I would have to give it to you regularly?"

If we were going to talk frank, then we were going to talk frank.

She said, "I'm a woman of practice. So if I practice it . . ."

I suddenly broke up and started laughing. *A woman of practice, huh?* I repeated to myself. I could take that plenty of places.

I asked her. "Are you smiling when you say this? Because you don't smile enough," I told her. I would have to break her out of her sternness. I know I was smiling.

"Maybe I am smiling," she told me.

I said, "Now, what about if I got some new shit I wanna try. Are you gonna practice that?"

She had given me something to run with, so I was running with it. She said, "There're always new things being introduced. I mean, I like knowing what I'm about to do, but new things are a part of life. Aren't they?"

I liked her attitude. She was still reserved, but she was willing to bend. Or at least that's what she was leading me to believe. But talk is cheap.

I thought to myself, *I'm gonna turn her ass out. This one woman. She ain't had sex in four years! Oh, it's gonna be lights out. But I gotta take things slow. I don't want to scare her. It'll be a day-by-day process. But if she can hold out for that long, then how many days can she have sex in a row? That's like having a virgin.*

My mind was off and running with the idea. I said, "Now, just out of curiosity, have you been using dildos or vibrators or anything like that?"

From what I knew about women's toys, they sometimes stretched a vagina to where a man could hardly feel the tug of the walls anymore. So a woman would have to use her playthings sparingly and correctly so as not to pull her natural elasticity out of place.

Michelle answered, "No. I just work out, and enjoy time with my daughter. I don't get involved in all of that extra whatever."

I said, "Well, let me ask you another question." I was on a roll with her, so I kept it going. "Now this hotel room and all is nice, but what if I want to stay with you and my daughter tomorrow night. Would that be a problem?"

She said, "Are you asking me if you can spend the night?"

"Yeah."

"Well, ask me then."

I was hesitant. I needed to understand her rules.

"Well, I don't know. I mean, I don't want to disturb your rules and everything," I told her. "You've been doing well for yourself."

She said, "I can explain it this way: I have rules for everyone else that I won't be willing to break. I mean, that's just how I live my life.

But then I'll have that special person who I'd be willing to break all the rules for. And after four years, trust me, I can't wait. So ask me what you want to ask me."

Man, she had my mouth wide open with that one. I said, "Aw'ight . . . so ahh . . ." I stopped and felt awkward for some reason. I just went for broke the first time I had been with Michelle. But now she was the mother of my child. That made a difference to me. Suddenly, I respected her more. But I still wanted to turn her out.

Finally, I backed down and changed the subject. I said, "You know, you didn't go about things the right way. What if I had gotten married or passed away or something, while you were out here walking around with my daughter?"

"That was the chance I took by waiting," she told me. "But there would have been no chance years ago."

"Well, if I wasn't ready then, what makes you so sure that I'm ready now?" I asked her.

First she chuckled. Then she said, "You should have seen your face when you saw Bree at the airport. That was a classic picture."

I laughed at that myself. Meeting my daughter for the first time was a hell of a moment for me. It was unposed and unpracticed.

"Yeah, you got me there. That would have been a classic picture," I admitted. "Have you collected any of my magazine spreads?"

I remembered that she collected things that meant something to her, like her brother's baseball stats and playing cards. So I figured I would ask her about my magazine photos. I had surely taken enough of them.

"Would you think I was weird if I did?" she asked me with a pause.

"No, I would just know that you were paying attention. I mean, you still collect your brother's baseball stuff, don't you?"

"You remember that?" She sounded excited by it.

"Yeah, I remember. I was around you when he first got called up to the major leagues."

"Yeah, you're right. Well, they're thinking about trading him now."

"Yeah, that happens to the best of them," I told her.

"But he wants to be traded to a West Coast team to be closer to us, you know; San Francisco, Oakland, Seattle, L.A. . . ."

I was happy for her brother and all, but we had our own business to take care of. I didn't want to get too far off track with talk about baseball. So I went back to my pictures.

"Okay, so, how many of my spreads have you collected?" I asked her.

She said, "Oh, well, I did it for my daughter."

"So she's seen me in a bunch of pictures?"

I panicked for a second. How long had Michelle been mapping this all out? But Briana didn't say anything about it. A kid would talk about seeing someone in pictures, especially over and over again. She would have already been familiar with my face.

"No, not yet. I just wanted to save them until everything came out," Michelle explained.

I settled down and said, "Oh, okay." Then I thought about it and started smiling. I was imagining what Briana would do. "She's gonna look at me like a hero," I predicted.

"Mmm hmm," Michelle agreed. "She already looks at her uncle Sean that way. But is there a problem with that? At least she'll never be starstruck. She's already around it."

I stopped and thought again about my own sister. I could be the big uncle and hero to her child. And once Michelle reminded me of her brother's connection to them, I figured he had helped her out financially just like I would with Juanita. It wasn't definite, but I strongly assumed it. It would have been only natural for him to help out. More important, I began to wonder what he would think about me.

"So, are you gonna ask me what you want?" Michelle questioned.

"Huh?" My mind was in another place and on another subject.

"I said, are you gonna ask me what you want?" she repeated. "You were saying something about not liking the hotel room. I tried to get you the best room I could get you."

"Oh, yeah, I, ah, wanted to see how you and, umm, Briana lived."

I had to get back on track to what we started off talking about.

I guess Michelle was paying a lot more attention to the subjects than I was.

"Well, ask me then," she pressed me.

I didn't expect her to be that assertive about rekindling a relationship with me. Up to that point, she was just being Briana's mom. I didn't know what she felt toward me anymore. So I got ready to ask and got stuck. I just wanted it to sound right.

"You want me to stay over at the house with you and Briana tomorrow night?" I asked her.

She said, "I thought you would never ask. Yes, I would like for you to stay over. Now tell me what *you* want."

I hesitated again. Did she really want to know what I wanted?

Hell, I went for broke again. I said, "I want you to make love to me like you haven't had it in four years."

I just couldn't get past that. Her four years of nothing was turning me the hell on.

Michelle started laughing. She said, "If that's what you want, then that's what I'll do. You just make sure you stay consistent."

I said, "Can you stay consistent with me?"

"I can't ask you to do something I won't do. So I'll make sure that it's my job, and it's my pleasure," she told me. She said, "I understand now what guys need in a relationship. I need it, too. And . . . I'm not . . . I'm not gonna deny it anymore."

Boy, my two heads were jumping for joy! She said she would make it her *job* and her *pleasure, consistently* to give me what I need. I liked the sound of that a lot. But then, talk was cheap. Still, if I remembered anything about Michelle Deveraux, she was dedicated to her job, and she was always even-tempered. But I called her bluff anyway.

"Yeah, well, seeing is believing."

She said, "Okay. We'll see tomorrow night then. So don't let your daughter tire you out. Save some of your energy."

You believe that? I could see Michelle loosening up her tight drawstrings already. So the more I was around her, the more I would get her to open up.

• • •

I HUNG UP THE PHONE and didn't know what to feel, really. I mean, this woman calls me up out of the blue, talking about she has a daughter that she wants me to see. I'm pissed off about it. Then I fly out there to see the daughter, and find out that she's a happier, prettier me. Then her mother tells me she's been holding out for four years to break all the rules with her daughter's daddy.

You gots to be kidding me! And the mother is finer than she was when I first met her, plus she has her life in order.

I smiled in my hotel bed from ear to ear.

"You lucky motherfucker!" I told myself. I hadn't felt that giddy to be sucked in by a girl in years. Then I thought about how everyone else would respond to it:

"She did what?"

"For how long?"

"Get the hell out of here!"

"And what did you say?"

"And you trust this girl after that?"

"Man, is you crazy!"

"Are you serious, man?"

Long pause.

"Shit, man . . . you just lost your damn mind!"

And I wouldn't even give a damn. Nobody helped me to make the decisions I made to get involved with all the women I was involved with in the first place.

Like my mother said, I was thirty-three years old, and I needed to get the hell off the streets and stop knocking on doors. Well, Michelle was offering me a good home. And unless she did something unexpected and outrageous, I was planning on taking her offer . . . for keeps.

Epilogue

AFTER THE LIFESTYLE I was living, Michelle and Briana couldn't have come at a better time. They had me thinking about marriage and more kids, and smiling about it. Of course, I took the paternity test first, and there were no surprises there. The doctor confirmed what we already knew. I was the father. So I got all involved and ready for the meetings and greetings on Michelle's side of the family and mine. I didn't want to look like some deadbeat, MIA dad, like my own father.

Fortunately, we didn't have any family uproars or anything. Her family liked me, and my mother and sister liked her.

"Now that's what I'm talking about," my mother whispered to me when I flew Michelle and Briana to Indiana. "She's a good girl. And you did it all by yourself. But why she wait so long to tell me about my precious granddaughter? Is that girl out of her mind? But don't tell I said that. I'm just expressing myself."

That's my mother for you. She's liable to say anything.

Juanita went ahead and had her abortion the same week I met my daughter, and I was terrified how she would respond to the situation. Surprisingly, my sister was openly supportive, and she loved my new daughter.

"Just call me Aunt Nita," she told her.

I pulled Juanita aside when I got a chance to, and she said, "You don't have to apologize about anything, Tee. My situation would not have turned out like yours. And you know, I'm proud of you. You're not as selfish as you think you are."

Then she cried into my arms. "She is beautiful, Terrance. She is so beautiful."

That part scared me. I had no idea how Juanita may act later on, but so far so good. She was happy to be a new aunt and not a new mother.

Kim O'Bannon sent Briana a bunch of designer clothes as a gift, and asked us when we wanted her to start off modeling.

"The girl has pedigree. You have to do it," she joked.

Kim decided that adoption would be the best route for her own desires to have a child. She finally determined that an adoption would make things a lot less complicated for her.

Judi was so excited for me that she wanted to be a bridesmaid in the wedding. I told her there was no wedding yet. We were still feeling everything out.

"Well, let me know when. And your daughter is gorgeous," she told me. "I am so happy for you. Only way I could be more happy is if it were me."

Then I told her about Michelle's four years of abstinence.

Judi said, "You see that? Just when you thought it was crazy. I bet you think differently about it now."

And I did. Of course, Michelle had a lot to learn in the sex department, but she proved her mettle in her willingness to learn, so I was satisfied with her forward progress.

My girl Danni continued to grow in her modeling career, and she started dating movie, sports, and music celebrity types. That fit her perfectly. With the way those guys turned relationships over—who's hot who's not—her attitude would fit right in with their revolving doors.

TaShay straightened up her act and left Taniva alone, and she was now on her way up the professional ladder with wings on. She had landed wholesome retail brands like Gap, Benetton, Banana Republic, and Old Navy, while staying away from the brutal competition of trying to land premier designer names. But all modeling money was good money to me, and I was still making mine, too.

I also forced myself to be real and break the bad news to all of the women out there who still had their hopes for me, including Victoria and Rachel. I mean, what can I do? One man can't have them all and keep out of trouble while doing it. The bad news would have happened sooner or later, and they all took it with dignity.

"Well, let me know if you get bored with her," Rachel joked to me. Or maybe she wasn't joking. I wouldn't put it past her, but I didn't plan on going there.

As for Andrea, Corey, and Marcus Vissel—well, like they say, if you can't say anything good about them . . . I wish them all well, but I won't be back. Everybody has dark secrets in their closet somewhere. I planned to leave that closet door alone forever. I had a respectable family to raise.

Everyone started asking and rushing us about wedding dates. But Michelle and I were in no hurry. We were dating like a new couple to start things off on the right foot, and I invited my new woman and daughter to as many weekend locations as I could. That's when I popped the question, six months later in Shanghai, China.

You already know what Michelle's answer was. A marriage and family was what she wanted, even after the wait. And you know what? It took me a while, but I found out that's what I wanted, too. As for everyone else out there, well, personally, I can't make a dream come true for every woman. Nor can any other man. So the women out there all have to find out what they want for themselves, find out who's willing to give it to them, and get what they can get while they can still get it.

Move around! And good luck!

About the Author

New York Times bestselling author **Omar Tyree** is the winner of the 2001 NAACP Image Award for Outstanding Literary Work—Fiction. His books include *Boss Lady, Diary of a Groupie, Leslie, Just Say No!, For the Love of Money, Sweet St. Louis, Single Mom, A Do Right Man,* and *Flyy Girl.* He lives in Charlotte, North Carolina.

To learn more about Omar Tyree,
visit his website at omartyree.com.

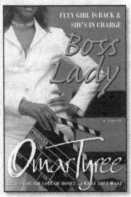